DANGER

"It seems, Miss Winthrop," Fortune said, stepping closer to her and tracing the soft edge of her jaw with one finger, "that for the time being you are mine."

"And how long will you keep me a prisoner?" she demanded.

"Prisoner?" He bent over, his lips hovering only inches above hers. "You are my guest, Miss Winthrop."

For long moments his eyes held hers, mesmerizing her. She caught the fragrance of the wine they had shared on his mouth and wondered absurdly what it would be like to taste it, to have him caress her lips with his. Abruptly, she tore her eyes away. What was she thinking? She could not welcome a kiss from a pirate. Especially not this pirate.

"Do you always make unwanted advances toward your guests, Captain?"

Michele Stegman

Fortune's Mistress

LEISURE BOOKS   NEW YORK CITY

To my husband Ron
and to my children Kira and Shana.

A LEISURE BOOK®

March 1992

Published by

Dorchester Publishing Co., Inc.
276 Fifth Avenue
New York, NY 10001

Printed in the United States of America.

Fortune's Mistress

Chapter One

One loop of the coarse rope binding Raven Winthrop to the mast of the pirate vessel was around her neck, chafing cruelly. Acrid black smoke from the cannons still hung in the air, stinging her eyes, burning her throat. She twisted her hands, trying to loosen the grip of the bonds that cut deeply into the tender flesh of her wrists, and strained against the ropes tied too tightly around her chest and narrow waist. Finally, she ceased her useless struggles, defiantly held up her head with its black, tangled mass of hair, and gazed at the carnage about her.

The ship she had been wrested from was sinking and the half-naked pirates hastened to finish their looting, tossing boxes and bags and bales onto the deck, heedless of the blood still pooled there. They leered at her, laughing and making coarse jests about the ways in which they would enjoy their captive once their work was done. Fear congealed around her heart, constricting her chest even more tightly than the bonds that held her, until she felt she could scarcely breathe.

On a second pirate vessel on the other side of the stricken ship, the pirates worked just as feverishly to unload the spoils of their victory before the sea stole their prize. The second ship was the smaller of the two pirate vessels but had taken the prominent role in the battle. Perhaps because it was lighter, sleeker, and more maneuverable it had taken the more dangerous positions, and its cannons had more often found their mark. Or perhaps it had been more skillfully handled, its crew more disciplined, its bottom less barnacle-befouled.

But it had not been an easy victory for the pirates. The gallant Dutch captain had put up a brave fight, all the braver for its hopelessness. He was outgunned, outmanned, and his fat merchant ship outmaneuvered. Raven wondered where the captain and his crew were now. Surely the pirates had not just killed ...No! She could not think about that now. She closed her eyes for a moment to the terror about her, gathering her shattered courage. A shout made her open her eyes to see the last pirate swing onto the deck in front of her before the little Dutch vessel shuddered and sank forever beneath the waves.

The pirates began shuffling the cargo into some sort of order and a table was set up on deck for dividing the spoils. Raven leaned her head back against the mast and tried to moisten her lips with a tongue dry from fear and thirst. She began to slip into a comforting oblivion when a touch on her throat jerked her back to harsh reality.

She opened her eyes to a face that was a grinning caricature of evil. A tattered rag held back his greasy hair, and little black eyes glittered avariciously at her. A low suggestive laugh bubbled up from a scrawny neck and tumbled over half-rotted teeth while his calloused finger ran down her shoulder then along the scoop of her gown to the dip between her full breasts, making her gasp in embarrassment. She tried to struggle away from his touch but the rope that held her was too tight, too expertly tied. Her gown was already torn, nearly exposing her left breast, and he was about to pull the last ragged strip away when an authoritative, *"Monsieur* De Lessops!" startled him, making him spin around.

The hail had come from a tall lean man with sun-bleached hair sauntering almost casually across the deck toward them. He picked his way nonchalantly through the carnage as if he were on an afternoon stroll through a meadow. He was smiling and walked with the lithe grace of a cat—or a master swords-man. But there was a tenseness about him, a hard-ness in his flint-blue eyes that, in spite of his easy manner, implied he was a man to be reckoned with.

Though blood and black powder stained his once white cambric shirt and two gnarled ruffians fol-lowed only a pace behind him, somehow, she felt that he was not one with the evil barbarians who had captured her. A brace of pistols were stuck into the red sash at his waist and a saber rode easily at his hip, yet Raven took a trembling breath of hope when she saw the man approaching.

Why she felt that he was a gentleman, a rescuer, she could not have said. He was bloodstained like the rest and gazed at the havoc about him with an eye as hard and as cold. Perhaps it was the trim fit of his doeskin breeches over his well-muscled thighs and the gleam of his expensive boots. Or his neatly trimmed hair or his face, sun-browned and angular but clean-shaven? It was a pleasant face, at variance with his profession and the other faces about her. But it was more than just his appearance. She sensed an almost tangible confidence about him that seemed to say he was a man who had no need to bully those beneath him to prove his own worth. The other pirates gave him a grinning respect and a wide berth.

He approached her now and she almost spoke to plead her cause. Hope leaped into her large black eyes and words trembled on the soft curves of her lips, but he gave her only a very brief glance before turning to DeLessops. "I heard you found a woman on board."

Her heart thudded in dismay. His glance had been swift and penetrating, as if in that second he had taken note of every detail about her, yet it had been indifferently brief. And now his words, his tone, were too casual, as if he asked about a bundle of silk or a keg of rum.

"She's mine!" snarled her captor, rounding on the newcomer.

A very slight arching of his brows was the tawny-haired pirate's only reaction. "I wasn't aware that the division of our prize was done. But at any rate, we agreed before the voyage that any captives were to be turned over to me."

Raven looked from one pirate to the other. She knew nothing of this tall, broad-shouldered buccaneer casually leaning on his saber, except that he was aloof, his speech and accent were that of a gentleman, and he seemed infinitely preferable to De-Lessops.

"The *crew*," DeLessops corrected, his lips twisting into a triumphant grin. "Our agreement was that you get the crew. We said nothing about passengers, Captain."

The merest flicker of irritation crossed the blond buccaneer's face before he shrugged, as if dismissing the problem altogether. He laughed and tapped the toe of his boot with his saber. "You're right, of course, DeLessops. I think you are splitting hairs with me, but you are right. You have as much right to her as I."

Raven shuddered at his cold dismissal of her. Why had she expected help from this man, anyway? She certainly had no claim on him. In spite of his elegant carriage and gentlemanly air, he was just as much a pirate, just as heartless and cruel as his unwashed companions. But the mere presence of a seeming gentleman had so raised her hopes that she now felt as if she had been betrayed. As nothing else had done, his casual words and easy laughter while the two pirates discussed her brought home to her the desperate reality of her situation. They spoke of her as if she were no more than any other piece of cargo. With horrifying certainty, she knew that whether they decided to try to ransom her, to throw her overboard, or to rape her on the spot, there was no one to whom she could appeal for help. And very little she could do to help herself.

"Tell me, DeLessops, what do you plan to do with her?"

DeLessops traced the path along her neckline once again with his grimy finger. "There is only one use that a man has for a woman," he said, licking his lips as though he would devour her. "And when I tire of her, there is always Maricaibo."

The smile did not leave the lean captain's face, but there was a tightening, a hardening about his eyes. "The slave market?"

Raven's eyes widened further in horror, but she was unable to shrink from DeLessops's touch. The bonds biting into her arms were too secure. She clenched her teeth and held her head another proud notch higher, determined to still the trembling she felt beginning deep within her.

The tall captain turned those cool, blue eyes upon

her, letting them travel the length of her, smiling appreciatively. And though they reminded her of two chips of glacial ice, his look did not chill her as DeLessops's had. Indeed, she found herself growing strangely warm beneath his scrutiny.

"A fine-looking wench. She'll bring a good price." He rested the tip of his saber on her shoulder, almost caressing her with it, as he slid it casually toward her throat. Then quickly, expertly, with an almost imperceptible flick of his corded forearm, he sliced through the rope about her neck, dropped the razor-sharp point once more to the deck, and leaned again on the pommel. "That is, unless you treat her as roughly as you usually do your women. Badly used goods do not sell well. Even in Maricaibo."

"I'll use her any damn way I please!" DeLessops snarled.

The other pirate shrugged and turned away as if the subject had begun to bore him. "Of course you may. That will be your right—as soon as you've paid for her."

DeLessops snatched at the taller man's sleeve. "What do you mean 'pay for her'? She's mine, I told you!"

One chilling glance from his fellow pirate was all the warning DeLessops needed. He dropped his hand quickly.

The smile was gone from the tall pirate's face and his body tensed. "As you pointed out, DeLessops, we made no agreement about passengers. She must be considered part of the booty and any ransom or sale money must be shared by all according to the articles we all signed."

"And in the meantime?" DeLessops screeched.

"In the meantime, she must be treated with every consideration. Any abuse would lessen her value and

12

I'm sure you would not want to cheat your men of their prize."

A growl and several mutterings came from the pirates who had gathered around, attracted by the heated discussion and the presence of a woman of uncommon beauty. Raven would have jumped at the sound had her bonds allowed her the freedom to do so. The glittering eyes and yellow teeth, the pressing, greedy bodies made her feel as if she were surrounded by a pack of hungry wolves ready to fight over every last one of her bones.

"But ransom is often hard to collect and Maricaibo is a long way off." The lean captain cast a meaningful glance at DeLessops and then turned his attention to the crew. "The only way to insure that these good men will not be cheated is to give them payment for the girl now."

DeLessops's evil grin returned and he chuckled. He almost clapped the other man on his back. For a moment he had been close to real hatred for his smooth-tongued partner but now he saw a way to satisfy his desire without facing a confrontation with his men. All he had to do was toss a pittance to his crew and the wench was his. And when he was through with her, he would gain their further favor by sharing her with them. If there was anything left. "That's fair," he agreed.

The ice-blue eyes again turned to study the ashen-faced Raven. By now she felt faint. Her hopes had been raised and cruelly dashed so many times in the last few minutes that she did not know what to think. And the tall pirate captain was an enigma which her battered sensibilities could not fathom. First he had criticized DeLessops for his treatment of women then he seemed to be smoothing DeLessops's path to her. When he cut the rope from her neck, she thought he was helping her. Now she wondered if he had done it only to make his point with DeLessops. The man she had at first hoped would rescue her now seemed to be the coldest, cruelest of them all. Again, she asked herself why she had ever thought he was any different from the other pirates leering at her. He, too, was leering at her. Or so it seemed. But when her eyes met his she thought she saw a momentary thawing of those icy orbs, a brief flicker of warmth in his smile.

And then he was again turning his back to her and she wondered if it was only desperation that made her imagine that his look was one of encouragement.

He spoke to DeLessops but he raised his voice to ensure that every greedy man there heard him clearly. "Aye, she's a fine-looking wench. She should bring at least three thousand pounds on the block."

DeLessops's good humor evaporated, incredulity etched into every grimy line on his face. "No woman is worth that much," he spat.

The broad shoulders in front of her shrugged indifferently. "I admit it is not often one goes for so much, but we have all seen it happen." There was a muttering of agreement from the gathered men. "In my opinion, this wench could easily fetch that much. Of course, if you are trying to cheat us of our rightful shares . . ."

The scrawny captain glittered with hate, and his fingers clenched just a bare inch from the pistols stuck into his worn silk sash. "I don't have that much and you know it. Not until we dispose of the cargo we've taken. Then I'll pay for her."

Now the look of incredulity was on the pleasant-faced captain—incredulity and amusement. "Are you asking us to trust you for our shares? To let you enjoy your prize now, then when she is worn and

14

spent and your pleasure's done, that you will pay three thousand pounds?''

There was a rising chorus of protest and angry mutterings. Not one of his crew would trust him that much and DeLessops knew it. ''Then we'll all have to wait 'til we reach port,'' DeLessops growled. ''None of us has that much coin.''

''I have.''

The words were quiet but everyone heard them and watched fascinated as the tawny-haired captain drew a heavy purse from his red sash and tossed it lightly into the air. He caught the solid chink of coins.

''Three thousand pounds, lads,'' he said, dangling the purse before them. ''Three thousand pounds to be divided among you now. Does anyone offer more for the wench?''

The only sound was a deep animal growl of outrage and hatred from DeLessops. Then the pirates burst into cheers of acceptance. The tall pirate tossed the purse to his first mate, who was in charge of the division of the spoils. A round, bookish little man, the mate caught the purse awkwardly and led the crew away to split their loot.

''You haven't heard the last of this,'' DeLessops threatened. Then he turned and stomped away.

A laugh rang out from her new captor as he stood, his arms akimbo, watching his adversary stalk away as if the ire of a pirate captain in control of a ship larger than his was no worry at all. Then he rounded on her, his saber still clenched in the fist at his waist, his feet widespread, and his head tilted to one side studying her. He was taller than average and well made, his broad shoulders tapering to slender hips and a lean belly. His shirt hung loose and opened halfway to his waist, exposing a hard, tanned chest sprinkled with light blond curls. Wide-topped boots came halfway to the knees of his long, well-muscled legs and he seemed oblivious to the gash on his left thigh. His laughter changed to warm appreciation as he looked at her, and she squirmed beneath so thorough a scrutiny.

His probing blue eyes roved over her black curls, her perfect oval-shaped face, her wide, black eyes fringed with thick, black lashes. They took in her pert nose and fragile rose-colored mouth. His eyes fell to the creamy column of her throat, hardening with anger at the angry red rope burn. They warmed again as they sailed over the crests of her full, round breasts and down the curve of her waist. "Aye," he said, letting his breath out slowly, "I was right. You are well worth three thousand pounds. Indeed, I fear I may have badly cheated my mates."

He then attacked her bonds, cutting away what he could with his saber, working at the knots close to her flesh. "I doubt that you have found our hospitality to your liking, so far," he said to her, "but you will soon be safe aboard my ship."

"And will I fare any better there than I would here?" she challenged, still blushing from his perusal.

His face was close to hers, and she could feel the warmth of his breath on her cheek as he paused. He grinned roguishly at her and amusement leaped into his eyes, turning them from ice to warm pools of blue. "That you will have to judge for yourself."

His answer gave her no reassurance. He bent his head silently to resume his task and she studied him. His nearly blond hair was streaked now with dirt and grime from the battle but it had been recently washed, as had his clothes. DeLessops, she was sure, could not have had a bath in weeks, and his clothes looked like he never took them off. As the captain stood close to her, his shoulder brushing hers, she felt his strength, and his fresh manly scent assailed her. His shirtsleeves had been rolled back and she could see the smoothly corded muscles of his arms and hands. His fingers were long and fine, and though his hands which grappled with her knots were blood-smeared and gunpowder-begrimed from the recent battle, his nails were clean and showed evidence of careful paring. She turned her attention to his face so near her own. His wide forehead was shadowed by a shock of nearly blond hair and his brows, a little darker than his sun-bleached hair, came together intently now above his deep-set eyes. His nose was straight and fine with nostrils flaring like a stallion's. But it was his mouth that captured her interest— full mobile lips, sensitive and sensual, yet lacking weakness. The kind of mouth made for kissing a woman, for holding her in thrall with its very touch.

Raven's bonds loosened all at once, surprising her so that she staggered forward. He caught her shoulders and his grip was shockingly strong, astoundingly tender. Though his grasp was gentle and his eyes reflected concern for her, she remembered that this man was a pirate. He had just violently attacked the vessel on which she had been a passenger, and he now held her captive. It was not just her shoulders, but her future and her life that he held in his hands.

She placed one shaky hand against his chest to push him away. Where his shirt was opened, her fingers came into contact with his flesh, warm and vibrant, hirsute and rock-hard. She gasped and withdrew her hand, still tingling from that touch, curling her fingers to her own breast. Swallowing hard, she tried to stand steadily before him. She let out a long ragged breath and drew her shattered courage about

17

her, lifting her little chin firmly before looking up at him.

She glanced meaningfully at his hands which still held her. She could feel their warmth spreading through her, quickening her breath. He was holding her close, very nearly supporting her, and she knew she could not have loosened herself from those arms any easier than she could have freed herself from the ropes that now lay at her feet.

Turning her around, he guided her steps through the carnage and chaos to the side of the ship. Now that the Dutch ship was gone, the second pirate vessel had drawn closer and grappling hooks kept the two ships from drifting apart. Sun-browned pirates leaped back and forth across the narrow chasm or handed parcels of plundered cargo from one side to the other as division of the spoils was made.

"My ship lies there," her captor said, indicating the other vessel. In dismay, she realized that she would have to make that crossing. And though the colorfully garbed buccaneers leaped easily from vessel to vessel, she doubted that she could. She looked down at the shadowed waves, and the empty expanse between the ships seemed to grow wider, stretching to an enormity she knew she could not conquer.

"I...I...can't..." Raven began, white-faced and wide-eyed. Her words were stopped, along with her heart and her breath when her captor swept her into his arms. Before she had time to struggle, he bounded to the railing ready to leap the expanse with her in his arms. With a cry, she flung her arms around his neck and buried her face against his chest. With a laugh, he easily made the crossing, landing safely on the deck of his own ship.

Raven lifted her head but her arms remained around his neck, seemingly of their own accord. After the harrowing events of the past hours and the frightening leap, she was trembling too hard to leave the relative safety and comfort she felt in his arms.

He, too, seemed reluctant to release her, letting her slide slowly down the lean length of him, supporting her closely against him. For a long moment he smiled at her, caressing her hair as if comforting a child. But his eyes were not comforting. He looked at her with appreciation for the woman she was—warm, desirable, and within the circle of his arms.

At last breaking the spell that bound them, he beckoned to a passing crewman, a short, wiry man, naked to the waist, and barefooted. "Rodney, take the lady below to my cabin and see to her needs."

"Aye, aye, Cap'n!" Rodney snapped crisply.

The captain bowed briefly to her as if she were a guest and passenger rather than a disheveled prisoner, then bounded back to the other ship, leaving her feeling very helpless and alone in the midst of the bustle about her.

The man in whose charge she had been placed touched his forelock politely. "If ye'll just come this way, milady."

Seeing no choice but to obey, she followed the man down into the ship. He opened the door to a cabin and she stepped inside. The cabin was large and spacious, the bunk neatly made, all was in order and clean. It was far different from what she had expected a pirate ship to be, as was the captain. A glimmer of hope sparked within her and she drew a deep relaxing breath. Of course ransom could be arranged. All was not lost. She would be treated with courtesy and allowed to continue on her way to her uncle in Barbados.

"Is there anythin' ye be needin', ma'am?"

Raven managed a smile. "No. Not now. Thank you, Rodney."

Again pulling his forelock politely, Rodney began backing out the door. "Then if ye'll excuse me, I've got me work. Captain Fortune will take care of ye later."

A trembling of her lips destroyed her smile, and the blood drained from her face. One hand fluttered to her breast, and she feared for a moment that her legs would not support her. "Fortune?" she managed to ask in a whisper.

"Aye, milady," the wiry pirate replied proudly. "The best captain in the Caribbean." Then he closed the door and was gone.

She did not check to see if the door was locked. It made little difference. She was a prisoner—and the prisoner of Jeffery Fortune! She collapsed onto the bunk, her hands over her face. Of all the pirates on the Spanish Main, how could she have had the misfortune to fall into his hands? She had been so eager to escape DeLessops. She should have begged to have been left with him. What mercy could she hope for at the hands of Jeffery Fortune?

Had he not vowed vengeance against her entire family? And had he not been taking his toll these last few years since his escape from slavery on her uncle's sugar plantation?

She almost laughed out loud. He had seemed such a gentleman! With his speech so refined, his elegant carriage, his easy manner, she had been completely fooled. Now she realized that it was only in contrast to DeLessops that he had appeared to be a gentleman. Now she knew him for who he was, a common felon, a traitor to his country, condemned to slavery and transported to the colonies for his crimes. His manners were only a veneer to impress his fellow buccaneers.

It was not her uncle's fault that Jeffery Fortune had committed his crimes and been sold into slavery. But it was Uncle Samuel's misfortune that he had bought him. In his letters he had told her and her father about the rebellious troublemaker who had escaped, laming him in the process and swearing vengeance on him and his family. He had heard no more of his escaped slave until three years ago when Fortune had acquired his own ship and began wreaking havoc on all of Uncle Samuel's shipping.

Now she found herself *his* slave. When he found out who she was, what form would his revenge take?

That the spoils were being shared aboard De-Lessops's ship was no accident. His was the larger vessel and the task would be more easily accomplished there. Though Captain Jeffery Fortune came late, his interests were well represented by Mr. Meachum, his first mate. One of the few of the motley band gathered on the deck who could read and write, Mr. Meachum sat at a small table with the logbook and the cargo manifests of the sunken Dutch merchant ship before him. Round and neat, having taken little active part in the fighting, Mr. Meachum looked more like a misplaced businessman than a pirate as his feathered quill scratched along the paper. De-Lessops stood behind Mr. Meachum, scowling over his shoulder with suspicion at the disposition of each box, bag, or barrel. His large, hook nose and glinting black eyes gave him the appearance of a vulture picking over the bits and pieces of his downed prey.

The men shuffled aside for Captain Fortune as he made his way to Mr. Meachum's side. Propping one foot atop a small keg, he leaned on his knee letting one hand dangle casually as if he had not a care in the world. But those who knew him—there were few in that band unfamiliar with Captain Fortune—would have noted that the captain's good right hand did not stray far from a brace of pistols that he had tucked into his belt, primed and loaded.

Captain DeLessops straightened his angular frame and it would have been hard to miss the sharp glint of hatred that blazed from his eyes when they alighted on his partner in this venture. "Do ye not trust us to make proper division, Captain?" he sneered. "I would have thought you would have other interests to occupy you."

Captain Fortune smiled crookedly and shrugged, ignoring DeLessops's reference to the woman. "I trust Mr. Meachum implicitly."

DeLessops stiffened further and his hand flew to the hilt of his saber. "Meaning that you do not trust me?"

Fortune waved his hand in the general direction of the assembled crews. "I'm sure you are as honest as any other man among your crew."

DeLessops gnashed his few remaining teeth at this reply, for without impugning the honesty of his own crew, he could not take offense. His long, thin fingers twitched once or twice before his hand fell away from his saber, and he returned his attention to the business at hand.

The division proceeded apace with each piece of cargo and loot being shifted to the correct vessel as its destiny was decided. Soon there were but three pieces left. They were traveling trunks and it was not difficult for Captain Fortune to guess to whom they belonged.

Mr. Meachum coughed nervously. "That's all that's left, sir. There was some disagreement about them earlier so we passed over them until last."

"The lady's, I take it?"

"Aye. The lady's. But you'll not be taking them." DeLessops stood straddled and menacing beside the trunks.

Captain Fortune pulled out his saber with a flourish, and DeLessops involuntarily stepped back. Captain Fortune prodded one trunk with the point of his saber. "I have more right to them than anyone, I think. I bought the lady. It follows that anything that belongs to her now belongs to me."

"Not to my way of thinking," DeLessops openly challenged. "Aye, you bought the lady. Nothing was said of aught else."

A chorus of assent followed DeLessops's words, mainly from his own crew.

Fortune shrugged. The paltry sum that the clothes represented was not worth a fight but he hated to deny the woman now in his keeping the comfort and necessity of her belongings. "Mr. Meachum, transfer some cargo of equal value to Captain DeLessops, along with a keg of rum for his men, and we will take these in their place."

He turned and headed for his ship but was stopped by a rough hand on his arm.

"Not so fast, Fortune! I have not agreed." DeLessops glanced from side to side, assuring himself that, indeed, more of his men than Fortune's were on deck. "There may be jewels in those cases," he said, winning the support of his crew. The men began dispersing, each moving a bit closer to his own captain.

"Meachum?" Jeffery asked.

"There were a few baubles, Captain. They were removed and properly divided."

"Then there should be no objection to the trade."

"But there is an objection, *Captain*," snarled

23

DeLessops. "I have an objection to you." He looked to his men for support but found them muttering. This was not their fight. They had just finished one with profitable results. But this one could lead to no good as far as they could see. What did they want with women's clothes, anyway? A good keg of rum was far easier to sell—or drink.

Captain Fortune motioned for his men to remove the trunks. They had already brought the rum and it now stood beside the trunks. But DeLessops placed a booted foot on the largest trunk. "Ye'll be taking nothing off my deck but yourselves, Fortune."

DeLessops men grinned and moved closer. Now this was something they understood. They did not object to a little brawl to gain both the trunks *and* the rum. Greed was their forte.

"Ye'll notice that you're outnumbered, Fortune." DeLessops spread his nearly lipless mouth into a mocking grin. "Ye'd do well to leave now or the face you present to the wench tonight may not be quite so fine as it is now. Unless you'd like to turn her over to me."

Only a slight flaring of his fine nostrils showed the contempt that Captain Fortune felt for DeLessops, as if a foul odor had suddenly sprung up. Otherwise, not by stance or action, did Captain Fortune seem to be affected by DeLessops's braggadocio.

The men from both vessels were clearly ranged behind their captains waiting only for orders, and in numbers, Captain Fortune was severely lacking. But this did not seem to weigh heavily upon him as he casually placed a foot on the keg and rested his arm across his knee, his saber dangling loosely in his hand. "The one mistake I made in this venture, DeLessops," he admitted, "was to take you as my partner. Do not think I would have sought you out.

Providence has given me a good lesson here. Never hope for a clean battle with scum on your side."

DeLessops and his outraged crew snarled and as a man stepped forward, aching for a fight. They were halted by the sudden appearance of a brace of loaded pistols, one in Captain Fortune's free hand and one in Meachum's. Captain Fortune still smiled and leaned casually on his knee, but his eyes missed nothing. The men had both heard and seen for themselves his deadly accuracy with a pistol.

"Now, lads," he said, slipping easily into the dialect favored by the less-schooled and lower born, "whilst ye've been muckin' about wi' the casks and cases 'ere, me own crew 'as been lookin' to their primin', so to speak."

His eyes shifted to the small group behind him then back to the larger group behind DeLessops. "And 'tis sure your eyes be as keen as mine and ye'll be notin' that the balance tips in yer favor...so it seems. But have ye noted the cannons pokin' their noses out of me vessel, ever so eager to blast this 'ere one to 'ell and back? 'Twould be an easy job with so many souls so eager to make the journey." He paused as the men looked nervously at the other ship. Pritchard, Captain Fortune's chief gunner, stood beside a cannon, the priming match glowing in one hand, awaiting only the order to fire.

"Now, lads. Ye knows what a broadside at these close quarters can do to a ship, even if yer captain don't."

There were nervous mutterings, tongues licking suddenly dry lips, and a cautious backward movement from DeLessops's men. Captain Fortune nodded to his men, and they carried the trunks aboard, sporting broad grins.

"I was a might anxious for a bit, Cap'n," Rodney

said, keeping a now merry eye on DeLessops's crew. "I should've known to trust ye. Ye've gotten us out of tighter scrapes than this."

"Should we take the keg 'o rum, too, Cap'n?" one cheery crewman asked hopefully.

Fortune laughed and shook his head. "Nay. We'll not be greedy—or unfair. Mayhap these fellows will remember that while they consume this keg. Captain Fortune never takes more—nor less—than he's bargained for."

When the last of his crew had clambered over the side, Jeffery bounded across to his ship, calling out to his men to cast off the grappling lines and to hoist the sails. "Sluggards they be, lads, but by the time they bring their cannon to bear I want to be showin' a fine pair of heels. Our stern is but a narrow target for such poor gunners, but I prefer to be out of range."

Captain Fortune glanced about the deck. The cargo from the sunken Dutch ship was strewn about, but his lads were busy stowing it away. The cargo had been divided between the two crews but it still had to be sold before a proper division could be made among his own men. But that would have to wait until they reached a safe port. For now, he had business below that could wait no longer.

Chapter Two

Raven took a deep calming breath and forced herself to sit ramrod straight on the bunk. She must not give way to despair! Jeffery Fortune did not yet know who his captive was. Her name would be on the ship's register, but Uncle Samuel was her mother's brother. His last name was not the same as hers. The chance was slight that Captain Fortune would know that Raven Winthrop was the niece of Samuel Parkington. She must keep that secret from him. Whatever his usual treatment of female prisoners, it could not be as bad as the vengeance he would take on the niece of his former master.

She looked down at her torn bodice, felt the disarray of her hair. Whatever his treatment of her, she would be better able to face him if she were more presentable. She stood up and looked around. The spacious cabin was very Spanish with heavy ornate carving on the beams and rich velvet hangings around the bed. The bed itself was unusually large, easily big enough for two. She blushed at the thought, hastily turning her eyes away. There was a large seat across the stern beneath a row of four large windows. Under the seat were shelves filled with rolled charts. Large built-in cabinets flanked the windows and to the right of the door was a small screened area in which she found toilet facilities, a basin and ewer of water, and much to her surprise, a small bathtub.

A long hot soak would have done much to restore her but there was not enough water in the pitcher, nor was it hot. But even a quick wash would be welcome, and she poured water into the basin.

Clean, soft towels were close at hand and a white, nearly scentless soap. She repaired the ravages of her capture as best she could, borrowing a comb and brush she found, all the while wondering how an escaped slave had managed to steal so fine a ship. A traitor he may be but at least he preyed upon the Spanish enemies of England as well as her Dutch friends.

The sounds of hurrying feet and the shuffle and scrape of cargo continued to reach her ears. Shortly, she heard shouted orders, the creak of block and tackle, and the crisp snap of sails opened to the wind. Then the motion of the ship changed. She knew they were under way, though her destination was yet unknown.

There was naught she could do but wait and that would not be easy. Near the window was a large table spread with charts, navigating instruments, and a few scattered volumes. Hoping to distract her thoughts, she approached the table and picked up a book.

She had just opened it when she heard the first scream. She gasped, and with a start, clutched the book, almost screaming herself. It came again followed by a stream of Dutch-flavored English alternately cursing and begging for mercy. Her heart thudded and her eyes widened in horror. She put her hands over her ears but could not keep out the rending sounds.

She flew to the door but paused with one hand on the latch, the other still holding the book to her breast. If the pirates were torturing the Dutch crew, what could she do to stop it? What would prevent them from adding her to their victims?

But with the next onslaught of screams, she knew she must act. She may not be able to help, she may only get herself into danger, but she knew she could not keep to the relative safety of the cabin while those horrifying sounds continued. She wrenched open the door, relieved to find it unlocked, and stepped into the passageway. The sounds were coming from below. Before she could change her mind, she hurried down the narrow steps, through an open door, and stopped in shock at the hell her eyes beheld.

Six men, four of them Dutch crewmen she recognized, lay on cots, various parts of their bodies red with blood. Two pirates held the gallant Dutch captain stretched on a cot, and the tall pirate captain loomed over him. Already liberally spattered with blood and with one large smear on his cheek, Captain Fortune held a grizzly saw in one hand, a bottle of brandy in the other. There was a grim set to his lips, and the setting sun added a bloody red cast to the scene.

Her hands flew to her face. So strongly was she expecting to see a horrible scene of debauchery and torture, and so strongly did the scene fit her expectations that she almost screamed.

But there was a familiarity about this carnage. Rolls of bandages lay beside the Dutchman and on a nearby table, surgical instruments were neatly laid out. The saw the pirate captain held was from a doctor's kit, the brandy a means to ease the pain of the wounded. The blue eyes that lifted from his work to meet hers were as clear and sober as her own. This was no torture chamber but a place for the wounded, both Dutch and pirate, from the battle.

For a moment she slumped against the door with relief. Even trembling with fear, she had been determined to try to stop the pirates' torture, even though she knew how important one woman would be. But this was a different situation altogether. A situation with which she had a long-standing familiarity and in which she felt eminently confident. The saw meant that someone needed an amputation and she moved closer to see.

It was the Dutch captain, Captain Van Doorn. His arm was stretched out and badly wounded, the bone broken just above the wrist. A tourniquet had staunched the worst of the blood flow but the flesh was badly mangled. Sweat beaded Van Doorn's brow, and though he had already been given a liberal dose of the brandy, his eyes focused on her and he smiled weakly.

"This is no place for you," Captain Fortune snapped at her. "Go back to the cabin."

She ignored his crisp command, though it was difficult not to hesitate beneath his uncompromising glare. Taking a fresh towel from a pile to wrap around her, she advanced to the cot. She was quite used to ordering men around in the surgery and to ignoring well-intentioned, but misplaced, commands, even from field commanders and generals. Then why were her hands trembling so much that it was hard to tie the towel around her waist? Was it because she knew she was this pirate's prisoner, and could not expect the gentlemanly respect she was usually afforded? She drew a deep breath and took refuge in the knowledge that Jeffery Fortune may be qualified to lead a scurvy crew of ruffians into battle but she doubted that he could equal her expertise in the treatment of battle wounds. "I'm not squeamish, Captain Fortune. And I won't faint. If you'll move aside, I'll see if I can save Captain Van Doorn's arm."

A trace of amusement crept into his cool blue eyes. But the trim, dark-haired young woman with snapping black eyes, standing there so quietly confident, made him hesitate uncertainly.

With difficulty, she kept her gaze steady, though she had never before had trouble in meeting a man head on. Was it because her captor was so tall, seeming to tower over her? She forced herself to hold up her head, to meet those cool, appraising eyes with her own as she said, "My father was an Army surgeon, Captain. From the time my mother died when I was eight years old, I was his assistant. We were no strangers to battlefields and I have set many bones and sewed many a gash. I may never have studied formally, but I assure you that I am quite competent and there is no need to amputate Captain Van Doorn's arm."

The pirate captain turned and asked a silent question of Van Doorn.

"Let Miss Winthrop try, Captain Fortune." His voice was a strained, hoarse whisper. "I don't think I will be much good without it. And I have reason to trust the lady."

With a last scrutiny that seemed to penetrate the very marrow of her bones, Captain Fortune nodded and stepped back to allow her access to the patient. It was narrow between the cots and her shoulder brushed against his chest as she passed, arousing within her the memory of being held against that rock-hardness, of the safety and comfort she had felt there. But there could be no safety or comfort for her in the arms of Jeffery Fortune, she reminded herself. Straightening her back to avoid any further contact, she edged into place beside the cot.

Reason to trust the lady. Raven smiled to herself as she bent to check the surgical instruments available. Captain Van Doorn was referring to an incident that had happened three weeks ago out of Rotterdam. Raven and her father had taken the first ship bound for Barbados, even though it was going by way of New Amsterdam in the northern American colonies. Her father, weakened from overwork and suffering from a fever, had at last relented to her pleas and resigned his battlefield duties to seek a milder climate in which to recuperate. Uncle Samuel had long praised Barbados so she had written and asked permission to make an extended visit. But her father would never see Barbados now for he had succumbed to the fever just before they docked in New Amsterdam.

It was while her father was ailing that a young sailor had fallen from the rigging onto the deck, breaking his left leg. Raven had insisted that her father not be disturbed. She had set the leg and sutured the lacerated flesh herself and the leg had healed well and cleanly.

But Van Doorn's arm was a different matter. It was badly mangled. Assured that the instruments were in order and surprisingly clean, Raven bent over her patient for a better view of the task before her, wondering how a pirate had come into possession of these fine tools. They were probably stolen, she thought, and shot a withering glance at her captor.

But her scorn went unnoticed. Captain Fortune's interest lay lower on her anatomy and with a start she realized just where. She had repaired her bodice as well as she could, but the rips, along with the already low cut of the gown, revealed much that she would have hidden from that probing gaze. Standing so tall and peering over her shoulder, he was in the perfect position to enjoy a most delightful view. A situation, she noted, that he had been quick to take advantage of. Angrily, she turned her shoulder but found it impossible to work in that position. It was a choice between modesty and the welfare of a patient who could no longer wait for help. She knew at once which was more important. With a proud toss of her head, she bent over Van Doorn's arm. The low chuckle from the man beside her seemed to wash over her in waves of heat.

Probing gently, she was thankful to find the main arteries intact and only the radius broken. But the bone was sticking up at a sickening angle and there was a possibility that there were small fragments in the mangled mass. It would have to be cleaned before she could assess the extent of the damage.

"I need some water," she ordered crisply, trying to focus her attention on her task. But she had never had such a distraction as the one who now stood by her side.

He put a pan of water into her hand and her fingers brushed his, sending another wave of heat over her. She longed to cool her hands, her face, her neck, with that water but instead, dipped in one slim finger and then put it to her lips.

"This is fresh. I need sea water to cleanse the wound," she said, pushing the pan back into the tall pirate's hand, carefully avoiding touching him.

"You would pour salt water into an open wound?"

She nodded. "I know it seems cruel, but wounds heal more cleanly when they are washed with sea water. No one knows why."

Michele Stegman

He hesitated only a moment before nodding to one of his crewmen who hauled a bucket of water to Raven's side.

She glanced once at Van Doorn and he nodded that he was ready. Taking a dripping dipperful of the briny water, she poured it gently over the wound. Van Doorn shuddered once, moaned, then fainted. Raven sighed with relief. With the Dutch captain unconscious, her task would be easier and he would not suffer. But speed was still of the essence.

She began to work with a concentration that eradicated all else. The tall man beside her who handed her a suture or scissors or who helped to sponge away the blood ceased to be her captor. He was only her assistant. He did naught to dispel that image for he deferred to her and responded to her terse commands as any trained assistant would, always ready with the instrument she needed next.

Carefully cleaning the wound, she picked out slivers of bone and cut away the badly shredded flesh, leaving a cleaner wound to be stitched. She aligned the bone as well as she could and then sutured the flesh. Then she bandaged the arm and tied a splint in place.

Straightening, Raven wiped away the perspiration on her brow with the back of her hand, leaving a bloody smear in its place.

"As fine a job as any surgeon could have done, my lady."

For one moment her eyes met the pirate captain's, no longer glacial shards but blue summer pools smiling at her in admiration. Warming from his praise and his look, she blushed and pulled her eyes away, looking to see what other work needed doing.

A youthful Dutch crewman lay on the next cot, his leg well-bandaged. Peering beneath the wrappings, she could see the stitches. They were not the work of a trained doctor but done well enough.

"It vas me dat vas screamin, miss," he said, hanging his head so that a long shock of pale blond hair nearly hid his reddened cheeks. "Da captain, he vas gentle, but it hurt ven he take out da ball and sew da hole."

Smiling, she patted his hand and started to move on to the next cot. But Captain Fortune was standing beside her and in her haste she ran into him.

One sandy brown brow traveled upward, seeming to pull the corner of his mouth into an amused grin, and his arms came around her. "Right into home port," he said.

She gasped and then stiffened as his meaning became clear to her, that in his embrace was where she belonged. She pushed away from him, her fingers seared from touching, once again, the warmth of that solidly muscled chest. She longed to wipe the smirk from his face with a slap but she dared not. She reminded herself that she was his prisoner, and though he was smiling now and apeing the gentleman, she had no way of knowing what mercurial moods this overbold pirate was prone to. A haughty glare was the most she dared and she had no illusions that it was her look that caused him to step aside gallantly. Even so, there was little room in the cabin and she was forced to once again brush close by him to get to her next patient.

A Dutch crewman lay insensible, a huge purple swelling on his head. She lifted his eyelids, noting the unequal dilation of the pupils, then probed the wound gently. "It seems to be a concussion," she pronounced. "Rest is the only cure."

It did not take her long to sew up a shallow saber gash across a pirate's ribs and to bandage a knife wound in a Dutchman's arm. The last injury was a clean bullet wound in a pirate's shoulder. The ball had passed completely through so there was little to do but to clean and bandage the hole.

Straightening from this final task, she found Captain Fortune waiting with a basin of clean water in his hands and a fresh towel over his arm. She sighed thankfully and dipped her bloody hands into the water and would have smiled gratefully at him if he had not been leering at her so boldly. Now that the needles and sutures were no longer in her fingers, the familiar ground was cut from beneath her and she felt the bonds of her captivity tighten once again. She did not like to think what might come next. Certainly she need not encourage the lust in his eyes with a smile that he would be free to interpret in any way he chose.

Seeking to delay the possibilities her mind conjured up, she pushed a stool beside Van Doorn's cot and seated herself firmly. "They will have to be watched carefully for a while."

She nodded her head as if to dismiss him, but he did not take the hint. Leaning over her, he braced his hands against the wall behind her, effectively trapping her between two steel-muscled arms. His sun-browned face bent near, a lock of his tawny hair nearly touching her midnight-black curls. The smells of sick bay, blood, wine, and the acrid taint of vomit, assailed her nostrils.

But it was his presence, she told herself, that suddenly made her feel slightly giddy, that made her heart beat an unsteady rhythm. One lean hand reached to cup her chin and she knew that it was fear that quickened her breathing and started a wave of warmth within her.

"Come," he said, and the heat within her seemed

to grow, fueled by the warmth she saw in his eyes. "You have done enough. Rodney will watch and call you if you're needed."

The wiry crewman nodded to her reassuringly. "Ye rest yerself now, miss. I'll look out fer 'em. I put a tray for ye in the cabin."

Two strong hands captured her shoulders, drawing her to her feet, and once more she felt that strange quickening of her heart when his flesh met hers. She had shared the company of rough men most of her life, on one battlefield or another, and she thought she had grown accustomed to their ways. But, she reminded herself, she had never before been so completely in someone else's power. Someone she had every reason to believe had no scruples about doing with her whatever he pleased and who had no fear of the laws that governed decent men.

Guiding her before him, they left the sick bay. All the way back up the steps she could feel his eyes upon her and she would have been even more fearful had she guessed how deeply her trim figure and gently swaying hips aroused him. Her own thoughts were far from calm as they neared his cabin. She felt as though she were being herded into a lion's den with a blue-eyed, tawny-maned lion close at her heels!

He leaned around her to open the cabin door and set his hand at her waist to guide her inside. Her heart beat a rapid staccato as if trying to escape her breast, which was as impossible as it would be for her to escape from his cabin. She heard the door close, sealing her doom, and stiffened as his hand caressed her briefly before it was withdrawn from her waist. She could feel the warmth of his body so close behind her and suddenly she felt almost giddy. She noted the tray Rodney had left on the table. It must be hunger and fatigue, she thought, putting one hand to her cheek.

Instantly, she felt his hand return to her waist as he guided her forward and pulled out a chair for her. He splashed something into a mug from a decanter on the tray and pushed it into her hand.

"Drink this," he ordered.

Numbly, she obeyed, choking on the brandy. But it revived her and she handed the mug back, smiling a timorous thank you up at him. Were his eyes really as full of concern as they seemed?

"I'm sure all this has not been easy for you, Miss Winthrop. And you have worked very hard helping the wounded. I want to thank you for that."

"I consider myself a doctor. I could do no less," she replied primly, trying not to let his smile warm her as much as the brandy.

"Nevertheless, I thank you," he said, refilling her mug with wine. He set it on the table next to her, making her heart leap at his nearness. "And I am sure Captain Van Doorn will have good reason to be grateful you were there."

"There is still a risk of infection," she cautioned, leaning back in her chair and putting a little more distance between them.

He filled his own mug and sat across from her. "Eat something, Miss Winthrop."

The tray Rodney had left was filled with slices of ham, beef, and cheeses. There were small rolls and fresh fruit. Very appetizing after weeks of salt pork and hard biscuit aboard the Dutch ship. But she was not sure she could eat with him watching her so closely over the rim of his mug. She felt very much like a mouse about to be pounced upon. But he expected her to eat something so she took a slice of mango and nibbled at it.

"You must keep up your strength, Doctor. Your patients may need you." He cut open a roll, stuffed it with meat and held it out to her.

She took it, starting as his fingers brushed hers, and forced herself to eat. She knew he was right. She hadn't eaten all day and she needed to fortify herself for whatever may come.

Captain Fortune ate with a hearty appetite that did justice to Rodney's efforts. Finally he pushed back his chair, stretched out his legs, and crossed his booted feet. She could not help noticing the long lithe form before her, the wide shoulders and lean, corded arms, the fine, strong fingers he laced together over the red silk sash that lay flat across his belly.

He studied her anew, a half-smile playing about his lips as his eyes traveled the length of her, warming on their way. "Now, Miss Winthrop, what shall I do with you?"

Sudden fear clutched at her heart but she forced herself to hold her head up proudly and smile back at him in an exact imitation of his amused half-smile. "What do you usually do with women you pay three thousand pounds for?"

His smile broadened at her spirit, and his eyes again touched her most intimately. "I've never paid that much for a woman before."

She shuddered inwardly, noting that he did not deny that he had bought women before, only that he had never paid so much. What then would he expect of her? "Then why did you pay so much for me?"

The smile left his face, replaced by a grim line. "I should think the answer to that is obvious."

"Not to me. If you plan to sell me in Maricaibo, I fear you have made a bad bargain. You can hope for little profit after paying so much. And if ransom is your hope, I must disabuse you of that notion also, for there is no one who will pay it." There was one other possibility, that he had purchased her for his own use, as DeLessops had planned to use her. But that possibility she would not mention and tried not to think about. Instead, she looked him square in the eyes, trying to retain the demeanor of one discussing the disposition of a piece of lace with a merchant.

"You are alone in the world?"

She thought of her distant cousins in England, so very far away and who knew so little of her, and dismissed them immediately from her consideration. Her only close relative was Uncle Samuel in Barbados. But what hope would she have if she were to say, "Oh, yes, I am the niece of your former master. The man you crippled. The man you hate so much. The man you have sworn vengeance upon and are bent on destroying." And she was not entirely certain that Uncle Samuel would be willing to pay so much for the release of a niece he had seldom seen and who might be unmarriageable after an encounter with pirates.

"There was only my father," she answered at last. "He died on board ship."

"I see," he said, and she thought there was a touch of sympathy in his voice.

"Set me ashore on Barbados!" She leaned forward and dared to lay a hand on his arm. "I am a good doctor. I can set up a practice and earn money. I will pay my own ransom."

"I think not, Miss Winthrop." Suddenly he got up and paced about the cabin. Then, with one arm braced on a beam, he stood looking out the stern windows.

"I know it is a lot of money and will take some time to earn so much." She got up and quickly came around the table to stand beside him, pleading with him. If she could just convince him to take her to Barbados, then when she was safe, she could ask Uncle Samuel for the money. "I give you my word. I will get the money to you. All of it. More if you want some profit. Just..."

Suddenly he turned on her and for one brief moment she saw pain on his face. Pain and hurt and anger. Then it was gone and she was not sure she hadn't imagined it, for his smile was back. The carefree, tilted smile that said that he hadn't a care and that the whole world was there to amuse him. "You forget, milady, that I am a pirate and can hardly go sailing boldly into the harbor in Barbados. The king's cannon and I do not get on so well with one another."

"But..."

"It seems, Miss Winthrop," he said, stepping closer to her and tracing the soft edge of her jaw with one finger, "that for the time being you are mine."

His touch sent shivers through her, spurring her heart to a more rapid beat. She edged away from him until she backed into the table, unable to retreat farther and sorry now that she had not kept the table between them.

"And how long will you keep me prisoner?" she demanded.

"Prisoner?" He bent over, his lips hovering only inches above hers. "You are my guest, Miss Winthrop."

For long moments his eyes held hers, mesmerizing her, quickening her breath. She caught the fragrance of the wine they had shared on his mouth and wondered absurdly what it would be like to taste it, to have him caress her lips with his. Abruptly, she tore her eyes away. What was she thinking? She could not welcome a kiss from a pirate. Especially this pirate. And somehow she must try to stop him from

41

taking any liberties with her.

"I've had little acquaintance with thieves and pirates. Do you always make unwanted advances toward your guests, Captain?"

He stepped back, then leaned casually beside the windows. "At times I am sorely tempted."

She took the opportunity to move as nonchalantly as she could to the other side of the table. She could feel his eyes following her, and she blushed at what he might be thinking. Her hand fluttered up in a small hopeless gesture to try to conceal what her torn dress seemed all too eager to reveal.

"But you must be tired, Miss Winthrop." He gathered up the remnants of their meal and held the tray. "I will bring you some hot water. Your trunks are in that cupboard." He left, closing the door softly behind him.

With a cry of surprised delight, she opened the cupboard. She had thought her trunks were on the ocean's floor and that she would have to make do with this one soiled and torn dress. Their return did much to lift her spirits. Hoping Captain Fortune would bring enough water for a bath, but thinking that chance was slight, she pulled out her small trunk and opened it. She was dismayed to find that the contents had been thoroughly jumbled but she managed to find her most modest nightgown and tossed it across the bed while she knelt to straighten the rest of her things.

She started and jumped to her feet when the door thumped open. Captain Fortune entered and set two steaming buckets beside the screened tub. Flushing, she snatched up her nightgown, thrown so provocatively across his bed, and hid it behind her while he crossed the cabin to the other cupboard. His clothes were neatly arranged within, and he quickly took what he needed.

"I will bathe on deck," he said, bowing briefly and leaving her alone once more.

She drew off her dress, laid it across the bed, and dimmed the lantern. Quickly, she took advantage of the captain's absence and settled gratefully into the tub. It was not a tub to luxuriate in but the hot water did much to soothe her and she dawdled much longer than was her usual custom, relaxing for the first time since her ordeal. If she had feared for her safety and her chastity, she let it slide now. Captain Fortune had not attacked her. He had, in fact, treated her with courtesy, except for that one awkward moment when she thought he would kiss her.

She leaned back smiling, thinking of his kindness in vacating his cabin for her. Only a gentleman would be so thoughtful. True, Captain Fortune was but a common felon, a traitor, and an escaped slave, but somewhere he had acquired at least the pose of a gentleman.

A small noise alerted her and she opened her eyes to see Captain Fortune leaning casually beside the screen, enjoying each delightful curve of her with a growing warmth in his eyes.

Chapter Three

Jeffery Fortune's presence sent fear crashing head-long into Raven's mind and her wits reeling. With a gasp, she sat up in the tub, exposing much of her body. Trying futilely to cover at least the most private parts of her anatomy with a hand that was woefully inadequate for the task, she groped for the out-of-reach towel with the other. There was no escape from his amused gaze which seemed to touch her everywhere at once, as she grew even more desperate to grab the towel.

A wide, leering grin sculpted itself across Captain Fortune's face as he watched the twin rosy peaks of her breasts play hide-and-seek with his eyes as they bobbed in and out of the water.

Realizing the hopelessness of reaching the towel from a sitting position, she stood up. She knew she was exposing even more of herself but attaining the covering was well worth it. Her initial fear at his unexpected return was quickly turning to anger. She had felt the strength of those corded arms and if rape was his aim, she knew she would be helpless within his grasp. For now, her only goal was to cover the fuel that fed the desire in his eyes and to rid his face of its smirk.

Little did she realize the impact her naked beauty would have on him. His quickly indrawn breath froze her action, and for one long moment she looked like some marble goddess carved by the hand of a master. But the long ivory limbs, softly curving hips, and rounded breasts glowed with a warmth and life that no marble goddess could ever hope to imitate. The smirk was indeed wiped away, replaced by a wondering awe as his eyes again traveled over her, this time as a pair of pilgrims worshipping the perfection they beheld. The heat of his gaze did not abate but grew apace until she felt engulfed in flame and her body warmed in that flame.

At last she forced her hand to move tremblingly to its long-delayed goal and she gathered the towel around her. The shelter of the partial covering gave confidence to her anger and she tossed her head, glaring at him.

"A gentleman would have left, Captain," she said gratingly.

He folded his arms across his wide chest and the smile returned to his lips. The towel, far too short for modesty and clinging damply to each curve, concealed far less than she imagined. Indeed, it did much to stir his imagination.

"But I am no gentleman. By your own definition I am but a thief and a pirate."

With great effort, she kept her knees from giving way beneath her. He did not make even a tenuous claim to be a gentleman. What restraint could she use to keep him from her? He seemed to have no compunction to restrain himself from whatever or whomever he desired. "What do you want of me? Why have you returned?"

He shrugged and continued to drink his fill of her. "I thought I had given you ample time to ready yourself for bed. When I entered and found the light dimmed, I thought you were already abed. 'Twas but a fortunate happenstance that I chanced to find you thus."

Her emotions continued to struggle between fear and anger, but she managed to gather enough courage to answer him in a coldly sneering tone. "Then if you have seen enough, Captain, would you please give me another moment alone?"

"Seen enough? Nay, love. For having glimpsed a moment of your beauty, I think that I am now a man condemned to forever wanting more." Once more his eyes roamed freely over her, devouring her hungrily, greedily. Then with an obvious iron-willed effort he turned away, crossing the cabin to busy himself at his cupboard with his back to her.

Much bemused at his words and gentle tone, she was relieved that he had not taken her then and there. Still wondering why he had returned, she hastened to dry herself and dress, pulling her robe around her and cinching the waist tightly. Securing her damp curls into a loose braid, its tip curled seductively around one breast, she came from behind the screen to confront him.

He had set the lamp on the table and adjusted it to a brighter light. As he bent over the table studying a chart, the flame cast a glow turning his sun-browned skin to bronze, while his hair, still damp, glistened like burnished gold, warm and alive. He wore his shirt loose and unsashed with the sleeves rolled almost to his elbows, and the light played through the fine cambric, clearly outlining his muscular torso. The corded muscles of his forearms took on a certain grace, softened by the play of light and shadow as he leaned on the table or made notations on a piece of parchment. He looked up as she stepped into the circle of light.

"If I am to sleep here, Captain, where will you stay?" she asked, hoping he would take her subtle suggestion to leave.

"Why, here in my own cabin."

Her face drained of color, though in the dim light she hoped it was not apparent. "Surely it would be better..."

" 'Tis my cabin, Miss Winthrop. My clothes are here as are my charts, navigating instruments, ship's logs, books, and other things I will need in the course of our journey. Here I will stay. However, I invite you to share my comforts. The only other place available to you is with the crew or on deck. Neither place would I advise for your safety."

Her arms akimbo, she cocked her head at a proud angle. "So it is the lion's den or the wolf pack. You say there is no safety for me there, but what of here? What guarantee of security can I have?"

"None whatsoever." He turned more fully to face her, and, even within the deep shadows cast by the lantern, she could see the amusement glinting in his eyes. "I would give you my word as a gentleman that you would be safe with me, but since you do not count me a gentleman you would but set aside my promise with your judgment. There is naught else I can offer you."

She seemed to have little choice. But if she stayed, would he then feel free to take her? Somehow she must make him know that, though she remained in his cabin, she did not also choose him. Turning brusquely, she took a blanket from the bed and began to make up a pallet on the floor. But a strong hand came out of the darkness and undid her work, gathering the blanket over a lean arm.

With a cry of protest, she turned. Captain Fortune stood over her dwarfing her. He towered in the darkness, and weird shadows, cast upward from the lantern, played over the lean planes of his face. For a moment fear accelerated her heart and widened her eyes as she wondered what he would do.

"You will find the bed more comfortable," he said, and spread the blanket back into place.

She backed away. If he took her, it would be by force. She would not climb willingly into this buccaneer's bed. "Perhaps I would be safer on deck, after all, Captain," she sneered.

A low chuckle came to her in the semi-darkness. "I can usually trust my crew with most things, Miss Winthrop. They are good men I have chosen to sail with me. But I would not tempt them beyond their capability to resist. And you are a piece too tempting by far. 'Tis best you remain here where I can protect you."

"And who will protect me from you? Or are you beyond temptation, Captain?"

He pulled down the covers on the bed invitingly then turned to face her. His eyes glowed in the lantern's light but their warmth came from within. "Nay, love. I am sorely tempted. I would take you this moment if you were but a shade more willing."

"I am not willing at all!"

"Then I must bide my time," he said with an impish grin. "Though you judge me a rogue, and I am in the eyes of all the world a lawless pirate, I do hold myself a trifle higher. I give you my bond, as the gentleman I call myself, to respect your chastity this night."

For a time she stood still, looking up at him, her lips parted softly, pondering his words. So gently were they spoken that she almost felt as if she could believe them. She shook her head as if to clear it from the spell he seemed to be weaving about her. "Still, Captain, I do not wish to strain your trust in yourself and prefer not to share a bed with you."

"Though I count myself a gentleman, I am no saint. It would indeed strain me to share my bed with you." He pointed to a dark corner. "Therefore, I have slung a hammock for myself."

Her eyes followed where he indicated and she saw the hammock in the shadowed corner. Whether he would indeed keep to it all night was still a question in her mind but one that only the passage of time would resolve. "Then good night, Captain."

He cocked a brow in a questioning arc. "Captain? Under the circumstances I think we might do well on more intimate terms. My name is Jeffery and I offer you free use of it. And yours?"

"Raven," she said through caution-stiffened lips. "But I think it best that we remain on more formal footing, Captain Fortune."

"Raven. The name suits you well."

His words, almost a caress, surprised her with their tenderness. She stiffened as he lifted his hand and again, she feared that his intent was further intimacy. But he merely chucked her under the chin as one would a child, though his smile was full of warmth.

"Good night, Raven."

He crossed the cabin, dousing the lantern on his way, and she heard a rustle in the darkness as he removed his clothing. The creaking of the hammock as he got in assured her that for the time being she would be left in peace. Breathing a deep sigh of relief, she climbed wearily into the bed, wondering just how safe she was. *If counting himself a gentleman is all that binds him*, she thought, *then I am lost indeed.*

Michele Stegman

For is he not, in spite of the gentlemanly veneer he hides beneath, merely a common felon, a traitor, and an escaped slave turned pirate?

As she sank wearily into the soft comfort of the bed and felt the aching weariness in her body, she thought that in spite of her fears, in spite of the precariousness of her position as a buccaneer's captive, she would have no trouble sleeping.

Then her eyes opened wide in the darkness as the full import of his words came back to her. He had not promised to do her no harm. His promise, if she could trust even that, had been extended for this one night only. Indeed, he had been quite sure that sooner or later she would fall willingly into his arms. Had he not said that he only bided his time until she were more willing?

That strutting jackanapes! The blackguard! The rogish knave! She expanded on her name-calling with a well-rounded vocabulary garnered from years of living in military encampments and battlegrounds.

Angrily, she pounded the pillow into a more comfortable form. He would learn that she was not some simple simpering maid eager for a tumble with the first man who offered her a tender word.

She was willing to grant that his form was fair. His long litheness showed not an ounce of fat. 'Twas muscle hardened into steel that clothed his bones. To that she could attest. She had felt his strength when he carried her in his arms. The grace of his movements she had already compared to those of a cat. A tawny-maned, blue-eyed lion. But there was more to a man than an outward form, a few soft-spoken words, and an eagerness to bed any willing wench who fell into his grasp. She would not let her head be turned by a felonious miscreant who probably should have been hanged before he could escape from well-deserved slavery to wreak destruction on the world.

She wondered how many other women he had captured, who willingly had assuaged his lust, thereby giving him such confidence in himself. She simmered briefly as she thought of him "biding his time." Did he think she would fall like a ripe plum into his lecherous hands?

His soft, even breathing came to her from across the room. The creaking of timbers and the gentle rise and fall of the ship seemed in harmony with it, as if his breath gave the ship life. The bed cradled her in its soft embrace. An embrace that carried a faint masculine fragrance. It seemed that even while he slumbered, she could not escape him. She crossed her arms and glared into the darkness. He may be an overconfident, swaggering rake, but if it was his intent to bed her, she would give him to understand that it would not be by her choice, but by his rape.

With that disconcerting thought and the soft motion of the ship, her exhausted mind and body at last found oblivion in slumber.

She awakened to the gentle slap, slap of a razor being plied on a strop. Or was it the soft singing of an old country air that had awakened her? Then the full memory of where she was came flooding back. 'Twas not her father's hearty, off-key bass she heard but a rich, quiet baritone. She lay still, facing the wall feigning sleep, waiting for Captain Fortune to finish his morning toilet and, hopefully, leave the room.

She heard the rasp of the razor as he shaved and the splash of water as he washed. She listened intently for his departure then sensed more than heard him bending over her. Her heart skipped and she was hard pressed to stay relaxed as if asleep. A low chuckle reached her ears as if he knew she was awake, then she heard the door open and close, his booted feet making scarcely a sound.

As soon as he was gone, she jumped up, took out a fresh gown, and dressed behind the screen, completing her toilet quickly, before she could be interrupted at another embarrassing moment. Her stomach rumbled hungrily and she wondered when and if she would have breakfast.

Sunlight slanted in long golden shafts across the floor, and she knew it was still early, but she had always been an early riser. She was just surprised to find her captor up so soon. She would have thought a pirate would be a slugabed, drinking and singing bawdy songs into the wee hours then snoring late in a drunken stupor, red-eyed and unkempt.

Her stomach growled again in angry protest, and she drank some water to quiet its demands. She had patients to attend to before she could eat.

Adjusting his hat to a slightly more rakish angle, Captain Jeffery Fortune, turned to Rodney, his erstwhile valet, and spread wide his arms asking silently for an opinion.

"Gor, Cap'n! Ye look like a bloody lord!" Rodney stood back, surveying his master proudly. From the jauntily plumed hat to the silver buckles on his shoes, no gentleman of the court could have dressed finer. His coat of deep blue accentuated his sun-bronzed skin, and the gold threads embroidered on his vest seemed specifically spun to match the luster of his hair. "All ye need is the periwig."

Jeffery grimaced in disgust at the curled mass Rodney held up. "I can't abide the thing. Style or not, on my own ship I'll wear my own hair."

Checking his appearance once more in the mirror, he thought again of the captive he was going to so much trouble to please. He was sure she would be surprised to see the elegance of the table he had ordered to be set. It was laid now with fine bone china and cut crystal accompanied by elaborate silver on a fine damask cloth. He did not often dine so elegantly aboard ship. Would she also be pleased to see him dressed as a gentleman? Would it help her forget, even for a time, that he was not a peer of the realm but one of the bretheren of the coast? Somehow he had to ease the fear from her eyes.

He thought of her as he had first seen her, frightened, but with her chin held high, and beautiful even as a bedraggled prisoner. There had been other women captured in the years of his piracy. Some had even been beautiful. But none had been so fiercely proud, so determined not to show their fear, so compelling, or so attractive to him.

When Raven had appeared in sick bay, he had expected her to fall into a ladylike swoon. Instead, she had taken over with a quiet authority, working competently to heal the wounded. He remembered the tantalizing glimpses of her rounded bosom as he stood over her, assisting her. And that reminded him of her naked beauty as she bathed, rising like Venus from the water, the waves of her dark hair pinned high on her head. He remembered her long slender limbs, smooth and glistening wet in the lamplight like polished marble. But no Greek goddess had ever been carved with the high roundness of Raven's breasts and the small expanse of her waist. He held out his hands and knew that if ever he had the chance, his two hands could easily circle that narrow waist. It had taken all his will to turn away from the sight of her. Even now, thinking of her, the heat of passion filled him.

Impatiently, he paced the cabin, waiting for Raven to return from her last check on her patients. Jeffery noticed Rodney fussing with the already-perfect table and glancing often toward the door. He, too, was anxious for their guest's arrival.

At last he heard her step outside the door and he struck a courtly pose, a wide smile lighting his face. She entered in a swirl of rustling satin skirts and he thought that the contrast between her sky-blue dress and her creamy skin combined with her slender frame gave her the appearance of a piece of delicate Delft porcelain. But her flashing black eyes gave a vitality and life to her that no statuette could ever hope to copy.

She stopped when she saw the table and Rodney standing stiffly at attention, and Jeffery saw a sweet smile light her face. Then her eyes found him, widening in admiration as they traveled over him. When they reached his face, she laughed happily, and his heart skipped a beat knowing that his efforts to please her had not been in vain.

Cocking her head coquettishly, she said, "It seems I was mistaken. I thought I had been captured by a nefarious buccaneer. But it seems I am actually a guest in the London townhouse of some great lord."

"I think that it is Captain Fortune who has been captured—at least his heart." A wry smile twisted his lips. "But for tonight, at least, the evil pirate has been vanquished and Lord Jeffery will take his place."

"But I sense that the pirate lurks close by and we will soon be forced to endure his return."

"Aye, milady. I fear it is so. We are not always privileged to choose the roles we must play."

With a flourish, he swept off his plumed hat in a low bow and she answered it with a deep curtsy, capturing his interest at the sight of the cleft of her breasts. It was with some difficulty that he freed his eyes to feast upon her face.

A light tap sounded at the door and a short, round man entered at Lord Fortune's response. He was balding and wore spectacles that threatened any moment to fall off the end of his nose. Jeffery thought that, as always, Meachum looked like a nervously misplaced merchant, but he noticed that his first mate ran an appreciative eye over Raven before bobbing a quick bow.

"Meachum, ma'am. First mate. Take care of the accounts. Sorry about your misfortune, ma'am. But good luck for us. Van Doorn and all." He paused a moment in his chatter to smile up at her and reddened as he added, "And uncommon beauty such as yours is always welcome."

Raven held out her hand to him and introduced herself.

With a touch of envy, Jeffery watched as Meachum's hand lingered on Raven's. Nudging his first mate aside, Captain Fortune held out his arm to Raven and said, "Shall we go in to dinner, milady."

Laughingly, she entered into the spirit of the occasion, and he thought how good it was to see her laugh. She was beautiful even disheveled and bound to a mast. Laughing, she was positively radiant. She took his arm and her touch was light and gentle. He wanted nothing more than to protect her, though from what he had seen, she probably needed less protection than most women he had known. He smiled down at her from his height, and as he seated her, he could not resist briefly caressing one satin shoulder which set his heart beating at a quicker tempo. As he bent over her, he inhaled the fragrance of her hair and enjoyed the excellent view he had of the ripe curves of her breasts. But before she could make some remark, he seated himself at her left and Mr. Meachum sat across from her. She smiled sweetly at the clerk, and Jeffery knew he had been right to include him at the table. Meachum's presence would do much to ease her fears.

Rodney, now dressed as a butler and looking very little like a buccaneer, placed a light soup before her. Jeffery kept up a banter of the latest fashions and tales of strange native rites. And always his eyes roved over her. *I feast, yet I hunger*, he thought. *The more I see, the more I desire. What witchery has she woven?*

"I am surprised at the excellence of your cuisine and the elegance of your table, Captain," Raven said, finishing the last scrap of a smooth custard.

"For a pirate?"

She reddened and he wished he had not reminded her of what he was. "For any ship," she corrected him.

"Different sailing in the islands. Always close to land, Miss Winthrop," Mr. Meachum pointed out. "Fresh provisions are easy to get."

"Having a French chef aboard is also an asset," Jeffery added.

"Oh, my, yes," the rotund accountant chimed in. "Before we captured him, the food was hardly fit to eat."

Captain Fortune swirled a fine Madeira in his glass and chuckled. "You exaggerate, my friend. But I, for one, am glad to have Jean aboard."

Raven's eyes widened. "The man was captured? Just how many prisoners do you keep aboard, Captain?"

"No! No! Oh, my, no! Jean is not a prisoner. Not exactly. I mean he . . ." Mr. Meachum spluttered to a halt.

Raven looked to Captain Fortune for an explanation.

"Jean was a slave aboard a Spanish ship we stopped. As a Huguenot, he was not treated very well. He was so thankful to be rescued, even by pirates, that he agreed to cook for us. But since he does not want to be hanged for being a pirate, he has never signed the articles and takes no part in the fighting. That officially makes him our prisoner, though he is free to leave us any time."

"You certainly have an unusual crew," Raven said. Then with a mischievious grin she added, "For a pirate."

"And a most unusual captain. Don't you agree, Miss Winthrop?" Mr. Meachum asked, finishing his wine and setting down his glass carefully as if afraid that he might break it.

"If Captain DeLessops would be considered typical, then I would certainly agree."

Captain Fortune pushed back his chair and got up. With a small bow, he held out his arm to Raven. "Would you care for a turn about the deck?"

"If you are sure it will be quite safe," she said with a merry twinkle in her eye.

"Absolutely," he answered, laughing and tucking her arm into his. "I will be with you."

"Which is exactly what worries me."

As he guided her up the steps to the deck, his hand resting on the soft curve of her waist, she thought that with the exception of worrying about her chastity, she had never felt more secure. Was it because he had rescued her from DeLessops?

She went to lean against the rail, closed her eyes, and lifted her face into the soft, cool breeze. Reveling in the play of the wind on her face and in her hair, she took great, deep breaths, grateful to be in the open air again.

"It is so refreshing here after spending all day below."

"Come on deck whenever you choose." His fingers trailed along her arm, sending shivers through her. "A bit of beauty to brighten a buccaneer's day is always welcome."

"I thought you warned me that it was not safe," she said, firmly removing his hand.

"I only warned you against inviting advances by sleeping on deck alone," he said, again allowing his hand free access to her arm. "My men are not quite the beasts you may think, Raven. I have chosen carefully those I allow to sail with me and they know well my feelings about abusing women. But every man has his limit of resistance."

"And yours must be very low." With a scornful frown, she again removed his searching hand which had begun to caress the inner crease of her elbow most intimately.

Sighing in momentary defeat, he leaned on the rail beside her, his shoulder brushing hers, and looked into the sea. "The wine-dark sea," he murmured.

She looked up in surprise. "Homer?"

"I always think of that line when I look into the night-darkened sea." Then he turned so that he could look at her. "You are very beautiful," he said, and this time his fingers found their way to her shoulder, tracing a searing path along the delicate arch of bone to the intimate hollow of her throat.

His fingers burned her like a brand, yet she shivered at his touch.

"Cold?" he asked. Without waiting for her answer, he put his arms around her and drew her back to lean against him.

She started to protest but realized that she was indeed more comfortable, protected by his embrace, and warmed. For a long time they stood together, gazing out to sea, watching the stars and the phosphoresence of the white-capped waves. She felt his cheek nuzzling her hair and heard a soft sigh of contentment escape him. Then he was turning her, tilting her face as his lips came down to claim hers.

For one panicked moment, she stiffened and would have pushed him away. But she tasted the wine-dark sea on his mouth, her world reeled with the motion of the waves, and her breath seemed gone forever on the ocean breeze.

Gathering all of her will, she broke away from him and turned again toward the sea, giving her heart time to steady its pace, letting her legs regain the strength that had drained from them. Could she be so afraid of a simple kiss? Was it fear she felt? Or something else? Something she was not prepared to name?

Trying to pretend that the kiss had never happened, trying to change the pattern of his thoughts and hers, she asked something that had been much on her mind. "Where are we bound, Captain, since it cannot be Barbados, and there is little profit for you in Maricaibo?"

He leaned back against the rail, crossed his arms, and looked at her in amusement. She was glad it was too dark for him to see her flushed face but she wondered if he could hear the pounding of her heart. She wanted to run but bravely she stood her ground, her head held proudly high, waiting for his answer.

"Tortuga."

Her face was no longer flushed. At the sound of that one word her face blanched. Tortuga. Pirate capital and hellhole of the world. Its infamy had spread even to the battlefields of Europe. It was hard not to let her voice tremble when she said, "It seems I will be going from the frying pan into the fire."

"Aye, milady. 'Tis a fine mess you've gotten yourself into," he said, grinning.

"I did not ask to be captured by pirates!" she protested, her black eyes snapping.

"An' did you not? A fat Dutch merchantman stuffed to the gunnels with fine European wares wallowing along right into my arms?"

"An honest seaman would not have been tempted by it."

"Oh, he would have been tempted. It just takes a pirate to be able to do something about his desires." He took her arm and began to pull her back into his arms, desire very obvious in his eyes.

She felt like a fish being drawn in, helpless within the net of his spell. He was a pirate, a thief, a rogue, she told herself. A traitor to England and her family's worst enemy. He had captured her in a violent act of piracy and was now taking her to the most evil, dangerous island in the Caribbean. How could she ever have felt safe with him? How could she even now feel so attracted to him? His irresistible charm was that of an unprincipled rake and something she must resist. "No!" she cried, pushing him away. Her heart pounding, she ran down to the cabin, closed the door, and leaned against it, determined to escape him, hoping he, at least, still considered himself enough of a gentleman to leave her in peace again this night.

Chapter Four

It was with some trepidation that Raven stood at the rail of the ship watching the approach to Tortuga. For two days she had stood there or paced the deck, scanning the sea, hoping, praying, for an English warship to appear suddenly over the horizon and to swoop to her rescue. But the only sail that had been sighted was a fellow pirate, and her captors had gone calmly about their business, cleaning decks, polishing fittings, and repairing the sails and rigging that had been damaged in their battle with the Dutch merchantman.

Captain Fortune helped with the repairs to his ship with unflagging energy, at times sitting cross-legged on a coil of rope to sew a sail and share a chantey like any common sailor. At those times, the crew swapped stories and passed a jug with him in easy familiarity. But when the captain took his place on the quarterdeck and snapped orders, the crew jumped to obey his crisp commands as quickly as any English seamen on one of His Majesty's ships. At times like that, it would have been easy for Raven to believe that she was on a well-disciplined ship sailing once again with her father to yet another battlefield hospital. But it took only one look from Captain Fortune to shatter her illusion. No English captain had ever been so bold as to so openly, so smilingly, and with such flagrant relish, enjoy her every movement.

Though Jeffery Fortune had kept his word and had pressed his desire no further than she would allow, she was constantly beseiged by his eyes. No matter how modestly she dressed, how high her neckline, his penetrating gaze had the uncanny ability to expose her most feminine charms, to bore through to her most intimate secrets. His infuriating grin only broadened when she haughtily turned away, trying most unsuccessfully not to blush. And still she would feel his gaze upon her, raking the long slant of her back, the delicate curve of her buttocks.

If she retreated to the cabin, she was reminded that she shared it with the bold buccaneer, that it was his bed she slept in, his tub in which she bathed. The charts on the table, the navigating instruments carefully placed, his boots, his clothes, all put their stamp on the room, declaring it his and surrounding her with his presence.

In sick bay, tending her charges, it was Captain Fortune's surgical instruments she used. Plundered from some other hapless ship, and first seen in his hands, they reminded her that there, too, all was under his domain.

On deck, scanning the sea was where she had found the most relief—and the most hope. But no brave English officer had come to her rescue, no royal warship had battled for her release, and now, all hope was gone that rescue was yet possible. Tortuga loomed before her.

She felt, more than saw, Captain Fortune standing close behind her. One of his hands reached behind her to grasp the ratlines at her shoulder. The other was braced on the railing, effectively trapping her between the railing and his body. She could feel the heat from his face and his golden hair, where the tropic sun had warmed them. Though his chest did not touch her, he was pressed close enough that she thought she could hear the quick beat of his heart. Or was it her own, speeded to an unnatural gait? But he did not seem bent on seduction. For once, his eyes did not rake her mercilessly but strained forward, instead, to that infamous island that lay dead ahead.

"Anxious to get home, Captain?" she asked.

He turned his eyes upon her and as always, when he looked at her, she was startled at their amazing blueness that could change so dramatically from smiling tropic pools to Arctic ice. They were warm now as they swept approvingly over her. His mouth, sensuous and full, lingered just a breath away, easily close enough for a kiss. Instead, it twitched into a humorless smile.

"Home? Aye. I would like to go home. But that is a place forever barred and dangerous to me." For a moment his knuckles whitened as his grip tightened on the ratline with the intensity of his emotion. Then his grip relaxed again, and his tone changed from one of thoughtfulness to one of lightheartedness. "Instead, I come here. 'Tis a safe enough haven for one such as I."

His answer surprised her. She had not thought of him belonging any place but in Tortuga. Was he not a pirate, a fugitive? It had never occurred to her that Jeffery Fortune had once claimed another place as home. Where was that home? she wanted to ask. But the business of docking claimed his attention and drew him away.

She watched him as he worked, calling orders to the crewmen aloft, yet never reluctant to haul on a

Michele Stegman

rope or two himself. His white lawn shirt, open at the throat and rolled to his elbows, revealed bronzed forearms where smooth muscles strained at their tasks. His bare feet easily scampered up a yardarm, yet his casual dress and behavior never seemed to diminish his authority when he strode across the quarterdeck.

Raven's attention was drawn to the dock where a sizable crowd of begging urchins, peddlers with various wares, and prostitutes were already gathered.

"Hey, Phillipe!" a grossly overweight woman called, swiveling her ample hips, "you ready to pay for what I got to offer?"

"Not if I got to pay by the pound!" a burly crewman yelled. "Ain't that much gold on the whole island!"

Raven thought the woman would have been incensed but she only laughed, showing a mouthful of gold teeth.

"Who's gonna put gold in me hand to get kissed by dis golden mouth? Bring you luck, sailor!"

"If I put gold in your hand, I better get more than kisses!" Phillipe laughed, throwing a rope to the dock.

"Angelique give you everything you been dreamin' 'bout while you out dere on dat ocean!"

The ship bumped the dock, more ropes were tossed and tied, and a gangplank lowered to the dock. The sailors who had been given shore leave filed ashore, almost as anxious to spend their gold as those waiting were to take it. In minutes every sailor had his arm around one or two women and had a bottle in his hand. Angelique did not lack for company as she waddled down the pier.

Raven wondered what part she would play in all this. How long would she be a prisoner here? Was

64

there more to the town than the miserable collection of waterfront bars and disreputable-looking buildings? Would she be taken ashore or would she remain aboard, sharing Captain Fortune's cabin? Now that they were safely docked, would his thoughts also turn to the nearest woman? One conveniently close whether willing or not?

"Hey, lady! You like to buy nice necklace?" A peddler dangled a cheap bauble up for her to see.

She shook her head but he was only encouraged, continuing to offer one piece after another.

"Here, Pierre! Buy Marie a new skirt before I see her!" A gold coin flipped past Raven's ear and into the agile hand of the peddler. He grinned a wide thank you and set off down the dock.

Raven turned to Captain Fortune, trying not to look as uncertain as she felt. Who was Marie? she wondered. Her eyes widened in surprise as she took in his elegant form. He was once again clad as a courtly gentleman. His bare feet were now shod with wide-cuffed polished boots. A vest and coat covered a spotless white cambric shirt, and a bunch of fine lace spouted from the carefully tied cravat at his throat. A wide-brimmed, plumed hat topped his tawny mane of hair. He seemed the epitomy of a proud lion when he paced the quarterdeck unshod and half-dressed. The rich clothes he now wore did nothing to dispel that image. He seemed temporarily tamed, but lying in wait, his energy coiled, the sword at his side like sheathed claws.

He held out his arm to her, no less gallant than any other gentleman or king's officer she had met. "If my lady is ready, I will escort you ashore."

"Ashore?" Her eyes darted nervously toward the waterfront hovels.

Taking her hand and pulling it through the crook

of his arm, he guided her to the gangplank. "You will be more comfortable at my house than aboard ship."

She looked up in surprise and missed her step. Instantly, his arm was around her, steadying her, holding her close to his side. Even through her clothes, the heat of his body seared her where it pressed against hers, the warmth of his hand branding her waist. But they were as nothing compared to the warmth she saw when she looked up into his eyes. His lips were parted, she felt the quickening of his breathing, and her own leapt to keep pace with his. Quickly flaming desire flared in his eyes and his square jaw tightened as if he fought to suppress his rising lust.

An answering flame leaped within her. But before it could intertwine with his, he released her. Once again, he was the courtly gentleman, his emotions held in check, a faint smile on his face. His fingers were cool and impersonal as he again drew her arm through his, letting her hand rest lightly on his arm as he led her to the dock.

They were instantly beseiged by a horde of peddlers and begging urchins. Deftly guiding her along, Jeffery laughed and tossed a few coins to the children, calling some of them by name and tousling a few heads as they walked along.

As they started up a narrow, dirty street, a woman with flaming red hair and a heavily painted face approached them, swaying in a provocative manner. Her dress was Spanish and had once been grand and expensive, but now was worn and ill-fitting.

"Captain Fortune!" she said huskily, batting her lashes at him. "I heard you were back and that you had a successful voyage."

"Don't he always?" Another girl laughed from a doorway from which emanated laughter and the sound of clinking bottles. "Come on in, Captain. Ye're always welcome here."

The red-haired woman ignored the other, coming closer to caress Captain Fortune's arm, rubbing her breast enticingly against. him. "I saved myself just for you, Captain."

"No one else would have you, you mean!" the girl in the doorway jeered.

Raven's face burned with embarrassment at the women's bold words. She looked up at her escort but far from being angry or embarrassed, he actually seemed to be enjoying himself.

He took the redhead's hand and swept her a courtly bow. "Another time, perhaps, Belle." Then he hurried on with Raven in tow.

As they left the women behind, Raven heard Belle sigh loudly and say, "Aye, that's what you always say."

"Your harem, Captain?" Raven sneered. She could just see him swathed in Turkish silks, being pampered by a dozen or more doting women. He would well fit the role.

"Jealous, love?" One brow was cocked and his lips threatened to twist into a grin.

Did he dare laugh at her? "Certainly not!" she snapped. "Enjoy all the women you wish."

He inclined his head. "Why, thank you for your kind permission, my lady."

She tossed her head but even as he said the words, a pang shot through her heart. For some reason, she did not relish the thought of him holding another woman in his arms. She held her head erect, proudly staring straight ahead. What difference was it to her what he did? she told herself. Except that, hopefully, he would soon be gone from her life.

The street led upward and became cleaner, the

houses better tended. They came out on a wider street of houses hidden behind high walls, nestled in shaded gardens. It was to one of these that Captain Fortune led her. The iron grill gate swung smoothly open at his touch, sounding a little bell. The door was flung wide and a broad Irish woman grinned at them.

The smile left her face and a look of surprise replaced it, her eyes becoming big, round *o*'s as she caught sight of Raven. "Ye've brought home a wee bit of a lass, Cap'n."

"Aye. Mary, this is Raven Winthrop."

"Come, come, come. Inside with ye, out o' the sun." She bustled them into the cool, tiled entry, taking Jeffery's hat and hanging it on a peg. Then she urged them on into a spacious sitting room, also with a cool, tiled floor but softened by rich, woven carpets. One large tapestry hung above a Spanish settee and smaller paintings hung on the side walls. The fourth wall was nearly all open to the garden at the back of the house.

"I've cool drinks for ye and a meal ready when ye are. As soon as yer ship was sighted, I started yer favorite, Cap'n."

She gave no one a chance to speak but her evident joy at having the master of the house home again was infectious. Raven could not help but return her smile.

"Now sit yerself down, lass. I'll get ye a cool drink and I'll soon have a room ready for ye." She patted Raven's hand solicitously as she pushed her into a chair. " 'Tis not an easy thing to be attacked by a horde of filthy pirates and stolen away from all ye know." She gave Jeffery a huffy glare but could not remain angry with him for long, even though she knew him for what he was. She threw her beefy arms around him for a quick hug. Then with teary eyes and a sniff she hurried from the room, flinging over her shoulder as she left, " 'Tis glad I am to see ye safe at home again, lad."

"It sounds like she speaks from experience, Captain Fortune. Did you also capture her?"

"Aye," he said, laughing. "Though it might be more accurate to say she captured me."

"Just how many women have you collected in your years of piracy?" she asked archly.

"Oh, hundreds," he answered, leaning casually against the wall and looking down at her, a wry smile on his face. "But I don't keep them all here."

He was laughing at her again. Did he always answer questions without giving any real information? She glared at him. She wasn't jealous, she told herself. He could keep his hundreds of women. She just needed to know how she fit in with his plans. What was to become of her? Would she ever get to her uncle in Barbados and get on with her life?

"Cap'n Jeffery!" a voice boomed. A big, burly man came in through the garden, his arms widespread. "Mary told me you were here."

Jeffery and the man grinned at each other, clapping each other on the back. Then the man spied Raven and he lifted a questioning brow.

"This is Raven Winthrop. Raven, Mary's husband, Joshua."

She offered her hand and it disappeared into Joshua's massive one. She did not even wonder why such a giant of a man was here instead of fighting by his captain's side. His touch and his eyes told her everything. He had to be the gentlest man alive.

"You're in good hands, Raven. I have to go now but I'll be back this evening," Jeffery said.

"You'll not be staying for lunch? Mary's put her

heart into it. She'll not take it well if you leave," Joshua said.

Jeffery took his hat from the peg, glanced nervously toward the kitchen, and said to Joshua, "Tell her I'll be back in time for supper."

"Me? Uh . . . I got to get back outside. Lots to do out there." Joshua edged toward the door.

Jeffery made his exit while Raven watched the two men in amazement. Then she threw back her head and laughed harder than she had since her capture. Those two big strapping men, one the terror of the Spanish Main, were afraid of one sharp-tongued woman!

The red silk was the most elegant gown she owned and she was determined to get into it. But Raven was having trouble reaching the last two buttons in the back. Her hands on her hips in frustration, she looked into the tall mirror before her. Her face was red and beaded with perspiration and a strand of hair had worked itself loose from her carefully arranged hairdo, tickling her nose. She blew it back out of her face and grimaced at herself in the mirror.

With her black hair and eyes, the red gown really did set off her coloring better than the blue one. But she might just have to wear the blue if she couldn't manage those last two buttons. Maybe she should wear the blue, anyway. Her host certainly didn't need the enticement that the low decolletage of the red dress offered. Not that a scrap of cloth could stop those probing blue eyes from searching out every detail of her anatomy, she thought, turning an even deeper shade of red.

Why did she want to impress the pirate anyway? Why should she care what that lowborn, rebel slave thought about her? A light tap sounded at the door, startling her.

"Who is it?" she asked tremulously, wondering if it might be Captain Fortune. She had heard him return home a few minutes ago.

The door opened a crack and Mary peeped in. "Supper is ready but I thought ye might need a bit o' help."

Sighing thankfully, Raven smiled and welcomed the woman into the room. "It's just these last two buttons."

Mary fastened the buttons then stood looking over Raven's shoulder at their reflection in the mirror. " 'Tis a fine gown. Captain Fortune will be pleased to see ye in it. I can see already that ye've taken his eye."

Raven tucked her comb in the wayward strand of hair, trying to ignore the beats her heart skipped. "It matters not. I hope to be on my way to Barbados soon enough."

"Ah, that's a loss then." Mary pursed her lips, appraising her. "Have ye a bit of jewelry? 'Twould set off the cut of yer dress."

Raven thought of the few pieces of inexpensive jewelry that were missing from her trunk then shook her head.

"Nay, nay, I suppose not. Not after...Well, yer own foin beauty will more than suffice. An' 'tis sure you have an abundance of it. What man would be lookin' at baubles when he could be lookin' at..." Her eyes strayed to the soft cleft exposed by the red dress.

Flushing, Raven tugged at the dress. But it had been designed to be revealing and was bent on doing that. Pursing her lips, she wondered once again at the wisdom of wearing this dress, but Mary was holding the door open for her and it was too late to change now.

Her head held high, Raven marched behind Mary to the dining room, feeling shaky and uncertain. On board ship, Captain Fortune had acted the gentleman. But now that she was in his house, her trunks moved in, and with little hope of ransoming herself, would he expect fair recompense for his three thousand pounds? He had paid dearly for her. Now that his mind was no longer diverted by the constant danger while at sea, and uninhibited within the walls of his own home, would he see her as fair game to be seduced? Or would he feel justified taking her, a slave, bought and paid for?

When she entered the room, Captain Fortune was bent over the table, lighting the candles. The light turned his skin to bronze, his hair to polished gold. When he looked up at her, his eyes smoldered with a fire of their own. He straightened slowly, studying her, taking his time to consume every part of her until she felt like the main course instead of a guest at his table.

"I thought I remembered how beautiful you are. But I have not remembered a tenth of what I see before me."

It was as if the flame actually touched her, beginning somewhere in the center of her being and flowing outward. It was fear, she told herself, that weakened her limbs, warmed her cheeks, speeded her heart. Fear realized. She would be a fool not to recognize the desire in those pools of blue fire. A worse fool not to know that he had the power to do whatever he wanted about it. And when he was done with her? She tore her gaze from his.

She did not know how he moved around the table and across the room so quickly. But suddenly he was there, smiling at her, taking her hand in his. If his eyes were flame, his touch was a conflagration. She tried to smile calmly, but her body betrayed her.

"You're trembling," he said.

She snatched her hand from his and held her head high. " 'Tis only my concern over what arrangements you plan to make to get me safely to Barbados."

He studied her a moment in silence then crossed to a table set with a decanter of wine and several fine crystal goblets and filled a glass for her. " 'Tis seldom an honest ship finds its way into these waters."

She took the glass gingerly, being careful not to let her fingers touch his again. "Are you telling me that I may be your prisoner for some time yet?"

He looked up from filling his own glass. "Prisoner? Surely not. Say rather you are my guest."

"An unwilling one."

He shrugged. "That, I cannot help."

"Can you not? If you were not a pirate, I would not be here."

"If I were not a pirate, you would now be the unwilling guest of Captain DeLessops."

"Should that make me happy that my ship was attacked and sunk and I was forcibly stolen and brought here?"

He sipped his wine, studying her above the rim of his glass. A half-smile played at his lips. "It makes me happy that you are here."

"Does that mean you have no intention of helping me get to Barbados?"

"It means just what I said. I am happy you are here."

Raven opened her mouth to spout a caustic retort but was interrupted by the entrance of Mary bearing a large tray.

Michele Stegman

Captain Fortune set down his glass to hold a chair for Raven. She wanted nothing more than to put her nose into the air and stomp from the room. But she was too proud to let him see just how shaken she was by his presence. She may be safe from him now but had he not told her aboard ship that he was only waiting until she was a shade more willing?

She watched him as he took his own place at the head of the table while Mary served them steaming bowls of seafood chowder. His gleaming, near-blond hair framed his face made golden by sun and wind. Her eyes dropped to his full, mobile lips. It was not difficult to remember how they felt on her own. In fact, it was uncomfortably easy to remember, impossible to forget. How long would it be before she found herself that shade more willing?

She watched as he spooned up his chowder, smoothed butter on a roll, sipped at his wine. *His manners are impeccable*, she thought, *at the table, as well as each time he has courteously offered me his arm or held my chair*. The brocade of his coat fit smoothly over his broad shoulders with neither a wrinkle nor a bulge to mar their perfect fit on his perfect form. He did not look awkward in gentlemanly dress but wore his fine clothes with the casualness of one well acquainted with wealth.

Sipping at her wine, she noticed the beauty of the crystal goblet she held. The table here, as well as on the ship, had been set with exquisite china, silver, and crystal. His house, what little she had seen of it, was furnished with the style and good taste of an aristocrat. How had a common felon acquired all the trappings of a gentleman?

Conversation for the rest of the meal was kept light, centering around the weather and the native vegetation. He offered to show her the garden after

74

dinner. But when dinner was finished and she stepped out into the warm, sultry night, alive with sounds of insects and flooded with moonlight, she wondered if she had not made a mistake.

His hand rested lightly at the small of her back yet it weighed heavily upon her mind. The garden was not large and they soon completed one circuit on the flagstone walk.

"Would you like to sit awhile?" he asked, indicating a stone bench set deep in an arbor.

The night was pleasantly beautiful and she would have liked to sit enjoying her first night ashore in the tropics. But here? With him? She did not want to dare it. "It has been a long day, Captain Fortune. If you will excuse me, I think I will retire for the night."

If she thought to escape him so easily, she was mistaken, for he took her arm to escort her inside and down the hall of her room. At her door, she said a firm good night to him but when she started to enter, his arm barred her way.

"I will be gone all day tomorrow, Raven," he said. "I want you to know that you have the freedom of my house, but do not leave it without me to escort you."

She turned to face him, resentment flashing in her black eyes. His lips hovered so close to hers that she could feel his warm, wine-scented breath. "I thought I was your guest, Captain. Why am I being treated like a prisoner?"

He leaned closer but she did not back away. "This is Tortuga, my lady. If you have not noticed, there are unprincipled pirates about."

"I did notice one in particular," she said, her eyes and her mouth softening.

Then that wonderful, firm, sensuous mouth was on hers. Gently at first, it tested, tasted, sampled the corners of her mouth, then the center. His arms enclosed her, one about her waist, the other around her neck, holding her secure for his next onslaught. When his lips firmly covered hers, probed, demanding entry, her defenses crumpled. Life became, at that moment, a swirling maelstrom, centered on two people pressed together. Her mind refused to think beyond that moment, her body refused to move beyond that point. She was pulled deeper, farther into that warm darkness, until his mouth lifted from hers, leaving her adrift and seeking a lifeline.

She exhaled deeply, unaware that she had held her breath, and opened her eyes, which she did not realize she had closed, to find him grinning down at her, mischief twinkling in his eyes. "I am very glad you are my captive and not Captain DeLessops's."

Then he released her and was gone, leaving her leaning against her door, weak and trembling. She put her hands to her mouth, so recently touched by his, felt her flushed cheeks. She could not have broken that kiss. How could he? Had he been totally unaffected? She thought of the merry twinkling in his eyes. He had known exactly what he was doing to her, working to make her that "shade more willing." Anger gave strength to her legs and she stomped into her room, slamming the door behind her. She hoped he heard it.

Then she hoped he hadn't. She didn't want him to think she was upset that he had left her!

"Out with ye!" Mary ordered good-naturedly when Raven appeared in her kitchen bringing her breakfast dishes. " 'Tis not your place to be my scullery maid and Cap'n Jeffery would have my hide if I allowed it. Out with ye, now."

Raven knew it was useless to protest so she fetched

her dress that had been ripped during her capture. She decided to sit in the garden and try to repair it. Stepping out into the bright sunlight, she looked around. Without the full light of the moon and a handsome buccaneer at her side, the garden appeared quite different. Joshua was sitting in the shade, polishing silver, so she sat on a nearby bench, hoping for some company while she worked.

"Mornin', Miss Winthrop."

"Good morning, Joshua." Raven watched the man work for a moment before she began to sew. "Have you been with Captain Fortune long?"

"Aye," the servant said, nodding. "He's a good lad."

"He's a pirate," she corrected dryly.

Joshua considered her statement a moment, shaking his head in agreement. "Aye. But he's a good one."

The corners of Raven's mouth twitched, then curled upward in an unsuppressible grin. The man was certainly loyal. "And is he also a good master?"

It was Joshua's turn to chuckle. "Master? He seems more like a son than my master. Mary and me, well, we only been married three years and too old to have children of our own. We keep this place for him, though at times it seems more like ours than his, he's gone so much. Driven by something and can't sit still 'til it's done. We look out for him best we can, tend his wounds."

Raven looked up sharply at that. She had never thought of Jeffery Fortune being wounded. In his profession, it must be an accepted hazard, though her hands shook when she thought of it.

"Do you never want to leave Tortuga? What happens to you if...if Captain Fortune were to be killed?"

Michele Stegman

"He's provided well for us in such a case." Joshua looked up to smile reassuringly at her. "Captain Jeffery takes care of his own."

They worked silently then, and when she had finished, she excused herself and went back into the house, wondering about the man who owned it. He had given her the freedom of his house and she decided to explore it.

The kitchen she had glimpsed this morning. The sitting room and dining room had impressed her last night with their rich Turkish carpets, ornately carved furniture, and fine tapestries. The delicate china and cut crystal was as fine as any she had ever seen. But what lay behind the closed doors in the long hall?

Her room was the first on the right. She went on to the second room which was another guest room, as elegantly furnished as her own but unoccupied. The last room on the right she knew was Mary and Joshua's so she did not go in. On the left were two rooms. She opened the door to the end room and found an overwhelmingly masculine room, obviously Captain Fortune's.

The bed had four massive posts, ornately carved and polished to a soft gleam. A tall armoire stood against one wall, and a large trunk along another. A table beside the bed held candles and two books. The book on navigation did not surprise her. The well-thumbed Bible did.

Raven knelt to feel the Turkish carpet on the floor. It was extraordinarily fine and soft, made of silk threads. She wondered about the man who, on one hand could attack a helpless Dutch merchantman, and on the other, read his Bible. A man who was a lowborn criminal, a rebel, and a traitor to his country, but whose tastes were as refined as any nobleman born and bred. She rose and left the room, closing the door softly behind her.

When she opened the remaining door, the one across from her own room, her mouth fell open in surprise. A library, filled from floor to ceiling, was the last thing she had expected to find in a pirate's lair. It was a room well suited for study. Several over-stuffed chairs invited one to snuggle into them with a book. A large, well-used desk sat under the window that looked out upon the garden. She ran her hands over the rows of books. There had been little to do between battles but read, and her father had been an avid teacher. Here she found many a familiar and well-loved title.

A box of books sat beside the desk and she bent to see what Captain Fortune was now adding to his collection. Familiar titles leaped out at her, *De Motu Cordis* by William Harvey, *Micrographia* by Robert Hook, *De Anatome Cerebri* by Thomas Willis. Familiar bindings. Suspicion filled her. She snatched up a book and opened it. *"Ex Libris De* John Winthrop," it read. From the library of John Winthrop. Her father's medical books!

She whirled to glare accusingly at the many rows of books in the room. From how many hapless wayfarers had Captain Jeffery Fortune stolen these? No wonder his shelves were so well stocked, his house so tastefully and extravagantly furnished, his life overlaid with the trappings of nobility. He had the wealth of the Caribbean, the offerings of every passing ship to choose from! All he had to do was train his cannon on them and help himself. Apparently, he had been doing just that! What else should she have expected of a pirate? She had come close to real admiration for Captain Jeffery Fortune. How could she have been such a fool not to remember what he really was? Angrily, she loaded her arms with her father's precious books, tears coming to her eyes, as she thought of the many times he had taught her from them. She carried them to her room and laid them on the bed. *Well, Pirate Fortune, here is one bit of loot that is being reclaimed!* she thought triumphantly.

Reclaimed? She laughed bitterly. Not as long as she remained his captive. How could she have been so blind? After last night it should have been clear to her that he planned to keep her just where she was. Had he not said he was happy she was here? She would have to find her own way to escape from Tortuga and the all too inviting arms of Pirate Captain Jeffery Fortune!

Even with the glow of several candles, Raven's room seemed empty. The pages of her father's books rustled loudly in the room and offered little comfort as she leafed through them. Mary and Joshua had offered some company that day, but for the most part they were busy with their duties.

Dinner by herself that night had been lonely but far preferable to facing another meal with her pirate-captor, Raven told herself. There was no good-night kiss to fend off, no eyes probing deeper than any surgeon's scapel, no leering looks to redden her cheeks and to discompose her. But the rattle of silverware, the clink of crystal, had seemed to echo off the walls with a hollowness that cried to be filled. Finally, she had been able to stand no more and had pushed back her chair, leaving her meal half-eaten.

It was not a pair of tropic blue eyes she missed, she told herself. It was the weight of her captivity that pressed upon her. At last she snuffed the candles and went to bed, planning one farfetched escape after another.

She slept and dreamed of her plans, but when she woke, her plans seemed far less realistic in the clear light of morning. She went to the dining room wondering how she could get out of the house to have a look around the town and see what the possibilities for escape from the island were.

She halted in surprise in the doorway. Captain Fortune was just sitting down to break his fast. A smile lit his face when he saw her and his eyes lost no time drinking their fill of her. Her breath quickened and she wished she had taken more time with her morning toilet. Then she raised her chin and marched to the table. What did it matter if he thought she were the ugliest hag in the world? Maybe then he would keep his roving hands and lusty kisses to himself.

Chapter Five

When Jeffery looked up to see Raven's trim figure standing in the doorway, a heat spread through him which had nothing to do with the temperature of the day. He took in the swell of softly curving breasts above that tiny waist he longed to encircle with his hands. Her smooth, creamy complexion seemed to glow against the backdrop of her midnight-black hair which seemed miraculous. The heavy length of it had been braided at her nape and soft wisps framed her face. Full red lips, now softly parted, seemed to invite kisses but the invitation was denied by twin orbs of jet that snapped with angry fire.

Was she angry that he had kissed her the other night? Or angry that he had stopped? She had seemed willing enough when he had held her. Indeed, he had been surprised, nay, shaken, by the depth of her passion. But he knew that hers was an inexperienced passion. She had no idea of the fires she kindled in him. Her response to his kiss had stirred him more deeply than he had expected, and he had known that if he had not left her quickly, he would have taken her regardless of any protests she might have made. When he looked at her, he wanted her with a boyish eagerness stronger than any he had ever felt.

Yet he must be sure that she wanted him equally. He was not ready to add rape to his list of crimes.

Therefore, it was with a forced calmness and an air of cheeriness that he rose to greet her as she marched into the room, her head thrust forward, stiffly proud and erect. He held her chair for her and it was with exaggerated and cool politeness that she accepted his courteous gesture.

As he leaned over her, the fragrance of her hair assailed him. He had felt those wispy tendrils brush his cheek when he had kissed her and knew them to have the texture of fine silk. He wanted nothing more than to loosen the heavy braid at her neck and bury his face in the heavy mass of curls that would fall free into his fingers.

He sat down and passed her tea, sugar, and cream and watched fascinated as her slender fingers stirred her tea to a rich whiteness. It was only after her first sip of the steaming liquid that she deigned to address him.

"Have you secured passage to Barbados for me yet, Captain?"

He sat back observing her. It amazed him that a woman who could become so warmly passionate so quickly, could so thoroughly deny that passion and sit across from him coolly spreading marmalade on a muffin. Truly, she could not realize how deeply her mere presence affected him. "I was busy with my own affairs yesterday."

"Finding a market for your plundered goods?" she asked archly.

"Precisely." *And I would have been home to dine with you last night if Monsieur Fournais had not been so pigheaded about the price he offered me for the Delftware*, he thought. He remembered the exasperation he had felt yesterday. Every merchant he encoun-

83

tered seemed determined to chatter on and on and haggle over every last penny. He was ready to give in to the lot of them, but he had a duty to his crew to get the best prices he could. He was not a captain to hold out on his men or make them wait any longer for their shares than he had to. The grog shops and brothels of the island called too strongly to make his crew wait too long for their shares.

It struck him that he had never before been so anxious to rid himself of his cargo, to take care of his crew, and to get home. When had it ever mattered if he came home early, late or at all? What difference had it made if he passed five days or six at home before he took to the seas again? But he had found his mind wandering time and again to the lovely captive waiting for him at home.

Sitting here with her now, playing dagger wits while his body cried out to immolate itself in the fires of her thinly banked passion, he wondered what it would be like to have her always waiting for his homecoming. If he had been anxious to get home to her snapping eyes and virginal fear, what would it be like to know she waited warm and willing, soft, pliant, and eager to please him?

The very thought inflamed him and he knew he dared not stand up or she would know exactly what he had been thinking about. He also knew he would like to come home to her that way. She still feared him, he was sure. And well might a beautiful woman in her circumstance. With no possibility of ransom and a very uncertain future, it was no wonder she was cold to him. And as he had felt aboard ship, he wanted to ease her mind, to make her laugh, to see her smile given to him freely.

His immediate business had been concluded and he had no pressing duties that could not wait until the morrow. He could think of nothing more pleasant than to escort her about the shops and markets of the town.

"Would you care to see what the markets and shops of Tortuga have to offer this morning?"

She looked up in surprise. "And is it a pirate I would have for escort?"

"Aye, my lady," he said, inclining his head. "What else would you find on Tortuga?"

A shy smile of childish eagerness lit her face and wrenched his heart. "Then I will have to make do. If you will excuse me, Sir Pirate, I will be ready in a moment."

He watched the provocative sway of her skirts as she left the room, and groaned. He must be a fool for offering to parade such a delicious temptation through a town full of horny cutthroats who had little better than the likes of Belle to ease their lust. He was hard pressed himself to retain his tenuous so-called honor which had become tarnished during the five years of his piracy.

He met her at the door with one of Mary's parasols.

She pushed it away, laughing. "I have grown up on battlefields where the fairness of my complexion was far secondary to my healing skills. Besides, I love the sun."

" 'Tis not the kind English sun that beams down out there but one as fierce and torrid as any pirate it shines upon." He placed the parasol firmly in her hand and clapped his hat firmly on his head.

She did not argue further. He had lived in the tropics. She had not. It was not long before she had to admit, at least to herself, his wisdom in insisting on the parasol. The sun seemed to press upon her with a tangible weight and fury. But beneath her shade and with the breeze, she found the day pleasant.

Jeffery also found the day enjoyable with his own bit of beauty constantly at his side, to ogle whenever he pleased. And it pleased him often to do so. She moved as if she were inviting one to dance, he thought. He kept her close and his hand near the sword at his side. The few ruffians who cast leering glances their way were quickly put off by a threatening glare from the well-known Captain Fortune. The women who eyed him were not so easily dissuaded and he found himself on several occasions having to disentangle their arms from his while Raven gave him disparaging looks.

The marketplace was a densely packed mass of milling humanity in every size and color. From ebony Africans to red-haired Irishmen, from dusky Indian natives to the fair-skinned English, for one reason or another their fates or crimes had delivered them to this pirate stronghold.

Jeffery was careful to stand close to Raven to protect her from the jostling as she made her way down the narrow path between long tables of goods. There were gleaming white heaps of salt, piles of sugar speckled with hungry flies, fish and fresh fruit, cloth and caps, lace and liquor. Pots and pans and baskets were strung up overhead.

The sellers were not loath to hamper their passage, hoping to make a sale, and it often took more than a smile and a shake of the head to discourage them.

Raven's every movement was a joy to Jeffery as he followed her through the market. He watched her finger silks from the Orient and native handwoven cloth in bright colors and designs. The smile on her face and the sparkle in her eye as she examined fringed shawls or ran soft ribbons through her supple fingers caught at his heart. He wished that just once she would give to him a taste of the sweetness she lavished on these paltry goods.

They had made their way down one aisle and were about to plunge into another when someone called Raven's name.

"Miss Winthrop!"

Raven turned, a puzzled frown on her face. Then she smiled as the blond hair and rotund form of Captain Van Doorn came into view. He huffed, red-faced from the heat, and guarded his splinted arm carefully. Otherwise he seemed quite fit.

"Captain Van Doorn!" she exclaimed happily, holding out her hand. "How is your arm? I should have a look at it again in a day or so. Does it trouble you?"

"A bit. But at least it's there, thanks to you." He turned to nod to Captain Fortune. "I was just on my way to see you, sir."

"Is there some problem?"

"Aye. 'Tis a poor repair job they want to do on *The Mermaid's* rudder. She needs a new one. The old rudder suffered too much damage. A repair job might hold on a clear day with a steady wind, but in heavy seas ..." He shrugged and shook his head doubtfully.

"I'll see to it in the morning," Jeffery assured him. "And we'll see about a small cannon or two as well. If you're to sail in these waters, you'll need them."

"Captain Van Doorn!" Raven's eyes were wide with undisguised horror. "Surely you're not thinking of turning pirate!"

The two men exchanged amused glances, then Captain Van Doorn hastened to explain. "Nay, Miss Winthrop. I fear I haven't the courage or the need for that. 'Tis an entirely honest venture. My crew and I needed a job. Captain Fortune has given us one and with far better terms and with a far better ship than I had."

"I acquired *The Mermaid* some weeks ago," Jeffery began.

"Stole," Raven corrected.

Her captor shrugged genially. "It had suffered some damage while at sea."

"Meaning you battered it to pieces with your cannon."

"While the common occupation here—"

"Piracy," she translated.

"Can be quite profitable—"

"Since there is no overhead on stolen goods," she put in.

"There are also considerable hazards."

"Getting caught and hanged," she interpreted.

"Therefore, I want to build up a fleet of honest merchant craft. But I needed a crew untainted by piracy and a worthy captain to sail her."

"To cover the fact that *The Mermaid* is actually owned by a nefarious pirate."

Captain Fortune grinned down at her, his eyes full of merriment. "You catch on very quickly, Raven, my love."

"And should anyone dare attack your semi-honest fleet . . ." she began.

"They will have two cannons and Captain Fortune to answer to!" Captain Van Doorn finished proudly.

"Then heaven help anyone who would dare it!"

"Aye!" Captain Van Doorn agreed with a satisfied sigh. Bowing awkwardly, he said, "I must get back now, Miss Winthrop. I will see you in the morning, sir." He gave the pirate captain a brief salute and it was not long before he was lost in the crowd.

"Could you not send me to Barbados via *The Mermaid*?" Her coy smile was not lost on Jeffery.

" 'Twill be some weeks before she is seaworthy." He watched her coquettish smile turn to disdain. He hated to disappoint her, yet he was glad he would have her to himself for a while.

Raven turned then to the next row of tables, and Jeffery was only too glad to trail along just far enough behind to admire the smooth curves of her figure and the gentle sway of her skirts.

A piece of lavender silk caught her eye and she ran her hand lovingly over its smooth surface.

"The perfect color for a dress for madam. Shall I measure off a length?" the merchant grinned. The stump of an arm gave evidence that he was most likely a disabled pirate turned salesman.

Her fingers quickly left the cloth and she shook her head. But her eyes were more reluctant to leave the lovely lavender.

"Measure off enough for a dress for the lady," Jeffery said, pulling a purse from inside his vest.

"No!" Raven said, whirling to face him and laying a hand firmly on his to keep his purse shut. "I'll not take more from you than I must. Food and shelter I cannot help, but expensive gifts I will not accept."

" 'Tis but a paltry sum," he said. "One I can well afford."

"Yes, I suppose you can," she said. "The Dutch merchantman was a rich prize."

She looked up at him with a pride and a haughtiness that made him want to throttle her but at the same time he wondered if she knew how kissable she looked when she tilted her head at that precise angle.

"It would please me to give it to you as a gift," he cajoled.

"I will not accept it from you." She crossed her arms firmly to emphasize her point and succeeded very well in emphasizing the fullness of her breasts.

"Then perhaps you will accept it from me." A tall stranger tossed down sufficient coins to buy three dresses. "Don't forget the thread and a bit of lace, too," he told the merchant who lost no time following the order.

"Alex! I didn't know you were in port." Jeffery grasped the outstretched hand of the stranger and clapped him vigorously on the shoulder.

As tall as Captain Fortune, though more slender of frame, he was a handsome man. His brown periwig and gray eyes lent him an air of gravity that his reckless grin completely destroyed. He dressed well, almost, but not quite like a dandy.

"I arrived just this morning. And I was not ashore five minutes before I was informed by at least three people that you had taken a rich prize and"—his eyes came to rest on Raven—"a beautiful woman."

A pang shot through Jeffery when he saw the brilliant smile Raven gave Alex. His friend had always affected women that way, making one easy conquest after another. It bothered him that his Raven should be one of them. But he could not avoid introducing them. "Alex Jamison, Miss Raven Winthrop."

Raven gave him her hand and he bowed over it in a most courtly fashion, lingering a bit too long to suit Jeffery.

"You seem to know each other well. Are you a fellow pirate, Mr. Jamison?" Raven was openly flirting and Jeffery could have strangled her for it since he was sure she did it deliberately to goad him.

Alex's eyes widened in surprise and he threw up his hands defensively. "Not I! Though there are some who might call me one. My work keeps me well within the law."

"Captain Jamison is a privateer," Jeffery supplied. "His only target has been the Spanish."

"Ah! An honest man among thieves."

Jeffery gritted his teeth watching Raven give to

Alex the warm smiles and sweet words he longed to hear for himself. An honest man, hah! He doubted that such a thing existed.

The merchant handed Captain Jamison a neatly wrapped parcel which he took and extended to Raven.

"She has already said she will not take it," Jeffery said, placing his arm possessively about her waist.

Raven stiffened at his touch and a spark of defiance leaped into her eyes. Tossing her head at him, she turned her sweetest smile on Alex.

"I said I would not accept it from Captain Fortune." She took the parcel and held it to her bosom, throwing Jeffery another defiant glare. "I will accept your gift and thank you for it, Captain Jamison."

The saucy wench! he thought. He felt like ripping the package from her fingers and dragging her home, but he knew that was the worst thing he could do.

"Come along, Raven," he said. "There are some shops I'd like to show you." He glared at Jamison. "I'm sure Captain Jamison has business to attend to."

"Why, not a thing this morning," Alex said, flashing his reckless grin.

"Oh, then you could come with us!" Raven said, smiling up at Alex with the most coquettish expression Jeffery had ever seen. Just what was she trying to do, anyway? She probably didn't realize that she was playing with fire. Alex might be his friend, but he was also a rake, and far too experienced for Raven, judging from the two kisses Jeffery had shared with her.

Ignoring Jeffery's discouraging glare, Alex took Raven's arm in his. "I can think of nothing more enjoyable than to accompany a beautiful woman wherever she wishes to go."

They headed down the narrow aisle together, effectively shutting Jeffery out, leaving him to trail along in their wake, scowling at the tall form that had taken his place. He had to agree with Alex. It was enjoyable to accompany a beautiful woman but he preferred to do it alone.

They browsed through several shops and then entered a jeweler's. Raven's eyes swept from one table of gleaming gold and silver to another of shining stones of every kind, her fingers touching here and there. But they did not linger long until she came to a gold necklace. It was a simple pendant with a lustrous pearl nestled in the scoop of a golden shell. A small exclamation escaped her lips and Alex was not slow to notice it.

"Put it on, Raven," he said, handing it to her. "I'll buy it for you."

When had he started calling her by her first name? Jeffery wondered. He gritted his teeth. He'd buy the necklace for her if he wasn't certain that she'd throw it in his face.

"No," she told Alex firmly. "I've accepted one present from you today."

"One present a day. Is that your limit?" he teased.

She laughed. "Especially since it is a far more expensive and personal one than I should have accepted from someone of such short acquaintance."

"Then I shall have to lengthen our acquaintance so that I may shower you with gifts."

Sighing, Raven replaced the pendant.

"Why don't you buy it yourself?" Alex suggested.

"I haven't any money at present," she answered, giving Jeffery an accusatory glare.

"Oh. Of course not. I suppose the pirates took everything," Alex commiserated.

"Yes."

"Really, Jeff, I thought it beneath you to prey on helpless women."

Alex's tone was light and bantering, but the words still left Jeffery looking like a blackguard. Raven did not seem loath to paint the picture darker yet.

"To make matters worse, I find myself indebted to Captain Fortune for three thousand pounds."

Alex turned to Jeffery, a surprised look on his face. "Only three thousand pounds ransom? 'Tis a paltry sum for such a beauty, Jeff. I will pay it gladly and take her off your hands."

" 'Tis not her ransom she speaks of," Jeffery said, a mischievious gleam in his eye. If she wanted to portray him as a dastardly rogue, he would play the role and see how well she liked it. "Three thousand pounds is what I paid DeLessops for her, thereby saving the fellow a trip to the slave market in Maricaibo."

Jeffery noted Raven's look of surprise at finding herself being discussed like any other piece of merchandise in the market. He eyed her speculatively as if judging her worth, and when he spoke, it was with a grin on his lips and merriment in his eyes. "I have not yet set a resale price on her, but I think it will be somewhat higher so I can turn a profit. It depends, of course, on how well she behaves."

She looked in appeal to Alex but he was also enjoying the little game, grinning from ear to ear. "Do let me know when you've set a price, then. I might be interested."

For a moment she looked from one to the other, not quite certain whether they were serious until Captain Fortune began to chuckle. "You're both insufferable!" she said, stamping her foot. Turning on her heel, she marched proudly out of the shop.

* * *

When Raven came in to breakfast the next morning, Captain Fortune was just finishing but he sat back in his chair, watching her over the rim of his cup. It was a moment before she spied the small package with her name on it set beside her plate. She pushed it toward him. "I told you I would not accept presents from you. I have not changed my mind."

"It is not from me."

Curious, she picked up the parcel and turned it in her hands. "Then who . . ."

"It was delivered this morning." He shrugged. "I know naught else."

When she untied the string, the gold shell pendant fell into her hands along with a note. "Good morrow on this new day. One present a day. Alex."

She would have to return it, of course. But how? She had no idea where Captain Jamison lived. Well, she was sure to see him sooner or later since he was Captain Fortune's friend. Then she would have to make it clear to him that she would not accept one present a day from him—or any at all, for that matter.

She caught Captain Fortune's curious eyes on her. He wanted to know about the package, she thought, but he would never deign to ask. She held the necklace up to her throat and preened. "It's from Alex," she told him. "I shall have to thank him next time I see him."

His eyes narrowed. "I think, Miss Winthrop, that it is advisable that you do not see Captain Jamison again."

She cocked her head at him. "But you do not forbid it, do you, my Lord Gaoler?"

He set his cup down with a rattle and stood up abruptly. "I will be gone most of the day. Do not leave the house alone." He grabbed his hat from its peg and slammed the door behind him.

She let her hands fall to her lap. Why did she have to goad him? If it was jealousy she was hoping to provoke, she had failed miserably.

After breakfast, Mary helped Raven cut out the pieces for a dress from the lavender silk. Then Mary went about her chores while Raven began to sew the long seams of the skirt. She had no idea when or where she would ever wear it, but she was going to make the most elegant dress she could from the material.

A knock sounded at the door and not seeing either Mary or Joshua, Raven went to answer it.

It was Alex and he swept off his plumed hat in a low, gallant bow. "My lady, you grow more lovely every day."

"And you, sir, are an inveterate flatterer." She laughed lightly and beckoned him in. "Captain Fortune has just left. I'm sorry you missed him."

"It is not Jeffery I have come to see but his lovely slave." He stepped inside followed by a boy in servants' livery carrying a large basket. "I come to offer an afternoon of freedom and a lunch with a most excellent view."

A picnic on such a beautiful day would be lovely, she thought. A day alone sewing paled by comparison. And she could not deny Captain Jamison's charm. But she hesitated, remembering her captor's admonition at breakfast.

"You can't deny me, Raven," he pleaded, taking her hands. "I badgered my cook all morning to have this done on time and to make something special for you."

It was all too tempting to refuse. Jeffery Fortune

may have bought her for three thousand pounds, but he didn't own her as far as she was concerned. As for his admonition, should she languish alone in the house on such a day if he could not be with her? She could do as she pleased. And it pleased her to go on a picnic on this beautiful day with a companion who was bent on charming her, whose eyes smiled at her pleasantly without making her feel devoured, and to whom she owed nothing at all.

"I would love to go with you, Captain Jamison. If you will excuse me a moment, I will fetch my parasol." She hurried to her room, put her sewing away, and got her parasol and the necklace she had to return. She poked her head into Mary's room to tell her where she was going, then rejoined Alex.

"My carriage awaits!" he said, taking her arm to lead her outside and help her in.

They made room for the boy and basket, and Alex took up the reins, urging the horses farther up the hill until the houses and road faded away.

Alex was right. The view he had chosen was wonderful. While the boy set out their lunch, she and Alex walked along the crest of the hill. The town lay beneath them and the curve of the bay sheltered several ships, looking like gulls on the nest of the sea.

Raven pulled the necklace out of her purse and held it out to Alex. "I appreciate your kindness and thoughtfulness in sending this to me, Captain Jamison, but I really must return it."

"I thought you would accept one present a day from me?" he said, his reckless smile slashed across his face.

"You are the one who said it, not me. I really must insist, Captain Jamison, that you give me no more gifts." She stood holding the necklace out to him, a firm set to her chin.

He looked at her a moment then folded her hand over the chain, holding it closed with his own. "I will strike a bargain with you, Raven. I will promise not to inundate you with gifts if you will accept this last one."

She started to protest, but he put a finger across her lips. "Unless you want to return something to me every day, you had better agree."

At last she relented, laughing. "Very well. But no more presents."

He took the necklace, turning her to fasten it around her neck. "While I am getting concessions from you, there is one more I crave."

She felt his fingers touching the back of her neck, caressing her shoulders. It was a pleasant sensation. His fingers were warm and gentle but there was no fire where he touched her. No rising tide within her like there was when Jeffery Fortune but looked at her. He took her arms, holding her close to him, while his lips nuzzled softly in her hair. "Call me Alex. We may not be acquaintances of long standing, but I would like to be."

It would be so easy to call him Alex, she thought. She felt so comfortable with him. It was easy to enjoy his company, to stand there leaning against him, looking out over the bay.

"Lunch is ready, sir."

Raven pulled away from Alex then turned toward him, laying her fingers on the pendant. "Thank you for this—Alex." She put her arm through the privateer captain's and pulled him along to the lunch spread out under a tree for them.

She wouldn't have believed that a picnic could be so delicious or so elegantly served. Wine was poured into crystal goblets, spiced rice and fish were eaten from thin china with fine silver. Afterward the boy put everything away and judiciously disappeared while they sat on the cloth and talked.

They exchanged childhood tales. Hers were full of battles and wounds healed and nights spent studying with her father. His were of boisterous pranks and rough tumblings with a houseful of brothers.

When they finally climbed into the carriage to return home, the sun was nearing the horizon, spreading a red sheet across the sky.

By the time the carriage stopped outside Captain Fortune's door, twilight was upon them. Alex helped her down and his hand did not leave hers as he accompanied her up the walk. When they entered the house, she was laughing at some remark he had made but the laughter died on her lips as her eyes met the glowering ice-blue ones awaiting her.

Chapter Six

Captain Fortune was dressed in much the same way as Raven had first seen him—a white shirt open at the throat with sleeves rolled to the elbow, a red sash, and wide-topped boots. All he lacked was a saber at his hip and a brace of pistols. But the stains that marred the perfect whiteness of his shirt and streaked his tawny mane were the pitch and grime of honest toil, not the blood and gunpowder of battle.

His eyes were also the same, hard, glacial chips of ice she had seen before. Though he came toward them with a casual step and a lazy smile, there was danger in those eyes. Even in her short acquaintance with Captain Jeffery Fortune, Raven had learned to recognize that characteristic.

Alex must have recognized his friend's mood, too, for he stepped forward as if to defend her with his body and his words.

But Jeffery cut his friend short, his words and his tone brooking no argument. "Good-bye, Alex. I'll see you later. I have something I wish to discuss with Raven. Alone."

Alex glanced at her and Raven gave him a quick, reassuring nod. Now or later she would have to face Captain Fortune and it might as well be now. He may be angry but, strangely, she knew she had nothing to fear from him. Nothing but her own desires.

Alex left then, and Jeffery came to stand close to her, his eyes resting for a moment on the shell pendant before his hands tenderly gripped her shoulders. "Are you all right, Raven?"

His question and his tone surprised her. Why would he worry about her being with Alex? Could it be that the danger she read in his eyes was not directed at her, but at some unknown he wanted to protect her from? "Yes. Of course. Why do you ask?"

"I warned you not to go out," he said, and she was not sure which was uppermost in his words, worry or anger.

"You warned me not to go out alone," she corrected. "I was with Alex."

"And who was there to protect you from him?" he sneered.

"From Alex?" She laughed. Was it a touch of jealousy or did he really think, after growing up in army encampments, she could not fend off an unwanted advance. But, then, she had not done very well defending herself against his advances. "He was a perfect gentleman. And I'm not a child."

His eyes raked her with blue fire, hungrily consuming her like dry tinder. "Yes. That is plain to see." His hands dropped away from her. "But stay away from him. He is not what he seems."

Her anger flared. Could he be serious? He who was a rakish buccaneer one moment, a gentleman the next? "At least he is an honest seaman and not a pirate!"

His eyes hardened more dangerously. "Don't be fooled, Raven. There is but a thin line between pirate and privateer. We are in much the same business, he and I."

"But the line is there," she said haughtily, moving a step or two away from him. "And he, at least, is on the right side of it!"

"Yes, he is on the right side of it," he agreed, and it seemed to her that there was some bitterness in his words. "But that only limits who he can attack at sea. It does not mean that his intentions toward you are honorable."

She turned questioning, puzzled eyes on him. "How can you so malign him? Is he not your friend?"

"He is. But he is also a rake!"

"And what of you, Sir Pirate?" she asked, incensed that he would find fault with Alex when he was equally guilty. "What makes me any safer with you than with him?"

"You are under my protection, Raven." His words were spoken softly but through clenched teeth.

"And who will protect me from you? What is to keep you from doing whatever you like with me any more than him?"

Suddenly she found herself caught in his arms, pressed close against his hard, lean body, his lips hovering above hers. His eyes had changed in an instant from ice shards to blue flame, hungrily lashing over her as if they would consume her in an instant.

"Nothing!" he growled.

She felt an answering flame rising to warm her body and to quicken her breath, rising to heat her limbs to a sudden weakness, rising to color her throat and cheeks with a red heat that demanded a joining of their two fires.

Then his mouth covered hers and there was no room for words or breath or thought between them. There was only the fire, swirling them into a heady ecstasy, flame answering flame, heat answering heat, passion answering passion, until there was but one flame, one heat, one passion.

His lips moved from her mouth to her cheek to the soft hollow of her throat, and the flame followed. Another flame followed the caress of his hand on her waist then rose upward bringing his hand with it. There seemed to be little choice in the matter. The flame was leading his hand ever upward over the crest of her ribs to tease the base of her breast, then to conquer the soft, rounded mound.

It was only then that the cool core of reason rose to quench the flame which struggled within her, fueled by the touch of his lips and the caress of his hand. But she knew she must fight it, must push him away. Her hands slid between them, up the hard muscles of his chest, and she pushed, her face turned from his seeking mouth. Then, with a wrench, she twisted away, fleeing like a frightened doe from the rush of a forest fire.

She ran from that conflagration, lifting her skirts to aid her in her flight, not stopping until she reached the relative safety of her room. She slammed the door shut between her and the dangerous passion without. Leaning breathless and trembling against her door, her eyes shut, her head back, Raven tried to find a small bit of tranquillity to cling to in the tempest swirling in her mind.

Without a doubt, she knew now that she had to leave his house, this island. Like a raft within reach of her drowning soul the thought came to her. She was much too attracted to her captor. What was there about his very presence that sent her senses reeling, destroyed her logic, and crumpled any sham of defense she had? How long before she found herself that "shade more willing"? Feeling the trembling in her knees, the quickness of her breath that still remained as evidence of his touch, she knew it would not be long.

It was not so with Alex. He was handsome, charming, and not an outlaw. She enjoyed his company. She even found his touch pleasant, yet it was only when Jeffery Fortune came near her that she had to fight for her very breath. His touch, his kiss seemed to engulf her in flame and drown her at the same time, confusing her, bringing her to an ecstasy that admitted no reason.

Why hadn't she ever felt this way about any of the other men she had met, officers, gentlemen, nobles, even one certain privateer? Was she so lost to good sense that she could only be attracted to an outlawed pirate?

She had to leave. And she could not look to Captain Jeffery Fortune to help her. There were at least a dozen ships in the harbor. Surely by this time he could have found one going to Barbados or to some other lawful English port. Yet he had not found passage for her. He had no reason to help her, but every selfish one to keep her right where she was—conveniently close beneath his hand for whatever purpose he chose, whenever he chose. Had he not just said that there was nothing to stop him from doing whatever he wanted with her? And had he not proceeded to do just that with his kiss?

Yes, he had every reason to keep her here. She had no reason to stay.

If he would not find passage for her, she would have to find it herself. And she would have to be careful. She had no illusions. If she tried to leave, he would stop her. She would have to slip out in the morning after he had left. Hopefully, she would have booked passage on some ship and be safely aboard before he knew she was missing. For money, she would have to thank Alex, she thought, touching the shell pendant. It was not much but it would buy her passage. After that, well, she would deal with her problems as they arose.

Raven pulled open the tall wardrobe where her dresses hung. Her small valise was all she could carry and she would have to be careful in her selection of clothing. Her fingers slid longingly over the lavender silk, lovely but still unfinished. It would have to be left behind. She had no room for crushable silk, nor any use for party dresses when she would have to work for a living. With a determined toss of her chin, she hastily pawed through her dresses, tossing two stout serviceable ones onto the bed. One to wear and one to pack. A change of undergarments landed on top of the dresses. A nightgown was too bulky to take. A chemise would have to do.

It took only a moment to pack the valise. But there was one more thing she wanted to take—her father's books. She hated to leave any for the profit and enjoyment of her captor, but there was very little room left in her valise. She laid them out across the bed, touching each one lovingly, reliving the memories each of them evoked.

She had narrowed her selection to two books when a light tap sounded at the door. In a panic, she crammed both books into the valise, shut it, and flung it into the bottom of the wardrobe. It was probably Mary, come to tell her supper was ready.

Smoothing her hair, she went to the door. She would make some excuse for not coming down, and ask for a tray in her room. The last thing she needed was another encounter with a certain bold buccaneer to weaken her defenses, to crumble her will to go. The kiss would have to be farewell. She would never see him again. Ignoring the wrench in her stomach at that thought, she flung wide the door—and looked up into a pair of summer blue eyes, sun-bleached locks, and an impish grin.

Raven stepped back warily, trying very hard to swallow the lump in her throat. She noted that his ardor had abated somewhat, cooled, perhaps, by the recent dousing still evident in his hair, now dampened to burnished gold. His clothes, too, were clean, though his fresh shirt was open in front and rolled to the elbows. The fresh washed scent of him, of soap and sun-dried clothes, assailed her as he stepped into the room.

There was another smell, too, sweet and heady, and she wondered briefly if he had used some of Mary's scent by mistake. Her puzzlement ended when he brought a large bouquet of flowers from behind his back and presented them to her.

"For you, my lady," he said, as if nothing at all unusual had passed between them only moments before. Except that, perhaps, there was even more confidence about him when he looked at her, as if he knew what he had caused her to feel. Grinning, he brushed the floor with his fingers in an exaggeration of a gallant bow and again held the flowers out to her as if he were gallantly trying to lighten the tension between them.

She laughed at his antics, relieved to take this playful attitude with him. Taking the freshly picked and hastily arranged blooms, she swept him a deep curtsy.

"I thank you, my lord, for your gifts and your gallantry."

He took her hand and she gasped. But he barely touched the tips of her fingers, holding them as if for a minute. Then bending over her hand, he kissed her fingers with a resounding smack.

"Will my lady do me the honor of dining with me *al fresco* tomorrow evening? There will be music and dancing, fine viands and rare sweets, heady wines and rich liquors."

Tomorrow? She stole a guilty glance at the wardrobe door which stood slightly ajar. If all went as planned, she would not be here. That thought did not please her as it should have. Was it his touch on her fingers that weakened her will to go? She looked up into his face which suddenly seemed so boyishly hopeful. If the evening turned out half as well as he promised, she would be sorry, indeed, to miss it. What would it be like, she wondered, to dine with him in elegant style outside in the cool garden, lit softly with candles? Did he plan to hire musicians to play quietly while they ate? Then would they dance to their strains until dawn streaked the sky? Could she, for one evening, pretend that he was not a traitor and a pirate and she was not his unwilling captive? It would be one last memory to carry with her all her life. She would go. But would one more day make so much difference?

"Perhaps I could be persuaded," she said, her resolution weakening. She buried her nose in the blooms, taking in their sweet fragrance, feeling the soft petals on her cheek. Turning, she began to arrange them in her water pitcher.

"And what could I do to persuade you?" His voice was a low, throaty whisper, close to her ear. She could feel his breath upon her hair. His hand slid around her waist.

She let herself be pulled back against him and his arms came around her, caressing her shoulders, her throat, her waist. Almost of its own accord, her head leaned back onto his shoulder and she closed her eyes. He bent to nip at her nape, to nuzzle at the

106

curve of her shoulder, to nibble his way to her ear.

When he pulled her ear lobe into his mouth to tease its tip with his tongue, she gasped. A wild thrill shot through her from her ear to the pit of her stomach.

One hand continued to caress her shoulder while the other began nimbly to untie the fastenings at the front of her bodice. His mouth slid across her cheek, seeking her mouth, and, finding it, sought sweet access which she granted.

The last fastening fell to his conquering fingers, letting the fullness of her breasts tumble free. His hands were not slow to catch their rounded softness, to caress the swelling mounds, and to tease their peaks to hardness. He turned her then to possess her mouth. His hard muscled chest confronted twin peaks whose rosy tips taunted him as he pressed her closer to him.

Thigh touched thigh, hip pressed into hip, and she was startled to feel his eager manhood. Tomorrow? He knew very well how to persuade her. At his lightest touch, her every resolve melted like candlewax in flame. She fought to stiffen her determination to leave but the only thing that seemed to be stiffening was his swelling desire. Everything in her was only weakening, softening, opening, for him.

She sought wildly for some release but her body had divorced itself from her mind, and, as if it had a will of its own, went willingly with him as he moved toward the bed. He drew her after him, her body completely within his power.

No! her mind shouted. *Tomorrow you will be gone. You cannot allow this to happen to you!* But her body ignored the warnings.

He was easing her onto the bed, his mouth still claiming hers as if by right, when her hip encountered something hard beneath her. Her fingers searched under her to remove the offending object, and felt one of her father's books. Instantly, her mind was in control again. Her eyes flew open and she twisted away from him, taking the book with her. Her father would certainly not have approved of what she was doing. She wasn't sure she did either, especially with the pirate who had captured her desire as easily as he had captured her body.

No, she was sure this was not what her father would have wanted for her. Not an illicit relationship with an outlaw, a traitor to his country, an escaped slave. So often had he envisioned a fine marriage for her, perhaps even to some rich lord.

Raven skittered away from him and stood.

"Do you know what this is?" she asked, holding the book out, shaking it at him accusingly.

He gave her a slow, easy grin, his eyes roving over her. "One of my medical books," he answered, reaching for her.

She avoided his grasp. "My *father's* medical book, you thieving pirate!"

He shrugged. "I make you a gift of it. Maybe this one you will not refuse."

"Oh!" she cried. Her hair had come loose and cupped her face, her lips were swollen from his kisses, and her breasts bobbed unshielded before him. But she paid no heed. Throwing the book aside, she advanced toward him but with angry fire blazing in her black eyes. "A gift of it?! 'Tis not yours to give!"

Shoving a finger into his chest, she continued her raging attack, railing at him. "You rogue, you blackguard, you knave! You rob a lady of all her possessions, steal her, then try to rob her of her chastity as well!"

His rakish grin told her that he was completely unperturbed by her tirade. "It seems to me 'twas not robbery. My lady seemed intent on making me a gift of her chastity."

Her outrage was shoved to new heights, and she pounded his chest with her fists. Though her efforts were no more to him than a fly, he retreated before her onslaught, with his arms up and a lecherous grin on his face, then scrambled to his feet. That he refused to take her seriously only fueled her fury. "Satyr! Seducer of women! Profligate libertine!" With each epithet, she pushed him closer to the door.

"Ah, Raven, my love," he defended himself with a twinkle in his eye, "what would you have of me? Your beauty urges me onward, your passion mounts with mine, then you deny me. I shall die of wanting you."

Her fists planted themselves angrily on her hips, and she stamped her foot when she saw that his eyes fell on the rose-tipped beauty that spilled from her open bodice.

"Oh!" she gasped, grabbing her dress and holding it closed with one hand. She shook the other hand at him. "If it were possible for a man to die of his desires, you, Jeffery Fortune, would have been dead long ago!"

His continual grin was infuriating.

"Nay, love. Until you came into my life, I have had no trouble satisfying my desires. 'Tis only you who thwarts me."

She drew herself up as proudly as her dishevelment would allow. "I will continue to do so. If you would satisfy your desire, you will either have to resort to rape, or"—and here a mischievious twinkle lit her eye—"seek solace with your friend, Belle!"

"Belle!" he said, nearly choking on the word. Then he cocked a brow and rubbed his chin as if giving the idea serious thought. "Aye, I may do just that."

A strangled growl and a hard stamp of her foot

were Raven's only responses.

He was almost out the door before he turned back to her. "I take it that you accept my offer and will accompany me tomorrow evening? Until then, keep close to the house. The streets of Tortuga are not safe."

Then he was gone, the door closed behind him.

She felt like pounding the door, throwing things. Whether it was in anger or frustration, she did not know. She flung herself onto the bed, still warm from his body, and she thought she could still faintly catch the smell of his soap and sun-scented clothes.

He was so sure of himself, she thought. So sure that she was waiting breathlessly for each crumb of himself that he offered. So sure that she would be anxious to dine with him on the morrow. He would not be so sure of himself when he found her gone.

Now she knew without a doubt that she must leave in the morning. She couldn't fool herself that tomorrow night would not be a repetition of tonight. Where would their kisses lead if there were a next time? She had to admit that he was at least gentleman enough to leave when she asked him to. The problem was, would she find the strength to ask him to go if there were a next time? She couldn't take that chance.

She would depart in the morning and his warnings about the danger in the streets of Tortuga would not stop her. She had twice walked through the town with him and had seen no evidence that she would be immediately set upon if he were not with her. The only one who had been bothered was him—by every loose woman they passed! Certainly she had naught to fear from that source.

Her mind made up, she undressed and went to bed, giving one last check to her waiting valise.

* * *

" 'Ere, lass, give me a good buss, eh?"

Raven shook off the grimy paw that clung to her arm and shouldered her way past the drunken pirate. But there were others in her path and all of them seemed to think that she was fair prey, that she was anxious for their foul embraces. Did every man on the island think that every unescorted woman was a prostitute?

It seemed a very long way to the dock through the gauntlet of erstwhile admirers. And the closer to the waterfront she got, the more arduous they became. She passed several taverns from whence issued squeals and coarse laughter, the bang and clatter of mugs and bottles, and smells she would rather not identify.

She set the valise down for a moment's rest. The street was as narrow and as dirty as the rest, and women stood in doorways or hung out of windows displaying their questionable charms.

"Ye'll not set up shop here, sister!" an overpainted harridan shouted at her from a doorway.

Raven tried to ignore the woman but a clot of filth from the open sewer narrowly missed her head, splattering on the wall beside her.

"G'wan! Go someplace else. Pickin's is lean enough as it is!"

Several other women joined the first in urging her on and she was not loath to go. She picked up her valise and continued down the sloping street.

Her problems were not over once she reached the docks. There were just as many amorous hands to push away, just as many glares from the women who thought they had a new competitor.

Raven looked at the ships bumping gently against the dock. There were also several anchored out in

111

the bay. How did one go about booking passage? She had never had to worry about it before. Her father or the Army had taken care of her traveling arrangements. Did she go aboard each ship and ask where they were bound and if they would take her along? What about the ships out in the bay?

She chewed her lip. She had to do something. And soon. She couldn't just stand there. The longer it took for her to get safely aboard a Barbados-bound ship the more likely it was that she would be found by Captain Fortune.

Loud guffaws sounded behind her. "Hey, me beauty! Lookin' fer a pair of lovin' arms?"

Hoping the pirates would pass her by if she stood primly straight and ignored them, Raven put her nose into the air and stared out to sea.

But her disinterest did not dampen their enthusiasm. An arm was thrown across her shoulder, a face reeking of rum even at this early hour was thrust into hers, and she was pulled into burly arms.

A hand pulled at the strong arms that held her. " 'Ere now, Sebastian! Lemme see what you got there!"

Sebastian released her, and a cold shiver of fear shot through her as she came face to face with an evil leering grin sporting half-rotted teeth, glittering black eyes, and greasy locks covered by an equally filthy red bandanna. Captain DeLessops.

"Why, 'tis the wench Fortune stole from me!"

He stepped closer and she tried to back away but Sebastian was as a solid wall halting her retreat.

DeLessops shoved his face into hers, nauseating her with a breath reeking of sour wine and the leavings of several past meals. "Has Fortune tired of ye so soon?"

Thankfully, he stepped back to survey her and she

was able to draw a relatively clean breath, tainted only by the offal and sewage of the street.

"Why, ye seem hardly the worse for wear. Hardly used at all, me girl!"

"I would advise you to leave me alone, sir. Captain Fortune will take a dim view of anyone bothering me." She tried to voice the words with a certainty she was far from feeling.

"If he feels so strongly about ye, where is the good captain?" DeLessops pulled her close and twined his thin, but wiry arms about her. "Seems ter me he should keep a better eye on ye or someone's bound to steal ye away. Bein's yer such a comely lass."

"Let me go!" Raven pushed at the bony chest, trying to escape from his grasp, but the sinewy arms held her fast.

"Be still, wench," he said, squeezing her until she could scarcely breathe, "or I'll have ter teach ye some manners. A little kiss fer me now and the rest can wait 'til I've got ye safe aboard me ship."

She tried to twist away from him but gasped in pain when he grabbed a handful of her hair and yanked her head around to face him. His fetid breath was in her face and his mouth was reaching for hers.

There was a flash of light on metal, and Raven felt the hard edge of cold steel on her throat. But it was a blunt line she felt. The sharp cutting edge of the saber was tucked beneath DeLessops's chin. DeLessops froze at the first touch of that glittering length of steel, and his eyes rolled wildly, searching for the adversary whose bladed hand held him at bay.

" 'Tis me property ye're makin' s' free with," a voice growled in the rough dialect common to the pirates. "If ye'll be s' good as ter release the lass, we'll be having' a discussion o' sorts. I've never taken kindly to them as trespass on what I consider mine."

Raven felt the slow release of DeLessops's arms. She was sure he was holding his breath as he backed slowly away from her, held almost on tiptoe by the threat of that razor sharpness. Already a red drop oozed at its tip.

Steel fingers suddenly bit into her arm, jerking her almost roughly to the side, yet holding her firmly to steady her. At last she was able to turn to see who it was that had rescued her from DeLessops but who now claimed her as his own. From his common speech she had expected a fellow pirate. And she was right. She looked up into a pair of familiar blue eyes, glacier cold and as dangerous as a tumbling avalanche. And all of it was falling upon her erstwhile tormentor.

"He has not harmed you?" Captain Fortune asked, raking those eyes over her in a glance both quick and complete to reassure himself that such was the case.

She could do no more than nod before his attention was once more focused on his adversary. The tip of his saber had not left DeLessops's scrawny neck for an instant. Even beneath the hot tropic sun, she shivered. She had felt that hard edge of steel against her own throat and seen the threat in the steel hardness of Captain Fortune's eyes and she did not envy DeLessops at that moment.

She had not thought to fall prey to such a one as DeLessops and though it was from Captain Fortune she was trying to escape, she had to admit that she was extremely glad to see him. Where he had come from or how he had managed to arrive in time to rescue her she had no idea until she caught sight of the figurehead on a nearby ship. The figure of a mermaid. The sounds of hammering and sawing emanated from the vessel and she guessed that this must be Captain Fortune's ship, *The Mermaid*, which he was repairing. When she had laid her plans and cleverly waited until Captain Fortune left that morning, she had been foolish not to realize that his destination was the same as hers. The next time she must plan more carefully to avoid both Captain Fortune and any ruffian who might bar her way.

At last the point of Captain Fortune's saber left DeLessops's neck, and that cocky bantam instantly made a show of brave belligerence. His saber rang from its sheath and an evil gloat spread across his face.

"Ye've interferred with me pleasure for the last time, Fortune!"

Captain Fortune flexed his wrist, sending the point of his saber in hypnotic circles. A hard smile lit his face, and his eyes, though still dangerous glacial shards, glittered in anticipation. "So! Ye choose a saber to do yer talkin'. Ye'll find me own tongue a sharp one!"

Raven scarcely dared to breathe. She had no doubt that whoever was the victor would claim her as his own. Though she wanted to escape from her captor's beguiling clutches, she did not want to do it by falling into the iron grip of DeLessops. Nor did she wish the death of Captain Fortune.

There seemed to be no way for her to halt the coming duel. She could only pray that Fortune's skills were sufficient to defeat DeLessops. Certainly he must possess some skill or he would not be able to captain a crew of cutthroats. But how practiced was that skill? A lowborn felon would not have the training in weaponry that a gentleman would have. The tawny-haired pirate's skill could only be acquired as the result of his piracy. And how thorough could that training be? How instructive of the finer points of fencing? As for DeLessops, how much longer had he had to depend on his skill for his very life? DeLessops didn't get to be a captain by being an indifferent swordsman. On the other hand, she could well believe that Fortune had become a pirate captain by saving his spoils and at last purchasing his own ship.

The duelists had begun to circle cautiously, testing each other with brief feints.

"Ye'll be fishbait when I've done wi' ye, Fortune!" DeLessops taunted.

Captain Fortune laughed, full-throated and free, as if his best friend had just told him a joke over mugs of ale. " 'Twill take more than one piece of offal to accomplish the task."

Raven stared at Fortune in wide-eyed horror. How could he laugh and joke as if he were enjoying this? Was he too dense to understand how desperate his situation was? How desperate *hers* was?

DeLessops feinted quickly to the left then thrust deeply—into thin air. Captain Fortune had sidestepped the blade as gracefully as if he were executing a dance step. Raven gasped, then gritted her teeth when he did not riposte but spread wide his arms, allowing his opponent time to recover. That kind of gallantry might be acceptable in a practice match with a friend, she thought, but the gesture would be wasted on a pirate.

But it was not entirely lost on the wiry captain. It angered him so that he slashed wildly and viciously at his rival, muttering a stream of epithets that even her wide experience on battlefields had not introduced her to. Tiring, and his anger spent for the moment, DeLessops narrowed his eyes in a glare of hatred, and he settled down to serious swordplay. This was to be no quick and easy victory as he had at first supposed, but as yet he could conceive of no other end to the fray than that Captain Fortune would eventually fall beneath his blade.

Bright blades flashed in the tropic sun. DeLessops feinted low, circled his saber and thrust, to meet steel instead of flesh. Fortune disengaged, riposted, and recovered so quickly that Raven was not sure it had happened at all until she noted the bright crimson slash along DeLessops's ribs.

Surprise and a new respect for his opponent's skill spread over DeLessops's face, and he grimly prepared to wrest the victory as best he could. Sabers flew so fast then that Raven could not follow the play. But every few moments when DeLessops would thrust or cut, expecting this time for his saber to bite into something more substantial than air, a new slash would appear as if by magic on his own arm or leg or chest.

DeLessops's expression had changed to one of desperation as he fought now for his very life. Fortune's grin had not wavered, though Raven thought she saw little enjoyment there for the havoc he was creating.

At last DeLessops stumbled to his knees, slashed once more through the air where Captain Fortune had stood just a second before, then fell forward on his hands. Fortune's blade pricked him beneath the chin.

"Do ye yield?"

DeLessops's eyes, black clots of glittering hatred, glared up at the other man. He had not the strength to fight on, even if that blade did threaten to end his existence in one quick, easy stroke. When he spoke, his voice was more of an animal growl than human, so much hatred did it carry. "Why don't ye finish the job?"

117

"Do ye yield?" Captain Fortune asked again more insistently.

"Aye!" DeLessops spat and his neck was at last freed from that sharp edge. He glared up at Fortune and his words were as venomous as a viper. "Aye, I yield. But 'tis not the last ye've heard from me! There'll come a day ye'll wish ye'd finished me whilst ye could!"

He nodded to his man and Sebastian came forward quickly to help him to his feet and down the street.

Raven looked at Captain Fortune. That she had been trying to escape him there could be no doubt and she wondered what he would say to her, what he would do. But it was not until after he had pulled a kerchief from his sash, wiped his blade, and sheathed it, that he turned those blue eyes upon her.

Chapter Seven

When Jeffery Fortune's blue eyes looked in her direction, Raven was fully prepared to answer the full blast of his anger with her own, which had been augmented by the heat of the last few minutes. But the glitter in those azure depths was not due to icy anger but amusement.

"Out for a bit of a stroll on this lovely day, are ye?" he asked lightly, as if that were exactly what she was about. "If you've had enough of an outing today, I'll be seein' ye home."

He picked up her valise in one hand and held out the other arm to her. She was speechless at his blithely dismissing his duel and its dangers both to him and to her had its outcome been different. How could he look on her escape attempt with nothing more than the amusement one would show to a kitten trying to climb out of its box? Was she then so thoroughly trapped?

Angrily, she stamped her foot, turned on her heel, and began to march back the way she had come, ignoring his proffered arm. For now, at least, she had no option but to return to his house with him.

"Now, now, lass. 'Twill do ye no good to take on so," he said, catching up to her in two long strides and tucking her arm in his. " 'Tis no way to show yer thanks to yer rescuer."

She glared up at him briefly. Did he expect her to thank him? Thank him that she was a pirate's captive? That she had no freedom to go where she would, do what she wanted?

He had been right about the danger of the streets, she was forced to admit, at least to herself. She felt she would never be clean again after the mauling and pawing she had received on her way to the docks.

But did he have to speak to her in that low-class brogue? she wondered angrily. He certainly used it with facility! So accustomed had she grown to his gentlemanly speech and manners that she had forgotten the commonness of his birth. She was well reminded of it now, though his skill with a blade had surprised her.

She glanced up at him striding along so easily beside her. Piracy sat well upon those broad shoulders, she thought. He was a rogue born, a rebel bred, and a raider by vocation. Yet none of it weighted his step, lessened his grin, or dimmed the twinkle in his eye.

"If you were indeed the rescuer you claim to be, you would set me now on board some ship bound for honest waters," she said.

" 'Tis in vain ye'll seek one here."

"Yes, since you keep me prisoner!" she accused. "And must you speak like a guttersnipe as well as act the rogue?"

He laughed and his eyes still twinkled with amusement. Changing his speech pattern as easily as one changes hats, he said, "Why, Raven, love, I thought you liked it, since in spite of my warnings about the dangers of Tortuga's streets you seemed so intent on throwing yourself into the arms of DeLessops or his like."

She tossed her head. "I am not trying to throw myself into any pirate's arms. I am trying to free myself from them!"

"Are you sure you want to?" he asked, pulling her close to his side and speaking low.

"Am I sure I...Oh!" She floundered to a stop, temporarily speechless at his arrogance. "Do not flatter yourself, sir. I was not on the docks to seek you out but to seek escape from you."

"But as you have learned, love, escape from one pirate's arms but leads into another's. You might as well remain in mine."

"And what makes your arms the better choice?" she asked, struggling to free herself from his grasp.

"Ah, love," he said, turning a very wounded look on her, "I thought I had already shown you. But if 'tis another lesson you need..." He stopped and pulled her into his arms, his lips hovering near hers.

She wrenched away from him but not before her heart had had a chance to skip to a betraying beat, to weaken her limbs, and to warm her blood. " 'Tis not your kisses I want, rogue!"

She walked on and again he pulled her arm through his to walk with her as if they were sweethearts out for a stroll. "What is it you want from me? My protection, perhaps?"

"Protection? Hah! You and DeLessops want the same thing from me. You are just more subtle! Asking you for protection is like setting the fox to watch the hen."

"If my attentions grow overbold, 'tis yourself you must blame," he said, his tone softer.

She looked up at him with puzzlement to find his expression one of warmth and longing.

"Your beauty clouds my reason. The midnight of your hair, as black as a moonless night at sea, sweeps me along with no light until I am lost in the labyrinth of its waves. The deep blackness of your eyes pulls at me, draws me in until I feel I am falling down a bottomless well. Your lips beguile me, teasing, taunting, letting fall gentle words as from an angel on those who also feel your healing touch. But for me, when I draw near, there is only the caustic lash of sea water on the open wound of my heart. At last, I stretch forth my hand to caress the velvet of your skin, to hold within these arms the soft curves of your form. But your denial is as the fruit which ever dances tempting, enticing, but always out of Tantulus's reach."

Much bemused by his speech and the seriousness of his tone, she was spared the necessity of replying by their arrival at his door, and he ushered her inside.

Once again, his mood changed and he gave her a boyish grin as he said, "Since you are still my guest, I take it you will be accepting my invitation to dine with me tonight. Wear your oldest dress and shoes and bring a shawl. Until then, stay in the house. I've work to do and may not be close at hand to slay another dragon for you."

Before she could retort that she had no intention of dining with him nor did she need his protection, she was staring at his retreating back, a merry tune carried to her in a lilting whistle.

Angrily, she fled to her room and slammed the door, determined to stay there through dinner even if she were starving. Then his words began to stir her curiosity. Had he not promised fine fare and music? Why then should she wear old clothes?

"Jeffery Fortune," she said with her hands on her hips, "you are an unprincipled rogue. But quite an intriguing one." Perhaps she would accept his invitation.

* * *

If her dream of an elegant garden dinner surrounded by musicians was shaken by Captain Fortune's injunction to wear an old dress and shoes, it was completely shattered when she saw him waiting for her at the front door of the house. His shirt was an old one tied just above his slim waist rather than buttoned. His pants were cut off below the knee, and he wore simple sandals. Peeking out of the top of the two buckets he carried, one inside the other, she could see a bottle of wine.

She had been too intrigued to refuse his invitation. Besides, she rationalized to herself, the more she saw of Tortuga, the more she could learn of possible ways to escape.

"My lady!" he said, sweeping her a low bow. "Dinner awaits!"

"But where . . ." she asked, puzzled.

He only chuckled, and led her out the door and down the street swinging their joined hands between them.

They walked away from the town, down toward the beach. The houses thinned to a few fishermen's huts strung with nets, then they too were left behind. Climbing a rocky hill, they looked down into a perfect crescent-shaped beach, small and private, with sand in its center and rocks at both tips of the quarter-moon beach. He helped her scramble down the rocks to the sand.

Throwing out his arms to the sea, he said, "Here we are!"

She looked around at the wave-washed cove. Sand and sea and surf she saw, but no place to dine. "But where is dinner?" she asked.

"I think milady is over preoccupied with her stomach. Does Mary not feed you well enough?" He looked her over as if to see if she were fat or thin.

"Aye, milord," she said, dropping him a small curtsy, "but I remember a promise of rare wine, fine fare, and music."

"Music?" He began to sing a sea chantey that set her to giggling. His voice was rich and full and he did not hold back, as if he were singing for all the gulls and rocks and waves. Suddenly he stopped and looked at her with a wickedly cocked brow. "The rest is not for a lady's ears. The sound of the wind and waves will have to suffice for our music."

The cove was enchantingly beautiful. The crash of the waves was indeed like music, she thought, its beat regular, its voice hypnotic. "I could not ask for finer."

Raven looked around. "The music I hear, the wine I see, but where is the fine fare?"

" 'Twill be a gift from Neptune. But first"—he spread wide his arms and a mischievous light lurked in his eyes—"he demands the sacrifice of a virgin!"

Kicking off his sandals, he charged at her, and squealing, she picked up her skirts to run. He was too fast for her. Grabbing her up in his arms, he headed for the waves, chuckling evilly. She struggled vainly in his iron embrace.

"Let me go! Put me down!" she pleaded, convulsed with laughter.

He paid no heed but continued toward the water and splashed into the waves.

"You wouldn't dare!"

He cocked an eye at her. "Is that a challenge?"

The waves were lapping about his knees and she stopped struggling for him to put her down. Instead, her arms wrapped more tightly about his neck. "Captain Fortune! Take me back!"

"Captain Fortune still? 'Tis many days hence that

I gave you the use of my first name. If I do not hear it now, you will get the drenching you deserve." His arms loosened and she slid a bit.

She yelped and clung harder to him. "All right, all right! Jeffery!"

"From now on?" Again, his arms opened a little.

"Yes! Yes! Now put me back on the beach."

He carried her to the sand then, still holding her, turned back toward the water. "Ah, but I forgot. There is the matter of a sacrifice."

"Jeffery!"

He stopped and looked down at her. The boyish mischievousness was forgotten, the music of the waves was forgotten. Not even the skreeing of the gulls could be heard above the mutual beating of their hearts. He released her knees and let her body slide slowly down along his until just her toes touched the sand.

"Perhaps Neptune will be satisfied with a kiss," he said, his voice husky with desire.

"And where is Neptune?" she asked in a sultry whisper.

"Here!"

The impact of his lips meeting hers jolted her, stealing her breath, shocking her with a new intensity, and she thought that perhaps being sacrificed would have been easier. For this was a death of a different sort, a piecemeal sort of dying, her soul being stolen bit by bit, her heart captured fragment by shattered fragment. And she knew that, as surely as he had stolen her bodily, he would soon possess all that she had left of herself to give.

How long the kiss lasted she could not have said; a day or a year were all the same. Time could have no meaning while her lips clung to his, his tongue gently teasing, probing, demanding. At last he released her for she could not have torn herself away.

"Aye," he breathed softly, "Neptune is well satisfied with a kiss. Yet having tasted, he hungers for more of the maiden."

The kiss had shaken her to the core of her being and while her body cried for more, her mind warned her that such sampling would be heady fare, food only the gods dare touch. Reluctantly, summoning the shreds of her willpower, she moved away from him, forced a light tone to her voice, and a playful grin to her lips that only moments before had been touched with sacrificial flame. "There will not be enough left of this maiden to consume if someone doesn't feed her!"

He laughed, taking up her lightened mood. "Raven, my love, I think that by the time you are ninety, you are going to be fat."

He knelt then to empty the contents of the buckets. There was a freshly baked loaf of Mary's bread, wrapped in a napkin, the wine, some raw potatoes, and a hunk of meat that was well past its prime. There were also some pieces of string with lead weights attached and a small net.

"This you call fine fare?"

"Patience, love. Neptune has not yet added his gift. Nor you yours," he added, glancing at her.

"Mine? I thought the kiss was my contribution."

"The kiss was but an appetizer to a meal you deny me. Therefore bring something more substantial. Yon firewood, for instance." He pointed to the piles of driftwood strung along the beach then gave her a hungry leer. "To build the sacrificial fire with."

There were so many small pieces of dry wood close by that it was little effort to gather enough for a fire. By the time she dumped it at his feet, he had cut the meat into small chunks and tied two pieces onto the ends of the string.

"Now we will see how skilled, patient, and brave you are." He handed her one of the lines and led her out onto the rocks.

Waves dashed against the rocks, wetting the hem of her dress, then sucked away as if trying to drag the land with them.

"There." He pointed to a protected pool. "Put the meat into the water. When you feel a tug, pull it up very slowly."

"What will we catch? Fish?"

He only looked askance at her and did not reply.

It seemed a long time to her before she felt a gentle tug on her line. Startled, she gasped and jerked the string out of the water. It was empty, the meat half-eaten.

He laughed. "You have the patience. The skill needs work."

"And the bravery?" she asked, piqued at him for laughing at her failure.

"It will be tested when you catch something."

Intrigued, she dropped the bait back into the water, determined that the next time she would be careful to pull the string out slowly.

But when the next tug came, it was on Jeffery's line. She watched as he carefully drew up the line, reaching out with the small net to scoop up a crab and plop it into the bucket.

"Crabs?"

"Food for the gods." He grinned at her. "Neptune's gift."

They caught several crabs in the next half-hour, then she watched as he turned over rocks along the water's edge and captured two lobsters. Jeffery carried the bucket up the beach and started a fire, setting the second bucket full of water on two rocks. The potatoes were buried deep in the hot coals, and Jeffery lay back on the sand, pulling her down beside him.

She came into the curve of his arm, feeling as though she belonged there. Her head rested on his shoulder and it wasn't long before she snuggled closer to him.

He turned toward her and she lifted her face to him, closing her eyes, expecting his mouth to capture hers. But she found herself suddenly dumped onto the sand as he jumped to his feet.

"Wha—" she began, then she shrieked. Their crabs were scuttling in every direction. When he had turned over, Jeffery had accidentally knocked over the bucket. She scrambled to her feet to shake two from her dress, and Jeffery scurried to scoop them up and return them to the bucket.

An irrepressible giggle started somewhere within her and bubbled to the surface followed by another and another. Soon she was sitting on the sand, holding her sides, watching through tear-clouded eyes, the fierce pirate who had captured her grab at fleeing crabs.

Most of the crabs were recaptured and were soon boiled and eaten along with the two lobsters. The potatoes, ashey-skinned and hot, had been pulled from the fire, dusted off, popped open, and eaten. The bread and wine had been shared between them. The fire, one bright spot in the gathering darkness, was dwindling while the fires of heaven were being lit in the blue-black arc above them.

"Well, wench," Jeffery said, pulling her so that she rested on top of him, "have I fullfilled my promise of elegant fare *al fresco* to your satisfaction?"

Raven sighed and smiled her replete contentment.

Laying her head down on the broad expanse of his chest, she listened to the thud of his heart as rhythmic and as restful as the wash of the waves. Her fingers played with the blond crisps of hair that covered his chest.

How strange that she could feel so sated, lying on a deserted beach, with a buccaneer captain, sandy, wet, bedraggled, her future anything but certain. She wished the evening would never end, that she would never have to think about leaving this island, this pirate stronghold, these arms.

His arms were around her now, the fingers of one hand tangled in the depths of her hair, the other caressing her back, one shoulder, then the other, down her spine, back up to one shoulder, then the other, as regular as his heartbeat. As the wind on water, his breath fell on the waves of her hair. His hand slipped lower to add her buttocks to his massage.

With a moan, Jeffery rolled over with her and their lips met in the darkness. His hand trailed down her thigh, pushed aside her skirt, and with tender fingertips, touched the soft silkiness of her skin.

I'm drowning, she thought, and the seductive sound of the surf added to the illusion. The tangible warmth of the night enveloped them, drawing them close. His mouth, warm, wet, tender, nibbled its way down her throat, was stopped momentarily by the line of her dress. But his hands, as nimble as his mouth, pushed her gown off one shoulder, loosened the ties of her bodice, and then moved to her breast. She gasped as his mouth followed, sucking slowly at the sweet nectar of the rosy tip.

She was lost in the swirling depths of unreason, never again to surface to sanity. Her hand found the hair that curled at his nape, her other hand gloried in the hard play of muscles on his back. Her lips buried themselves in his hair, chasing the faint flickers of firelight that glittered in its burnished gold. She moaned, urging him to taste more deeply of the rose he had found. His hand slid along the soft length of her thigh and she felt that her soul was stretched between his mouth and his hand. For long moments he sucked pleasure from the depth of her being. It flowed outward in a never-ending stream, clouding her reason, silencing any protest before it could be born.

Then his mouth moved to taste hers, and his hand slid between her soft inner thighs. Suddenly she found the strength to form the one word she needed—no. It was long moments surfacing and even then her body cried for her to abandon voicing it. But at last she was able to say, "No," so weakly that at first it sounded like a prayer for love.

He lifted his head and his hand stopped its sweet torment and she was able to repeat it again, stronger. "No."

"Hmm?"

"No!" She shoved him away as she breathed a sob. A sob that almost begged him not to hear her no, not to heed her push.

She sat up, pulling her bodice together, refastening the ties with trembling fingers.

He covered her hands with his, stopping her with a grip that almost made her wince, a grip born of frustration. He pushed her back down upon the sand and his mouth sought hers.

From somewhere she found the strength to turn her face away, though a tear formed at the outer corner of her eye.

"Raven, love, will you not yield to me?" he asked raggedly, his voice husky and filled with the warmth of the night, the sultry wind, the calling wave.

All that and more stirred in response within her, but she shook her head, summoning all her strength to push him away. "No," she whispered.

"You push so weakly, love, but with a strength I cannot seem to conquer—the strength of that one little word."

His fingers brushed along her jaw, rousing the fire within her once more. Pinned helplessly beneath him, she could feel his long, muscled length where he pressed against her. The strength of those rock-hard limbs held her easily, and fear began to rise within her. Compared to the corded thews that held her, her no was nothing. What was to keep him from taking her now? She blushed when she thought that she was not entirely sure she would mind. Yet reason took control and told her she must not let it happen.

Forcing herself to lie limp and still, and putting all the scorn she could muster into her words, she asked, "Will you let me go, Captain? Or will you rape me?"

She felt him stiffen, heard his teeth gnash as he clenched his jaw. In one fluid motion, he rolled off her and came to his feet.

"You do tempt me, love. And sorely. Yet though I am besotted and bewitched, I am not ready to resort to that foul means to have you."

He stripped off his shirt and she looked up at him with widened eyes, wondering if his actions would belie his words. But he tossed the garment to the sand and turned to run into the waves, plunging beneath that ardor-cooling tide.

She sat on the sand, her arms clutched tightly about her knees. Through tear-blurred eyes, she watched him swim out into the dark purple waves, disappearing from sight in the dim starlight.

When at last he returned, he busied himself with gathering their things, dousing the fire, putting on his shirt. Then he reached down for her, pulling her to her feet, and brushing the sand from one cheek.

"Raven, love,'tis time to go home."

They walked silently, hand in hand, through the black streets. Once she heard the angry curses of drunken pirates fighting among themselves and though it was some distance away, she moved closer to Jeffery. He put his arm around her shoulders and held her close to him until they reached his home.

Raven picked up her sewing again and tried to concentrate, to stop thinking about a certain bold freebooter who had captured her and whose mouth could rob her of her senses. Even when he was not present, thoughts of his hands roaming over her body brought a quickness to her breathe, a tingling to her every cell.

She sighed and thought of last night. She had been sandy, wet, rumpled, nearly bitten by crabs, almost sacrificed to Neptune, yet it was the most happily content picnic she had ever had. She compared it to the picnic with Alex, drinking from fine crystal instead of from a wine bottle, using silver instead of fingers, being served well-prepared food by a servant boy instead of having to catch and prepare her own. Alex had been charming, the perfect gentleman. Yet of the two outings the one with Jeffery had left the most pleasant memories.

When she thought of the night before, a tingling came to her lips where Jeffery had kissed her. She could almost feel once again the caress of his hand on her back, her thigh, the press of his lean body against hers. She warmed with the memory. How difficult it had been not to....

How would she ever be able to refuse him again? Yet she must, she resolved. Where could their passion lead but to a bastard babe in her belly? She must be strong and keep him at arm's length. Nay, farther. For to touch him even with her fingertips would so weaken her as to destroy all her resolve. If he kissed her, she would be doomed.

How could she avoid contact with him, living daily in his house, totally in his power? Somehow she must get away. The thought still plagued her. But how? There must be a way and she must find it before she was lost.

Perhaps tonight would provide the answer. Surely all the most important officials would be present at the governor's ball. Perhaps there would be someone she could appeal to for help.

When Jeffery had told her this morning that they were invited to Governor Ducasse's ball, she was surprised that the French governor would invite a pirate captain into polite society. But there were probably very few officials on the tiny island, fewer Frenchmen still who would have chosen to live in this pirate port. Who else was left but pirates? And as pirates went, she had to admit, that Captain Jeffery Fortune was most socially acceptable.

At least he had the outward manifestations of a gentleman. He dressed well, he had acquired the proper manners, and he could speak with all the refinement of a duke when he chose. Of course most of the conversation tonight would probably be in French. Having learned it as a child, hers was adequate. Jeffery must surely have picked up enough to communicate since he lived on a French-owned island, but she could always translate for him if necessary.

She held up the lavender silk gown. With Mary's

help, she had nearly finished it. She only had to stitch the hem into place. Fingering the silk, she wondered what it would be like to dance tonight in the arms of her pirate captor.

Raven patted the last of her piled hair into place and picked up the frontage. She had made it from a piece of the lavender silk, pleating it, and trimming it with a bit of the lace. Mary had starched and ironed it so that it would stand up stiffly when she pinned it into place in the front of her hair.

"Here now, lass, let me do that for ye," Mary said, taking the frontage and fastening it deftly. She smiled into the mirror over Raven's head, looking as proud as if Raven were her own daughter. "Stand up and let's see ye now."

Raven stood up and turned around. The lavender silk rustled pleasantly. The neckline of the dress was cut low and trimmed with lace. The bodice fitted firmly above her narrow waist but gaped open down the front between the ties to show off her embroidered stomacher. The silk skirt trailed behind her but was pulled back in front to reveal her fringed underskirt which she had trimmed with the rest of the lace.

"Ye look like a duchess!"

"Thank you, Mary." Raven was reaching for her shell pendant when a deep voice from the doorway shot through her, ricocheting off her heart, rebounding off every cell of her being.

"I would say an angel were it not for the blackness of her hair."

It would have been hard to believe that the elegantly clad gentleman who leaned negligently in the doorway was a notorious pirate if it had not been for the air of vitality about him, the feline energy coiled and ready to spring. There was not one inch of Captain Jeffery Fortune that could not have been presented at court. He wore a periwig tonight, artfully curled and arranged, yet it did not detract from the lean masculinity of his jaw nor the wide set of his broad shoulders. His lace-edged cravat hung in perfect pleats, and his wide-cuffed coat was buttoned neatly and correctly at the waist. The coat, form-fitting to the waist and deeply pleated, hung nearly to his knees over close-fitting breeches. Large silver buckles gleamed on his shoes, and under one arm he held a large hat trimmed with ostrich feathers. Peeking through the pleats in his coat was a slender sword. Raven could not see much of it but she could tell that it was not worn for mere ornamentation, but was a strong and serviceable weapon.

Raven's eyes grew wide, and she swallowed with difficulty as she viewed her escort for the evening. *Not only his touch, but his very voice stirs me*, she thought. *How will I ever make it through the evening with his hand on mine, his arm about my waist, his tall body dancing so near to mine?*

"You flatter me, my lord pirate," she said, and her words came out shakier than she would have liked.

He came to stand behind her, to look over her head into the mirror at her as Mary had done moments ago while Raven was still seated. Where was Mary? Had she traitorously left her alone?

Her breath caught when his hand came up to caress the curve of her shoulder. A glitter of gold and stones fell from his fingers, and she was overcome with the beauty of the necklace he was fastening about her throat. Pale, smokey amethysts almost the exact shade of her dress shone from their setting of polished gold.

Her fingers closed tightly around the shell pendant

135

she had been about to put on. It was hard to think with him standing so close, the warmth of his body reaching for her, his breath falling softly on her cheek, his fingers lightly touching her nape. She looked at him in the mirror. He was so tall that his chin could easily rest on the top of her head. She took in the long, golden lashes over his downcast eyes, the lean brown fingers fastening the necklace, fingers that were nimble enough for that delicate task yet strong enough to wield a saber with deadly force. A lock of his periwig fell forward to curl about his jaw and she longed to push it back, to trail her fingers along that hard square ridge of bone to his well-molded lips, firm, sensitive, and warm.

She tore her eyes away. There was something she had to say but her mind refused to work until his hands finished their task and settled on her shoulders.

Thrusting her chin up firmly, she forced herself to be cool. "I have already told you I will not accept gifts from you, Captain Fortune."

His brows furrowed into a pained expression. "Captain Fortune? I thought I had extracted a promise from you to call me Jeffery?"

Relenting a bit, she smiled. "So you did. Though it was under duress, I will try to keep it. But I did not also agree to accept gifts from you."

"Then call it a loan. Wear it tonight to please me and return it when we come home."

His fingers gently kneaded her shoulders, and the smile he gave her caused her heart to lurch. At that point she did not think she could have denied him anything. "Very well, Jeffery."

He gave her a quick kiss on the cheek. "Shall we go?"

Taking her arm, Jeffery led her outside and helped

her into the carriage. Joshua took up the reins and, slapping them lightly on the horse's back, drove them the short distance to the ball.

Governor Ducasse's home was set high above any other house on the island. From the front there was a panoramic view of the town and the bay. French windows opened in the front as well as the back of the house, allowing cool breezes to flow through the house from the extensive garden in back. The light strains of a French country dance floated out to Raven as Jeffery helped her from the carriage, and she could hardly wait to dance.

There had always been dancing in her life. Army officers seemed obsessed by it, particularly before a battle when there could be little reassurance that they would ever dance again.

Inside the foyer they were greeted enthusiastically by a tall spare man in his early forties. "Jeffery, *mon ami!* Is this the lovely captive I have been hearing so much about?"

Jeffery inclined his head. "I was not aware that my affairs were the subject of gossip. But if you heard that she is beautiful then for once gossip is right. May I present *Mademoiselle* Raven Winthrop? Raven, His Excellency, Governor Ducasse."

"Your Excellency." Raven swept into a low curtsy, for the moment speechless. Jeffery had spoken in flawless French. It was possible for a lowborn, escaped slave through perserverance to learn the mannerisms and speech of a gentleman. But Raven knew that to speak another language so perfectly required its being learned in childhood. And his French was not the patois of the islands, not the French of the streets. It was the cultivated French of the nobility.

"Welcome, *Mademoiselle*, to my home. May I present my wife?"

Raven also curtsied to the short, plump woman by the governor's side and was rewarded with a sweet, welcoming smile.

"You must reserve a dance for me, *Mademoiselle*," the governor said. "My wife does not dance but generously allows me the pleasure of dancing with every other beautiful woman present. As long as it is within her sight!"

"Certainly, sir," Raven said. "As long as *Madame* truly does not mind?"

"Of course not, *ma cherie*," *Madame* Ducasse said. "He is a fine thoroughbred and needs some exercise now and then—and a little loosening of the reins."

"Then I will look forward to our dance, Governor."

They moved on so that the governor could greet his other guests.

Raven's eyes swept the ballroom which was lit by myriad candles. There were very few women present. But those few were dressed in the latest fashions made with the finest materials. They wore jewels as lovely as any Raven had seen. And why not? she thought. The plundered wealth of the Caribbean passed through this port. It was not surprising that some of it would remain in Tortugan hands.

A girl in pink-striped satin caught Raven's attention. She was slipping inside from the garden, looking very much as if she had just had a tryst with a forbidden lover. Her hair was slightly mussed and the ribbons of her gown were crookedly tied as if done in a hurry by shaky hands. And though she had just come inside, her cheeks were flushed and she fanned herself nervously.

Raven hid her smile, absently wondering what swain would sheepishly appear momentarily from the garden. But the man who entered was far from sheepish. He was cool and urbane, with warm gray eyes and a reckless smile. Alex Jamison!

She felt Jeffery stiffen beside her and his fingers tighten possessively on her arm.

A quick glance at the adoring look the girl gave him confirmed that it had indeed been Alex in the garden with her. The girl's eyes followed him hungrily, but Alex had spotted Raven and his youthful friend was forgotten as he strode across the room, his hands outstretched to greet her.

Chapter Eight

"Raven! How lovely you are." Alex took her hands in his and kissed her fingers.

"Thank you, Alex," she said, slipping her fingers from his grasp. "And thank you again for the silk."

He stood back to admire the dress, nodding in approval. "It is the most fortunate piece of material in all the Caribbean!"

Alex held out his hand to Jeffery. "How are the repairs to *The Mermaid* coming along, Jeff?"

Jeffery took his friend's hand, though she noted that he pulled her closer at the same time. They were like two schoolboys, she thought. Good friends yet jealously wrangling for a prized possession. Jealous? She wondered if that could be true then dismissed the idea. Jeffery was only protecting his property. Whatever the reason, she had no wish to be a bone of contention between the two friends. But Alex was too good a friend for her to stop seeing just because Jeffery thought he owned her.

"Slower than I expected. But she should be sea worthy in two or three weeks."

Repressing a grin, Alex said, "I heard that you had to take time out yesterday to take care of a large-sized rat."

"Doesn't this town have anything to talk about but my affairs?" Jeffery growled.

"You should have killed him, Jeff. Scum like that..." Alex let the thought dangle.

"Give piracy a bad name?" Jeffery suggested.

"Never forget a grudge. You'll be looking over your shoulder until he's hanged."

"Jeffery?" Raven placed a shaking hand on his arm. She knew that DeLessops was the worst kind of pirate but that her escapade could further endanger Jeffery's life frightened her.

Jeffery looked down at her and gave her a reassuring grin. "The ball is about to begin. If I don't see a smile on your face in one second, I will take you home."

"And spoil the party for the rest of us?" Alex cried, holding out his arm to her. "Allow me the honor of the first dance and let me take you away from this cad, Raven."

Jeffery held her arm firmly on his own. "I might let you borrow her for one dance later, Alex. But her first dance goes to her escort."

"I am going to exert my authority and take her from both of you."

Raven turned to see Governor Ducasse standing behind them, and smiled up at him almost as she would to a rescuer. He bowed to her. "Will you do me the honor of opening the ball with me?"

"With pleasure!" Raven swept away on the arm of the governor, leaving two very chagrined-looking men behind.

Raven and Governor Ducasse stood in the middle of the dance floor, hand in hand, and the musicians struck up a lively tune. They danced the first measure alone then were gradually joined by other dancers. Alex danced with the girl from the garden, but Jeffery just stood at the side and watched her as if he could not wait for the dance to be over so he could claim her for his own once again.

"Captain Fortune seems very happy to have such a lovely lady in his home," the governor said, smiling down at her.

"He must be," Raven replied, taking the opening to appeal to the governor for help. "He has refused to let me go."

"Refused? Surely he is but waiting for your ransom to arrive."

They executed an intricate turn, and when she came back to the governor's side, she continued her appeal. "There is no one to ransom me. I have offered to pay my own ransom yet I still find myself his unwilling prisoner. Can you do anything to help me?"

"Your French is perfect but you are not French, are you?"

"No, Your Excellency. I'm English."

"By any chance was your mama a Frenchwoman?"

"No. She was English also."

"Then, *ma cherie*, there is nothing I can do for you. If one of your parents had been French or if our countries were not at war, perhaps I could, but *c'est la vie*." He gave an eloquent Gallic shrug.

Raven's heart sank. She had counted, perhaps too much, on being delivered by the government officials. She tried not to seem too disappointed, forcing a smile to her lips and concentrating on her dancing. The governor was an excellent dancer and a typically charming Frenchman as well. It was not long before her smile was genuine, and her heart was lightened.

When the dance was over, Governor Ducasse led her to the refreshment table and placed a glass of red wine into her hand. Jeffery was being kept busy by *Madame* Ducasse, but Alex soon joined them with his dance partner.

"*Mademoiselle* Winthrop, may I present my daughter, Jeanne?" Ducasse indicated the girl who had entered the ballroom from the garden.

Raven smiled and shook hands with her.

"Oh, Miss Winthrop! I heard about the duel Captain Fortune fought!" she said ingenuously, her eyes wide. "Is it so very exciting to have two men fighting over you?"

Raven laughed. "Actually, it was quite frightening."

"But, oh, so romantic, was it not?"

"There is nothing romantic about two men fighting, bleeding, and perhaps dying," her papa reprimanded. "Come, *ma petite*, and dance with your papa."

"Would you like to see the garden, Raven?"

Raven looked up at Alex with a mischievous gleam in her eye and nodded toward *Mademoiselle* Ducasse, dancing with her father. "I thought you had seen quite enough of the garden for one evening, Captain Jamison."

For a moment Alex looked surprised then laughed. "Then you must dance with me, Raven," he said, plucking the wine glass from her fingers, "before Jeff pries himself loose from *Madame* Ducasse and snatches you away."

Alex danced superbly, subtly leading her through the steps with feather-light suggestions from his fingers.

The last strains of the music had not died away before another hand took hers from Alex's. Raven had no need to turn to see who it was. The thrill that ran from her fingertips straight to her heart identified the source of that touch. Jeffery's other hand came around her waist to pull her close to his side. Her body brushed against the hard length of him and she gasped. Did he expect her to dance with him? Like this? Her knees were so weakened by his nearness, she was not sure she could even stand.

Jeffery's eyes locked with Alex's and Alex sighed with resignation, his reckless grin playing across his lips. "Until later, Raven." He bowed and chose another partner from the several women, young and old, who were looking hopefully at his tall, handsome form.

"You've tormented me enough, wench," Jeffery growled into her ear. "Now you will pay!"

Raven looked up at him in puzzlement, and he swept her into the next dance.

"Twice I've watched while you dance with another man. Graceful as a gazelle, supple as a cat, your smiling eyes flashing sparks that ignite the desire in every man's loins. Twice I watched from across the room, watching these fingers touch the hand of another, and I hungered for them."

He brought her hand to his lips, pretending to kiss her fingertips but actually nibbling at them with his teeth, his tongue sending weakening waves of warmth to her cheeks, her chest, to the secret place between her thighs.

"What witchery have you woven that draws my eyes to you, that makes my arms ache to hold your slender form, my hands long to caress your sweet hidden places?"

The steps of the dance separated them for a moment, giving her time to reclaim her thoughts, her soul, so that she was able to laugh up at him as though his words meant no more than any man's flirtations. But her voice, when she spoke, was not as steady as she would have liked. "Now must I pay yet another ransom, Sir Pirate?"

"Aye! I will not surrender you until you have given me an equal tally of dances."

He guided her through the dance with a sureness that was masterful. There was nothing unusual about the placement of his hands on her waist, her arms, yet she felt as if it were the first time any man had touched her there. When the movement of the dance drew them close together, her heart tripped to a faster beat and she found the warm embrace of home within the circle of his arms.

When the dance ended, he held her fast until the music started again, glaring down several men who approached them eagerly.

Throughout the second dance, his eyes never left her, growing warmer when he caught a tantalizing glimpse of her slender ankle and heating to a blue blaze when he took her in his arms and looked down into the valley between her breasts, lit by the glitter of the amethysts that rested there.

At the second dance's end she pulled away from him and went to stand in the cool breeze from the garden windows. The warmth she felt, she knew, was not entirely due to the exertion of the dance. If the heat from Jeffery's eyes and the growing tendril of flame within her met, there would be a conflagration she would not be able to contain. Her next partner would have to be someone other than Captain Fortune. The rhythm of the dance was too seductive for her to endure it in his arms.

"I have paid the full tally, Sir Pirate. The ransom is met. Have I now leave to go?"

"And leave me adrift? Bereft? Alone? Nay, fair maiden. The web of witchery you have woven is too strong."

"You, sir," she said, poking her finger into his

chest, "are a rogue, a thief, and a knave. If ever I get away from you, I will have to escape, for it is clear you will never let me go."

"Then I will keep you fast by my side." He pulled her to him, looking down at her as if he could devour her on the spot. "I do not think I shall mind dancing every dance with you."

She pushed away from him and looked up at him with a grin. "I think my bold buccaneer needs to be taught a lesson. I will not dance with you again until I have danced with at least three others!"

He opened his mouth to protest but was interrupted by a harsh voice grating brusquely, "Cap'n D'Arnot, ma'am. Dance?"

A short, heavy-set man with a black bushy beard and balding head held out his arm to her. He was dressed more casually than Jeffery, wearing a long leather jerkin and wide-topped boots, as if he had just come from a voyage. A gold earring dangled in one ear and a serviceable saber hung at one hip.

Uncertainly, she looked up at Jeffery but he only shrugged noncommittally and said, "One."

Dancing with Captain D'Arnot was like stomping through spring plowing with an ox. He spoke not one word, concentrating on each plodding step. When the dance was ended, he returned her to Jeffery, bowed a brief thank you and was gone.

She had no lack of dance partners and had soon gone through dance two and three. Jeffery immediately swept her onto the dance floor and claimed two more dances from her.

Alex presented himself to claim another dance, but she shook her head. "I couldn't dance another step just now. But I promise you my next dance."

The reckless grin appeared on his face. "Perhaps now is my chance to show you the garden?"

She could barely contain a smile. "I'm sure you know it well."

"Yes, I do. There's a bench in the back where we could sit and talk quite privately."

Her arm was through Jeffery's, pressed against his ribs and she felt, rather than heard, the low growl rumbling dangerously within him. She did want a stroll in the cool air but she did not want to go alone with Alex. Although she was sure he would be a gentleman, she did not want to provoke an incident between the two friends. Sliding her free arm into Alex's, she smiled up at both of them. "I would love to get some air—with both of you."

They found the bench Alex had mentioned, and Raven sat down, her wide skirts leaving room for only one of the men. Alex sat quickly beside her, leaving Jeffery the bole of a tree to lean against. He crossed his arms and glared down at them, listening but adding little to their chatter.

"If you are rested, Raven, I would like to claim that dance now." Alex took her hand and they stood up. He slipped his arm through hers, and the three of them ambled back inside.

A thin man with a large hook nose and an elegantly curled periwig bowed before them. The man was beribboned and ruffled to the point of being a dandy, and he sniffed haughtily at a perfumed, lace-edged handkerchief. But his brown eyes were hard, his stance one of officious pride, and Raven sensed that his foppery was but a shield over a nature as cruel as any pirate's could be.

"I'd like a dance with your woman, Fortune. Or d'ye intend to keep her all to yourself? You guard her well enough. Is she such a valuable prisoner?"

Jeffery smiled at the man, but she noted that his

arm slipped from hers and he stepped just far enough away to give him free access to his sword.

"She is valuable enough to guard her against scum and villains, Fournais." Jeffery's tone was calm, even pleasant, and his smile never left his face, but his eyes had hardened to blue sapphires and if the man had had any feelings, he would have frozen in their chill glare.

Fournais stiffened, his nostrils flaring. He nodded toward Alex. "Is the guarding of her too much for you to handle that you bring your hound to help you?"

Alex had tightened his hand on her as if ready to thrust her out of danger, but now she felt his hand slip down to free the hilt of his sword from the folds of his coat. She could not let Jeffery fight another duel over her, especially at the governor's ball.

"*Monsieur* Fournais, I refuse to be discussed like a piece of baggage as if I were not here. Though I realize that the worst sort of pirate is present, you are dressed like a gentleman. If you wanted to dance with me, you should have asked me. I am perfectly free to accept any partner I please but I would have told you that this dance is taken. If you will excuse me?"

She looked up at Alex sweetly and coyly. He took her arm and led her into the dance barely able to restrain a chuckle. Fournais could do nothing but grit his teeth and stomp away.

"I wonder how long before the bonehead realizes he is the worst sort of pirate you referred to?"

"Why, Alex," she said in wide-eyed innocence, "surely you don't think I insulted a gentleman?"

Alex grinned down at her, his gray eyes full of admiration. "A gentleman, no."

For the rest of the evening, most of her dances

alternated between Jeffery and Alex. Occasionally the governor asked her to dance or D'Arnot. He seemed harmless enough, and though Jeffery might not have approved of the man, he did not seem to disapprove of him either and she accepted, stomping around with him in silence until the end of a dance.

Dancing with Alex was a pleasure. He was smooth and expert. His leading was subtle. But it was when she went back to Jeffery's arms that she felt she had come home.

While they were enjoying some refreshments, Raven heard loud voices coming from the next room. Several men had been drinking during the evening but there had been nothing disturbing except for a few off-key songs sung louder and louder. But this was something else. The voices were drunken and strident.

Jeanne had long since been sent to her room and several other ladies were leaving when Jeffery went to get his hat and her shawl, leaving her in Alex's charge.

He looked down at her, his gray eyes growing warm, his smile more gentle than reckless now. He took her hand, drawing it to his lips to kiss her fingers. "I thought you looked lovely when you arrived. Fresh, your eyes shining with anticipation. But now, with your cheeks flushed from dancing, you are breathtaking. Have you truly grown more lovely as the evening progressed?"

Raven smiled sweetly at him. "I have enjoyed the evening, Alex. Any woman would enjoy herself dancing with you."

Suddenly a hand grabbed her arm, spinning her around and jerking her roughly into the burly arms of a pirate reeking of rum. Alex reached for her but two others grabbed him from behind, pinning his arms behind him. Alex struggled ineffectually in their grasp.

Strong arms held her fast, bleary eyes glittered at her, and the man laughed. " 'Tis only a little kiss we'll be wantin', *Mam'zelle*. A little kiss fer each of us. Ye've been givin' out more'n that to the two that's been guardin' ye all evenin'. We figured it was 'bout time we got our share."

The man was too drunk to reason with. She tried to kick him but missed and he chuckled. "Don't take on so. It's just a bit of a kiss I'm wantin'."

"Let me go!" Raven said as calmly and firmly as she could.

"Get your hands off her, Boudreau!" Alex growled.

"Now, now, lad, don't get so riled up. We've shared many a cup betwixt us. I'm only askin' that ye share the lass a bit. I won't hurt her none."

She couldn't see Alex but she heard several thumps and oofs then the zing of a sword being unsheathed.

Then Jeffery's voice sounded, clear and cool, "Some things are shared between comrades, Boudreau, other things are not. I suggest that you let the lady go."

Jeffery stood behind Boudreau and Raven felt the man stiffen, his arms loosen their grip.

"I'm lettin' go, Fortune. I didn't hurt her none."

Sweat began to bead on the man's brow as he very carefully released her. She quickly stepped away from him. The two men who had held Alex lay insensible against the wall, and Alex had his sword in hand. Jeffery stood unruffled and unperturbed, a smile on his face. Raven's eyes widened when she saw that it was not a sword or a pistol that Jeffery had poked into Boudreau's back but the end of his finger.

She looked up at Jeffery and he shrugged with a

grin. "He's not such a bad fellow, are you, Boudreau?"

The man shook his head frantically from side to side.

"He just forgot his manners for a space. 'Tis not a tavern you are in. Apologize to the lady and go back to your drinking." Jeffery's voice was calm, almost as if he were speaking to a child. He poked Boudreau's back again with his finger.

"Sorry, *Mam'zelle*." Carefully, Boudreau eased back toward the room he had come from, bowing profusely all the way.

"Had yourself a bit of a scuffle, did you?" Jeffery asked, grinning.

Alex sheathed his sword, and his smile was a bit chagrined. "Nothing I couldn't have handled, but thanks, anyway."

Raven looked back and forth between the two men. She had been frightened out of her wits and they acted as if they were having the time of their lives. No wonder they were so good at their professions! Men! Stamping her foot, she snatched her shawl and left them.

She said her good-byes to the Governor and *Madame* Ducasse then went to the carriage. Joshua was there to help her in, and she plopped down into the seat, crossing her arms angrily. Shuddering, she thought of Boudreau's greasy face pushed into hers, his rum-reddened eyes. She pictured the beads of sweat that had popped out when he thought Jeffery held a gun at his back. It was only Jeffery's finger and his reputation but they were enough to scare the man witless. Perhaps, as Jeffery had said, the fellow was not so bad after all. She started to giggle at the thought of holding a pirate at bay with one finger and the audacity of Jeffery to do such a thing.

The carriage dipped as Jeffery climbed in beside her. He pulled off his feather-trimmed hat and periwig and tossed them into the seat beside Joshua. "The long way home, Josh," he said.

Joshua nodded and the carriage moved off, climbing to wind along the crest of the hill, giving them a view of the moon-drenched bay.

"I wonder, Sir Pirate, why you bother with guns when your finger is so effective?"

"Not everyone I attack has his back turned," he said, sliding closer to her.

She poked her finger into his chest to halt his advance. "I wonder how effective my finger will be to hold this pirate at bay."

"Not effective at all," he said, and drew her fingers to his lips, beginning to kiss them.

"Stop that!" She snatched her hand away. She had no intention of letting him seduce her and she could not let him even begin, for it would be too difficult to stop. She would not have the will.

He bent to nibble at her ear, easing his arm around her shoulders.

"Behave yourself," she chided, pushing against his chest.

But he brushed aside her hands and put his other arm around her waist, pulling her to him. His hand slipped downward over the curve of her buttock and he lifted her onto his lap. Her head fell back onto his arm and his mouth claimed her throat, nibbling gently with his lips, his tongue sending shivers through her.

"Don't," she pleaded weakly.

"Why?" was all he asked and she had no answer except a silent, *Why not?*

She fought against the robbing of her reason. But his mouth was now attacking the smooth curve of her shoulder, his hand loosening the ties of her bodice.

"Jeffery, stop. There's no point to this." She grabbed at his hands but his nimble fingers foiled her, continuing their work with dexterity.

"There's a very good point to all this, my love," he whispered against her shoulder. "I am going to make you fully and completely mine."

"Three thousand pounds does not give you the right to rape me!" she cried, but her hand betrayed her words, moving inside his coat to stroke the lean flesh over his ribs.

The last defensive tie was loosened, and her breasts spilled forth into the moonlight, into his waiting hands, his mouth. She gasped as his tongue lashed the rosy peak into a taut hardness. Her fingers dug into his side as he drew ecstasy from the core of her being with the gentle pull of his mouth.

"No," she moaned, rolling her head back and forth on his arm. But he ignored her voice, listening only to her body which invited further conquest.

She felt her skirt being pushed up, his hand gliding over her ankle, her calf, pausing to tease the back of her knee, then onward. His fingers trailed along her thigh then along her inner thigh. The tension of waiting for his fingers to reach their goal kept her breathing shallow and quick.

Suddenly the carriage jerked to a halt in front of Jeffery's home and she sat up with a cry, realizing what a disheveled state she was in. Joshua was the soul of propriety as he got down from the high seat, keeping his eyes carefully averted, but her cheeks flamed as she hastily, and with shaking fingers, retied the bows of her bodice.

Chuckling, Jeffery reached over to help her, but she slapped his hands away.

"Restrain your attacks to the sea!" she snapped.

"Does that mean you would prefer to continue this aboard my ship?" he asked with a lazy rolling chuckle.

Her black eyes flashed at him. "It means I would prefer not to continue this at all!"

Arching his brows, he let his hand fall onto her thigh but she brushed it away with a frown.

"Joshua is waiting," she said.

With a sigh, he climbed down from the carriage and reached up to help her down.

She looked down at his arms, outstretched to welcome her, and she longed to throw herself into them, let them hold her close, and find whatever comfort she could within their encircling embrace. But there was only one place that could lead. She tossed her head proudly. "Don't touch me!"

Holding on to the door, she climbed down but at the last moment, the treacherous door swung away and she stumbled, twisting her ankle. Her cry of pain had not left her lips before she felt Jeffery's supporting arms gathering her to him, lifting her against his broad, hard chest, cradling her head on his shoulder.

"I . . . I can walk," she said, flexing her foot.

"No, you can't," he said huskily. He held her firmly against him and she could feel the quick thudding of his heart. "I won't let you. I may never let you walk again."

He carried her up the walk, kissing her hair, her forehead. Her arms were around his neck, her fingers twining in the hair at his nape. His hand reached nearly to the crest of her breast and she longed to twist into its grasp, to feel once again the teasing play of his fingers.

He carried her inside, across to the hall. His shoes

clicked on the cool tiles, each click carrying her closer to her room, her bed.

The door to her room was kicked open, then shut, and his mouth found hers, hungrily, devouring, probing. She opened her lips in a gluttonous invitation to him, as hungry for him as he was for her.

His lips never left hers as he lay her across the bed. Once again, his fingers began loosening the ties of her bodice but this time, she helped him. The buttons of his vest and shirt were vanquished and at last her hands found what they sought—his warm, hard flesh. She kneaded the strong muscles of his chest, stroked the leanly fleshed ribs, pulled gently at the hair that spread over his chest and trailed downward.

His shoes dropped to the floor, then hers. He turned to remove her stockings, rolling the sheer silk downward, his lips nibbling a trail along her calf in the wake of his hands. His own socks were less ceremoniously flung away, his shirt pulled off and tossed aside.

Her breasts were freed, the dangling stomacher pushed away, her underskirt and chemise banished into the shadows.

At last he lay beside her, flesh to flesh, warm life to warm life.

Every part of her face was kissed, her eyes, her cheeks, her lips. Gently, he sought her mouth again then thoroughly claimed it, affirming it forever as his own.

His tormenting fingers tickled over her stomach, up her side, around the mounds of her breasts, retreating just short of the waiting peaks.

Moaning against him in protest, her own hands moved across his chest, found the downward trail of hair and followed it across the hard, flat, plain of his belly. Her fingers splayed into the widening delta of hair at his loins and in response he conquered one pink tip of her breast.

She sighed contentedly but the relief was short-lived. Like an addict, her body cried for more, more hungrily than before. Chuckling, he denied her, rolling her to her stomach to torment her further by trailing his tongue along her spine, kneading her rounded buttocks, lifting the tumbled midnight of her hair to nip playfully at her neck.

Unable to stand his teasing torture any longer, she twisted beneath him and wrapped her arms around his neck to pull him closer, to bring his mouth once more to hers. He let her taste the fullness of his kiss before he tore his mouth away to plant it on her breast. His hand glided over the smooth skin of her belly and brought her to new heights of anxious longing when he found the soft, secret recess between her thighs. A raging flood was building within her, demanding release.

He lifted himself above her, then came down, pressed for entry, and found her welcoming warmth.

There was one quick moment of pain then the tide of heat within her climbed, nearly stopping her breath, threatening to drown her if it did not soon find release. She arched to meet him, filling the aching void within her until the flood crested, then tumbled over, carrying them both away in a raging, surging torrent, rhythmic as the cycle of life.

When the deluge abated and his ragged breathing became calmer, more even, he nuzzled her ear, whispering into it, "Now you are mine. Now and forever."

For the moment she was content to let it be so. Whether he had purchased her with three thousand pounds or with a night of love, it mattered not. She was his.

Gently, he lifted himself from her to lie beside her,

his hand tangled in her hair, his face pressed into the curve of her shoulder. She snuggled closer, ran her hand once more over his warm, well-muscled back, then slept.

Chapter Nine

The heady, musky scent of Jeffery clinging to sheets and pillows, enveloped Raven in its sensuous embrace, making her want to burrow deeper into the bed. But the morning was too full of promise, her heart too full of memory. She stretched like a cat, rolled over and stretched again, enjoying the feel of the warm morning bedding sliding smoothly against her naked skin.

She ran her hand over the place beside her where he had slept, the impression of his head still clearly pressed into the pillow. When had he left her? She seemed to remember a predawn rousing, a hasty kiss brushed onto her cheek. She ran a hand through her hair, thoroughly touseled from their lovemaking. Why had he left? Was the work on *The Mermaid* so important that it could not have waited one hour past her waking?

What had she expected? Frowning, she sat up to an empty, lonely room. She had expected him to be there when she awoke. She had expected morning kisses and caresses, sweet whispers of love and devotion, a long, lingering breakfast shared together. If he must go, the parting would be prolonged and reluctant.

She flounced from the bed to gather the clothes that had been scattered in such hasty, wild abandon the night before. Her hands were full of silk and chemise when she spotted the torn scrap of paper on the dresser. "Dinner tonight," was scrawled across a piece of ledger paper. Was it a promise, an invitation, or an order?

She wadded it and threw it into a corner. Most likely it was an order. He certainly seemed to think he owned her. What place did she hold in his life? Did he think of her only as his slave to use for his own pleasure? There had been no promises of marriage, not even any words of love. At the outset he had told her he would bide his time until she was ready. Well, she had been ready last night. He had plucked her like a ripe plum, used her to satisfy his needs, then left her with orders to await his return.

Am I expected to wait patiently in his house all day, bathing in scented water, rubbing fragrant oil into my skin, donning soft silks like a good odalisque, all for his sybaritic pleasure, when he at last appears? she thought, glaring at herself in the mirror.

What was it he had whispered so huskily into her ear last night? "Now you are mine. Now and forever." He had bought her for three thousand pounds. Right now it seemed like thirty pieces of silver.

The glitter of the amethysts she had worn last night winked up at her from the folds of the lavender silk, the silk he had wanted to buy for her but she had refused. She looked about the room with its silken Oriental carpet and fine polished furniture. She could not deny that he was generous to her. Nor could she deny that he had been gentle and careful with her last night. Her skin still tingled with wanting his touch. But where was her freedom? Barbados was still a dream. He had had plenty of time to find passage for her away from here. But still she was confined to this island. He had told her not to leave even the house without him or Joshua with her. She was very much a prisoner and he seemed to be in no hurry to grant her her freedom.

And why should he? He had wanted her and now she had given herself to him. He would expect her to be here waiting for him whenever he wanted to use her. He was a very tender master and she had all too easily become his. She ran her hands over her arms, thinking of the pleasure of his touch, longing for it even now. Was she not becoming even more of a slave—to her own passions?

What happened when he tired of her? Would she cling to him and beg him for one more caress, one more kiss? What would happen to her then? Would he see her safely to Barbados or sell her in the slave markets of Maricaibo?

She must get away. Somehow she must get away.

Dressing quickly, she set the room to rights, grabbed the parasol, and left the room. She had to get some air, get away from this house and all that belonged to Captain Jeffery Fortune, even if just for a while.

But when she opened the front door, she saw Joshua sitting on the patio, his hands busy with a pistol he was cleaning. Had he been set there to guard her comings and goings? Certainly he would not let her go out alone.

She gritted her teeth in frustration, wondering if there might be some way to get around him when the front gate opened and Alex came up the walk, more casually dressed than usual in a simple coat of blue linen and beige buckskin breeches.

Raven ran out to greet him. To his surprise, nearly throwing herself into his arms. He put an arm about her and she also slipped hers around his waist, leaning against him and feeling very much like crying on his shoulder.

Joshua nodded a hello to Alex but only scowled at her, clearly disapproving of her behavior. He had seen how she had behaved in the carriage last night, had seen Jeffery carry her to her room. Doubtless he knew that Jeffery did not come out again until this morning. Now here she was with her arm around Alex. No wonder he had nothing but a frown for her.

But she found an odd comfort with Alex. She wasn't going to let an old retainer, obviously loyal to his master, keep her from being with someone she considered a good friend.

"Alex!" she said, smiling up at him, "I'm so glad to see you."

He cocked a brow and his grin this morning was more wistful than reckless and there was a glow in his gray eyes when he looked at her. "If I had known I was going to receive such an eager welcome, I'd have come earlier."

"If you've come to see Jeffery, I think he's at the harbor working on *The Mermaid*." She looked at Joshua for confirmation and he shook his head.

"I've seen him," Alex said. "Up to his armpits in pitch. Since he is busy, I thought you might be in need of companionship."

"I'd love some." She turned him toward the gate. "Let's go for a walk. Out. Anywhere."

"With pleasure," he said, and his eyes, gleaming softly, took in her form.

Joshua put down the pistol and got up to follow them, but she stopped him with a hand on his chest. "I shall be perfectly safe with Alex. There's no need to take you away from your work."

Joshua looked doubtful. "Master Jeffery said I was to stay close by ye, lass."

"I'm sure he meant that you were not to let me go out alone, Joshua. But I'm sure that Jeffery's good friend will not let any harm come to me." She emphasized the "good friend" and noticed a slight wince on Alex's face so fleetingly that she was not sure she had really seen it.

Heaving a giant sigh, Joshua finally nodded his assent and went back to his work, letting them go alone.

Lighthearted at getting away as well as having a pleasant companion for the day, Raven held to Alex's arm and chatted happily, her skirts swinging gaily.

Alex looked down at the beautiful woman swaying along so provocatively at his side. If she were merely beautiful, he could walk away from her, with only a slight regret that it was not to be he who seduced her. After all, she belonged to his best friend. Not only was she Jeff's by right of capture, but he had seen the way Jeff looked at her. Jeff was as smitten as he was.

And there lay the problem. There was so much more to Raven Winthrop than mere beauty. Jeff had told him of her surgical skills. He had seen for himself her smile, her charm, her sweetness. Her cleverness. He chuckled anew whenever he thought of her standing up to Fournais, outwitting him, and preventing what could have been a serious brawl.

He wanted her. And he was willing to risk his friendship with Jeff if that's what it took to gain the prize.

He would have to move carefully with this one. She was not a naive young girl he could take into a garden for a few quick kisses. Nor did he want to.

He wanted more from her. Much more. Looking at her, he could almost feel the silkiness of her skin. His hands itched to cup the fullness of those rounded breasts, to suck their sweet nectar with his mouth. But he held back cautiously. Not until the time was right would he make his move. Not until he was sure he would be successful.

That time could not be far away, he thought. The welcome she had given him had been far warmer than he had expected. How trustingly she had come along with him, leaning on his arm, smiling up at him, chatting happily, not once asking where he was taking her.

"Would you like to see my ship?" he asked, and his heart gave a strange lurch when she looked up at him with that piquant expression. For him, it was almost as if the whole future of the world rested upon her answer.

"Yes. I'd like that very much."

The softness of her tones, the vibrancy of her voice thrilled him as much as her answer and he could not resist putting his arm about her waist for a brief hug, then worried that he had gone too far, too soon. But to his relief, she did not pull away or look up at him in scorn. She merely accepted the hug and continued on her way with him. Yes, the time was not far off when she would be his for the taking.

The Brigand lay at anchor out in the bay so they took a boat out to her. Helping her mount the rope ladder up the side of the ship, he took delight in their enforced closeness, the sight of her trim ankle, the necessary placement of his hands on her slim waist, a steadying hand on her thigh. Even through the myriad layers of skirt and petticoat, the firm feel of her heated his blood so that it was hard to resist further intimacy.

A crewman saluted smartly as they came up onto the deck. "Welcome aboard, miss, Captain."

"Lunch in my cabin, Sturgis," Alex ordered.

"Oh, Alex," she said, laying her hand lightly on his sleeve, "could we have it on deck? The day is too beautiful to waste."

Her large black eyes were so appealing, her skin glowing in the morning light, her touch so sweet, he did not think he could have denied her anything at that moment. "Of course." He nodded to Sturgis who went off to prepare the meal.

"She's English built, isn't she?" Raven asked.

Alex nodded.

"She's so narrow for an English ship!" Raven exclaimed, looking across *The Brigand*.

"She's quite new. The English are finally beginning to realize that round-bottomed stability and storage space are not the only desirable qualities in a ship."

"She must be fast."

"Speed is of the essence to a privateer."

"Which reminds me," Raven said, looking up at him with puzzlement, "I wanted to ask you something. How does an English privateer come to find refuge on a French-held island when the English and French are at war?"

Alex laughed. "Maybe it's my charm?"

At her look of complete incredulity, he offered a more believable answer. "Tortuga is French, yes. But mostly it is pirate. Any valuable cargo is welcome if the French government is given its cut. Secondly, it is well known that I have never preyed on the French. Only the Spanish. My mother is French and would box my ears if I did. But I suppose the most helpful little detail"—and here he grinned—"is that my mother is a distant cousin to Governor Ducasse."

"An important detail!" She laughed and turned to study the rest of the ship.

He watched her look up at the tall masts which seemed to rake the clouds drifting by. How he longed to trail his fingers down the slim column of her throat.

Alex followed her contentedly about the ship, showing her every part, answering her questions which were surprisingly knowledgeable.

"How do you know so much about ships?" he asked as they sat down to lunch.

"I've spent much of my life on them," she answered, stirring her tea to creamy whiteness. "From war to war, from battlefield to battlefield, the Royal Navy was our transport. The voyages were sometimes long and the officers were always happy to indulge me by answering my questions."

He could just imagine it. Raven would be a pretty distraction from any long, tedious voyage.

They lingered over lunch then talked until their conversation died away. Raven absently stirred a half-empty cup of cold tea and sighed. At times during the day she had seemed distracted, at other times, her chatter seemed to be full of false happiness. Now there was no denying that her thoughts were far away and from the look on her face, those thoughts were not ones to gladden the heart.

He reached across the table and took her hand in his, squeezing gently. "Is anything wrong, Raven?"

She looked up startled, then smiled brightly. "I'm sorry. I must have been woolgathering."

She started to butter another piece of bread but he took the knife from her fingers, holding her hand firmly and looking seriously into her eyes. "What is it, Raven? What's wrong?"

The pain in her eyes was clear when she looked up

at him, but she gave her head a quick shake and her hand held his gratefully. "I would rather not talk about it, Alex. I'm sorry if I haven't been very good company."

"I could have had none better!" he said brightly. If she would not talk, the least he could do would be to cheer her up.

"You're very kind, Alex."

"Kind?" Then he became as serious as she, bending close to cup her chin in his fingers. "I want to be more than kind. If ever I can do anything, help you in any way, even just to listen, I want you to promise that you will tell me."

Tears threatened to spill from her eyes but she smiled them away. "I will, Alex. I feel sure I can trust you." She stood abruptly. "But I think it is time you took me back."

He wanted nothing more than to sweep her away with him but reluctantly he took her back to her captor, ordering a carriage over her protest. They arrived laughing and he helped her down, allowing himself the indulgence of holding her a moment longer than necessary.

She stopped him at the gate, reaching on tiptoe to kiss him lightly on the cheek. He very nearly lost his breath and would have swept her into his arms and carried her back to his ship, his cabin, if he thought she would have gone willingly.

But she stepped away from him. "Thank you, Alex. It was a wonderful day."

Then she was gone, leaving him feeling very much like a lifeboat cast adrift and lost.

Raven opened the door to Jeffery's town home, and, swinging her parasol, headed for her room. She would have been lying to herself if she did not admit

166

that she was glad that an angry Jeffery had not been waiting for her. She was sure that Joshua would make his report as soon as Jeffery returned and she was equally sure that Jeffery would not be happy that she had spent the day with Alex.

She tossed her head prettily. *Just like a child*, she thought. *He can't spend time with me so he doesn't want anyone else to.*

"Good evening, Raven."

Her hand froze on the latch of her door and she turned to see Jeffery leaning casually in the doorway of his room. He wore only a loose, unsashed shirt, rolled to the elbows, and black breeches. The evening sunlight streamed through the windows of his room, spilling through the doorway, and she could see the outline of his muscular torso through his shirt. Droplets of water glistened in his freshly washed hair and it curled enticingly at his neck. The sunlit edges of his hair were shining gold, but his face was in shadow, his blue eyes hidden in darkened recesses.

She held tightly to the latch to support knees grown suddenly weak at the sight of his long, lean length. A sudden warmth sprang up deep within her, speading through her, robbing her of breath, of speech, of reason. Tearing her eyes away from his tall, lithe body, she tried to remember that she was supposed to be angry with him.

"Good evening, Captain Fortune," she said as frigidly as the warmth within her would allow.

She lifted the latch to go into her room without looking at him again, but he stopped her with, "You're playing with fire, you know."

For a brief moment she wondered if he meant the heat that played within her whenever he was near. Could he really see into her very being? Then she realized that he meant Alex. Holding up her chin, she chanced a scathing glance in his direction, being careful to concentrate on his face, not that spare frame lit with fire from the sun.

"What I do is no concern of yours."

"I am making you my concern." He pushed away from the door frame and came toward her, almost, she thought, like a stalking cat. She backed against the door, one hand still on the latch behind her.

"By what right?" she asked, lifting her chin defiantly.

He leaned a sun-bronzed hand on each side of her door, trapping her. He bent close to her and she wondered if he could hear the pounding of her heart. "By right of capture. Because you have no one else to protect you."

She faced him squarely, using the door for support, determined neither to run nor to throw herself into his arms. "I'm a grown woman. I can protect myself."

"Even from the likes of Alex Jamison?"

"Alex has been nothing but a perfect gentleman. Which is more than I can say for you," she threw at him.

"Then he's up to something." He leaned closer, gripping her chin in the fingers of one hand, searing her with his firm touch. "Stay away from him, Raven."

She shook free of his fingers but could not escape his closeness, the clean smell of him, the heat emanating from his body. "I thought he was your friend. Friends trust each other."

"He is my friend and I would trust him with my life. But I wouldn't trust him five minutes alone with an innocent woman." His words were hard, a clear warning, but his hand toyed with a loose strand of her hair.

She slapped at his hand.

"Innocent? You can call me innocent after last night?" she snapped, then colored and turned her eyes away, biting her tongue for mentioning what had happened between them.

A low chuckle rumbled from him and she looked up to see in his face all the desire and passion that she thought had been thoroughly quenched the night before. She could see she had been wrong. The night before had only been added fuel.

"You have no idea how innocent you are, how seductive his charm can be. You don't know his reputation."

"Is yours any better?" she cried. "At least Alex is not a pirate and can offer me honesty and honor. What am I to you but a slave? What can you offer me that he can't?"

"This!"

There was no space of time between the word and his mouth crashing down upon hers, spilling liquid fire between them. Her hand left the latch, found those crisp, damp curls at his nape. The fire flowed through her, was spread by his lips, blazing a burning trail down her throat.

His arms came around her and he bent to lift her to him. She made no protest as he carried her into the golden light of his room and lay her on his bed. A candle had been lit, and the scent of burnt wick and beeswax mingled with the heady fragrance of tropical flowers from the garden. His own smell came to her, too—soap and musk, sea air and sun-scented skin.

Raven's eyes glided over him. The slanting rays of the setting sun cast a golden-orange glow over him, burnishing his hair to bright gold, brightening his eyes to deep, burning sapphire, turning him into an ancient Greek god of bronze and gold.

But this god was warm and alive. The flesh beneath her fingers vibrant and pulsing with passion. The lips that once again found hers were sensitive and mobile, the fingers that slid her gown from her shoulders left a trail of tingling nerve endings that cried for the return of his touch.

One of his hands pushed downward, into her loosened bodice, drawing the fire from his lips onto her breasts. The other hand lifted her, sliding down her back, pushing her gown away from her shoulders, breasts, waist, hips. It took but a moment for her to kick free of the dress. His shirt and breeches followed in an arcing path to a far corner.

Both their bodies now glowed golden-orange in the sun's dying rays. The candlelight added its warm touch. But neither of those fires could match that which Raven felt burning between her and her pirate-god.

His hand found the hidden recess between her thighs, his tongue played a teasing torment upon her breast, and the fire blazed to new intensity. He rose over her, his knee breaking a trail for his swollen passion to follow. She arched beneath him, scorching the silken skin of her stomach against the flat, firm hardness of his.

He sought and found welcome entry to her inner richness but held back, drawing such sweet ecstasy from her that she moaned. Her fingers clutched his muscled buttocks to draw him closer, but still he taunted her, building the fire higher until in a bright, blinding rush, the flame flashed over her. It gushed over them, hungry tongues of fire ravaging through the dry tinder of their passion, leaving them burnt and spent, collapsed in each other's arms.

But the fire was not a destroying fire, leaving only

ashes. It left a glow, banked and ready for renewal at the center of their beings.

Jeffery kissed her forehead, her eyes, her lips, and she lay still, greedily holding on to this moment of being cherished. She tried not to think past its ending, to dinnertime when they would sit, fully clothed, coolly and properly across from each other to eat. She refused to think of the future when he would leave on a voyage to be gone long days while she worried if he were living or dead, captured and hanged, or coming home to her.

The thought of her own leaving was now unfathomable. Not while he held her. Not when it seemed that he might care a little for her.

The sun was but a memory. The candle began to sputter. He kissed her once more and rose from the bed, lighting a new candle.

Propped on one elbow she watched unashamedly as he moved about the room, gathering their scattered clothing. As a battlefield surgeon, naked male bodies were not new to her. But the one before her was easily the most perfect she had seen.

His skin was made warm and rosy in the candle-light, and his nearly blond hair flashed strands of fine gold. His arms were corded with muscle, his shoulders were broad and strong, and his hands were supple, long-fingered. His chest was wide and deep, his belly, flat and hard, displaying the ridges of muscle that lay just beneath the skin. His slim hips led to well-developed thighs and sinewy calves.

Multiple scars marred the smooth perfection of his skin but none were disfiguring. She wondered about them, resolving to have him tell her the story of each one someday.

He turned to her, his breeches in hand. "If your maidenly curiosity has been satisfied, may I dress?"

171

Her only answer was a pillow hurled playfully at his head.

Dodging it easily, he laughed evilly. "So! You want to play rough, eh?"

Like a primeval monster he formed his hands into claws and lunged at her with a savage growl. He fell on her, tickling her unmercifully.

Alternately laughing and screaming, she begged him to stop, none of her efforts to throw him off being successful. Finally he rolled her over and gave her a playful swat on the bottom.

"Up, me girl. Get yourself dressed. 'Tis nearly time for supper and the exercise of the past hour has given me an appetite."

Watching as she rolled away from him to get out of bed, trying unsuccessfully to cover herself with a sheet, he added, "And not just for food. I'll be wanting more of your sweet meat later."

Raven wrapped the sheet tightly about her, unknowingly showing off her shapely form, pushing the fullness of her breasts up in an enticing display. With an exaggerated swing of her buttocks, she gathered her own clothing under his lustful eye. "Is there no end to your hunger, my ravaging beast?"

"Nay. And fair maidens are my favorite food."

Slinging her clothes over her shoulder, she said, "Then this maid must make a quick escape 'ere she is devoured."

She opened the door and he lunged for her, but she made her escape, hurrying to her own room to wash and dress for dinner.

Somehow she got through the meal. She kept telling herself that it was her imagination that made Mary's looks seem smug and knowing. Was Mary really treating her even better tonight? Cutting choice sections of beef for her plate, adding an extra dollop of whipped cream to her peach pie, as if she could not do enough for Jeffery's woman?

And Jeffery. His conversation was light. No overt comment was made about what they had been doing short moments before dinner, yet every word seemed to hold a memory of that time, a promise of another. Each look he gave her was heavy with desire. An intensity burned in his eyes as they swept over her, lingering along the edge of her neckline where the full swell of her bosom was thrust into view. His gaze raked downward and where cloth concealed, memory revealed, and the dress she wore might as well not have been there.

The last of her pie was just disappearing when Joshua ushered Mr. Meachum into the room.

Breathless and hurried as ever, the rotund pirate-accountant bobbed her a quick bow then turned to Jeffery. "Sorry to bother, Captain. But news wouldn't wait. Can we talk?"

"Sit down, Mr. Meachum," Jeffery invited. "Have a piece of Mary's peach pie."

Meachum looked greedily at the pie and unconsciously rubbed his stomach. "Maybe just a bite," he conceded.

He was well into his second piece when he remembered the urgent business that had brought him there, "Must talk to you, Captain."

"Very well, Mr. Meachum," Jeffery said, finishing his own second helping of pie, "talk." He leaned back, toying with his knife.

Meachum glanced once at Raven as if not sure he should discuss piratical concerns in front of her. But at Jeffery's nod, he began to speak. And the first words he said riveted Raven's attention.

Michele Stegman

"Parkington's making a big shipment. May have left Barbados already."

Jeffery sat forward, the knife in his hand suddenly changed from an innocuous table utensil to a deadly weapon in his savage grip. "Sugar?"

"Aye. And rum."

Jeffery grinned, and the grin was one of demonic pleasure. "Shall we stir Master Parkington's sugar into salt water instead of tea?"

Meachum caught the grim humor. "And the rum?"

"The king's navy would not put it to as good a use as my crew. We shall use it to drink to the ill health of Samuel Parkington."

"There's one or two amongst the crew besides yourself who'll drink most heartily," Meachum answered.

Raven sat speechless as she listened to their talk, heard Jeffery issuing orders to round up the crew, to take aboard last-minute supplies, to ready his ship to sail by morning. Samuel Parkington. Her uncle. They were planning to raid one of his ships. And there was probably nothing she could do to stop it. But she could try. She just had to be careful not to let slip her relationship to Samuel Parkington.

At last Meachum took his leave, and she stood to face Jeffery, whose mind seemed to be mulling over his plans.

"You're planning a raid on a hapless ship?"

He tossed down the knife. "You heard our talk."

His eyes met hers but there was no passion in them. Nor were there any pleas for understanding yet she suddenly knew that he had deliberately made his plans in her presence. That he wanted her to understand just what it meant to be a pirate. "I have never tried to hide what I am from you."

As I must hide who I am from you, she thought.

What was he asking of her? To accept the fact that he was a pirate? Could she accept it?

Of course she had known what he was. But somehow she had been able to think of his raid on her ship with gratitude. He had saved her from De-Lessops, had saved Van Doorn and his crew, had given them new jobs. He had not been on another raid since she had known him and the past was, well, past.

But this was different. He was deliberately planning a future raid. A raid on someone she knew. It struck too close to shrug it off. Of course she knew he was a pirate. But now she was being asked to accept his piracy as part of who he was and she did not think she could do that.

"Why do you want to attack a sugar ship?" she asked, trying a new approach. "What profit is there in that? I would think a pirate would seek out treasure ships."

" 'Tis true there is little monetary profit in this venture, although we may sight another ship along the way. I have other reasons for attacking this particular ship."

"I cannot see any."

Jeffery shoved his chair away from the table and stood up. "Samuel Parkington is a cruel, evil man. I have numerous reasons for seeking his ruin, for attacking every ship of his that comes my way. I will show you but one of those reasons."

He came to her and, thrusting up the sleeves of his shirt, he held out his wrists to her. A line of faded, white scars circled each wrist. "A reminder of ropes and manacles I shall carry with me until the day I die."

Raven's eyes widened and she longed to reach out

to soothe that old hurt but she held back, waiting for him to continue.

"I was his slave, Raven. But I escaped. I will never be a slave again. I will die first. But for what I suffered in the past, and for other injuries done me, Samuel Parkington will pay, and pay as dearly as I am capable of making him pay."

His tone was quiet but so much anger smoldered there that she was sure nothing she could say could quench it. Still, for her uncle's sake, she had to try. "Others have been slaves. They do not seek unreasoning vengeance on their former masters."

"Unreasoning?" He laughed grimly and bitterly. "You have no idea of the horrors inflicted daily on the slaves of a sugar plantation. And you have no idea what that man has done to me."

"Then there is nothing I can do to stop you?"

"You have known from the beginning what I am. If my reasons are not good enough for you . . ." His voice trailed off and he shrugged.

"No," she said, and there was a building bitterness in her own words. "They are not good enough for me. I think your thirst for revenge is excessive and unreasonable."

Once more his eyes raked over her hungrily, hopefully, almost, but not quite pleading. "I do not have time to discuss this now. But when I return, we will settle things once and for all."

With an iron will she did not know she had, she watched him buckle on his saber, thrust the familiar brace of pistols into his sash, and clap his feathered hat upon his sun-burnished locks. She did not throw herself into his arms as she longed to do. She did not kiss him good-bye. She merely stood there, prim and dry-eyed, and watched him go. Stiffly, she walked to her room and shut the door. Then the tears came.

Chapter Ten

Darkness had seeped into the room, bringing with it the night sounds and scents of Tortuga before Raven's tears were gone. She went to her washstand and wet a cloth, pressing its coolness against her tear-swollen eyes.

She could not believe that Jeffery's slavery had been any worse than any other slave's. Nor could she believe that slavery could be as bad as he indicated. It would be stupid to mistreat slaves and then have to buy new ones and train them. Why would her uncle chain a slave? How would the slave be able to work? Jeffery had probably gotten those scars while he was in gaol and being transported. Surely Jeffery was blaming her uncle for things that were not his fault at all.

But he did blame her uncle. She had seen the hatred in his eyes, the cold frigidity that would never melt. Willing to risk his ship, his crew, his very life, to attack a ship for very little profit, and for the sole reason that it belonged to Samuel Parkington, and to continue to do so year after year, showed an excess of vengeance, a thirst for revenge that far exceeded his hurt. How could she love such a man?

Love? She lifted her face from the cool cloth to

stare at herself in the mirror. A face ravaged by tears, with swollen eyes and a reddened nose, stared back at her. Why else would she be shedding tears? Did she cry each time DeLessops or Fournais set sail? Did she care so fiercely whether any other pirate lived or died?

Her hands shook as she sat on the edge of the bed, and she clenched them in her lap to steady them. Would she have given herself so freely, with such abandon, with such utter joy to someone she did not love? What had happened to her that she could find herself willingly bedding a pirate with never a promise of marriage, never a word of love spoken, never a thought that she was his prisoner?

Perhaps the question was not *what* had happened to her but *who*. She could not imagine falling in love with DeLessops. Or even the more refined Fournais. Not even Alex stirred her blood as one touch from Jeffery's fingers or one heated glance from him did.

But where did all this leave her? Jeffery had never once spoken of love between them, of marriage. Even if he offered marriage, could she accept? Was this the marriage she had hoped for, the marriage her father had dreamed of for her? Marriage to a traitor, a common felon, an escaped slave, a pirate? Could she accept what he was, shut off her conscience each time he gave her a piece of lace or . . . or . . . Her eyes caught the glitter of the amethyst necklace still laying on the dresser. From what hapless traveler had that been stolen?

But he had not spoken of marriage. He had only said that they would "settle things." Just what did he mean by that? Tighter confinement to ensure she did not escape him? Already Joshua watched her every move outside this room.

She remembered the look Jeffery gave her just before he left. Maybe "settling things" meant that he was tired of her. She had finally given him what he wanted from her. Maybe now that the chase was over, the excitement was gone. He was ready for fresh game. What then would he do with her? She was not sure she wanted to know.

One thing was clear. She could no longer remain in this house. She had to make her escape while he was gone. No matter what he had meant, whether it was marriage, a continuation of their present circumstances, or something else, she could accept none of those choices.

She began to pace, her eyes roaming every corner of the room for some clue, some idea, of how to get away. Her eyes fell on the glitter of gold on her dresser. The shell pendant lay next to the amethyst necklace. Absently, she fingered them both. One was a loan from Jeffery, as if what he offered was but temporary. The other was a free gift from Alex.

Alex! Had she deliberately refused to see the escape that lay in the harbor? Had love so clouded her vision that she had not realized that Alex's ship was a possible means of escape? Alex was no pirate. He was a privateer, with letters of marque from the English. It would be no problem at all for him to sail into Bridgetown Bay.

She squared her shoulders, held up her chin. Alex had offered her his help. Would he help her even if it meant crossing his friend? Would Alex take her to Barbados? Perhaps if he knew just who she was, he might. She searched for and found a piece of paper then dug out her ink and quills.

"Alex," she wrote. "I need your help. Will you come to see me as soon as you can? Raven."

She sanded the note and waved it in the air to dry then folded it into a tiny square. Tomorrow, somehow, she would get it to Alex. Alex would come. Alex would help her. She would get away—while she could still force herself to go.

When Alex read the note the urchin had given him, he slowly crumpled it, smiling triumphantly. He had seen Jeff's ship leave the harbor this morning and had planned to give Raven a day or two to get very lonely before he rescued her from her boredom. But this! This was better than he could have hoped for. He could rescue her indeed from whatever petty little problem was pestering her and earn her undying gratitude. It would not be long before the fruit of success dropped into his hands, the ripe melons of her breasts, the luscious strawberry of her mouth, the whole tempting bowl that he had been so careful to keep his hands off of up until now.

He could not believe fortune had been so kind to him. Fortune? He laughed out loud. Fortune indeed. Captain Jeffery Fortune. He looked out to sea and flicked a quick salute in the direction Jeff's ship had gone. *Thank you, Fortune, for bringing a most enticing, desirable woman to Tortuga. And thank you for leaving just when you did.*

When Alex arrived at Jeffery's house, faithful watchdog Joshua was busy resetting the bricks in the walk. Alex nodded hello and let himself in—and was almost bowled over by silk and petticoats filled by soft, sweetly scented flesh, and topped by a mass of midnight-black tresses, softly curling in an intoxicating cascade down Raven's back.

"Alex! I hoped you would come. I *knew* you would come," she corrected.

Her glittering eyes looked up at him anxiously and he dared to put an arm about her shoulder, but did not let his hand stray, remembering that she would need comfort before love.

"What is it?" and he let himself add, "my darling," sure that soon it would be true.

She did not blink at the endearment but pulled him after her into the garden, guiding him to a bench in the far corner.

"Are we finally going to have our turn in the garden?" he asked, his tone pleasantly light, teasing, trying to reassure her that good old Alex was here. He was rewarded by the invasion of a brief smile into the worry on her face.

They sat down, and he pulled one of her hands away from shredding a fine lace handkerchief to hold it comfortingly in his. "Your note said you needed help," he prodded.

She turned to him, hope and despair in her pleading eyes. "Alex, will you take me to Barbados? Now? Before Jeffery returns?"

For a moment he was stunned. This was the last thing he had expected to hear her say. He thought furiously. The consequences of stealing a pirate's hostage away from Tortuga could be grave enough, but that the hostage belonged to his good friend gave him real pause. Yet there could be no thought of denying her. He had offered her his help and she was asking for it. And, he could not help adding to himself, a long sea voyage alone with her, with him in the role of rescuing knight, would doubtless offer endless opportunity to accomplish his final seduction.

"It need not be Barbados. Any friendly port will do," she said.

She must have seen his hesitation, he thought, and he hastened to reassure her, not wanting her to think, even for a moment, that he would fail to keep his promise. "If it is Barbados you want, Barbados it is."

"Oh, Alex! Thank you!" She threw her arms around him, her tears now falling freely, and he was not reluctant to hold her close to him, to caress her back in a comforting way that was more arousing than comforting to him.

At last she drew away, drying her tears on the remnants of her handkerchief.

"If you can have your things ready," he was beginning to plan now, "it would be best if we left on the evening tide. I will have to round up my crew, clean up a few loose ends, but *The Brigand* is nearly ready to sail now. I will send for your things this afternoon and come later myself to get you."

He started to rise but was detained by her hand laid lightly on his arm. "I cannot let you do this for me without explaining why I have to get away."

"It is enough that you want to go. You need not explain why."

She squeezed his arm, and the smile she gave him gave him promise enough and hope.

"I want to explain. I want you to know."

He nodded his assent and waited for her to continue.

"Jeffery has gone to attack a ship owned by Samuel Parkington."

"Jeff's hatred of Parkington is not secret on Tortuga. What does it have to do with you?"

"His hatred is no secret," she agreed. "But there is a secret I have kept from Jeffery." She took a deep breath. "Samuel Parkington is my uncle. I was on my way to him when my ship was sunk."

Alex's quickly indrawn breath told her, more than any words he could have spoken, that she had been wise to keep her secret.

"So that is why you want so badly to escape? Because he continues to prey on your uncle's ships?"

"That," she confirmed, "and other things."

He did not ask what those other things were. If she and Jeff had had a falling out, so much the better.

Pulling her up with him, holding her hands in his, he stood to take his leave of her. "I will send for your things in an hour. Can you have them ready by then?"

She nodded.

"I will come for you at six. We will sail at eight." He risked a chaste kiss on her forehead and was pleased not to be repulsed. Giving her hands one last, reassuring squeeze, he left her.

Not until Alex's men came for her trunks did Raven inform Mary and Joshua of her intent to leave. From then until Alex came for her, Mary was in tears, pleading with her not to go. Joshua only shook his head and lumbered away, making Raven feel that she was betraying the couple. They were treating her as if she were their own daughter, deserting them.

"Cap'n Jeffery will not be takin' this kindly," Joshua warned Alex, shaking his head dourly.

"The lady has a mind to go, Josh." Alex smiled his reckless smile. "And you know how it is when a lady makes up her mind."

Sighing heavily, Joshua nodded. Then he turned to Raven. "Have a care, lass," he said, and disappeared out the garden door, pulling a large bandanna from his pocket on the way.

Mary did not try to hide her tears, but blubbered openly, unable to say a word. But at the last minute she gave Raven a great hug and shoved a packet of food into her hand.

Raven did not tell her that she was sure Alex would

feed her well enough. She just took the packet and kissed Mary on the cheek, thanking her for all she had done for her.

When at last Alex lifted her into a carriage, Raven did not look back. A flood of tears was building in her own eyes. Why did she feel so strongly that she was leaving *home?*

Standing on the quarterdeck of *The Brigand*, Raven watched Tortuga until it was too dark and too far away to distinguish it from the black swells of the sea.

She had at last escaped from that pirate stronghold and from her captor, her ransom unpaid. She was doing exactly what she had wanted to do ever since her capture—continue her journey to Barbados. In four or five days she would be safe with Uncle Samuel. Why then did she feel this gripping loneliness?

She lifted her head into the wind, taking in the salt-laden air, heard the quiet wake of waves from the ship's passage, the soft, plucking tune from some sailor's hurdy-gurdy.

"Wine for milady?"

Alex had come up quietly behind her and now offered her a glass.

Smiling, she took it and sipped. "Thank you. And thank you again for helping me."

He shrugged. "I was ready to go to sea again. The only reason I had lingered so long on Tortuga was because of you."

"Now you are being both generous and flattering," she accused.

"Not at all. Don't you know how truly beautiful you are? How the spark in your eyes can light the whole day? How one smile from you can set a man's heart in a spin?"

His hand caressed her cheek, tilted her face to his as his mouth lowered. But she twisted away from his kiss, her own heart hammering. But it was not the same lilting beat that she felt in anticipation of one of Jeffery's kisses.

"Please, Alex. Don't."

His hand dropped and he stepped back. "I'm sorry, Raven. Forgive me?"

"Of course, Alex." He looked so wounded. Why couldn't she welcome his kiss? "It's just that right now, I—"

"It's all right." His finger touched her lips. "I understand."

"It's very late," she said, returning the wine to him, barely tasted.

"How thoughtless of me! You must be tired after today. Come. I'll show you to your cabin."

Until now, she had given no thought to their sleeping arrangements. She had simply trusted Alex with everything, and he did not disappoint her now.

"I've moved into this cabin," he said, indicating a door just outside the main cabin. "You should be comfortable in mine."

He opened the door for her but did not offer to go farther.

Relief that she had been right to trust him, that he would not force himself upon her, mingled with the deep gratitude she felt. Standing on tiptoe, she kissed him sweetly, not knowing the emotions she stirred within him. "Good night, Alex," she said, and entered the cabin. Alone.

The next day Alex was very attentive and entertaining. He showed her how to use the astrolable, holding it to let her sight along it to calculate their position. It was not unpleasant at all when his steadying arm slid around her shoulder, but it was

Jeffery she thought of. Later, they stood together at the helm. She took the whipstaff in her hands, but it took Alex's strength to hold them on course so she stood in the circle of his arms, his hands on either side of her. If he occasionally pressed against her, or let one hand stray from its post to hold her waist, leaning over her to nuzzle one cheek, she found no cause for complaint.

That night, she accepted his tentatively offered kiss. It was chaste and sweet and though it did not fill her with the excitement of Jeffery's, it was by no means unpleasant. He said good night then and left her at the door of her cabin.

On the third night of their voyage, he suggested that they dine alone in her cabin, away from the ship's officers with whom they had been sharing meals. Raven was not reluctant to agree to the arrangement. She would enjoy having time alone with Alex to talk and relax.

Alex smoothed his hair and straightened his cravat. He moved from side to side and craned up and down trying to see as much of himself as he could in the tiny mirror. Moving at all in his present cabin was difficult. There was but a narrow path between the door and his trunk and the rest of the cabin was taken up by a narrow bed. A most uncomfortable one, he thought, scowling at it.

He certainly did not regret giving up his own more spacious cabin for Raven. She was worth any amount of inconvenience. And, he thought, giving himself a cocky smile, if all went as he planned this evening, he would not have to return to this cubbyhole at all. The bed in the main cabin was easily large enough for two and he was intent on sharing it with a most beautiful companion this night.

He had moved slowly and cautiously with Raven. She was no naive young ingenue to fall panting into his arms at his first flattering words. How often he had held back when he wanted to sweep her into his arms, tried to appear content with kissing her fingers when he really wanted to nibble his way all the way up her arm to that luscious mouth. His careful advances of the past two days, the caress of a cheek, a simple kiss, a chaste embrace, had not been repulsed, and he was encouraged. Tonight, one way or another, he was determined that his patience would pay off.

The cook had been ordered to prepare his best meal and to keep the wine flowing copiously. Alex was prepared to supply the charm and the ice-breaking gift. Slipping into his pocket the packet that he had purchased for Raven before they left port, he left the cabin, being careful not to knock his shin again on the corner of the bed.

The door of the main cabin was open, and two cabin boys scurried in and out bringing the food and wine. Raven was waiting and Alex caught his breath when he saw her. She was again wearing the lavender silk but this time it was accompanied by the shell pendant, not pale amethysts. The pendant nestled in a pleasant valley between two rising mounds and it was with difficulty that he tore his eyes away from that enticing spot, especially when she sank into a low curtsy, revealing even more of her breasts.

"I am speechless before such beauty!" Taking both her hands, he drew her to him and kissed her on the cheek.

"And I am most fortunate to have such a handsome dinner partner," she responded.

Then her eyes softened and she looked up at him with such a sweet smile that he thought he would not be able to resist scooping her into his arms.

"You have been so kind, Alex. Helping me without question, entertaining me, giving up your cabin. And you have asked nothing in return. How can I ever repay you?" He had not let go of her hands and she squeezed his gently.

I will be amply repaid tonight, he thought. But he said, "There is no need for repayment, Raven. It is enough that you would come to me when you needed help."

"You have been a good friend, Alex. You don't know how much it has meant to me to have someone I can count on. Someone I could trust."

He tried to ignore the twinge of guilt her words caused him. When he seated her at the table, the view that met his eyes was enough to shove aside any guilt he might feel. And her heady fragrance made him hungrier for her than for the excellent meal his cook had prepared.

Waving the cabin boys who would have served them from the room, Alex shut the door and took his place at the table, pouring two brimming glasses of wine. He merely sipped at his but was careful to keep Raven's replenished.

"Have you visited your uncle on Barbados before?" he asked, again refilling her glass.

"Never. I'm afraid I do not know him well at all. I've only seen Uncle Samuel twice in my life when he made trips to England on business."

"Only twice?"

"Yes," she said, her brow wrinkling in thought. "The first time was about six or seven years ago, just after the Monmouth rebellion. Then again about a year ago when he started urging us to join him in Barbados."

"So you do not know him well?"

"Hardly at all. I can only hope that though my

188

father has died and I am now alone and penniless, he will still welcome me." A worried frown crossed her face and she chewed her lip pensively.

Alex reached to caress her hand. "I cannot imagine any man turning you out for any reason."

She smiled gratefully at him, fanning his desire for her.

"I am hoping that I can help him somewhat by serving as his hostess since he has never married. And perhaps my medical skills could be of use."

"Simply having your charming and beautiful presence at his table each evening should make him most grateful," he said, again topping off her wine.

"You are flattering me again, Alex," she said, drinking deeply and giggling.

He refilled her glass and pushed it into her hand, encouraging her to drink.

"Here's to Uncle Samuel!" he said, lifting his glass.

"I'd rather drink to you," she said, "and your kindness."

"And I'd rather drink to you. Shall we drink to all of us? One at a time? Then I shall offer a toast to each perfect and desirable part of you, starting with your eyes. But first Uncle Samuel."

He lifted her glass to her lips and urged her to drink, then refilled her glass, hoping that she did not notice that he was not drinking nearly as much as she.

They drank to each other, then to her eyes, to his, to her mouth which he kissed, more intoxicated by its rich flavor than by the wine.

His mouth lingered on hers, then slipped to kiss her throat, and he groaned with long suppressed desire as she fueled the growing ache in his loins with her warm response.

He nibbled at one tender ear-lobe while his hands

busied themselves with loosening her bodice. She sighed contentedly when he slipped a hand around one firm mound.

Her eyes were now bright and slightly unfocused. She backed away to peer intently at him a moment. "Your eyes are not blue. I thought they were blue. Ice sometimes. Or warm pools."

Then she giggled. "Silly me. You're not him. Not Jeffery. You're Alex. Gray eyes. Where's the blue ones?"

"Gone. You're running away from Jeffery, remember?"

"Thash ridiculous," she said. "Why would I run away from Jeffery? I love him."

He stiffened, halting his work of removing her gown. "And can you not love me?"

Her arms went around him and she kissed his cheek. "Yes, I love you."

Encouraged, he lifted her to carry her to the bed. She cuddled contentedly in his arms, causing his heart to race, to swell with the passion, the love, he felt for her.

"I never had a brother."

"A brother?"

"Not until now." She smiled up at him. "I always wanted a brother. Someone I could count on. Trust." Her eyes closed and her head lolled on his shoulder.

Pain stabbed at his heart. Was this the way she thought of him? How she loved him? As a brother? His feelings for her were anything but brotherly as he lay her across the bed, shoved her gown down around her hips then removed it. Her chemise clung seductively to her form.

He gazed down at her. She was so beautiful. He caressed her cheek, her shoulder. But it was not just her beauty that aroused him. It was *her*. He loved *her*. He had to admit that to himself now. He wanted her. And he wanted her to love him.

She stirred. Her eyes opened and she looked into his and smiled. She reached up and drew him down to her, searching for his mouth. "Jeffery!"

He sat up with a gasp, and she whimpered that he had left her unkissed. Again, he bent over her, touching his lips to hers and was surprised at the eagerness of her response, the hunger of her mouth.

But it is not for you she hungers, his mind told him. *The kiss you accept is not meant for you. For you, she has but the chaste kisses of a sister for a brother.* He tried to ignore the thought, sliding his hand around one tempting breast. She arched to meet his touch but he knew that it was not his touch she was seeking, but Jeffery's.

She was his for the taking now. She lay completely trusting, waiting for loving caresses. The chance he had long sought and planned for was his. For this, he had risked his friendship with Jeffery, his welcome in Tortuga. For this, he had helped her escape and was willing to take her to the ends of the earth if she would but acknowledge their love. He had his chance now to take her. She would not push him away. He would be gentle and caring. At last he could quench the fire that had burned in him from the first moment he had met her.

He let his eyes rove hungrily over her disheveled form and something stayed him. She had come to him so trustingly, had confided in him, accepted in good faith the help he had offered. Could he betray that trust by taking her when she was besotted with wine and love for his best friend? Could he make love to her knowing that it was another who stirred her passion?

He pulled away and drew a deep shuddering sigh.

No, he could not do that to Raven. Nor to himself. God, how he wanted her! How he loved her. But it was not his love she wanted, but Jeffery's. From him she wanted friendship. And a brother.

Then that is what I must give her, he thought. He could not merely use her for his pleasure. Love was more than that. It was giving to the loved one what she needed, not taking from her.

He squared his shoulders and gritted his teeth, looking down at the beautiful woman sprawled beside him, more asleep than awake. Well, what would a good brother do in a situation like this?

Gently, he removed her stomacher and underskirt, rolled down her silk stockings, resisting the temptation to kiss each one of her toes. Loosening her chemise, he moved her to the center of the bed and covered her with a sheet. Pushing a stray lock of hair from her forehead, he kissed her, sweetly, brotherly, chastely. Dousing the candles, he left, shutting the door quietly behind him. Hopefully, she would remember none of this tomorrow.

When Raven awoke, it was with a feeling of unfullfillment, of incompleteness, as if there were something left undone, something missing. Or someone. Her hand stretched across the bed encountering only emptiness. Where was Jeffery?

Her eyes flew open and she sat up as the memory of where she was returned to her. Not Jeffery. Alex. Jeffery was but a memory. She would never see him again.

Then what of last night? She pushed the sheet aside. The only thing she wore was her chemise. And that was loose about her, her breasts exposed. The last thing she remembered was telling Alex she loved him and his carrying her to the bed. There had been kisses. She vaguely remembered that. Kisses, and something more.

But what more? She looked down at herself, saw her gown crushed in the corner of the bed, her stockings tossed onto a chair, her underskirt and stomacher abandoned beside the bed. Was there any question of what more had occurred?

She hid her face in her hands, guilt flooding her as if she had betrayed her love. Was she such a wanton that any attractive man could seduce her into bed?

But had she really been seduced? She remembered her response to his kisses. She had been eager for them. Then she frowned. No. Not for Alex's kisses. For Jeffery's. But Alex was the one who was there, who had given her what she sought. Could he be blamed for taking her to bed when she had behaved so shamelessly?

But it was not Alex she desired. Last night, it had been Jeffery she made love to. It was Jeffery's arms, Jeffery's kisses, Jeffery, Jeffery, Jeffery. Did Alex know it was not him she had made love to when he held her? Could he be blamed for taking advantage of the situation? No, she thought, Alex was not to blame.

Alex had long desired her. She knew that. But until last night, when she had confused him with Jeffery, she had been unable to respond to him. His kisses were pleasant. She enjoyed his company. But there had never been any passion, never the fire, the undeniable excitement she had felt when she was with Jeffery.

She had tried to respond to Alex, tried to love him. And she did. But it was love of a different sort. The same love she had felt for her father. The love she would have given to a brother.

Jeffery was the only man she had been unable to

withstand, whose touch, whose glance, whose very presence, were enough to weaken her limbs, quicken her breath, speed her heart. No, she was no wanton. If she had made love to Alex, it was only because she had mistaken him for the one man who could set fire to her being, causing her to abandon every moral scruple for the touch of his body on hers.

She dressed quickly in the most conservative dress she owned then straightened the room while she tried to bring some order to her thoughts, her life.

What would Alex's attitude be toward her this morning? Would he assume that he now had full rights to her? It was an attitude she would have to discourage without hurting him, if possible. He had been good to her, and she would not lie to him about her feelings for him.

Taking a deep breath, Raven opened the door and headed up on deck. It would not be easy to look Alex in the eye after last night, to discourage his advances, but she must. As much as she wished it could be otherwise, her feelings for him could never be more than sisterly. Her heart had been captured by a bold buccaneer and never set free. Though she would never see Jeffery again, whether he knew it or not, he would forever possess that part of her.

A bright tropic morning and brisk breezes greeted her when she stepped onto the deck but Alex was nowhere in sight. She turned to look up at the quarterdeck and found a pair of warm gray eyes gazing down at her.

Chapter Eleven

Alex's familiar, reckless smile played upon his face, but it seemed to Raven that its cheeriness was a trifle forced, that there was more warmth than twinkle in his eyes.

"Good morning, Raven," he said, and she noted that his eyes remained steadily on her face, not raking over her as was his usual wont. Had he had his fill of her last night and now desired her no more? If such was the case, she was glad of it. She did not want him pressing her to give again that which she could never give him.

"Good morning," she said quietly, joining him on the quarterdeck.

"We've had a fair wind and made good progress through the night." He held up the gleaming brass astrolabe. "If the wind holds, we should be in Bridgetown tomorrow night.

"Alex, I—"

"Would you like to try your hand at navigation?" he asked, cutting her off, his tone a bit too cheery.

She smiled at his kindness, standing there holding out the astrolabe, trying to divert her from a topic neither of them would be comfortable discussing. Perhaps he sensed, perhaps he knew, that what had happened between them last night could never be repeated. She reached for the navigating instrument, not wanting to destroy the moment.

After the initial awkwardness between them, Raven felt completely at ease with Alex, and the rest of their trip together was pleasant. Never once did he mention what had passed between them that night. Never once did he make an advance that she had to stop. It was as if he knew how she wanted him to treat her, and was treating her just that way—like a younger sister.

Why his behavior suddenly changed she did not know. But whatever the reason, she was grateful for it.

They had played chess and cards to pass the time and he had named the islands they sighted in the distance.

It had been a relaxing time for her, but now it was ending. Barbados lay off the port bow. Bridgetown was but a few minutes away. White beaches edged the bright green of the land and glistening waves sparkled in the sun. If the rest of Barbados was as lovely as this, it was a paradise indeed.

Yet she had her apprehensions. What if she were not welcome at Uncle Samuel's? Oh, he would take her in. She was sure of that. But being an unwelcome poor relation was not a position she relished. There was always her medical practice, of course. But in spite of her assurances to Jeffery, she was not sure she could earn her way. She was a woman for one thing, and had no official schooling. Her father had taught her everything he had learned at Edinburgh, but that did not give her a diploma. It would take a long time to build a practice, to get people to trust her.

She could see Bridgetown now, the many ships

that were docked there, the spire of St. Michael's Church, St. Ann's fort, still unfinished.

The Brigand slowed as the crew took in sail and began the process of docking. She watched the town grow closer, and soon the ship was gently bumping the dock. The last sails were lowered in, lines were thrown and secured. Finally, Raven had reached her destination.

Alex hired a wagon to carry her trunks and wanted to hire a carriage, too, but Raven insisted that she could ride in the wagon. He had gone to far too much trouble and expense for her already. At last he relented but insisted on driving her to her uncle's plantation to be sure she was well settled before he left.

"Besides," he said as he lifted her up to the high wagon seat, "I want to know where this plantation is. For when I come back to visit you. I can come visit you, can't I?"

"I will be devastated if you don't!"

The drive to the plantation led through wide cane fields where Raven could see rows of workers toiling under the watchful eye of mounted overseers.

The man who had rented them the wagon had given them clear directions and they were soon pulling into the long drive leading to the Parkington plantation house. Raven leaned forward, eager for her first glimpse of her new home. At last she saw it, a long, low, rambling structure with small windows that looked as if a dozen different people had designed it, each adding a room or veranda wherever it suited them.

As they approached, she could see signs of neglect. There was nothing overt like dangling shutters or a collapsing roof. But the house could have used a fresh coat of paint, and there were weeds around the trees and along the walk. The lawn was clipped, but there wasn't much of a lawn and no flowering plants to soften the edges. The cane fields surrounding the house had crept closer until they pressed the house for room. It was clear that cane was supreme here, the house secondary.

No servant came to greet them or take care of the horse. Indeed, the place seemed deserted as Alex's knock reverberated through the house. With a creak, the door opened and a face blacker and more wrinkled than any Raven had ever seen peered out at them.

"Is this the home of Samuel Parkington?" Alex asked.

The door opened a bit wider to reveal a stooped, dried-up form of a man in shabby, cast-off clothing. "Yas, Master!"

"Is Mr. Parkington at home?"

The man only nodded but made no move to invite them inside.

"This is Mr. Parkington's niece. We would like to see him. Will you tell him we are here?" Alex tried to keep the exasperation out of his voice.

Nodding again, the man moved into the hallway, disappearing into the dark interior.

It was hot on the porch but the air coming from inside the house was even hotter. Jeffery's Tortugan home had been open and airy, with thick, rock walls and high ceilings for maximum cooling. Uncle Samuel's house seemed to be a hotbox, closed and airless, more suited to a cooler clime.

It seemed like an hour but it was only minutes later when Uncle Samuel came down the hall, hurrying as quickly as his limp allowed.

"Raven! My dear, you are here at last!" Uncle Samuel thumped his walking stick and gave her a studied perusal in place of a welcoming hug. Glancing at Alex, he asked, "Where is your papa? Ah, but I am forgetting myself. Do come in. My pardon for Cato's lack of manners but we don't get much company out here."

They were soon seated in an airless, tropical version of an English sitting room with hot cups of chocolate in their hands. Raven had introduced Alex and told her uncle about her father's death. Now she wondered just how much of the rest she should relate. Not all of it, certainly. Nothing about Jeffery. She had listened to Uncle Samuel rave about "that damned pirate" before. There was enough hatred on both sides without adding to it. At last she said only that she had been captured by pirates and while waiting for her ransom to arrive, Captain Jamison had rescued her.

A troubled look came into Uncle Samuel's eyes at that point which Raven was sure must be concern for her.

"I can see that you are unharmed, my dear. What of your things?"

"They are out in the wagon, Uncle. Could someone bring them in? I think Captain Jamison is anxious to return to his ship."

The smile returned to Uncle Samuel's face and he called to Cato, ordering him to have her trunks brought in.

When the bump and scrape of trunks had quieted, Alex stood up. "It's getting late. I must be getting back to my ship, Miss Winthrop," Alex said, using a more formal address in front of her uncle.

Raven came to her feet, her eyes beginning to fill with tears. She suddenly felt so alone. She didn't want to stay here, didn't want Alex to go. But what choice did she have?

"I'll see Captain Jamison out, Uncle. You needn't bother," she said, glad for a chance to escape for a moment into the cooler air outside.

"Very well. Then return here, child. We have a lot to talk about." He extended his hand to Alex. "Thank you for bringing my niece, Captain Jamison."

She shut the parlor door. She wanted a few minutes alone with Alex to say her good-byes. At the thought of his leaving, tears again brimmed in her eyes. But she forced a bright smile for Alex's sake. She would cry later. For all of it. For loving Jeffery but having to leave him, for not being able to love Alex, and the sure feeling that in spite of Uncle Samuel's smile, she was not really welcome here.

"Alex."

"Raven."

They spoke each other's names at the same time. She laughed but he took her hands in his and looked up solemnly from two steps lower. "You don't have to stay, Raven."

Tears were seriously threatening now. "I'll look forward to seeing you again."

"If you need me..."

"I know," she said softly. Bending forward, she kissed his forehead.

He stood stock still for the kiss, and she noticed that he even closed his eyes. Then, with a final squeeze to her hands, and with his cocky smile in place, he clapped his hat on, sprang onto the wagon seat, and slapped the horses into a quick trot.

She stood there until he was out of sight and she had swallowed enough of the lump in her throat to allow her to talk to her uncle. Then she went back into the parlor.

Raven took a second cup of chocolate, even though she didn't want it, just to keep her hands busy. Sipping from the steaming cup, she looked around the room for the first time while Uncle Samuel poured himself a brandy. *The wallpaper needs to be replaced,* she thought. It was streaked from the sun and had been patched none too skillfully in several places. The drapes were also sun-faded, a dull red in places, a brighter red in others. She felt a chip in her cup with her tongue. Where was the great wealth her uncle claimed was in sugar?

"So!" her uncle began. "You managed to hang on to your possessions even though you were captured by pirates?"

What an odd question, she thought but she nodded politely.

Uncle Samuel seemed almost too jovial. "Lost nothing important then, eh?"

Only my heart, she thought. Then she reddened. Did he mean her chastity? But, no, he had been talking about things, clothes and shoes. Surely that was what he must mean. "No. Nothing important."

Gleefully, her uncle rubbed his hands, sitting forward in his chair. "Then you still have the money."

"Money?"

"Yes, yes, the money. The money your father was going to invest in the plantation."

Was that all he cared about? No word of consolation about Father, no word of concern about her ordeal, only concern about the money. His happiness to see her, although there was no real warmth in his greeting, the shabbiness she saw around her, even his urging her and her father to come to Barbados, now made sense. Uncle Samuel was in desperate need of money. How welcome would she be when she told him the money was gone?

She set down her cup and folded her hands in her lap. Squaring her shoulders, she looked him in the eye. "There is nothing left. The pirates took it all."

It was as if someone had suddenly pounded him in the stomach, knocking all the breath, all the starch from his bony body. "All?"

She nodded, watching as his face changed from a faint white to an angry red.

"Surely you didn't bring it in *cash*?" He almost screeched the words, and Raven could hear the scorn in his voice as if he had actually added, "You stupid twit."

"Certainly not! Not all of it. But when ... when my things were returned to me the box with the cash and the bonds was missing."

"So you come to me with empty hands and with nowhere else to go," he said in an accusing tone, a sneer on his face.

"I am willing to make myself useful. I can take over the running of your house, for example, or—"

"I have slaves to take care of that sort of nonsense!" he snapped.

He was silent a moment. Then his eyes caught the glimmer of gold about her neck. "I see you managed to hang on to your jewelry," he said accusingly. "Perhaps ..."

"No, Uncle," she said, wanting to disabuse him of the thought that she had jewels aplenty. "I have nothing left." Gently, she clutched the shell pendant. "Except this."

She glared at him, almost daring him to suggest that she sell it.

He snorted. "I suppose it's worth something. But not enough to bother with. You can keep your bauble."

Incensed that he would even think of taking Alex's gift, that he seemed to think she was now under his total control, she rose to her feet. Fighting not to say anything in anger that she would later regret, she took a deep breath. "If you will excuse me, sir, I would like to freshen up."

Giving him no opportunity to say anything more, she marched from the room, shutting the door behind her. It was only when she reached the hall that she realized that she had no idea where her room was. Or even if she had a room.

She walked toward the back of the house until a movement startled her. A shadow, blacker than the surrounding shadows, stood up.

"Cato!"

"Yas'm?"

"Can you show me where my room is?"

"Yas'm." He shuffled off and she followed him. He stopped before a door and gestured but did not offer to open it for her.

Deciding that now was not the time to berate a servant on his manners, she merely thanked him and stepped into her room. She heard the slow scrape of his feet continue down the hall.

Her trunks were there, set willy-nilly about the room. And the room was even hotter and stuffier than the parlor. She went to the one narrow window and opened it, but there was very little air stirring.

The room was spartan in its furnishings which were shabby. One or two pieces might have once been fine, but they had been neglected.

She threw herself across the bed for a good cry before supper. She wanted all her tears shed before she had to face Uncle Samuel again. But the tears did not come as she stared at the hangings around the bed. It took her a moment to realize what they reminded her of. They were the exact shade of Jeffery's eyes.

* * *

Jeffery watched as sack after sack of Samuel Parkington's sugar was poured into the sea. The kegs of rum were more valuable and were being transferred to his own ship, *The Falcon*. He must remember to drink a toast to Parkington tonight for making it so easy to capture this ship, he thought, grinning in grim satisfaction. One warning shot across *The Siren's* bow was all it had taken to bring her to a halt. She was completely unarmed and the crew had offered no resistance.

No other pirate would have bothered to stop a sugar ship heading out into the Atlantic. Parkington had depended on deception to elude him, Jeffery knew, since the name on the ship's manifest was Webb. It was only due to his informer on Barbados that he knew this to be an alias of Parkington's.

The lads were nearly done with their sticky business and were anxious to get under way again. When the last of his crew was aboard, they cast loose from *The Siren* and let her go on her way. If the ship had belonged to Parkington, they would have kept it or sunk it. Other than revenge, there had been little profit in taking this ship. Yet his men had done what he had asked of them, quickly and efficiently. He would have to break out a keg or two of the rum for them tonight.

For now, he ordered his helmsman to set a course northward. He would seek a prize there then head west along the north coast of Hispanola, avoiding the danger of the English stronghold of Jamaica.

He hoped they would take a suitable ship soon. For the first time in his years of piracy, he was anxious to return to Tortuga. He gazed into the northwest as if to espy that island. No, it was not Tortuga he wanted to return to, but a certain midnight-haired temptress, who set his blood boiling just thinking of her.

A frown crossed his brow and he paced back and forth on the quarterdeck as he thought of their parting. He had deliberately let Raven hear him planning a raid. He wanted her to understand exactly what he was, what he did. But he had been surprised at the vehemence of her reaction. Would she ever be able to accept him in spite of the profession to which fate had set his hand? But could their relationship endure without that acceptance?

He had told her they would settle things when he returned. But what could he offer her? Marriage was out of the question. He would not even ask it of her. How could he ask a decent woman like Raven to marry a pirate? In the eyes of the law, she could be arrested for harboring a fugitive and perhaps share the guilt for any of his future crimes. But was it fair to ask her to remain his mistress, without security, without decency? Or worse, to continue to keep her an unwilling captive? The best course would be to set her on her way to Barbados as she wanted.

He gripped the railing so tightly his knuckles whitened. Was that a course he could follow? Could he give her up, knowing he might never see her again, even for her own good?

He cursed softly. What had she done to him? How had she become so important to him in so short a time that he would even contemplate keeping her against her will? But was that not exactly what he had been doing? Had she not accused him of it time and again?

His shoulders slumped. When he returned to Tortuga, he would have to set her free, to make sure she got to Barbados, and had enough money to see to her needs. Then he would have to cut himself out of her life. It would be like cutting out his own heart, he thought. But it was something he had to do for Raven. And for himself. What was he becoming that he kept an unwilling woman captive? Even if that woman responded to his touch with a depth of passion that only thinking about it could shake him, she was still a prisoner. And he was still a pirate with no right to ruin her life by keeping her. He would have to let her go—and ruin his own life.

"Sail ho!"

Jeffery dropped the sail he had been mending and leaped to his feet. Only two days before they had taken a rich prize. One more before returning to Tortuga would ensure a longer stay in port. Looking up into the mass of canvas and rigging, Jeffery cupped his hands around his mouth and called to the lookout, "Where away?"

"Two points off the starboard bow, sir!"

Taking the steps to the quarterdeck two at a time, Jeffery climbed onto the railing, steadied himself with one hand on a ratline, and peered into the distance. He was still not high enough to see the ship but he could detect the faraway booming of cannon.

"Can you make her out?" he called to the lookout perched on the mainmast's highest yardarm.

"Not yet, Cap'n. But there's three of 'em."

Three. Two against one. And in these waters they could be anything. French, Spanish, English, Dutch, pirate.

"Clear for action!" he called, and while the crew hastened to obey, Jeffery sprinted to his own cabin.

Quickly donning boots and a shirt, he checked the priming on a brace of pistols and stuck them into his sash. A knife was added to the sash at his back and he slung baldric and saber over his shoulder. He bounded back up the stairs to the main deck.

He could see the three ships in the distance and the cannon fire was more distinct.

"A Spanish frigate and galleon and an English fourth-rate ship of the .line, Cap'n!" the lookout called. "The king's ship won't last much longer!"

Gazing through his telescope, Jeffery confirmed the lookout's appraisal of the situation. The fourth rate was indeed in trouble with a broken mast and shipping water through a gaping hole at the waterline.

Jeffery's crew had armed themselves, cleared the deck of loose objects, and run out the cannon. Now they stood at the foot of the quarterdeck, waiting for instructions. But this was no disciplined corps of Navy-trained seamen. They were a rowdy bunch of free brethren. Though they fought well and took orders in a fight, they felt it was their right to offer an opinion about any situation. Captain Fortune stood silent, well aware of their need and their right to express themselves.

"I say we leave 'em. Let the Spanish have 'em!" a burly crewman said, spitting to emphasize his disdain for a representative of the Crown that made him an outlaw.

"It's not our fight, Captain," another crewman said. "And where's the profit?"

"But it's the Spanish out there, and the English are losin'," a stocky fellow spoke, and the way he said "Spanish" made it sound like a foul disease.

There were mutters of agreement to this last as they voiced the pirates' almost universal hatred of the Spanish.

Several others voiced their opinions, then they turned to their captain to hear his opinion.

Captain Fortune had listened carefully to both

sides of the argument. The prize they had taken two days before had not completely filled the hold, but there was sufficient booty and the men were anxious to get to port and spend it. There would be little profit in this fight and much risk. Yet it was not a fight he could sail away from.

" 'Tis true that there's no profit for us in this fight. But it's an English ship out there losing to the Spanish and you all know what will happen to them. If it's not an *auto-de-fe*, it's a little slower death in the cane fields, helped along by generous doses of the lash from those who feel they're doing God's work by ridding the world of another heretic.

"Aye, it's a man-o-war," he continued, "and would as soon as sink us as hang us for the pirates we are, but the common sailors aboard that ship are not so different from us. Shropshire lads and Devonshire farmers shanghaied into service or seeking adventure. I've little stomach for seeing stout Englishmen burn in the fires of the Inquisition if there's aught I can do about it."

The crew was silent a moment, then the burly crewman again spoke. "And what's to keep them from turning on us as soon as the Spanish are taken care of?"

Jeffery flung an arm toward the battle they were nearing. "A broken mainmast and a hole near the waterline that will need repairs before they can turn on anyone. What say ye, lads? Do we give them a hand and give the Spanish a trouncing?"

"I 'ave no reason to 'elp zee English," a French crewman shouted, "but I hate zee Spanish even more! I weel follow zee captain!"

A cheer went up from the men and Jeffery knew he had won the day. Not that it had been so hard to convince them to fight the hated dons.

Captain Fortune lost no time issuing his orders, setting his crew scrambling to obey. "Man your cannon, Barnes! And give a sharp look to those on the port side. Helmsman, change course! North, northeast. I want to come so close to the starboard side of that Spanish ship that we'll scrape off his barnacles. But let him think we're going to pass on his port side until the last second. Rodney, hoist the red-and-yellow flag."

Rodney hopped to obey then stopped dead in his tracks. "The *Spanish* flag? I thought we had declared for the English?"

Captain Fortune grinned devilishly. "Aye, but we don't have to tell the Spanish that just yet, do we? Shall we let a close broadside deliver our message?"

Jeffery looked up at the mainsail. It still bore the cross of Spain, though a bit faded. That, and the Spanish lines of his stolen ship would fool the Spanish long enough to deliver his broadside, then he would hoist the English flag.

With his first close view of the still-raging battle, it had been clear what his tactics must be. The fourth rate had not been remiss in delivering a pounding to its attackers. The Spanish galleon to starboard of the man-o-war was listing so heavily to one side that it could only fire into the rigging, while the English could continue pouring shot into its hull. For now, it could be ignored. It was the Spanish frigate to port that was inflicting the most damage. It was the one Jeffery intended to cripple with a full broadside, delivered at as close a range as he could manage. At the same time, he would put the Spanish ship between *The Falcon* and the man-o-war, using it as a shield against the English cannon until they realized he was a friend.

The frigate sent another round into the beleaguered

man-o-war and as *The Falcon* came at her head on, she began to signal frantically for Jeffery to cut between them and the English while they reloaded their cannon. If *The Falcon* had indeed been a friend to the Spanish, it would be the most logical move. But Jeffery had no intention of shielding the frigate from the English cannon fire with his own hull.

They continued to bear down on the bow of the Spanish frigate, giving no clue to the direction they would take. At the last possible moment, Jeffery shouted, "Now!" and the helmsman heaved on the whipstaff, sending them close enough to count the hairs in the Spanish captain's beard.

"Fire!" And *The Falcon* shuddered from the recoil of her own cannon.

Almost before the sound of the guns had died away, Rodney had hoisted the English flag and even above the sounds of the battle, they could hear the welcoming cheer from the English ship.

At the range it had been fired, their broadside had been murderous, and Jeffery ordered the sails slackened and the grappling lines thrown before the Spanish could recover enough to repel boarders. His crew, well seasoned in boarding and fighting hand to hand, leaped to the deck of the Spanish ship, hacking their way through those hapless men who were now too demoralized to offer much resistance.

Jeffery was among the first to board and he now fought his way through the milling combatants toward the high poop of the Spanish ship. There the Spanish captain still shouted orders and encouragement to his men to fight on.

Gaining a foothold on the quarterdeck, Jeffery shoved aside an armored Spaniard who stood in his way. With his knife in one hand and his saber in the other, he charged the steps leading to the poopdeck.

His charge was halted by a round giant of a man who stood spraddle-legged at the top of the steps. The man grinned in grim satisfaction, brandishing a saber. Suddenly the man slashed wickedly at Jeffery, but he ducked under the blade then plowed into the giant's knees, causing him to fall forward over Jeffery's back. Jeffery straightened, throwing the man over his shoulder to land heavily on the quarterdeck below.

The way to the poopdeck was now clear, and Jeffery lost no time scrambling up to plant his feet firmly on it. He and the Spanish captain stood alone, facing each other with drawn sabers. Glistening armor protected the Spaniard's torso and he wore a helmet on his head. A huge bell guard protected his sword hand, but lessened his wrist's flexibility.

Jeffery would have to depend on wounding him or disarming him. Though Jeffery wore no protective armor, having only his saber and his ability to defend himself, neither was he hampered by the weight and heat of armor beneath a hot, tropic sun.

The two men circled warily then the Spanish captain lunged and Jeffery parried. In spite of his armor, the Spaniard recovered quickly and Jeffery's riposte fell on empty air. Their sabers clashed again and again with neither able to gain the advantage. But the Spaniard was sweating heavily and beginning to tire. On his next lunge he was not so quick to recover. Jeffery's saber circled the Spaniard's, jerking it from his hand. It clattered to the deck, just out of his reach, and he found the point of Jeffery's saber pressing against his throat.

Proudly, he drew himself up, quietly awaiting the death blow.

"Yield to me, *Capitán*. Tell your men to lay down their arms," Jeffery said in passable Spanish.

211

Though the saber at his throat needed to press but an inch deeper to end his life, the Spanish captain's eyes looked steadily into Jeffery's, showing not the slightest fear. Calm with resignation, he said, "Kill me quickly, *Ingles*. I will not yield."

"Yield to me now and I will spare all your lives."

The Spaniard laughed shortly and bitterly. "To what end? I prefer to die here and now on the deck of my own ship than under the tortures the English inflict on their Spanish prisoners."

Jeffery could well sympathize with the man's feelings yet he was reluctant to run him through in cold blood. And he wanted the Spaniard's surrender to end the fighting quickly, to spare as many lives as possible.

"I am not exactly one with the English I have come to aid. But if you will accept the word of a pirate and surrender to me, I promise to give you and your men your lives, a lifeboat, and enough provisions to reach Hispanola."

"Pirate?" The Spaniard's eyes flickered with interest. "What is your name?"

"Jeffery Fortune."

"Even among your enemies you are known as a man of your word, *Senor* Fortune. Understand that I do not yield to the English but to you personally and trust you to keep your promise."

Jeffery lowered his saber and the Spaniard stepped to the rail shouting above the din of clashing weapons for his men to surrender.

The battle was over quickly then. The frigate struck her colors and the second Spanish ship followed suit.

When the delegation from the English man-o-war stepped onto the main deck of *The Falcon*, they were greeted by an elegantly dressed gentleman with tawny hair and an amused twinkle in his sapphire-blue eyes.

The captain of the English ship was accompanied by a young lieutenant, two men-at-arms, and a gentleman of about sixty who looked around with great interest.

It had been decided, after the wounded were taken care of, to meet on *The Falcon* since she had suffered no damage in the battle. While tending the wounded, Raven had been constantly in Jeffery's thoughts, and he wished she were with him to help with her knowledge and skill.

"I am Captain Matthew Symmonds. I would like to thank you for coming to our aid." Captain Symmonds held out a slim, well-manicured hand nearly lost in a froth of lace. But it was a competent hand and grasped Jeffery's firmly.

"This is Lieutenant Evans, my first mate," Captain Symmonds continued in a slow drawl. "And Sir Charles Bradford. And whom do we have the honor of thanking for our rescue?" He arched one aristocratic brow and glanced skeptically at Jeffery's nondescript crew, still armed and wary. "From the look of you, I would guess that you are not some Jamaican rum merchant."

Jeffery grinned. "No, sir. I am a buccaneer."

"We suspected as much, Captain. Though why you have come to our aid still puzzles me."

"You are English. That is sufficient reason."

"And your name?"

"Jeffery Fortune!" Sir Charles answered before Jeffery could speak, and held out his hands in greeting as if to an old friend.

Jeffery took the proffered hand, looking with puzzlement into Sir Charles's face. "Have we met, sir,

213

that you know who I am?"

"No," Sir Charles replied, "but I knew that the son of my good friend, John Fortune, was a pirate somewhere in the Caribbean. You are your father's image."

"I take that as a compliment, sir," Jeffery said, warming quickly to this man who had known his family in better times.

"You should. Your father was a good man."

"He was hanged for treason," Jeffery said bitterly.

"A lot of good men were hanged for treason after the Monmouth Rebellion." Sir Charles studied Jeffery for a moment. "And a lot were transported, some of them quite innocent of any wrongdoing."

Jeffery saw no need to repeat the protestations of his own innocence. It had done him little good in the courts. It would do less here. "May I offer you gentlemen some refreshment in my cabin?"

They were soon settled at the table in Jeffery's cabin, each man with his choice of wine, brandy, or rum. The spoils of the battle were quickly divided to the satisfaction of all, one ship to Jeffery, one to the English. The prisoners were to be set free according to Jeffery's promise.

"Are you always so magnanimous with your prisoners, Captain Fortune?" Sir Charles asked, casually sipping his wine.

"Whenever possible, sir. I try not to take lives unnecessarily."

"Isn't it unusual for a pirate to be concerned about innocent lives?"

It was as if Sir Charles were deliberately goading him, Jeffery thought, or probing for something, but he refused to take offense. "I admit that I am a pirate, sir. It would do me little good to deny it. But I also claim to have once been a gentleman and I try to cling to what bit of honor I can, even though the profession I have been forced into is seldom a pleasant one."

"I take it you would prefer another occupation?" Sir Charles swirled the wine in his glass, and his question was nonchalantly phrased, as if he were but making conversation. But Jeffery noticed that Sir Charles was studying him surreptitiously.

Jeffery stood and crossed to lean by the stern windows, putting the light at his back, giving him a better view of his inquisitor but putting his own face in shadow. "What I prefer is of little consequence since I have no choice. To sail into Barbados and to try to take up once again the life of a planter would be to choose hanging sooner rather than later."

"I understand that you once had extensive holdings on Barbados?"

"My father's estates were confiscated by the Crown. They are now being run by a neighbor, Samuel Parkington."

"Ah, yes, Mr. Parkington," Sir Charles said, joining Jeffery by the window, forcing Jeffery to turn more fully into the light. "The king has had numerous reports from Mr. Parkington and his friends complaining of your depredations against him and demanding that you be caught and hanged."

"Is that why you are here, Sir Charles?" Jeffery asked, smiling, his brow raised in amusement.

Sir Charles looked surprised at the question then laughed. "If it were, I would be foolish to admit it to you while aboard your ship with the warship that brought me here laying helpless! But to answer your question, Captain Fortune, the king is indeed concerned with ending piracy in this part of the world. At the same time, England is in need of fighting men and ships because of the war with France. I hold a

commission from the king to seek out certain well-
known pirates and, using my own judgment, offer
some of them pardons in exchange for their help in
the war. Your name is high on my list. Your name
has come before him many times. Many of the reports include acts of mercy, kind treatment of captives, even one or two incidents of your helping some
ship. Now I have witnessed for myself your tactics,
your comportment, and your mercy. And having
known your family, I have no compunctions in offering you, here and now, a full pardon in exchange
for your help as a privateer against the French. Will
you accept it, Captain?"

The look of amusement left Jeffery's face and, too
moved for the moment to speak, he turned to gaze
out the stern windows, unmindful that the light now
played fully upon him, giving Sir Charles a chance
to study the younger man. "A pardon?" Jeffery said
the words as if they were sacred, unable for the moment to speak further as the full implications of what
Sir Charles offered him sank in. Once more he would
be able to walk the streets of England, sail freely into
any English port. Raven. He could marry her, live
openly and honestly with her, never again be shamed
by the name of pirate. He turned to Sir Charles and
again asked, "A pardon?" unable to believe that the
courtly gentleman before him was truly serious.

"In exchange for your help against the French,"
Sir Charles confirmed, excitement also growing in
his eyes. He had little doubt that Captain Fortune
would accept the proferred pardon and that he could
successfully carry out his commission earning the
king's gratitude—and that of one other person who
meant so much to him.

Jeffery's eyes began to dance as the expression on
his face changed from disbelief to joy, then narrowed

as he began thinking of other concerns. "What of my men, Sir Charles? There are those on this ship who would be glad of a pardon."

"Any who continue to sail with you will be included in the pardon." Sir Charles grinned broadly.

"And will my estates be restored to me, my father's name cleared?" Jeffery asked, his growing excitement evident in his face.

"I have been empowered to restore your estates to you," Sir Charles answered. "But"—he shrugged—"your father's name will have to be cleared through the courts. For that you will need proof of his innocence."

Some of the joy left Jeffery's eyes, but he nodded his acceptance of a situation neither of them could help. Gravely, Jeffery extended his hand, and it was with difficulty that he kept his hand from shaking with the emotion he felt. "Gladly will I accept the king's pardon, Sir Charles, with the hope that I will find some way to prove my father's innocence."

Sir Charles took Jeffery's hand in a firm clasp. "It will be gratifying to report to the king that not only have I rid the seas of a dangerous and most successful pirate, but gained him a most formidable ally."

"May I offer my congratulations, Captain Fortune?" Captain Symmonds held out his hand to Jeffery. "And welcome you to the service of the king?"

Jeffery shook his hand and Lieutenant Evans's.

"I will prepare your pardon and your letter of marque for you," Sir Charles said, standing to take his leave, "and have them for you before you sail."

"Now that we are on the same side," Captain Symmonds said, "may I importune you to escort us to Jamaica, Captain? My ship is barely afloat and would hardly stand a further attack."

"Certainly," Jeffery agreed. His eyes took on a far-away look and it was more to himself than anyone that he added, "Then I have some important business on Tortuga before I take up my duties as a privateer."

Chapter Twelve

When Captain Jeffery Fortune at last sighted Tortuga, his heart was light, the wind was fair, and his pardon rode comfortingly against his breast. Yet his ship seemed a sluggard, the wind but a puff of a breeze, and it seemed to take an agonizingly long time to heave into the bay at Tortuga.

He came with a light ship and a rested crew. The last of his piratical gleanings had been sold in Jamaica and for a far better price than he could have gotten in Tortuga. He needed but a day to settle the last of his affairs on this pirate stronghold.

And about a minute to propose to Raven, he thought, smiling to himself. What would she do, he wondered, when he placed his pardon in her hand and told her that he was no longer an outlaw, a fugitive? He could imagine her black eyes shining with joy, filled with happiness for him.

What if she turned down his proposal? Insisted on her freedom? No, he laughed, shaking his head, it was not possible. He knew with what passion she responded to him. Her only objection to him had been that he had been a pirate and held her captive against her will. That was over now. She had wanted marriage with a man she could live openly and honestly with. He had not been able to offer that to any woman. Now he could. And the woman he wanted to offer it to was Raven Winthrop.

As they sailed into the harbor, Jeffery noticed that Alex Jamison's ship, *The Brigand*, still lay at anchor in the bay. A frown clouded his face momentarily. Was that hound still sniffing around Raven's skirt?

As soon as *The Falcon's* hull bumped the dock, Jeffery was over the side, jumping down to the wooden boards, not waiting for the gangplank to be run out. He shrugged off the women who brushed suggestively against him, almost without noticing them and, with a bounce in his step, headed up the narrow streets toward his house.

When the familiar gates of his home came into sight, his heart thudded happily, and he ran the last few yards, knowing that he was only moments away from Raven's arms, her lips. She would have seen his ship coming in, of course, and would be waiting for him.

He flung open the door, glancing around, his eyes not quite able to pierce through the shadows after the bright sunlight outside. "Raven!" A face and form appeared in the hallway, but even in the dimness, he could tell that it was not Raven's slender, supple figure and inky hair, but the more heartily proportioned Mary.

"Mary!" Jeffery stepped forward and, grasping the woman by the shoulders, bussed her on both cheeks. "Where's Raven? I've something to tell her." He looked around her expecting any moment to see Raven appear.

Sniffing loudly, Mary turned away, swiping at her nose.

Jeffery's brows creased and fear clutched at his heart. "What is it? Where's Raven? Is she all right?"

His eyes had adjusted to the light now and when Mary looked up at him, he could see her worried look and the tears that reddened her eyes. "She's gone, Captain Jeffery."

"Gone?" His heart suddenly felt hollow, and a sick wrenching twisted in his gut. Had Raven tried again to escape and some disaster befallen her?

"Where? When?" he demanded. His fingers bit into her arm and he ignored her wince of pain.

"The day after you left. Captain Jamison came and got her."

"Alex!" The name came out almost a snarl.

"Yes, sir." Mary sniffled. "She packed her things and went with him. I don't know where."

"Then she is on the island," he said hopefully. "Alex's ship is still in the harbor."

He turned to go but was stopped by Mary's hand on his arm. "I doubt ye'll find her, sir. They sailed the day after you did. Captain Jamison just returned this morning, towing that little Spanish prize he took."

"I'll find her," he growled. "Alex will tell me where he took her if I have to put him on the rack."

He clapped his hat on his head but turned back to Mary with his hand on the latch. "I've been pardoned, Mary. I'll be going back to Barbados to live after I find Raven. Pack all my clothes and personal belongings. If you and Joshua want to come to Barbados, you can come with Van Doorn and the rest of the household goods on *The Mermaid* in two weeks. I'll be leaving in the morning."

Joy lit her face and he left quickly before she could throw herself into his arms, blubbering her congratulations. It was not her arms he wanted about him, but another's. And he would find that proud, hardheaded piece of baggage if he had to search every island in the Caribbean!

But first he would have to find Alex. His fists clenched as he strode purposefully down the hill toward the Lion and Dagger. It was the only tavern on the island that could make even the slightest claim to some small leanings toward decency, and it was there that he was most likely to find Alex if he were ashore. An ache pounded in his chest where his heart should have been, and he could only hope that their long-standing friendship had prevented Alex from hurting Raven. Not that his friend had ever physically abused a woman, but he had a habit of seducing a woman then deserting her for the next skirt that crossed his path, leaving a trail of shattered hearts and sullied reputations.

Even before he reached the open doorway of the Lion and Dagger, Jeffery could hear the raucous singing of drunken men, their words of anger and ribald jesting, the calls to the harried barmaids. To step inside was to enter an atmosphere thick with smoke and smells. The acrid taint of sour, spilled wine, cheap ale, and oceans of rum assailed him in a palpable wave, but he spied his quarry slumped in a corner, mug in hand, and he plunged in, striding purposefully across the sawdust-strewn floor.

He stopped, spraddle-legged and angry before Alex's table, and glared down at the privateer. "Where is she?"

Alex looked up with unfocused eyes and a sad, vacuous look on his face. His normally spotless clothes were rumpled and wine-stained, the lace at his throat torn, his shirt open. Jeffery had gotten drunk with Alex on more than one occasion, but he had never seen his friend in this state. Usually, he was a happy drunk, smiling and jesting, and even at his drunkest, still perfectly groomed.

A small spark of recognition lit Alex's eyes when he saw Jeffery. He pushed a cup toward him and splashed some wine into it, sloshing as much on the table as in the cup. "Wine for solace," he stated, his voice surprisingly unslurred in spite of his condition.

"Where is she?" Jeffery demanded again and when there was no response, he grasped a handful of the soiled shirt and gently shook Alex. He felt like driving a fist into that drunken face but managed to control his anger. Information was what he wanted now, and a softer approach would yield more results than a good pummeling.

Alex seemed to sober a bit, sitting up and straightening his shirt. Again, he pushed the cup of wine toward Jeffery. "Drink up, my pirate friend, we've both lost her."

Jeffery saw little alternative but to humor the drunken privateer. He took the cup and sat down, wincing in distaste when he sipped the wine. Now he was certain Alex was deep in his cups. His friend would never have countenanced such rank stuff otherwise.

"Where is she, Alex?" he asked for the third time.

"Where you can never go and where it will do me no good to go. I thought if I took her away from you, took her where she wanted to go, I could ... But she ... she said ... Right when ... right when ... Aw, hell."

He lifted his cup to drink again, but Jeffery stayed his hand. "Tell me where she is, Alex."

"I've lost her, Jeff. One of us should have her. But you can't go to Barbados so you've lost her, too."

"Barbados?" Jeffery pounced on the information. Of course. That is where she wanted to go. "Is that where you took her?"

Alex shook his head and Jeff probed deeper.

223

"Bridgetown? Holetown? Where?"

The familiar reckless grin spread across Alex's face. "To Bridgetown. To her uncle. You never knew she had an uncle on Barbados, did you? She was afraid to tell you. Afraid of what you'd do."

"Afraid?" Jeffery asked, frowning.

Alex leaned across the table. "Her uncle is . . ." He hiccuped. "Samuel Parkington." Then he laughed, loud and long.

Parkington? Raven was Parkington's niece? He sat back dumbfounded, his anger at Alex forgotten. Of all the people in the world she could have been related to, why did it have to be his worst enemy? No wonder she had been so anxious to escape him. She had been afraid that he might use her to get back at Parkington.

He shook his head, watching Alex take another deep drink, wondering what had happened to make his friend so morose. He had come here to find out where Raven was then take his revenge on Alex. But what revenge was there to take? In his drunken state, he doubted that Alex would know what hit him. Besides, it was hard to fault Alex for loving and helping Raven. He knew how easy it was to love her. He could only wonder how his friend had found it so easy to sail away and leave her. At least he knew now where she was and that she was safe.

When Jeffery left the tavern, he could still hear Alex's laughter, but it had turned into a sob.

Walking back the way he had come, he thought of Raven, the waves of her hair, so inky black it was like being lost at sea on a moonless night with only the two bright stars of her eyes to guide him safely to port. He remembered the silkiness of her skin, his fingers caressing her cheek, tracing the column of her throat, the curve of her shoulder, to the crest of her breast and beyond. Thinking of her, he felt a rising desire to hold her once again, to feel the stirrings of her deep response, and he knew that it mattered not to him who her uncle was. It was Raven he loved and Raven he wanted.

But would she have him? She might forgive him for having been a pirate, for holding her in captivity, but would she disown her family for him? Having lost her temporarily, he realized just how much he loved her. Somehow, he would find a way to make her his own.

Sweat beaded Raven's upper lip even at the early breakfast hour. Dabbing at it with her napkin which was stained from long use and indifferent cleaning, she forced herself to eat from the choice of poached eggs and hot, thick, English gravy, doughy biscuits, and fried pork. She could not help comparing this breakfast with those she had shared with Jeffery. There had been fruit with whipped cream, thinly sliced bread with butter, and rice pudding, cooled somehow by Mary's magic.

And there had been a breeze. Jeffery's house was opened to catch every errant breath of air and direct it inside. Uncle Samuel's house was small-windowed, low-ceilinged, and airless.

Under cover of her skirts, Raven slipped out of her shoes to place her bare feet on the somewhat cooler floor. She had done away with as many petticoats as she could and wore her coolest Indian muslin dress. But the last three days had been nearly unbearable when she was in the house. She had quickly learned to make her escape to the cooling breezes under the shade of a tamarind tree.

It was also the best way to escape Uncle Samuel's glares and snorts of disgust whenever he happened to glance her way. Other than that, he had said very little to her since the first night of her arrival. Their meals were taken mostly in silence, broken only by Cato's shuffle, the clatter of dishes, and an occasional sharp word from her uncle to one of the servants.

There were but three servants to see to the house, Cato, Liza, the cook, and Mae Jo, a flighty girl who managed to find an excuse to get out of any job Raven asked her to do. Raven had finally rounded up some polish and rags and cleaned her room herself. Then she had started on the parlor. But her uncle had put a stop to it, insisting that she would shame him by doing "slave's work." She bit her tongue to keep from retorting that if his slaves would do the work she would not need to. After that, she had confined her cleaning to her own room, determined that it, at least, would be clean.

She had explored the low, rambling house and the nearby buildings—kitchen, smokehouse, tool shed— and found them all in a similar state of neglect. Once her exploring was done and she had repaired all her clothes, she had nothing to occupy her time. She had begun to gaze at the cane fields, half of them already harvested, and wish she could ride farther afield to explore. Surely Uncle Samuel could see nothing amiss in a lady riding. So this morning she had determined to ask him if there was a horse she could use.

"A horse, eh?" her uncle said in response to her question as he poured gravy over a split biscuit. "I'm surprised such a high-and-mighty miss is not asking for a carriage and driver."

"Oh, no," she said, pretending that she thought he was offering one to her, "I wouldn't want to trouble you for that. Just a horse. You need not even assign a groom to ride with me. I'm an excellent horsewoman and can take care of myself."

"You'll have to," he snarled. "We're shorthanded with the harvest going on."

"Thank you, Uncle! I'll ask Cato to have a horse ready for me right after breakfast every morning," she said, smiling prettily. She knew he hadn't actually said she could have a horse, but she had trapped him. There was no way he could deny her now without being downright nasty.

He snorted and turned his attention back to his plate. "I suppose it will keep you well out of my way. But be sure you're back in time for supper every day. I'll not waste my time or my slaves' searching for you."

She nodded her acquiesence to that one demand and left the table, happy to leave that scowling face and oppressive house.

The sense of freedom Raven felt when she rode away from the house lifted her spirits in spite of the plodding gait of the animal beneath her. His name was Lightning, and she could only assume that it was because of the jagged white blaze on his forehead and not because of his speed. With the clear blue skies and spreading fields of ripe cane, the fresh breezes, the long rows of slaves chopping at the cane in the distance, she could well believe she had found her way to an earthly paradise.

She rode down main roads and tiny lanes between cane fields, finding her way to the land's edge by midday. Sitting on a bluff overlooking the sea, watching waves lap into the sheltered cove beneath her, she ate the lunch of bread, cheese, and wine she had brought with her. Were there crabs in these waters? she wondered. Hastily, she turned away from that cove that reminded her so much of the one on Tortuga and began gathering the remnants of her meal. She did not want to think of a tall pirate with sun-bleached hair and slim hips whose eyes of blue fire could set her aflame with one scorching, lustful look.

That episode in her life was behind her. Over. She must give her thoughts to the present and the future, not to a brief dream in the past that could never come to fruition.

Remounting Lightning who protested with wheezes and snorts, she urged him to his greatest speed away from that cove. If she had had a decent mount, she could have skimmed over the fields, leaped the fences, and perhaps outrun the haunting memories that whirled within her. But mayhap even that would not have worked, for everything she saw stirred fresh ones. The ripe cane, golden and lustrous like his hair, ebony trees like the ones in his garden, the very air she breathed, tangy with the salt smell of the sea and heavy with the smell of tropic vegetation, were like what she had first encountered on Tortuga.

She headed across a partly cut field back toward her uncle's plantation. Right now, she needed something besides memories to occupy her mind. She had not yet explored the slave quarters and the working buildings of the plantation. That should provide some diversion. Other than the house servants, she had never seen slaves up close, but she thought they could not live too differently from the tenant farmers on an English estate.

Ahead of her a line of slaves, supervised by an overseer, hacked at the tall cane, piling it into wagons. As she approached, one slave threw his bundle of cane stalks onto the high pile on the wagon. But the load was already high enough and perhaps a bit unbalanced, for it came tumbling down over the side, causing the overseer's horse to shy. With an angry curse, the man leaped from his horse to begin pummeling the helpless slave with the butt end of a wicked-looking whip he carried. Blows and curses rained indiscriminately over the head and shoulders of the slave, who cried piteously but uselessly for mercy.

So intent was the overseer on his brutal thrashing that he did not hear Raven's cry of outrage, nor her order for him to stop. He was not even aware of her presence until he felt the sting of her riding crop across his own shoulders.

With a snarl, he turned, raising his whip to beat off whoever had dared to attack him. When he caught sight of the blazing black eyes, creamy skin, and shapely figure of a mounted Englishwoman, his face paled. This must be Parkington's niece whom he had heard about, and he had almost struck her. He lowered his arm and snarled an order over his shoulder for the slaves to get back to work.

"How dare you thrash a helpless man for something that was no fault of his?" she snapped, her black eyes flashing.

His head came up. A moment before his eyes had been filled with fear because of the enormity of what he had almost done to the niece of his employer. Now they began to fill with anger. Fresh from England, this one was, he thought, or she would know better than to come between an overseer and a slave. It was typical of the breed, he thought. Their little hearts bled for the poor, downtrodden slaves—until they learned that there was nothing they could do to change the system. Then they realized that as long as some dumb beast was sweating out his life to harvest the cane there would be a steady supply of money to buy whatever furbelows they wanted to bedeck themselves with. That's when they learned to turn a deaf ear and a blind eye to what went on in the fields and barracoons and pretended to themselves that it didn't exist. Well, this little missy was due for her first lesson.

"How dare you interfere with the disciplining of a slave?" he growled up at her.

"Discipline?" Her black eyes narrowed dangerously as she glared down at him from her high seat on the horse's back. "There is a big difference between discipline and brutality, sir."

She slid down from her horse to stride over to the beaten slave. He had returned to his work, repiling the cane onto the wagon, but he turned at her touch. He was a large Negro and he stared at her with an aloof, almost hateful expression, as if he little appreciated the help she was trying to give him. There was a two-inch gash above his eye and Raven made him bend over so she could examine it.

Oh, Lord, the overseer thought, *this is one of the meddling ones. She'll never be content to cry on someone's shoulder for a day or two and then let it drop.*

"This wound should be tended to immediately," she told the overseer.

"I'll see to it right away, miss," he said in a mocking tone.

She turned a sharp, hard eye on him. "A wound like this could fester, cause a fever."

"I'll sit up all night nursin' 'im meself," came the sarcastic answer.

She gritted her teeth, trying to keep back a useless retort. Striding back to her horse, she struggled into the saddle. It was not easy since it was a side saddle and she had no mounting block or stone to stand on but the man stood by watching insolently, making no move to help her.

Straightening her skirts, she glared down at him. "You may be sure Mr. Parkington will hear of this."

"I'm sure he will, miss," the overseer drawled, and he touched his whip to the brim of his hat in mock salute as she rode away.

Raven rode straight for the house. She didn't look for her uncle. She could talk to him later. Right now, that wound had to be tended to. She collected her sutures, bandages, salves, and herbs into her bag, climbed back into the saddle, and headed back to the cane field.

The slaves were still swinging along at an even pace. As she slid down from the saddle, the overseer glared at her but she ignored him and, pulling the injured slave aside, made him sit down so she could tend the wound.

Dried blood mingled with sweat provided an attractive feast for the flies which were attacking the slave's brow hungrily. Carefully, Raven cleaned the wound then stitched the edges together, covering it with a bandage.

Another slave had surreptitiously watched the whole operation and now siddled close to Raven, continuing to cut cane.

"You be a witch woman?" the slave asked.

"I'm a doctor," she answered.

"Can you fix me, too?"

"I can try. What's wrong?"

Without missing a stroke, the slave indicated a large boil on his back. Nodding, she took him aside, lanced the boil, applied a salve and sent him back to work.

Under the hateful glare of the overseer, Raven marched down the row of working slaves, looking

Michele Stegman

each of them over. Nearly all of them bore the scars of past beatings, three were encumbered with heavy leg irons, all were malnourished and overworked.

About twenty-five slaves labored in this gang. Raven knew that her uncle owned about one hundred fifty slaves. The others must be cutting cane in other fields or working in the mill. She was determined now to seek them out and do what she could medically for them. *Then I will have a talk with Uncle Samuel tonight*, she thought. Surely he would not want his property so abused.

Smiling at the overseer, Raven turned to the slave with the boil. "Would you help me to mount, please?"

The slave glanced apprehensively at the overseer but seeing nothing but the usual scowl, he stepped forward and formed his calloused hands into a stirrup to help Raven onto her horse.

With a sincere smile and a thank you to the slave and a cold nod to the overseer, she rode away to seek out the rest of the slaves.

By the time she had visited three more gangs, her anger could barely be contained. The first gang she had visited was not unusual. It was typical. Even those gangs under the supervision of a fellow slave suffered abuse. She sewed several overseer-inflicted wounds and dosed various other ills. Surely if her uncle knew what was going on he would not allow it, she thought. It must be his crippled leg that prevented him from properly overseeing his own property.

After she had treated the worst cases among the slaves, it was nearly time to return to the plantation house. But Raven wanted to stop by for a quick look at the slave quarters. On her way from England she had imagined neat rows of white-washed houses.

After having her illusions about the slaves so severely shattered, she shuddered to think what kind of housing she would find.

But when she stood in the doorway of one barracoon, her nostrils were assailed by a stench so dreadful that her stomach, even accustomed as it was to the smells of surgery and sickness, was wrenched with nausea. It was worse even than her revised imagination had pictured.

The room was long and low with small barred windows which admitted little air. One end of the room had been used too long as a toilet and flies buzzed everywhere. She could not bring herself to go farther than the doorway. How the slaves endured night after night in that hellhole was beyond her.

As she staggered to her horse, she noticed that the preparations for the evening meal were beginning. She had only to glance into the huge pots to realize that the slaves' diet was also bad, consisting of an unpalatable mass of poorly cooked vegetables.

By the time Raven reached the house and turned her horse over to Cato, it was nearly time for dinner. She did not bother to change but charged straight into the parlor, booted and spurred.

Uncle Samuel was waiting for her but not with his usual scowl. Tonight it was worse. There was an angry set to his jaw and his shaggy black brows nearly met over his flint-hard black eyes. The knuckles on the hand that clutched his cane were white.

"What's this I hear about you stirring up trouble all over the plantation today?" he snapped before she could open her mouth. He totaled the list of her crimes on the fingers of his free hand. "Interfering with the proper disciplining of slaves, slowing work at harvest time, criticizing the management of my property." He shook his cane at her. "I'll thank you to stop your meddling!"

Raven's own black eyes blazed. Did he condemn her before she even had a chance to speak? She drew a deep, calming breath before plunging into an explanation. Surely when he heard the truth, he would make the necessary changes to improve the lot of his slaves.

"Uncle, one of your overseers beat a slave unmercifully for an accident," she began.

"I know the overseer and I trust his judgment. The slave was probably a troublemaker long overdue for a beating."

She gasped at his callous dismissal of the beating but naively plunged ahead. "If the wound had not been treated, it could have festered, led to a fever. In this climate, it is not unlikely he could have died."

Her uncle shrugged. "It would have served as a deterrent to other troublemakers."

Surely her uncle could not be this unfeeling! "The slave quarters are filthy styes. Many of the slaves are thin and malnourished. Nearly all of them bear the scars of beatings. Surely they are not all rebels."

His mouth twisted into a sour scowl. " 'Tis not my purpose to coddle them! They belong to me and will work until they die or until I have no further use for them! If they are slow or rebellious, they deserve to be beaten. As for food, they are given an assortment of native vegetables and, once a week, dried salt cod which I import at no little expense. If they weaken, 'tis no fault of mine. If they then die, so much the better. They can be replaced easier than nursed and dosed back to health."

He paused to pour himself a brandy then rounded on her. "If your fine English sensibilities have been offended, then I suggest you stay out of the fields and away from the barracoons."

Cato appeared in the doorway to announce dinner. Untasted, his brandy was put down and her uncle marched into the dining room.

Undaunted, Raven strode after him. "It seems only logical that if a slave is well treated, he will not only be more able, but more willing to work."

Her uncle snorted as he dashed mashed potatoes onto his plate. "You know nothing about slaves. Less than nothing. You've been here three days and now you presume to tell me how to run a plantation I've lived on for twenty years."

Raven began filling her own plate, feeling guilty when she thought of the rations the slaves would have this night. Swallowing her pride along with a forkful of lumpy potatoes, she decided on a softer approach. "Uncle Samuel, I admit I know nothing about growing cane. It only seems that if the workers were fed better, their hurts tended, their barracoons cleaned, you would find more profit in them in the long run."

He shook a fork at her. "I would find more rebellion, more demands. The more you give a slave, the more they want. They're lazy and shiftless and must be driven to obtain even the least amount of work from them."

"It is hard enough to work in this heat," she said, "and some of the men are ill or hurt. If they were treated, I'm sure—"

"A doctor is the last thing I'll waste money on!" her uncle snapped.

"But it needn't cost you a thing, Uncle," Raven said, brightening, thinking that at last, she had a wedge to use on his resistance. "I am a perfectly capable doctor and willing to treat the slaves."

Samuel Parkington looked askance at his niece,

rolled his eyes and went back to eating.

"I worked with my father for years and—"

"And it's far different really treating ills than sitting by the bed of a wounded soldier and writing home for him," he interrupted her.

Indignant, she glared at her uncle. The flintlike set of his black eyes, the hard line of his mouth, his fork jabbing at his food told her that there was no use talking any further to him. She bent over her own plate. But she was far from defeated. Tomorrow she would continue treating the slaves and she would get those barracoons cleaned somehow. Better rations might be more difficult, but surely there was a way. And she would find it.

Then with a forkful of food halfway to her mouth a sickening thought hit her. Jeffery had been this man's slave, had been penned in those barracoons. She had seen the marks of the lash on his back, the scars from the manacles he had worn. It no longer surprised her that he had escaped. It only surprised her that he had been able to. Now more than ever, she was determined to do all she could to aid the helpless slaves in her uncle's power.

Chapter Thirteen

They were gone. It was barely daylight when Raven arrived at the barracoons but already the slaves had been sent into the fields. Only three ancient, slow-moving black men were left, and they were busy chopping vegetables.

She pursed her lips in exasperation. She had skipped her own breakfast, hoping to arrive before the slaves had left for the fields. Not only did she want to appropriate two or three of the slaves to help her clean the barracoons, but she wanted to see what they had had for breakfast.

Sliding down from her horse, she approached one of the men. "What was served this morning for breakfast?"

The man looked blankly at her, his rheumy eyes full of fear. "Breakfas'?"

Smiling to dispel his fear, she asked her question again.

"Dey doan hab nothin' dis mornin', missy. In de middle of de day, dey come back and eat dis."

"They toil in the sun until midday with nothing in their bellies?" Raven asked incredulously.

The man only shrugged and turned listlessly back to his work.

She could see a line of slaves in the distance and she decided to requisition two of them to help her. She was remounting when she spied the whipping post. Well spattered with blood, it gave evidence of much use. Shuddering, Raven spurred her horse toward the field. Was it tied to that post that Jeffery had gotten the stripes he would carry for the rest of his life?

The overseer in charge of the gang she approached glared up at her. She had had a run in with Mr. Thorpe the day before when she had treated the slaves in his gang.

Nodding a greeting, she said, "Mr. Thorpe, I shall require two of your men to help me this morning." Without giving the man a chance to argue, she motioned to two of the workers. "You and you. Come with me."

The two men, a huge black and a burly redhead, looked uncertainly at their overseer then dropped their machetes to follow Raven.

Raven pulled at Lightning's reins to turn him around but a meaty paw came up to grab at her skirt. Instantly, she lashed down, laying an angry red welt across the overseer's arm with her riding crop, causing him to jump back. Glaring down at the man with all the pride and disdain she could muster, she said, "Do you dare to lay hands on me, Mr. Thorpe?"

Her only answer was a strangled snarl. The man realized that he had overstepped his bounds and would not push her further.

Motioning for the two men she had chosen to precede her, she looked back at Mr. Thorpe. "My uncle will hear of this, sir!"

"You can be sure of it, *Miss* Winthrop!" he muttered. But he made no further move to stop her, and she led the two men back to the compound.

By the time the slaves returned for their midday meal, Raven had made great progress in cleaning up the barracoons and the compound. Uncle Samuel might have to drive the slaves to work, she thought, but the two she had chosen to help her had needed little urging to shovel out the filth they had been forced to live in for so long. Willingly, they had carried buckets of water and sluiced down the inside of the barracoons and now were busy raking up the clutter in the compound.

Thanking them, she dismissed them to their meal and though her own stomach was rumbling, she did not think she could force down the mess the slaves were being offered. Reluctantly, she returned to the house to eat.

Mr. Thorpe passed her on the porch on her way into the house. He nodded and stood aside for her but he glared at her with eyes glittering with hatred and a jaw clenched in anger while he fingered the welt on his arm that was still red and swollen.

She was sure her uncle had had a full report of her day's activities, and was equally sure that he would not be pleased.

If the overseer's glare had been angry, it was nothing compared to the one her uncle gave her when she joined him at the table. But her conscience was light, her stomach empty, and she was well pleased with her morning's work. No matter what Uncle Samuel thought or said, it would not deter her appetite or her sense of well-being. She helped herself to slices of roast beef, carrots, and potatoes.

"You've been meddling again!" her uncle shot at her as soon as he had swallowed the mouthful he had been chewing when she came in.

"I'm sure you were pleased to hear what I've

done," she replied, smiling. Before he could either die of apoplexy or sputter a retort, she continued, "The barracoons, though still far too small for the number of slaves who are crammed into them each night, at least are clean now and no longer the pest-holes they were. This afternoon I plan to draw up a list of supplies we will need to supplement the slaves' diet."

Her uncle's bony fingers clutched his knife and fork, and he sawed at his beef as if he wished it were her neck. "It will do you no good. I am satisfied with my slaves' diet as it is. But prepare all the lists you like, if it will please you. Only"—he stopped his cutting long enough to focus all his hateful attention on her—"stay away from the slaves and the barracoons. It is no place for you and I will not tolerate any further interference."

"Interference!" she cried. "I have done much good this day both for the slaves and for you! Your slaves will rest easier this night in clean quarters. They can be stronger tomorrow if they are better fed."

"You breed discontent and rebellion and I will not have it!" He wiped his lips and threw down his napkin. Rising to his feet, he pointed a thin finger at her. "Stay away from the slaves or you'll find yourself afoot. You'll find it a little harder to get around without your horse."

Raven jumped to her feet to face him before he could get away. "Then I will walk if I must! But I will treat their injuries and illnesses. I may never have officially sworn the Hippocratic Oath, yet I abide by it. While it is in my power, I will not let suffering go unattended!"

White-faced and shaking, her uncle fought to control his anger. Raven stood stalwart before him, her head held high and determined.

At last, letting out his pent-up breath, he said, "Very well. Tend them. But only when their work is done in the evenings. You are to stay out of the fields and away from the barracoons at all other times. And," he again emphasized his words with a jabbing finger, "if I hear of you interfering once more in the discipline meted out to them, no matter how 'unjust' you think it is, I will have you locked in your room!"

Smiling at her uncle's retreating back, Raven felt very proud of herself. She sat down to finish her meal and to plan the afternoon's activities. Having gained one concession, she would not invoke her uncle's wrath by going against his commands. She would restock her medical supplies in readiness for her evening clinic. And she would make up her list of needed provisions and present it to him. She would urge the slaves to clean the barracoons themselves and do whatever else she could to mitigate their suffering.

It was completely dark when Raven at last slid from the saddle. For a long moment she stood holding onto the pommel, leaning against Lightning's side. A touch on her arm roused her and she realized that she was almost asleep.

"Liza, she kept your supper warm in the kitchen, missy," Cato said.

Without protest, she let Cato pry her fingers from their grip on the pommel and direct her around the house. Warm, yellow light spilled into the darkness, welcoming her to the kitchen as she had never been welcomed into the main house. An enticing smell of cinnamon and pungent fruit met her as Liza pushed her into a chair and shoved a plate in front of her.

She had had to miss dinner in order to be on hand to treat the slaves. Halfheartedly, she stuck a fork into the food before her and began to eat, then looked up at Liza in surprise. Surely the delay and her added hunger alone could not have made the roast beef seem so much juicier, tenderer, the potatoes smoother and creamier, the carrots done to perfection in a lemon-and-butter sauce. Nor could her tiredness have made the pie crust so light and flakey, the whipped cream so sweet and thick.

"Liza, this is delicious! I didn't know you could cook like this!"

"Master Parkington, he don't know it neither!" Liza said, and then chuckled.

Raven looked at the round, black face in surprise then started to laugh. What justice, she thought. Uncle Samuel had a jewel of a cook yet he suffered through meal after meal of soggy biscuits, doughy dumplings, half-done meat, and lumpy potatoes. It could not make up for his cruelties, but it gave at least one slave on his plantation some satisfaction.

"They say you been a real angel, Miss Raven. Even fightin' with your uncle. Whenever you miss your dinner, you just come 'round here to the kitchen an' I fix you up good."

Raven finished the last scrap of pie and stood to go. "I'm sure I'll be missing a lot of dinners from now on, Liza." On impulse, Raven gave the cook a quick hug and kissed her cheek. Then she headed tiredly to bed, missing the tear that brightened Liza's eye.

The next morning Raven was surprised to find a large bouquet of flowers brightening the table. And her place had been moved farther from her uncle's. When Cato served the food, she understood the reason for the screening flowers. Her biscuits were light and flakey, her scrambled eggs fluffy and well-seasoned. She managed a peek at her uncle's plate and his food was the same mess as usual.

She looked up at Cato, but he only rolled his eyes innocently and shuffled away. Raven was not about to reveal Liza's secret. Restraining a chuckle, she ate her breakfast.

"Here is the list of supplies we will need to supplement the slaves' diet," Raven said, placing a sheet of paper at her uncle's elbow.

His only answer was to crumple it into a ball and throw it contemptuously onto the floor before stomping out, leaning heavily on his cane.

Raven enjoyed a leisurely breakfast, then as she left the table, she took a lump of sugar for Lightning. The horse nickered and shook his head when he saw her, reaching out to nibble her fingers in search of the treat he had now come to expect. She fed him the sugar and caressed his velvet nose. "Where shall we go today, Lightning?"

She looked up and down the road. She had the whole day to spend as she liked as her clinic for the slaves would not open until the evening. Mounting, she turned the horse around, kicked him once, and gave him his head. He chose to go left and she was content with his choice. Plodding down the road, Raven enjoyed the sweet smell of fresh-cut cane. She waved to the slaves she passed, and one or two were brave enough to wave back. The others smiled when they saw her, their grins giving encouragement to her determination to help them any way she could.

Soon she passed the borders of her uncle's plantation, but the cane fields continued endlessly onto the adjoining land. Within a few minutes she came to the gates of the neighboring plantation. If she had been shocked at the condition of her uncle's property, here the neglect was even more obvious. Only the cane fields were tended. Weeds grew rampant along the fence lines and the once-white fence was grayed and completely fallen away in places. The tall iron gates hung askew on the tilting pillars that still tenuously held them, and the road was not only neglected and potted, but seemed seldom used, making Raven wonder if the place was inhabited at all.

She urged Lightning through the gates and down the lane, shaded by twin rows of large symmetrical trees, strong-limbed and stout-trunked.

She first saw the plantation house through a screen of leafy branches and caught her breath at its beauty. But drawing nearer, the neglect and ruin became apparent—the faded patches of paint, the crookedly hung shutters, broken gaping wide windows, and the badly damaged roof.

It saddened her to see the decaying house, its once proud beauty bearing witness to the love that once was lavished on it. Dismounting, she climbed the three shallow steps onto the veranda. She felt good being there, as if the house welcomed her, as if this place had once been filled with so much love and laughter that even the years of abandonment could not diminish it.

It seemed a practical house for this climate with its high ceilings, the grated transoms over each wide window, and shaded verandas on every side. Who had lived here? she wondered. And why did they leave? Were they of that breed of landlord who had made enough money to return to England in splendor, leaving an overseer to continue working the land and the slaves? Somehow, that did not seem right. Well built to begin with, the house still seemed stout enough to salvage. The owners had built the house with the intention of staying.

Leaving her horse tied to a porch post, Raven walked around the house along the wide veranda. Tamarind trees spread their branches over the desolate gardens that spread from every side of the house, and yellow love-vine twined at the edges.

The kitchen, a separate building at the back, was large and must have once been a busy, bustling place.

A nearly overgrown path caught Raven's eye and she followed it through a grove of ebony trees, coming out on a weed-choked compound. Rows of once neat individual cottages bound the edges of the compound. No barracoons here!

Raven threaded her way back along the path and around the house to her horse. Thoughtfully scratching the jagged white blaze on the horse's forehead, she thought that she would like to have known the people who had once made this their home. Reluctant to leave, she sat on the steps and ate the lunch Liza had packed for her, listening to the steady crunching of her grazing horse.

There was a certain peace here, Raven thought, and she decided to come again, perhaps with a book or two. Remounting, she headed back to Uncle Samuel's. She could not think of the place where she lived as home. Stopping Lightning, she turned for one more look at the house. This, she thought, would be easy to call home. Kicking the horse into a bone-jarring trot, she headed down the lane.

As she passed through the pillars at the plantation entrance, she noticed something carved into one pillar and now nearly hidden by weeds. She got down and pulled the weeds away, hoping to find some clue to who had lived there. The letters were carved fine and deep, bordered by never-fading stone flowers. Her eyes widened as she cleared away the last of the weeds and read the two words carved there. "Fortune's Fancy."

Her hand trembled as she traced over the letters. Surely it had to be a coincidence. Merely a name

245

someone had picked for their plantation. Jeffery Fortune had been a slave on Barbados, her uncle's slave, not a plantation owner.

She straightened, taking a deep breath. Even in a name a certain pirate captain haunted her. She had escaped from his grasp, fled his island home, traveled over a thousand miles away. But she was beginning to feel that she would never be free of him.

Remounting, she kicked Lightning into a trot. Liza had promised to have her dinner ready before her clinic tonight. Raven smiled in anticipation now that dinner was something she could look forward to again. Not only had she been promised another delicious meal, but she would not be eating with her uncle.

Her thoughts wandered again to the abandoned plantation house. The fields were still being worked. Only the house and buildings had been left to decay. Her mind was still on the neighboring plantation as she went around the house to the kitchen.

After dinner, she had some time before she had to leave so she sought out her uncle in his study. He would know about the neighboring plantation. Perhaps, she thought, if she acted sufficiently humble, he would tell her what he knew.

The door of his study was ajar, and she leaned in the doorway a moment, watching her uncle pour over his ledgers, scratching along with a long feather quill. One whole wall of the study was crammed with papers, boxes, and ledgers and she thought that Uncle Samuel must never have thrown out a single document since he lived here. She cleared her throat to get his attention and he looked around with a scowl. His scowl deepened and he gave her a raking glare of disapproval.

"So it's you. What do you want now?"

Ignoring his caustic tone, she asked, "Who owns the plantation next to this one?"

He started, causing his pen to leave a splotch on his ledger which did not help his mood. Blotting the ink, he looked over his shoulder at her. "Why do you ask?"

She shrugged and crossed her arms. "It's such a beautiful piece of land yet the house has long been abandoned. I only wondered why the people left and who they were."

"It belongs to the Crown. It was confiscated from the Fortune family when they were condemned as traitors after the Monmouth rebellion," he replied curtly, and turned back to his work.

Raven's heart seemed to tumble within her chest. Trying hard to keep her voice from shaking, to keep it sounding nonchalantly interested, she asked, "Fortune? The pirate you told my father and me about?"

"A likely nest of rebels!" her uncle muttered almost incoherently into his ledger.

"Was the whole family condemned?"

"John Fortune was hanged deservedly for his crimes. His wife"—he shrugged—"I don't know what became of her."

Raven waited breathlessly for her uncle to continue, but he seemed to have forgotten she was there. She almost ground her teeth in frustration. Did she have to beg for every bit of information? What made Uncle Samuel so reluctant to talk about them? She wanted to shriek at him to finish telling her. Instead, she calmly urged, "And were there any others?"

His hand clutched the quill so tightly that it snapped, sending drops of ink splattering across the page. "Yes, the son. Damned insolent rogue. He was condemned, too. But not hanged. Cursed be the judge who thought the evidence not sufficient to implicate him. Mercy was granted and the whelp was merely transported for his part in the rebellion."

He turned around to face her. "I tried to help the lad. Bought him myself. But he ran off and became a pirate. Which just proves what kind of character he was. Styles himself a captain now. Captain Jeffery Fortune. 'Tis he who is bent on destroying me, and is damn near succeeding. As if I were responsible for his family's crimes!"

She gave him time to calm down before she asked her next question. "You say the property now belongs to the Crown but who works the fields? They are well tended but the slave quarters are empty."

"I do."

"You?"

He opened a drawer at the side of his desk and pulled out a box from which he drew out some papers. Carefully replacing most of them, he shoved one of them across the desk toward her. "I was instrumental in helping the Crown prove its case against the Fortunes. In gratitude for my services, I was given King James's commission to work the land. I need only send him a fifth share. The rest is mine for my efforts. I have tried to buy the land but so far have been unable to."

Raven looked at the papers, somehow feeling very glad that her uncle had been unable to buy Fortune's Fancy. No wonder Jeffery hated her uncle so. Not only had he been a slave here, but he had seen his family destroyed, largely due to Uncle Samuel's efforts, and his plantation put into Uncle Samuel's keeping.

As Raven rode through the gathering dusk toward the barracoons, her mind kept turning to thoughts of Jeffery and Fortune's Fancy. She had told herself

that his gentlemanly manner, his fine speech and
education were but a veneer to hide a common felon,
a slave, a traitor. But she had fallen in love with him
anyway. Now she found that she had been wrong
about Jeffery Fortune. That he was, indeed, a gentleman born. Although it did neither of them any good.
She would never see him again. Whether born a
gentleman or noble, pauper or slave, he was an out-
cast now. A condemned traitor, a pirate. To return
to Fortune's Fancy, to walk the streets of Bridgetown
was to ask for a hanging. He could never come to
Barbados and she would never return to Tortuga.

Sometimes, like now, as she rode along through
the coming night, she longed for his arms about her
once again. But she was sure she had done the right
thing to escape him. Perhaps he had been a pirate
too long, she thought, taken on too many of their
ways. Perhaps that was why it seemed to bother him
not at all to keep her a prisoner and seduce her with
never a promise of anything more than a warm bed
until he tired of her. Even if by chance he would have
wanted to marry her, could she be happy married to
a traitor? There were certainly many, including herself, who had been glad to see the last of King James.
But her feelings had included no overt act of treason.
If he had asked her, could she have married Jeffery
knowing that each time he left her it was to commit
an unlawful act? Could she forgive him for those he
had committed already?

No, there was no future at all for her and Pirate
Captain Jeffery Fortune.

Her reverie was interrupted by the sound of a whip
striking flesh as she entered the slave compound. The
slaves were gathered in a silent knot around the
whipping post between the barracoons. One of the
slaves, a white transportee from England, hung by

his wrists, his back already a shredded mass of bloody meat.

Clapping a hand to her mouth and biting her lip to keep from retching, Raven watched in horror, unable to look away, unable to move, as one of the overseers finished his brutal work. She had seen the grisly results of savage battle, but she had never before witnessed a flogging, the deliberate mangling of a helpless human being.

When the slave was cut down, his limp body dropping into the dirt, Raven was finally able to move. Dismounting, her legs shaking, she pushed through the crowd of slaves.

Bending over the unconscious form, she bit back angry accusations and questions. She knew that any interference from her would result in her being locked in her room where she would be no help at all to the slaves. Shedding tears would not help either, she chided herself, wiping her eyes with the back of her hand. It would only slow down her work. And right now she must do what she could for the man's back before he regained consciousness.

The slaves hurried to do Raven's bidding as they never hurried for their overseers. She called for water and it appeared almost before the words were out of her mouth. She asked for her medical bag and it was at her side and opened for her. Gently, she washed the wounds, sewed the worst of the gashes, and applied a healing salve. There was nothing more she could do but see that the man was comfortable in the barracoon before she went on to other patients.

She glanced around the barracoon and was satisfied to see that the slaves had been making some effort to keep it cleaner. Asking one of the slaves to stay with the battered man, she went outside to treat the lesser ills.

* * *

The next day was much the same except she worried about the battered man as she rode through the fields. After her dinner in Liza's cozy kitchen, she collected her medical supplies and was on her way to the barracoons when she was halted by her uncle's voice.

"Come into my study a moment, girl!"

"I was just on my way to the barracoons, Uncle Samuel. May I see you tomorrow?"

A brief scowl crossed her uncle's face but he hid it quickly, even managing a bit of a smile. "I would think that your future is more important than a few boils and imagined ills."

She thought that she had not seen her uncle looking so pleased with himself since he thought she had money to invest in the sugar business. "They are hardly imagined, Uncle." But she followed him into his study, intrigued by his reference to her future.

Waving her into a chair, he sat at his desk and picked up a piece of paper. "Are you acquainted with a Randolph Kenfield, Baronet?"

Raven sat up, her full attention and her suspicions aroused. Baronet Kenfield had been quite unrelenting in his attentions to her just before she had left England. At first he had tried only to seduce her but when that had failed, he had sworn that he had fallen deeply in love with her and wanted to marry her. On her part, she had seen the baronet as an arrogant, overbearing aristocrat who seemed to think that his title would cause any woman to fall languishing into his arms. Not that he didn't have charms enough of his own. He had been an engaging conversationalist and was handsome in a thin, snobbish way. But his touch had left her cold, his manner was more annoying than seductive, and she had tried to discourage his interest.

"I have met the baronet a time or two," she hedged in answer to her uncle's question, wondering what connection there was with her uncle, the baronet, and her future.

"I have received a letter from Baronet Kenfield," her uncle said, rattling the paper in his hand. "Or rather, your father did. But since I am now your legal guardian, I took it upon myself to open the letter since it may have contained something of importance."

Raven's eyes blazed indignantly and she reached for the letter, thinking that he had used his legal position to snoop into something that was none of his business. "You have opened a letter to my father without even consulting me?"

He held the letter out of her reach. "As I said, I am now your legal guardian and it is my duty to deal with any of your matters which might be of some importance. It seems my feelings were correct since the baronet writes that you refused his offer of marriage and asks your father to intercede for him. Can it be possible that you refused to marry a baronet?"

Rising to her feet, Raven held her head up proudly. "I refused to marry a pompous, overbearing man for whom I had no feelings. Whether he was a baronet, a duke, or a pauper had no bearing."

"Do you realize that the baronet was willing to marry you even without a dowry?" he asked, his voice rising incredulously.

"It matters not, since I do not plan on marrying the baronet in any case."

"Ah, but you will, my girl! As your legal guardian—"

Raven cut him off, her black eyes as flint-hard as

his. "May I remind you, Uncle, that I am of age and cannot be forced into a marriage?"

He sat back and glared at her. "So you are. I should think that at your age you would jump at the chance to marry or you'll soon be too old for any man to want you!"

"I hardly think marriage is the only option open to me," she said in a calmer tone.

Her uncle rose to his feet, sneering into her face and striking the letter with the back of his hand to emphasize his words. "Just what *do* you plan to do? Do you think I want a meddling spinster on my hands for the rest of my life?"

"I shall do what I can to earn my keep, sir. My medical skills—"

"Bah!" he interrupted. "Get yourself a husband, girl. It is your only choice in life. You will find few enough men to suit your high-and-mighty notions. Best take the baronet and learn to like it. There's more advantages in such a match than you realize. And not just for yourself. Think of the influence you could have at court, the connections."

The determined line of her mouth hardened. She had thought of all those things. The baronet himself had not been loath to point them out to her.

"Aagh!" he snorted with disgust, throwing the letter down. "Think of it, girl. Think of your position here. No more than a poor relation, unwanted. Think of what Kenfield offers you. You're thick-headed but you are not stupid. I'll give you a week or two before I write to the baronet. Mayhap by that time you'll have come to realize what you're throwing away before it's too late." He waved a hand at her, dismissing her. "Now get along to your good deeds. At least it has given me back my solitude at dinner."

* * *

As the days passed, one very much like another, Raven had plenty of time to think. Except for an hour or two each day when she tended the slaves, she had little else to do. She made a list of things she would need to set up a medical practice in Bridgetown, what kind of office to look for, how much money it would require. More than she had. She made lists of food for the slaves' diet, and lists of improvements that could be implemented. But whenever she brought up the slaves' diet or complained about the frequent floggings, her uncle only scowled and turned a deaf ear.

She had memorized every road and lane around her uncle's plantation, and often haunted Fortune's Fancy, eating her lunch there and walking on the veranda. She had even weeded one of the gardens, pruning the roses, and giving new life to the patterns of flowers that still grew there.

But she was lonely and bored. There was never any company at Uncle Samuel's and she knew no one to visit. She began to think that about one thing at least her uncle was right. She should accept Baronet Kenfield's proposal and return to England. What was here for her but to grow old alone, tending slaves and flower gardens? She knew he was right. But the thought of marrying a man she could barely tolerate made her blood run cold.

Raven was sitting in the side garden of her uncle's house, mending a ripped seam, when she caught a movement at the garden's edge. A tall, elegant gentleman was coming toward her, a familiar set to his broad shoulders. He wore a broad-brimmed hat pulled low over his brow, but she could see that it was in the height of fashion with its trimming of ostrich plumes. Shading her eyes with one hand, she rose slowly to her feet, her heart beginning to pound erratically. It was a neighbor, a visitor from town, a recent arrival from England. It could not be who it seemed. Had she imagined this form and face so often that it had become real? Could it really be Jeffery Fortune strolling so casually through her uncle's garden?

Sweeping off the plumed hat, the gentleman bowed low before her, his eyes merry summer pools. His mouth twisted itself into a smile and when he spoke, the warmth and vibrancy of that voice shot through her with sudden flame.

"Good morning, my love."

Chapter Fourteen

Raven's mending—needles, thread, dress—fell un-heeded from her trembling fingers. Her breath came in short, quick gasps and she felt as if the day had suddenly grown exceptionally warm. It was impossible, she thought. He was not really there. She stretched her fingers to disprove his existence with her touch.

He took her outstretched hand in his, bringing it to his lips to kiss, as would any gentleman. But this was no gentleman. This was a pirate. He did not satisfy himself with only a chaste touching of lips to the back of her hand. He kissed it then nibbled at her fingers as if hungry for her. He turned her hand up and caressed all the tender places of her palm with his searching, searing mouth, his wayward, wanton tongue.

His touch was still the same. Even in the shade on this cool, breezy morning, it made the heat rise in her cheeks. A wave of flame passed through her, and her breath caught on the constriction in her throat.

"Jeffery!" she breathed, unable at that moment to say more while her eyes greedily took in each detail of his face.

Then her eyes widened even further. He was in

danger. If he were caught, he would be hanged. "What are you doing here?" she asked in alarm.

He chuckled and drew her closer, the blue flame of his eyes dancing over her. "I've come to reclaim that which is mine."

She gasped and snatched her hand away. It was madness. Surely he was not so bold as to follow her to Barbados, courting death to regain a captive? Yet the danger did not weigh heavily upon him. He seemed most lighthearted. She remembered how nonchalant he had been amid the carnage of battle when she had first seen him and later when he had fought DeLessops. It was almost as if he thrived on danger. But to come where he was well-known and officers of the king were within easy reach, was madness indeed.

"Jeffery, you must get away while you still can!" She pushed at him, trying ineffectually to turn him around, to make him go. "Do you want to be hanged?"

"It gladdens my heart to know that you would not take pleasure in my hanging," he said, laughing.

He reached out to pull her to him, but she stepped back, a staying hand on his chest, rock-hard beneath the soft ruffles of his cambric shirt. "Can you laugh with the noose nearly about your neck? At least hide yourself!" She plucked at his sleeve with one hand and lifted her skirt with the other, looking for a safe place.

He grasped her by the shoulders to still her efforts and laughing, said, "Raven, I've been pardoned."

She stopped and turned and her eyes searched his face. Could it be true? "Pardoned?" she asked softly, at first uncomprehendingly.

He nodded his head. "A full pardon. My lands restored. I—"

Raven threw herself into his arms, flinging her arms about his neck, stopping any further conversation.

His mouth fell upon hers, devouring, insatiable, and she responded with a deep, long-denied hunger. They stood entwined, and he moaned as his lips kissed her cheeks, her eyes, her forehead, buried themselves in her silken tresses.

"Raven, I want you to marry me," he murmured into the blackness of her hair.

For a moment, her heart stopped. She looked up into his face. There was no mockery there, only love. Could he really mean it? Her brow creased. "Jeffery, do you know who I am? Who my uncle is?"

He smiled. "I know."

"You!" a grating voice shrieked. "Get your foul hands off my niece!"

Instantly, Jeffery thrust her behind him, his hand instinctively reaching for the sword that hung at his hip.

Samuel Parkington stood on the porch, a cane gripped tightly in his uplifted hand, as if threatening Jeffery with that improvised weapon. "Cato!" he called over his shoulder to the wizened black. "Find Billings and the other overseers. Bring them here immediately!" He chuckled in evil satisfaction. "We'll see this strutting peacock trussed up in fine style!"

"That won't be necessary, Mr. Parkington," a voice drawled from the corner of the house. A uniformed officer of the king lounged against a porch post, casually pulling an enameled snuffbox from his rumpled vest.

"Lieutenant Mason, arrest this man!" Parkington's glee was almost palpable.

"I think not, sir," the lieutenant replied, sniffing a

pinch of snuff then sneezing violently into a well-used handkerchief.

"This is Jeffery Fortune, the notorious pirate!" Parkington yelled, shaking a bony finger at Jeffery. "There is a price on his head! And he belongs to me! He is an escaped slave. I demand that you arrest him!"

"I have come on a different errand altogether, Mr. Parkington," Lieutenant Mason said calmly, stuffing his handkerchief into a large pocket.

"What can take precedence over this?" Raven's uncle shouted. "A dangerous criminal stands before you. His crimes are beyond number. Hanging is too good for him. He should be arrested and returned to slavery in chains."

"He has been pardoned, Mr. Parkington." Lieutenant Mason pulled a mango from his voluminous pocket and began to peel it with a penknife.

"Pardoned? Pardoned!" Parkington spluttered incoherently for a long moment, his face mottled a splotchy red.

"Yes, sir. Pardoned. I am here to ensure the proper restoration of his land and property. I believe that you were given the wardship of Fortune's Fancy?" The lieutenant turned the fruit in his hand, looking for a likely place to bite.

"You are being flummoxed, Lieutenant! This is all some clever trick!"

"I assure you, Parkington," Mason said between juicy bites of the fruit, "the papers are quite in order."

"Papers!" Parkington snorted. "It is not so difficult to forge papers."

"True," the lieutenant said, studying his mango to decide where the next bite should be placed. "But people can't be forged. Captain Fortune has brought

Sir Charles Bradford along to attest to the genuineness of his pardon. I am well acquainted with Sir Charles." Raising his eyebrows and looking at Parkington over his mango, as if admonishing a schoolboy, he said, "You will now consider your wardship at an end. Fortune's Fancy now belongs to Jeffery Fortune. All slaves or an equal number will be returned to him."

Her uncle's eyes bulged and his skin reddened until Raven began to fear he would suffer an apoplectic attack. "All the slaves?"

"Or an equal number," Mason said, tossing the pit into the bushes and wiping his hands on the all-purpose handkerchief.

"Two hundred and fifty slaves," Jeffery supplied the number. "One hundred twenty-five men, seventy-four women, and fifty-one children. Most of whom should be grown now."

"I keep no women or children," Parkington sneered. "They were sold."

Raven heard Jeffery's quickly indrawn breath, saw the tightening of his jaw.

"Then I suppose you will have to return one hundred twenty-five men and sufficient funds to replace the slaves you sold," Mason said. "I'm sure a judge can decide the exact amount. Until then," he said to Jeffery, "I'm sure you can make do with the men who should be returned to you by this evening. Now if you will excuse me, I will return to my duties in Bridgetown."

"This evening? How will I finish my harvest?"

Lieutenant Mason shrugged.

Parkington limped after him, pulling at his sleeve. "I don't have the money."

Picking Parkington's fingers from his rumpled sleeve as he would a leech, the lieutenant said, "I'm sure after the sale of your harvest will be soon enough."

"But most of my harvest is at the bottom of the Caribbean." He turned with a feral snarl, pointing an accusing finger at Jeffery. "Thanks to him! I was counting on the harvest from Fortune's Fancy to recoup my losses. We were to begin cutting cane there tomorrow."

"And so I shall," Jeffery said. "I will expect my men this evening. As for the money, I am willing to be generous and give you until next year to pay it, since I well understand the reasons you are in short supply."

"You can wait until hell freezes over!" Parkington said through clenched teeth.

"I suppose a judge can decide that as well," Mason said, climbing onto his horse. Kicking it into a lope, he gave a vague wave of his hand as he rode away.

"I will also take my leave of you," Jeffery said, giving her uncle a mocking bow. Then once again he took Raven's fingers in his and bowing low, kissed them. "May I call on you tomorrow?"

Without waiting for her answer, he mounted his horse, touched the brim of his hat with his riding crop, and with a barely perceptible command to the prancing stallion, cantered away.

"Have ye no shame?" Parkington rounded on Raven, giving her a hard, backhanded slap. "I saw the way you were draped around that bastard's neck. Will ye throw yerself at the first thing that comes around here on two legs? So high and mighty ye are that ye turn up yer nose at a baronet but ye go sniffin' after one of my slaves!"

"He is no longer one of your slaves, Uncle," Raven said, drawing herself up proudly and ignoring the pain in her smarting cheek. "Nor has he been for some time."

"No, he's been worse! A lawless pirate, a thief, a blackguard of the lowest ilk."

It seemed he would go on but she cut him off. "He's been pardoned."

Her uncle sneered. "A pardon doesn't change what he's done. Or what he is. 'Tis best ye give me yer consent to write to Kenfield before ye ruin yerself. That way we can both mend our fortunes."

"I will think on it, Uncle," Raven said meekly. But her eyes followed the thin trail of dust receding down the road.

"Aargh!" Parkington said, and stamping his cane he limped away.

Raven's eyes stared at the dissipating dust, but she did not really see it. She was thinking about what her uncle had said. She had been so overjoyed when Jeffery had told her he had been pardoned. But what her uncle said was true. It did not change what Jeffery had done, what he had been.

Yes, he was pardoned. He could live openly and honestly with her. He had asked her to marry him. Her heart could not help but warm to the knowledge that he wanted her for a wife and not just a temporary bedmate. But could she accept his proposal knowing what he had been? A pirate, a traitor. Was this the good marriage her father had wanted for her?

Her father had been intensely loyal to his country. True, he had had little love for King James's politics and less for his religion, but he had remained loyal, nonetheless. Would he have sanctioned her marriage to a man who had been condemned for overt acts of treason?

And what of Captain Jeffery Fortune's depredations against her family? Her uncle was nearly ruined because of him. Yes, Uncle Samuel had mistreated Jeffery when he was a slave, but Uncle Samuel had not been the cause of Jeffery's treason.

She buried her face in her hands. What kind of man had she fallen in love with? What was wrong with her that her heart could choose Jeffery and spurn Baronet Kenfield? Or Alex Jamison?

Rubbing her eyes which threatened to overflow, she stiffened her resolve. She could never marry Jeffery Fortune.

Although she slept poorly, Raven was up early the next morning as was her usual wont. Through a long, thoughtful night, she had decided that the wisest thing she could do would be to consent to marry Baronet Kenfield. It would be impossible to live next door to Jeffery without seeing him. And if she saw him, she would fall into his arms the first time he touched her. She knew the limits of her resistance where Jeffery Fortune was concerned. He had proven them weak indeed on Tortuga.

She would tell her uncle tonight of her decision. It would be a week or two before she was packed and had passage on a London-bound ship. Until then, it would be best to avoid any contact with the former pirate who haunted her dreams. He had said he would call on her today. She would not be there. She would continue her exploration of the area—in the direction away from Fortune's Fancy.

After a quick breakfast, she mounted Lightning. Her daily rides had given new life to the horse and Raven was able to stir him into a canter. She was just leaving the gates of the plantation when she saw Jeffery riding toward her.

Sighing, she reined her horse to a halt. There was no way Lightning could outrun the magnificent stallion Jeffery controlled with such ease. It was bound to happen that their paths would cross. She could only hope to hold him at arm's length and let him know that there could be naught between them.

"Good morning, Raven," he said.

No tropic sun had ever warmed her the way his gaze did. Raking boldly over her, his eyes revived the memory of his caresses on each part of her he had touched. His hand on her hair, his lips on her cheeks, her mouth, her breasts. Gasping, she turned away, her cheeks flaming.

"Good morning, Captain Fortune," she replied as coolly as she could, holding her head high.

"Such a cold good morning belies the warmth of yesterday's greeting," he said, his glance lingering hungrily on the soft curve of her shoulder as if he would like to taste its sweetness.

Her brows arching haughtily, she looked him over with a well-feigned air of detachment. He was dressed as she had often seen him, both in Tortuga and on the deck of his ship. He wore no coat or vest and his white cambric shirt hung open at the throat, the sleeves rolled nearly to the elbow. A red silk sash bound his waist and smooth-fitting breeches were tucked into his wide-topped boots. A serviceable saber and baldrick were slung across his wide shoulders and a brace of pistols in a saddle holster completed the perfect picture of a pirate. When he smiled at her so rakishly and fired her blood with the blue flame of his eyes, the elegant gentleman of the day before seemed even more remote, even more of a pose put on and taken off at his convenience. Here she was seeing the real Jeffery Fortune—rogue, rake, pirate.

Had her uncle been right about him? That a pardon would not change what he was?

"I've come to ask for your help, Raven," he said, the rakish look on his face replaced with one of worried concern.

"My help?"

"One of my slaves was..." He paused, searching for the right word. "Wounded. His leg is badly infected and I think it might have to be amputated."

"I'll get my bag," she said, starting to turn Lightning.

She was stopped by his hand on her arm. " 'Tis not a pleasant sight," he warned.

Her mouth set in a hard line. "Suffering never is."

Raven was amazed at the change in Fortune's Fancy. It was not the main house so much, though a few weeds had been pulled and the windows replaced. Most of the work had been done in the slave compound. Several of the cottages had been newly whitewashed, their roofs repaired, and small gardens dug. But she had little chance to look around as Jeffery urged her into one of the cottages.

Her patient lay on a clean cot in the corner of the one-room building. The only other furniture was one chair and a table. But she noticed that a tray was on the table and that it held a large bowl of a savory-smelling stew and a chunk of thickly buttered bread. Pushing open the shutters to let more light into the room, she turned for a look at the man lying there, a man she recognized named Jenkins. A second slave, the huge black who had helped her clean her uncle's barracoons, pushed the chair over for her.

Jenkins smiled weakly at her, his face flushed and beaded with perspiration. "I don't want to lose me leg, mum."

Raven smiled reassuringly at him but said nothing to commit herself until she had had a chance to examine the wound. She bent over the leg and Jeffery hovered at her shoulder. Jeffery was right about one thing. It was not a pleasant sight, red and swollen, oozing with pus, and hot to the touch. But it was not the ugliness of the infection that caused Raven to suck in her breath and clench her teeth in anger. The wound was an even series of cuts across the bottom of the foot and up the leg almost to the knee. The cuts had been rubbed with hot pepper. She rounded on Jeffery, her black eyes flashing. "This is no 'wound.' This man has been deliberately tortured!"

"It weren't Mastah Jeffery who done it, Miss Raven," the black said. "It were Mastah Parkington."

Jenkins confirmed the accusation with a nod. "Said I was too insolent. Am I going to lose my leg?"

Raven bent again, looking carefully for the telltale signs of gangrene and for the life-threatening streaks of red traveling up the leg. Finding none, she sat back with a sigh. "It's a very bad infection. But as long as it doesn't turn gangrenous or poisonous, I'll try to save your leg."

She cleaned the wounds, poured brandy onto them, and stitched them closed. Applying a large poultice, she promised to return the next day to check on him.

"How could Uncle Samuel do that?" Raven asked angrily when she and Jeffery left the cottage.

"The rage he has against me was turned on several of the slaves before he sent them over," he said, his lips set in a hard line. "There are a couple more I'd like you to take a look at while you're here."

He ushered her into another cottage. She felt the warmth of his hand resting lightly on the small of her back and it was with some difficulty that she kept from turning into his arms.

Two men lay face down on cots, their backs shredded from recent floggings.

"Is my uncle also responsible for this?" she asked between gritted teeth as she bent to do what she could for the two men.

"There are no whips at Fortune's Fancy," he answered.

She looked up at him and saw the tight set of his jaw, the ice in his eyes, and knew that there would never be whips at Fortune's Fancy. Was it because he had had too close an acquaintance with those whips himself?

She had soon done all she could for the men. Time would have to be the healer now. Gathering her things into her bag, she stood and brushed past Jeffery on her way out the door. In that brief contact she could feel his desire for her, warm and inviting. Or was it hers for him? Then she was in the open air walking beside him to her horse. She lifted her face into the breeze, hoping it would cool more than just her skin.

Jeffery set her on her horse and she was conscious of the warmth of his hands circling her waist. But his eyes were even warmer, touching her where his hands dared not follow with so many eyes to see.

"I'll see you home, Raven," he said, mounting his stallion.

" 'Twill not be necessary, Captain Fortune," she said, remembering with difficulty her vow to be cool to him. "I was going for a ride this morning anyway."

"Then it will be my pleasure to accompany you." He smiled, again setting her ablaze with a rakish glance.

She gripped the reins tightly, afraid that if he looked at her like that again, she would throw herself off her horse straight into his arms. She needed a good, hard ride, the wind whipping in her face, and having to concentrate on controlling her mount. She

Michele Stegman

did not need Lightning's slow plodding with Jeffery at her side, brushing her thigh, his eyes constantly upon her.

She could not think like this. *Remember*, she told herself, *that this man is—or was—a traitor, a pirate. Remember all the reasons why you can have nothing further to do with Captain Jeffery Fortune. Think of ways to discourage his advances.*

They rode down the tree-shaded drive and onto the road. Nudging their horses down a shaded lane, Jeffery had to hold his prancing stallion with an iron hand to keep it abreast of Lightning's ambling gait.

"I was happy to hear of your pardon, Captain. Will you miss the sea? Or will it content you to be a planter?" She smiled coyly, knowing she was goading him.

"I shall not miss the sea at all," he replied. She looked up in surprise and he continued, "Since I will not be giving it up."

Her eyes widened and her lips parted in a gasp. Without even realizing it, she reached over to place a hand lightly on his arm. "Jeffery! Surely you don't plan to continue ... They'll never pardon you a second time!"

He laughed, placing his hand over hers. "So you do remember my first name."

Snatching her hand away, she tossed her head. "You were born to be hanged, Captain Fortune."

"Ah, ah," he said, wagging a warning finger at her. "You gave me your word that you would use my first name. Or will Neptune get his sacrifice after all?"

"He certainly will!" she snapped. "When your ship is sunk. Oh, Jeffery," she continued in a pleading tone, forgetting her vow to be cold to him, "don't go raiding again."

"I must," he said, barely restraining a laugh. Then

268

he explained, "Along with my pardon I had to accept a letter of marque to privateer against the French until the war is over."

Relief warred with anger across her face. Relief that he was not, after all, returning to his piratical ways, anger that she had been made a fool of. "So a mere scrap of paper has given legal sanction for you to continue what you are so naturally wont to do."

"Was it not you who condemned piracy as a heinous crime but hailed privateering an honored profession?"

" 'Twas you who taught me what a small difference there really is between the two."

"Ah, but the difference is there," he said, echoing the words she had thrown at him on Tortuga.

The path narrowed so that they were forced to go single file. He restrained his stallion, letting her take the lead. Ducking beneath overhanging branches, she was sure she could feel his eyes on her. Glancing back, she found that she was right and was surprised that the heat glowing from his eyes did not set her clothing aflame. It certainly set her blood boiling. What was she doing riding down this lonely lane with a confessed, but scarcely redeemed, pirate?

The lane ended on a bluff overlooking the sea. She could hear the crash of the waves against the rocks below and the skreeing of the gulls. Far in the distance a white sail flashed in the sun before it disappeared over the horizon.

Strong, sun-bronzed hands reached up to lift her from her saddle, caressing, nearly circling her waist. Her hands held his bare forearms, and she gloried in their hard strength. Her body slid along his until her feet touched the earth but even then he did not let her go. Grasping her shoulders, he crushed her to him, his mouth falling onto hers with all the weight of his long-denied lust. Flame met flame, intertwining them, consuming them, swirling them into a vortex where only the two of them existed. They clung together, his hands exploring anew the marvels of her body, her body responding in fond memory of his fire-kindling touch.

"Marry me, Raven," he said, his voice husky with desire.

His words brought the swirling vortex to a halt. All the reasons she had given herself for not marrying Jeffery flooded again into her brain. That those reasons did not affect her heart was something she would have to control.

"I can't," she said, pushing away from him, trying in vain to steady her heartbeat, to cool the burning that had launched shafts of flame into her loins.

"Can't?" he asked, looking down at her with amusement as if she could not be serious.

She tried to look into those warm, blue pools without melting into them, to appear cool and calm, casual. "I have decided to accept the proposal of marriage to a certain Baronet Kenfield."

"What?" He laughed, still not believing that she was serious.

"He wrote and I plan to write back and—"

"He *wrote*?" he asked contemptuously.

"Yes. I have decided that it would be an advantageous match." Even as she said the words, she realized how ludicrous they would seem to Jeffery.

His face darkened and his eyes turned hard and cold, threatening and dangerous. He snatched her to him, one arm holding her close in an iron grip while the other found all her wild, sweet places, reminding her of what his touch could do to her.

"Will an 'advantageous match' be sufficient when your body cries out in the night for this?" he asked, tormenting, teasing, his hands working their will upon her breasts and her buttocks, his thighs searing hers. "Will your mincing, milk-and-water lordling satisfy that which my touch has awakened in you? You, with the fire and passion of a Venus?"

She struggled to free herself, not only from the steel-hardened arms that held her but from her own mounting passion. But her struggles were to him no more than a kitten's. His mouth and hands played over her angrily, drawing the response from her body he could not draw from her voice. The anguished, pleading yes he longed to hear her speak was wrenched from her breasts hardening with desire beneath his touch, from her tongue and lips feeding upon the kisses he gave her, from her arching body, grinding into his of its own volition. Her struggles to free herself converted into writhing desire.

Suddenly she found herself free of his arms. Swaying without his support, she grasped Lightning's saddle, leaning heavily against the horse.

Jeffery stepped away from her, his eyes thawed not at all by the heat of passion that had left her limp. "Think on that, Miss Winthrop, when you compose your letter to the baronet."

Anger gave her the strength to retort, "Do you think me such a wanton that only a savage pirate can satisfy me?"

A twinkle began to melt the edges of those glacial shards as he turned to mount his pawing stallion. "If that is what it takes, may I be the first to offer my services?"

Settling into the saddle, he held the quivering stallion steady. His eyes now melted into mocking blue pools, he touched his crop to the brim of an imaginary hat in mock salute. "I will call again tomorrow. Perhaps we can go riding again, Miss Winthrop."

Then he was gone. The stallion, at last released from restraint, thundered down the lane.

It was not a question or a request. It was a command. But it was a command she fully intended to defy.

That night, in her airless room, stripped of all but her lightest chemise, she lay wakeful, watching the progress of the strip of moonlight across her bed. She could not marry Jeffery Fortune. She had already decided that. So why did she feel such an ache within her when she thought of him? And why did she think of him constantly?

Angrily, she turned over and shut her eyes. But it was a long time before sleep came. She was half awakened by seductive fingers playing over her, rousing her to passionate desire. A roguish mouth touched hers, and she responded, but it seemed to melt away before she was satisfied. "Jeffery!" she murmured as his mouth kindled fire on her breasts and his lithe thighs slid between hers. As she began to respond with wild, wicked abandonment to his body touching hers, she came to complete wakefulness. Jeffery, so real to her but a moment before, faded into the wispy dream world from whence he had come.

Jumping from the bed, she went to her washstand and dashed cold water in her face, mixing it with her tears. Now he was invading her dreams!

Returning to her bed, she pounded her pillow in frustration. If she were to marry Baronet Kenfield, she would have to purge Jeffery from her life completely.

Perhaps she could avoid him by remaining in her room all day. But the thought of wasting even one glorious tropic day cooped up inside the hot, airless room was too much to bear. Besides, she thought, why should she let Jeffery Fortune cause her to alter her plans in the least? She would continue with her normal routine, eating an early breakfast, riding and exploring most of the day, then tending her uncle's remaining few slaves in her clinic.

But in the morning, just for once, she thought, perhaps she could leave a little earlier than usual. She did not doubt that Jeffery would come by. But if she were already gone, what could he do?

But when morning came and she got up to dress, she felt so nauseous that she had to lie down again. It was the second morning she had felt sick. Was it Jeffery who was making her so upset or had she eaten something? Whatever it was, it passed quickly but it made her late enough so that when she came out onto the veranda, settling a broad-brimmed hat upon her head, she saw Jeffery riding at an easy canter up the drive.

He rode sitting tall and straight yet relaxed, the reins held almost negligently in one hand. The magnificent stallion responded immediately to the almost imperceptible commands from his strong, masterful hands. It was a picture of beauty and grace and strength that mesmerized her until he pulled the horse to a pawing stop before her.

"Good morning, my love. Ready and waiting, I see."

Her only answer was a contemptuous toss of her head as she reached for Lightning's reins.

"I've brought you a present." Throwing a leg over the stallion's neck, he leaped to the ground and drew a second horse he had been leading from behind the stallion.

So intent on stallion and rider, she had scarcely noticed the second horse until now. She froze, her hand dropping the reins she had gathered, and stared at the horse he had brought. A glistening chestnut mare with white face and feet, deep of chest and long of leg, it was full of life, spirit, and beauty. No sluggard here! Already bearing a side saddle, it tossed its head at her as if it were as anxious to get moving as the stallion was.

Unable to resist the mare, she ran a hand over the gleaming, satiny neck. "Jeffery, she's beautiful!" she said, feeding it the sugar she had brought for Lightning. "What's her name?"

"Anything you choose to call her, Raven. She's yours."

"Mine?" Her eyes widened and, shaking her head, she reluctantly withdrew her hand from the mare's neck. "I couldn't. It's too much."

"Still not accepting presents from me?" He chuckled. "Do you really prefer riding a plowhorse?"

Raven looked from one horse to the other, from the chestnut's gently arched neck and firm, gleaming flesh to Lightning's bony frame, from the chestnut's bright, spirited eyes to Lightning, who looked as if he would much prefer to remain in the stable today. It was sorely tempting to snatch up the chestnut's reins and dare Jeffery to take the mare back. It had been so long since she had had a decent piece of horseflesh beneath her. But she could hardly refuse to marry the man one day and accept such a wonderful gift from him the next.

"I really can't accept her, Jeffery," she said softly.

He sighed with exasperation, shaking his head. "Then at least ride her today since I intend to ride with you and it's too cruel to hold Star back to keep pace with that rack of bones you ride."

Once more she looked at the two horses, wanting desperately to ride the chestnut but feeling that it wasn't really right. Then she heard a low chuckle. Cato had been watching the whole scene. Laughing, he took up Lightning's reins and led the horse away.

She started toward the chestnut then stopped. "I'd like your promise that you'll take no liberties with me today."

Cocking one brow in distaste, he said, "I never make ridiculous promises I can't keep." Then giving her no chance to protest, Jeffery lifted her into the saddle, his hands lingering on her waist then dropping down to caress her rounded buttocks quickly before he turned to his own mount.

Realizing that, for better or worse, she was committed to the ride, Raven decided to make the best of it. Touching her heels to the mare, she took off down the drive at a gallop, the pounding hooves of the stallion close behind.

Racing down the road, leaping fences, tearing across cut fields, the mare seemed never to tire. Raven gave her her head, letting her run, sharing joy with her. Coming to a straight stretch of road, Jeffery's stallion came alongside to race neck and neck with the chestnut. At the turning to the lane they had taken the day before, Jeffery nudged the mare to the side, forcing her to slow and take that path.

They followed it to the same clearing atop the bluff, and Raven reined in her mount, jumping down from the saddle before Jeffery could take her into his arms. Letting him lead the horses to a grassy spot so they could graze, she strolled to the shade of a low-growing tree. The leaves of the tree were shiny and smooth-looking and she reached up to pluck one.

Brown, sinewy fingers grabbed her wrist in a painful, viselike grip, jerking her backward so quickly she stumbled against a rock-hard chest and familiar arms came around her to steady her. Her anger rising

275

Michele Stegman

at his rough treatment of her, she twisted in his grasp to berate him. But before the angry words could leave her mouth, he spoke.

" 'Tis a manchineel tree. Did you touch it?"

Alarmed at the worried frown on his face, she could only shake her head.

He relaxed his grip on her wrist, but his arms continued to hold her close to him, thigh to thigh, hip to hip. "The manchineel tree is poisonous," he said. "Even water dripping off the leaves after a rain can raise painful blisters."

"So there are serpents in Eden," she said, trying to sound lighthearted. Placing a hand flat against the solid wall of his chest to push him away, she added, "And one devil."

His arms tightened around her, and she could feel the acceleration of his heartbeat beneath her fingers. His breath quickened and his eyes burst into twin flames. "And one lovely Eve."

His mouth found hers before she could protest, and once their lips touched, all thought of protest was consumed. The flame in his eyes found an answering conflagration within her. The touch that she had dreamed of the night before became real and warm and breath-stopping as his hand wandered lustfully over her waist, back, and breast.

Her hand on his chest found its way inside his shirt to the living, vital flesh beneath. This was no midnight phantom of her mind, no hungering dream that vanished beneath her searching grasp. The muscles within her fingers' grasp were hard and solid and real. They rippled smoothly beneath the warm skin of his back as his arms lifted her, carrying her to a shaded spot of grass.

He lay down with her in his arms and his fingers soon banished her bodice to lift one rosebud-tipped breast to his greedy lips. Her gasp became a groan as she tore at his shirt, wanting, needing, to press her naked body against his.

Long-denied and starved for each other, their fingers flung aside impeding garments while their mouths kissed hungrily, insatiably. Lying on the pile of discarded clothing, she reached for him, her nails clawing lightly at his back, drawing him down upon her. Wet and wanting, she parted her thighs and, like silk, he slid between them, the evidence of his own deep desire demanding entry.

Her blood pounded in her ears, underscored by his quick raspy breathing. As one, they moved in a steadily building rhythm, until they reached a throbbing, crashing crescendo, fully in tune with one another.

Afterward, as they lay entwined, the melody continued in birdsong, and breeze-ruffled leaves, and the soft tread of his trailing fingers across her shoulder. Raven watched white puffs of clouds scudding across the sky, and Jeffery tickled her nose with a blade of grass.

Sighing, Raven sat up, reaching for her chemise. When she lifted the light fabric above her head, Jeffery nuzzled at her breast. Pushing him away, she pulled at her other clothes, trapped beneath him. Tossing his breeches at his head, she shoved him aside, freeing her clothes, and continued dressing. He lay on his side watching her, his eyes avidly taking in each bit of her flesh before she covered it.

"I would much prefer watching you undress," he said.

She looked at him lying there, propped on one elbow in unashamed nakedness, his golden skin sun-and-shade-dappled, and she longed to run her hands over the smooth line of his strongly muscled form. "You, sir, are an insatiable rogue!"

His arm snaked out and pulled her to him. Nibbling at her neck, he teased her nipple to a hard peak with his hand. "I think, my love, that I am not the only one."

"Oh!" She moved away from him, standing to finish her dressing.

He grinned at her while pulling on his breeches and boots. When he finished dressing, he stood before her and lifted her face to his. "How can you compare an 'advantageous match' to this? Marry me, Raven."

She stiffened, the color draining from her face as all the reasons she had for not marrying him vied in her conscience with what she had just done. Was she such a wanton that her morals dissolved at the mere touch of Jeffery's hand? How could she coolly plan to marry Baronet Kenfield one moment and the next find herself writhing in wicked abandon beneath a rakish pirate? Perhaps the baronet did not offer passion but, in spite of Jeffery's sneering, it *was* an advantageous match her father would have approved of. She admitted that she had enjoyed her dalliance with Jeffery. But it must remain just that. And it must stop. He would have to agree not to call on her again.

"I can't," she said, turning toward the tethered horses.

He grabbed her arm, turning her back to face him, his face a hurricane held barely in check. "Can't?"

"I ... I have reasons."

"Reasons!" he spat. "The reasons are only within you. They have no substance otherwise."

She shook her arm free and untied the chestnut. "They are still my reasons. I will not marry you, Jeffery Fortune. And I will ask you not to come calling upon me again."

In deadly silence, they rode back to her uncle's

plantation. There, she quickly dismounted and handed the reins to him. Without a further word, she went into the house, her back straight, her head high, and her heart breaking.

Chapter Fifteen

Raven awoke feeling as if she were back on board ship, and that the ship were being tossed about in a storm. Only there was no howling wind, no pitch and toss of the bed she lay in. There was only the pitch and toss of her stomach, a roiling, greasy churning that threatened to turn her inside out any moment.

Throwing aside the thin covering of the sheet, she sat up, knowing from the experience of the last two mornings that lying down did not help. Holding one hand over her mouth, she groped with the other for the steadying bedpost. She managed to stumble to the nightstand, to soak a rag in the tepid water and apply it to her face.

What was wrong with her? she wondered. Was it Jeffery's return that had so upset her? Or was it something she had eaten?

Standing in front of her long mirror, feeling almost but not quite sick enough to retch, she pulled on a yellow gown sprinkled with small gold roses. She had not worn this gown in some weeks and was surprised to find that the bodice was a bit snug in the waist. Uncomfortably snug.

Her eyes widened into large black disks, and she slowly raised her head to look at herself in the mirror, trying desperately to keep her breathing even, to keep the fear corralled at the back of her brain. Her hands trembling, she turned to her small trunk, threw open the lid, and rummaged hurriedly, frantically, through its contents, throwing books helter-skelter about her until she found her journal. She had neglected writing in it of late, but there was one thing she always recorded—the dates of her menses. Almost tearing the pages in her hurry, she at last found the page she sought opposite the calender. She counted the weeks quickly, then counted them again, telling herself that in her hurry, she must have made some mistake.

But there was no mistake. It had been six weeks since the beginning of her last menses. *Six* and a half weeks, not four. Nausea, a thickening of the waist. She felt her breasts, full and tender. All the signs were there. She was pregnant.

"Oh, Jeffery," she whispered. "What have you done to me?" But even as she said the words, she knew that she could not place the blame entirely at Jeffery's feet. He had not forced her. Seduced her, perhaps, but certainly never forced her. She was as much to blame as he.

Her head snapped up. What if the babe were Alex's? She had been with him last month, too. How could she know who the father was?

Carefully, one at a time, trying desperately to calm herself, she replaced the books.

Standing once more before her mirror, she ran her hands over her still flat stomach. She did not look pregnant. There was no protruding stomach, no ungainly gait. But that took time.

A baby. Smiling, she tenderly caressed her stomach. A new life, sweet and tender, growing within her. It was a wonderful thought. She frowned. Or would have been under different circumstances. What was she going to do?

Methodically, logically, she thought of her options. She could no longer consider marriage to Baronet Kenfield. She might have been able to convince him of her innocence in spite of her lack of virginity, but she was sure he would not walk down the aisle with a woman who was carrying another man's child.

She could continue as she was, living with Uncle Samuel. But that thought she discarded as soon as it came to her. More and more every day she had considered her own stay as temporary. She certainly would not raise a child beneath this blighted roof.

She had wanted to move to Bridgetown and set up a medical practice, had even begun to collect some of the things she would need. In spite of her lack of capital, she had been determined to do it. But now, with the baby, that was too uncertain. People did not always pay doctors. And would they even come to a woman? Especially an unmarried, pregnant woman? If it were only herself, she would not mind taking the chance. But she had to think of the child, too.

And the child needed a father. She did not want to raise a bastard who would suffer insult and sneers because its mother was not married to its father. So she must marry. But who? Alex or Jeffery?

She could marry Jeffery. He had asked her often enough. Would he still want her, not knowing whose child she carried?

Sitting down on the bed, she folded her hands in her lap and looked out the window at the tamarind tree in the garden.

Alex or Jeffery. She must ask one of them to marry her, knowing that she carried a child who could belong to either of them. Alex was not here. She did not know when he would be. Nor, she thought, had he ever asked her to marry him. She needed a husband now. She would have to swallow her pride and ask Jeffery. Ordinarily, Papa might not have approved of the marriage, but surely it was better to marry a former pirate and traitor than to let this scandal befall her and the innocent life she carried.

After yesterday, it would not be easy. What if he refused her? She clenched her hands. She could marry him and then tell him about the child! She shook her head. No, she would not begin a marriage with deception. There would be problems enough if she married Jeffery. She would tell him and hope he would understand.

The ride to Fortune's Fancy was usually a pleasant one. But this morning Raven was too worried to enjoy the warm morning sun and the fresh, cane-sweetened breeze. Dismounting in front of the big house, she almost hoped she would not find Jeffery home, and was relieved that he did not come out to greet her. Yet in another way, she wanted to get it over with.

Having come on the pretext of checking on her patients, she went through the garden and down the path to the slave quarters. She was surprised to find Jenkins sitting out in the sun with his leg propped on a table, a mug of ale in one hand, a smile on his face. The day before when she had come by the infection in his leg was still rampant.

He waved happily to her. "Pardon, Miss Raven, if I don't get up, even though me leg's a sight better than it were, thanks to you."

Raven laughed. "Thanks to your own hearty constitution and the good care you've received."

She checked his leg, changed the bandages, then

saw her other patients. She took her time, talking to several of the men, hoping that Jeffery would show up before she left. Pray God she did not have to ask where he was, go chasing after him, humbling herself further.

When Jeffery reined in his stallion before the neglected mansion that was once again his home, he could not miss seeing Raven's nag of a mount. He was certain she had come to see her patients and not the master of Fortune's Fancy. *But,* he thought, grinning, *I am not so reluctant to see her.* How much longer would she hold out to salve her pride, he wondered, before she agreed to marry him? Her body had already given him the answer he wanted to hear. If only Raven would respond to him with the same eager passion her body did.

Just thinking of her as she had been in his arms yesterday aroused him. He dismounted and stood for a moment absently rubbing his stallion's neck, taking several deep breaths. It would not do to let her see him in his present state.

He walked through the garden and was starting down the path to the slave quarters when he saw her, sun-dappled, beneath the overhanging branches of the sandbox trees. Light and shadow played over her flawless skin and danced in the deep waves of her midnight-black tresses. She was tanned by the tropic sun, her cheeks a deep, glowing rose. Walking slowly and thoughtfully with downcast eyes, her lashes thick, black fans against her cheeks and the gentle sway of her slender body beguiled him. Each of her luscious curves teased his eyes, kindling his desire. Stopping to readjust the strap of the medical bag she had slung over her shoulder, her eyes met his.

Grinning lustily while his eyes continued their

feast, an earthy remark sprang to his lips. But it died there when he saw the pain, the need, in her eyes. Silently, he opened his arms to her and without reluctance she came into them, putting her arms about his waist and leaning her head against his chest. For long moments she stood there with closed eyes, soaking in the unquestioning comfort he was so glad to offer her. Though the reason for her trouble worried him, he could not help but be glad that it was he she had chosen to come to with her problem.

"Jeffery, I need to talk with you," she said, her voice muffled against his chest.

He took her bag, and with his arm about her waist, he led her to a secluded spot in the garden and they sat down on a bench.

She sat licking her lips and looking down at her hands clenched in her lap. It was hard for him to wait patiently for her to pour out her heart to him. Knowing that whatever she had to say must be difficult for her, he took one of her hands in his and squeezed it reassuringly. It was cold and trembling, but the gentle pressure of his fingers must have given her courage, for she squared her shoulders and lifted her chin. Her eyes were full of ... Was it resignation?

"Jeffery, if you still want to marry me, I am ready."

So surprised was he at her pronouncement that for a moment all he could do was stare at her. Then such joy filled him and bubbled to his lips in happy laughter. "*If* I still want you!"

He reached to take her into his arms, to prove to her with the heat of his kisses, how much he still wanted her. She stopped his advance with a hand held firmly against his chest.

"Before you commit yourself, there is something I must tell you."

"Some terrible secret about your past?" he asked.

Knowing now why she had come, he could not help but be happy and it was hard to hide the smile that nudged at his lips.

"I'm pregnant."

He threw back his head and laughed joyously. "I could not be happier! To be told within the space of two minutes that not only will I become the husband of the most beautiful, the most desirable woman I have yet seen but the father of her child, is joy unspeakable."

Again, he reached for her, putting his hands on her shoulders, but yet she stayed him. There was no joy in her eyes. A chill swept over his heart as he looked into them and he knew that what she still had to say was the terrible secret he was not sure he wanted to know. When she spoke, it was as if each word was a spike being driven into his heart.

"I cannot be certain the child is yours, Jeffery."

His hands dropped from her shoulders, the smile from his lips, the joy from his heart. She had been a virgin when he first took her on Tortuga. Between then and now, there could be but one person she could have betrayed him with. Betrayed? No, she had never uttered one word of love or commitment. If she had gone to Alex, it was no betrayal. It was but a further testimony to her adamant refusal to accept anything from him but advances she was powerless to stop. "Alex!"

She nodded and again lowered her gaze to her clenched hands. He knew she was waiting for his answer, that it had been hard for her to come to him needing a husband yet not knowing whose child she carried. But his own pain was too great just then to speak. He had been so sure that despite his capturing her and holding her prisoner, she cared for him, and that her feelings would eventually deepen into love.

She had attracted him from the first moment he saw her. And that attraction had only deepened as he got to know her, as he deliberately seduced her to force her to return the growing feelings he had for her. Had Alex had to seduce her? Or had she gone willingly into his arms? Did she, even now, prefer Alex? Was she willing to wed him only because Alex was not around? How had she phrased her proposal? Not, "I want to marry you," but "I am ready." As if it were an ordeal. He had been right to read resignation in her eyes.

He clenched his fists, thinking of Alex. He could understand his friend's rakish progress across the Caribbean, taking his pleasure where he found it, winning hearts and breaking them. But not when it came to Raven. How could any man who won her love walk off and leave her? Especially if he had once tasted her flesh, felt the rapture of her moving urgently beneath him? If Jamison had no plan to wed Raven, why had he taken advantage of her innocence? For virgin or not, she was still an innocent in the hands of such an experienced libertine.

But willing or resigned, she needed him. And he still wanted her. Though she might prefer Alex, Alex was not here, nor, apparently, had he asked her to marry him. For now, Jeffery was here for her. Perhaps in time, she would come to love him.

Taking her face between his hands, he lifted it until she looked up at him. Seeking to lighten her heart and to infuse a little joy back into the situation, he smiled and said, "There is but one condition I would put upon our marriage." At her questioning look, he continued, "That you will finally accept gifts from me!"

When he saw the relief flood her eyes and the smile light her face, he could no longer resist kissing her.

287

Tenderly, he touched his lips to hers, chastely, as if this were his first kiss to his betrothed.

But the chastity did not last long. Almost of its own accord, the kiss deepened, expanded, his tongue probing the richness of her mouth. Breathless, they parted, though their eyes held.

"I must go into Bridgetown this afternoon," he said, "and make arrangements with the priest. What day shall we marry?"

Lightly touching her stomach, she said, "The sooner, the better."

"So I feel, though for different reasons." He laughed. "Do you want to marry at St. Michael's?"

She looked up at him pleadingly. "There will be few enough people in attendance, can we marry here?"

Cocking a brow and looking toward the house, he thought of the shabby rooms, the broken furniture, the rotted drapes and wallpaper. Only the master bedroom had been given any attention and it was still but barely liveable. He had focused his energy on the slave quarters and the harvest. He had planned to leave the house until that was done. How could he possibly have a wedding here?

But her eyes were so large and luminous he felt he could drown in them and never regret the merging of their beings. Smiling ruefully, he wondered just what he was getting himself into. Any time their wills clashed all she would have to do is look at him like that and he would give her anything she wanted.

"I suppose one room of the house could be cleared and cleaned in time, though it will be shabby," he warned.

She laughed softly. "I'm sure it will be some time before the house is in order. I was thinking more of a garden wedding."

His eyes lighting, he nodded with pleasure. The garden had been cared for by someone and would need little to ready it for a small celebration. It was the perfect spot for their wedding. Then he looked at her in surprise. "Was it you who tended the garden?"

At her shy nod, he laughed. "I wondered whose hand had cleared my mother's roses. But why? Did you know whose house this was?"

"Not at first. But even in near ruins, the beauty of the place touched me and I spent much time here."

"And will spend much more, beginning with our wedding," he promised. "Will Wednesday morning please you?"

"Yes." She rose to go. "I will come about ten o'clock. If there is any problem, you can send me word."

"I will send a carriage for you," he said, also standing. A frown crossed his brow. "I suppose your uncle will give you away?" he asked. He hoped she would say no. Though he knew Samuel Parkington was her only relative, it would gall him even to allow the man on Fortune's Fancy, let alone accept his bride from the man.

Raven lowered her eyes to her tightly clenched fingers and he feared that he had offended her. Were her eyes flashing sparks beneath those demurely lowered lids?

When she looked at him, it was with that proud determination he had come to know so well. "I am of age. I do not need Uncle Samuel to give me away."

He only nodded and escorted her to the front of the house. When she took up the reins to her nag, he put his hand on hers. "Shall I saddle Cinnamon for you?"

"Cinnamon?"

"Your chestnut mare." He grinned. "Remember that you must accept presents from me."

She tossed her head proudly, but a teasing smile played about her lips. "We are not yet wed, Sir Pirate!" Her grin widened. "But when we are, I shall be happy to call her mine."

"You are too proud by half, wench. I shall consider it my first duty as your husband to teach you due humility." Laughing, he lifted her into the saddle. It was with difficulty that he tore his hands away from that still-slender waist.

"Is it not humbling enough that I am forced by circumstances to marry a pirate?" she asked. A teasing smile played about her mouth, but he wondered if she did not mean what she said.

"A former pirate," he corrected.

Her eyes raked over him, her brow cocked uncertainly. "I am not so sure."

Gathering her fingers together, he kissed them, lingering over each one, reluctant to let her go.

"Thank you, Jeffery," she said softly, and he thought he heard a catch in her voice. He looked up at her, but she snatched her fingers away and kicked Lightning into a canter before he could be certain whether there had been a tear in her eye.

"You *what*?"

Samuel Parkington's snarl of rage and the angry twist of his features as he came out of his chair startled his niece, causing her to take a step backward. That was as far as she could retreat from his fury as she was backed against the door she had shut behind her for privacy.

When she had entered Uncle Samuel's office to inform him of her pending marriage, she had known he would not be pleased with her choice, but she had not expected the vehemence of his outburst. Now his face, contorted with fury, was thrust into hers.

"Are ye a dimwit?" he raged. "Or are ye determined to be as perverse a twit as your mother?"

Her eyes widened at the insult but she knew not what to say. She had known her mother only as a sweet, caring person totally devoted to her and her father.

"Aye," her uncle continued less loud but just as angry, as he surveyed her as if seeing her for the first time. "Ye're just like her. She was the granddaughter of a marquis. And a beauty. I was willing to give her a dowry to wed well but she chose your father instead. The fourth son of a petty baron whose poor lands were all entailed. No prospects at all. Where did it ever get her? Following him from camp to camp, never any real home, never got to court, never had any influence with the right people. Is that what you want? To repeat her mistake?"

"Perhaps it was not a mistake, Uncle," Raven ventured quietly. "They seemed quite happy together."

"Is that what ye seek with that rake? Happiness? How did he so quickly turn yer head, girl, that ye cannot see him for what he is?"

"I know very well what he is," she answered, lowering her lashes.

"Do ye now?" he sneered. "Then why do ye persist in wanting to marry him? A traitor, a pirate, a nobody!" His voice became softer. "Why not accept Baronet Kenfield? You could be on the next ship for England! 'Tis not too late."

You do not know how late it is, Uncle, Raven thought. But she kept silent, clenching her teeth to do so. Her uncle was enraged enough as it was. He would not take the news of her pregnancy lightly.

"Kenfield could give you money, position, influence. You could go to court, get to know all the right people," he urged softly. She could hear the greed in his words and knew that it was not for her that he wanted those things.

"None of that would matter if I could not love him, Uncle."

"Bah! You seemed to have learned fast enough to love this pirate!" He turned back to his cluttered desk, shoving a handful of papers into an already stuffed slot. " 'Tis his fine looks that fool you. I should have scarred that pretty face instead of his back one of those times I had him trussed to the whipping post!"

Raven's heart lurched sickeningly, thinking of Jeffery bound to the bloody post in the slave compound, feeling the full force of Uncle Samuel's unreasoning hatred. Perhaps it was her pregnancy that made her suddenly feel closed in, sickened to be in the same room with the hatred emanating from her uncle.

"If you will excuse me, Uncle," she said, groping behind her for the latch, "I have a lot to do."

"Ye're set on wedding this pirate, then?" he asked. "Even though he's the bastard who's damn near ruined me, raiding my ships year after year? Who crippled me?"

She could do no more than nod.

"Ye'll get no dowry from me!" he said in a last attempt to sway her.

Her fingers had at last found the latch and opened the door. "I expected none," she said proudly. When she made her escape and closed the door behind her, her last glimpse of her uncle was of him snapping a quill in his angrily clenched fist.

When Jeffery's carriage arrived Wednesday morning, Raven was ready and impatiently waiting, her trunks packed and hauled onto the porch. *Not that I am eager to wed Jeffery Fortune,* she told herself. But wedding or no, she was sure she could not stay another day beneath her uncle's roof. His roiling hatred of Jeffery now seemed to include her, leaping out at her whenever she passed the open door of his office, oozing out at every meal, seeping into every corner of the house.

After Jeffery's men loaded her trunks, they helped her into the carriage and she turned for a last look at her uncle's house. She caught a movement at one window and realized that, even now, he was glaring at her. Another movement at the corner of the house caught her attention and she smiled. Liza and Cato stood smiling and waving, happy for her. She smiled but did not want to get the two slaves into trouble by waving back.

Smoothing the skirt of her blue silk gown, she looked straight ahead as the carriage started forward at a smart pace to carry her the short distance to her new life. The blue silk was not her best gown, but she did not think Jeffery would have appreciated wedding her in the lavender one Alex had given her.

As they approached the house at Fortune's Fancy, she was surprised to see several carriages in the driveway. Jeffery would have friends there to see him wed and it saddened her to think that she had no one at all. No one to give her away, nor even a woman to stand up with her as bridesmaid.

Jeffery must have been waiting, for the carriage had not quite pulled to a stop when he reached up to help her down. For a moment, the elegance of his attire took her breath away. The dark blue brocade of his coat lay smoothly over the wide set of his shoulders. The gold embroidery on his cream satin vest set off the golden gleam of his hair, and the gush of lace at his throat matched the froth that fell over his sun-browned fingers.

"I have never seen a more beautiful bride," he said, lifting her down.

She noted that his eyes were different than she had ever seen them, warm when they looked at her, but also sparkling with happiness like sunlight on the Caribbean shallows. Pulling her arm through his, he led her around the house to the side garden. She stopped in awe at the transformation he had wrought. She had kept the worst of the weeds at bay in the garden but now there were none at all to be found. The roses had been mulched and stone pathways she never knew existed had been dug out of their covering of debris. Was it her imagination that the flowers bore an extra covering of blooms today?

Chairs had been set in the clearing at the center of the garden, and a small arch had been decorated with more blossoms and ribbons. Near the house, long tables laden with food had been set up for the guests who now awaited her arrival.

"Jeffery!" Raven exclaimed. "It's so beautiful! I never expected so much!"

" 'Twas not all my doing." He laughed.

"Then who . . ."

"When Jenkins and some of the other slaves you had tended heard of our impending nuptials, they volunteered to weed and hoe. The food—"

"Raven, love!"

Raven looked for the owner of that familiar voice, knowing she was responsible for the delicacies, and found her when she was nearly smothered in Mary's motherly embrace.

"Mary!" Raven smiled, happy to see a familiar face. "I didn't know Jeffery brought you from Tortuga."

"Two days ago we arrived aboard *The Mermaid* with Captain Van Doorn. And 'tis lucky now that we arrived when we did what with the weddin' and all. Josh and me would not be wantin' to miss seein' the young master finally settle down. And with such a foin lass, too."

"Aye, that you are," Josh said, red-faced, extending his hand.

"And is Captain Van Doorn here, too?" Raven asked.

"Did I hear my name mentioned?"

Raven turned to greet Captain Van Doorn but he did not content himself with a handshake and embraced her like a daughter. And that was the way she felt about him, too. He had been such a great comfort to her when her father died.

"Captain," Raven said with sudden inspiration, her eyes flashing, "will you stand in for my father this day and give me away?"

Van Doorn's ruddy cheeks turned even redder. "I would be proud to, Miss Winthrop!"

An older gentleman approached and Jeffery introduced her. "Sir Charles, may I present Miss Raven Winthrop? Raven, Sir Charles Bradford."

Raven curtsied politely. Jeffery continued to surprise her, she thought. A few weeks ago she would never have believed that he could count members of the aristocracy among his acquaintances.

"I have been looking forward to meeting you, my dear," Sir Charles said. "You are every bit as lovely as I thought you'd be." In a more conspiratorial tone he added, " 'Tis a fine family you're marrying into."

More than anything, that surprised her. How could he say that about a family who had been condemned for treason? She wanted to ask him what he meant, but Jeffery was pulling her along to introduce her to the few remaining guests, three local planters and their families who had also known the Fortune family in former days.

The introductions over, the guests seated themselves while she and Jeffery took their places under the archway, a beaming Captain Van Doorn holding tightly to her arm, Sir Charles standing up with Jeffery. The priest began the ceremony and she knew that there was no turning back now. In a few moments she would forever plight her troth to this tall pirate who stood beside her.

When the priest asked who gave the bride, Captain Van Doorn spoke up proudly, "I do, in her father's place."

Jeffery said his vows in a firm voice, gazing down at her with a warmth that shook her to the core. Her own vows were said in a voice that she managed to keep steady, though her hand trembled when Jeffery slipped a wide gold band onto her finger.

The rest of the morning and the afternoon passed in a blur of polite conversation, nibbling at pastries Mary had labored long and lovingly to make, saying good-bye to new acquaintances with promises to call in a few days, accepting invitations to dinner.

When the last guest left, Jeffery stood beside her, watching the carriage disappear down the drive. Putting his arm about her waist, he drew her to him. "Shall we go in to dinner, Mrs. Fortune?"

Raven started at this first use of her new name, then smiling shyly, allowed him to lead her around to the garden where Josh had set up a small table for them. Although the meal Mary served them was an excellent one, Raven scarcely tasted it. She kept stealing glances at Jeffery, wondering what it would be like now that she was married to him and he had complete rights to her body. What would it be like to give herself freely and without guilt? Would he still ply her with gentle words and send fire coursing through her veins with each seductive touch? Or would he simply take her quickly to satisfy his own needs?

The looks he was giving her told her that she would not have long to wait to find out, for his eyes were bold and burning. Yet there was something new in his eyes, too, a sort of gentleness.

Though she had to force herself to eat, she lingered long over each dish, prolonging the time when he would lead her into the house and into his—their bed.

But finally there was no more delay. Mary had cleared the dishes, the last of the wine had been sipped from her glass, the sun had set. But the flame in Jeffery's eyes was rising, leaping brightly each time he looked at her, brushed her hand, or when his knee met hers beneath the table. Taking the empty glass from her fingers, he rose to lead her inside.

She went with him without objection, not because he had as usual eroded her will to resist with his kisses and his hands, but because she, with the vows she had spoken, had abdicated her right to resist.

Jeffery ushered her through rooms filled with rubble, his hand claiming a place at the small of her back. Plaster crumbled from the walls and ceilings. Broken furniture was piled in the corners. Some effort had been made to clear at least the center of the long hall that led to the bedrooms in the back wing of the house.

Stopping before a door, Jeffery flung it open and she entered, aware of his presence beside her. It was a sitting room, but unlike the rest of the house, it was immaculate, though like the other rooms, plaster had

Michele Stegman

crumbled in places and the wallpaper, once a cheerful gold stripe, was spotted and peeling.

Jeffery stood close behind her, his breath falling lightly on her hair. He indicated a door. "The bedroom is through there," he said, his voice husky, his hand a burning brand where it still rested on her waist. "Shall I give you a few minutes before I join you?"

Suddenly too shy to speak, she could only nod and start toward the door. But he held her back a moment, saying, "I will not be long, my love. It has already been a hundred years since last I held you."

Chapter Sixteen

Raven stood inside the bedroom where she would spend her wedding night. It had once been papered in a delightful design of yellow roses that was now spotted and peeling. But fresh clean linens covered the bed, and all the furniture had been repaired and polished. A plush Oriental rug she remembered from Tortuga covered the floor. Large windows, now covered with slatted shutters, were along the wall that must look out onto the rear garden.

Mary had unpacked the small trunk for her and laid her nightgown across the bed. It was of white lawn and maidenly modest. She undressed quickly, her fingers shaking as she untied the bows on her bodice. Raven slipped on the gown then stood before a long mirror to take down her hair. Pulling her hair over her shoulder to brush its waist-long length, she paused to look at herself in the mirror. Even with her tan, she could tell that she was pale and drawn, her flushed cheeks the two bright spots on her face.

What was wrong with her? True, this was her wedding night, but she was no untried virgin. She wanted Jeffery so much that even thinking of him coming through that door to touch her, caress her body, sent an unnatural warmth surging through her. Yet there was still a part of her that could not accept, could not respect, the man she had married. Her husband was a former pirate and was still little better than one. And he had been a traitor to England.

She worried about how Jeffery would feel about her now. She had seen the look of anguish on his face when she had told him that the child she carried might not be his. Would its parentage forever be a shadow between them?

"You may have had little choice of husbands," she told her reflection, "but you married Captain Jeffery Fortune, privateer, traitor, knowing what he was. For better or worse, he is yours and you are his. There is no turning back now."

Her words gave her some comfort, and she tried to think only of this night, of the two of them, and not how the world and she had judged him.

She stiffened, the brush halfway through the long length of her hair, when she heard the door open behind her. She did not turn around, but her heart speeded to a faster tempo as she listened to the soft tread of Jeffery's slippered feet coming closer, saw his tall, muscled form in the mirror behind her. The rich brocade of his deep burgundy dressing gown lay smoothly across his shoulders and the wide lapel was open, exposing the crisply curling blond hair on his chest. Jeffery bent toward her and she felt his arms circling her waist. As his hands caressed upward to the base of her breasts, she sighed and leaned back against him with her head on his shoulder, all else forgotten but his touch. Bending, he kissed her throat, sliding his hands farther along their predetermined path to tease the tip of her breast beneath the thin lawn of her gown. She was held in the circle of Jeffery's arms and already her body was responding to his nearness. At this moment, it mattered not what he was or had been. Only his caresses mattered, and his kisses, and their response to each other.

Lifting her hair, he fingered its silken texture, burying his face in its fragrant blackness. "I have never made love to you with your hair unbound," he whispered raggedly into her ear. "On my ship when I first captured you, I would watch you as you readied for bed and it was all I could do to keep from sinking my fingers in these maddening waves."

Raven turned in his embrace, twining her arms about his neck. Standing on tiptoe, she lifted her mouth to his, and he claimed her gift, tasting fully and deeply of its rich nectar. He took her face between his hands, caressing her jaw, then his fingers drifted down the smooth column of her throat. His hands moved to her shoulders, pushing aside the fabric of her gown, edging it off to fall in a billowing heap on the floor.

She was no less bold, untying the belt of his robe, opening it wide, and stepping into its confines to press her naked body along his hard, lean length. Already his manhood pressed against her, warm and eager, fanning her desire for him.

Yet he seemed hesitant to take her. Why was he holding back? His kisses were tender, yet restrained. His hands, though pressing onward, seemed to do so reluctantly. Had he married her, after all, only out of duty because she might be pregnant with his child? When he carried her to the bed, he did not seem anxious to consummate what he had so gently begun. He lay a little apart from her, lightly touching, scarcely skimming the surface of her need for his touch, until she wanted to cry out in frustration.

Now that the chase was won, did he already tire of the game? Was he aroused only when she fought him, when their love was illicit? Would he be one of those husbands who found more interesting sport outside the bounds of matrimony?

Finally she pushed his hands away, pulled the sheet around her, and sat up. "Jeffery, you don't have to do this if you don't want to."

He looked as though he had been struck. "Don't want to?" He took her hand and placed it on the swollen evidence of his desire. With his other hand, he grasped a handful of her hair and pulled her close to him to rasp raggedly in her ear. "Does that feel like I do not want you? I am consumed with wanting you. All day I have been in agony waiting for the moment when I could have you all to myself. I watched you arrive today and wanted then to kiss your eyes, to taste the sweetness of your lips, to feel the softness of your naked body next to mine. If I do not soon find release within the warm moistness of your honeyed cavern, I think that I shall surely go mad!"

She listened to his words, looked into his eyes, alight with sincerity, and wanted desperately to believe him. "Then why don't you claim me, Jeffery? Why do you hold back? What is restraining you?"

Gently, he touched her cheek, his hand shaking. He smiled at her, his eyes dark sapphire pools in the light of the single candle. "I do not want to hurt you."

It didn't make sense. They had made love before. Why did he suddenly think she was so fragile? "Hurt me?"

"Because of the baby," he explained. "I don't want to hurt the child within you."

Relief flooded her and she laughed until tears began to flow. Then she threw herself at him so hard, wrapping her arms around his neck, that she knocked him over. He rolled back onto the pillows with her on top of him, trying to cushion her fall with his body.

Grinning, she faced him nose to nose, her lips nearly brushing his. "Jeffery Fortune, I was pregnant the other day when you rode me so roughly on the bare ground. If that did not hurt me, how can you hurt me on a soft bed?"

His eyes glinted brightly. "You are certain our lovemaking will not hurt the child?"

"I am certain. And if, my bold buccaneer, you do not very soon completely possess your captive, she is going to claw your back to shreds and make the scars it now bears seem as nothing!"

Chuckling, he rolled over, pinning her beneath him. "Then, my love, I will not spare you nor give you quarter!"

Bending low, he nipped at her shoulder and chewed his way to her breast where he feasted lavishly, drawing moans of pleasure from her. He was still gentle, his lovemaking tender. But the restraint was gone. And there was no doubt that he wanted her as much as she wanted him.

When the upward path they took at last peaked in an explosion of ecstacy, they lay exhausted in each other's arms. Raven found sleep quickly, the worry of the past few days and the pregnancy making her more needful of sleep than usual.

But Jeffery lay sleepless, looking down at his new bride, her black hair fanning away into the darkness of which it seemed so much a part. She lay on her back, one arm flung upward, lifting and rounding one perfect rose-tipped mound. Not that the other was any less delectable, he thought, his mouth again hungering to taste its sweetness.

Had any bride ever been so beautiful? His joy in her response to his touch filled him again, and he wanted to run his hand over that still-flat belly, curve around those tantalizing peaks, and seek out the secret hollow between her thighs. Yet he hesitated. He told himself it was because he did not want to disturb her sleep. But was it really because he was not yet sure of her?

That her body responded to his touch quickly and deeply he could not deny. But what of her heart? Would it ever belong wholly to him? Or would Alex forever hold preeminence in it?

Alex was certain to visit them sometime. Would Jeffery be able to welcome him into his home again, knowing that his wife preferred Alex? Not that he didn't trust Raven. Now that she had spoken her vows he had no doubt that she would keep them. Until death, he would possess her body, her fidelity. But could he content himself with that without also possessing her love? Could he remain friends with the man who did have it? A man who valued it so little that he had made free with Raven's body then left her?

He sighed and studied the perfect features of her face. Awake, they were animated with her sweetness; asleep, they were angelic. Except for that hair, he thought, fingering one silken curl. That was pure darkness, giving her the earthy carnality that he so delighted in, a lustiness that no ethereal angel could possibly possess. Would he ever be able to win her love?

I may destroy what chance there is for love between us if I pursue my present course, he thought. Yet he could not give up trying to prove that it was her uncle who was the traitor and not his father. Somehow Samuel Parkington had been able to shift the blame for his crimes onto John Fortune so that his father was hanged, Jeffery condemned to slavery, and his mother left to the charity of relatives in England after the confiscation of Fortune's Fancy. One day he would find out how and prove it. Would Raven's loyalty to her family twist the bit of love she did have for him to hatred?

He must have groaned aloud, for Raven stirred in her sleep, her face turning closer to his, her lips parting softly, an invitation beyond resisting. If he turned his back on Alex and branded her uncle a traitor, he would risk losing her. But for now, she was his, and though the pain of having her spurn him would be trebled if he let himself love her any more than he already did, he was drawn to her as a moth to flame. With a moan of agony, he claimed her mouth, stirring desire within her and plunging into it.

High on her makeshift ladder, Raven strained to reach a little farther. If she could just reach one more inch, she could unhook the bar that held up the tattered curtains. Raven dared not look down at her precarious perch—a rickety chair atop a shaky table—for fear of upsetting its delicate balance. Perhaps if she stood on tiptoe it would give her that extra inch she needed.

The chair beneath her began to teeter and she gasped, grabbing the drapes for support. But the rotted material could not take her weight and began to shred through her fingers just as the chair leg gave. Desperately, she clutched the material tighter, hoping to at least break her fall. But as she started sliding downward, strong hands circled her waist, plucking her from her predicament, and she found herself safely ensconced in her husband's arms.

She turned to him with a smile to thank him but found his face contorted with anger.

"What do you think you are doing, madame?"

Surprised at his anger, the smile left her face and

her black eyes snapped with her own anger. "If you will be so kind as to put me down, Jeffery Fortune, I will continue trying to make this house habitable!"

His arms tightened about her. "Not if it means you will break your lovely neck!" He let her stand but gathered her into his arms and spoke more softly, his anger evaporating now that she was clearly safe once more. "If your own neck means little to you, at least have a care for the life of our child, Raven."

She noted that he said "our" child. Had he accepted it as his, even though there would always be some doubt or did he merely use that term to please her? Either way, she could only love him more. Pressed against him, his arms holding her tightly, she could smell his morning's work—horse and leather, the sweetness of cut cane, the too-sweet smell from the mill, and the warmth of the sun. "It was foolish of me, I admit. But I wanted to get these musty things out of here and to clean out the rubble. I'd like to get one room suitable for callers."

"I'll send one or two of the men to help you, then. I don't want you getting hurt climbing around."

"No, you won't," she said, shaking her head. "I know how shorthanded you are while the harvest is going on. I promise not to do anything else careless and Mary can help me."

One of his hands slid down to squeeze her rounded buttock and a lusty leer spread across his face. "I think I can find more suitable work for you than cleaning, wench. Leave the musty curtains to a less comely lass and come entertain me for an hour."

She wriggled her hips enticingly against him, feeling his quick rise of interest. "Only an hour, milord?" she asked in her best imitation of a low-class maid. "I've heard ye're a might more lusty than that. 'Tis said ye're nigh insatiable."

He chuckled and gently tweaked her breast. "If I've lingered in the bedroom more often these past three days, 'tis that wench I've been bedding of late," he said, sighing. "She never wants to let me go."

"Oh!" she cried indignantly.

But he only chuckled and scooped her up again. "I do have an hour or so to spare, lovely maiden. Will ye spend it in sweet dalliance with me?"

She looked up at him with mock fear on her face. "I fear I must come quietly or my rapacious pirate lord will carry me off by force."

He laughed and turned with her in his arms. "Aye, madame, I just might after the enticement you gave me a moment ago."

But the sound of carriage wheels crunching gravel in the driveway halted them. Mutual sighs escaped them, but the looks they gave each other as he set her on her feet promised completion of their dalliance at a later hour. Straightening her dress and removing the scarf she had tied around her hair to keep the dust off, she followed her husband out to greet their guest.

"Sir Charles!" Jeffery said, extending his hand to help the older man alight from his carriage. "How good to see you."

"And you, Jeffery." Sir Charles bowed over Raven's hand. "You are looking even more radiant than at your wedding, my dear. I would not have thought it possible."

"You are so kind, Sir Charles. Will you join us for lunch?" Raven asked.

"I would be delighted, Mrs. Fortune."

He offered her his arm and she led him around to the side garden. "I am afraid we will have to ask you to put up with a garden setting. I am trying to bring some semblance of order to the house. Until I do, we have been taking our meals out here."

" 'Tis a lovely setting," he assured her. "But that brings me to the reason I have come calling so soon after your wedding." He pulled a folded piece of paper from his vest and handed it to Raven. " 'Tis a wedding present from me. When I came to the wedding, I knew immediately what you needed," he explained. "Open it."

Puzzled that a sheet of paper could be a present, Raven unfolded it and read aloud, "Roger Horn, cabinetmaker, promises to build one dining-room table and eight chairs to your specifications." She looked at Sir Charles, feeling very warm toward this gentleman she had known for such a short time but to whom she owed so much. "Thank you, Sir Charles. It is a very generous gift. And one we can certainly use! May I invite you now to eat as many meals at our future table as you will?"

"I will take you up on that invitation." Sir Charles laughed. "You may grow quite tired of me!" He turned to Jeffery. "Van Doorn asked me to tell you he found a buyer for the cargo of the French prize you took. And there is more damage to *The Falcon* than he suspected. She may not be seaworthy for some weeks yet."

Raven's brows knotted. Damage to *The Falcon*? A French prize? Why hadn't Jeffery told her that already he had been privateering? Had he hoped to keep it from her? she wondered. Or were danger and fighting so second nature to him that he had not thought it important enough to mention?

"I will ride in to Bridgetown tomorrow to see him," Jeffery said. "Perhaps you would like to come along, Raven? You can put in your order with Roger Horn and see what the shops have of interest."

"Yes, I would like that," she answered distractedly, more concerned with the damage to Jeffery's ship and the danger he had been in.

Jeffery held a chair for her and they sat down to eat. Mary, as usual, had prepared a sumptuous meal for them, and they, as usual, did it justice. When they had finished, they sat relaxing and talking.

"Do you plan to rebuild the house or build anew?" Sir Charles asked.

"Fortune's Fancy is my home," Jeffery answered, his jaw set with pride in the house and a determination to keep it. "The house is basically sound, though there are many repairs to be made. Seven years take their toll, especially in this climate."

"Seven years!" Sir Charles shook his head.

"Aye. And I'm no closer now to proving my father's innocence than I was then."

Raven looked up in surprise. She had never thought that Jeffery and his father might be innocent. Had they not been duly tried and condemned? But there was such an intense bitterness, an anger, in Jeffery's face that it made her wonder whether justice, this once, might have gone astray.

"Your father was a fine man, Jeffery If he had supported Monmouth, he would have done so openly. He would have fought by his side as so many other good men did, not gone skulking around spying and playing both ends."

"I thank you for your trust," Jeffery said. "But I'm afraid it will take more than your trust to sway a court."

"Perhaps your pardon and your return to Barbados will facilitate your investigations, since this Samuel Parkington you suspect of laying his own crimes on your father lives nearby," Sir Charles suggested.

Raven's fork clattered to her plate, dropped from trembling fingers she could not control. Uncle Samuel was no favorite of hers but surely he could not be guilty of such a crime? To not only be a traitor, but to cause another man to be condemned for that crime was detestable beyond belief. Feeling faint, she grasped the edge of the table for support.

Jeffery jumped from his place, setting her wine glass to her lips, forcing her to swallow a few drops.

"Mrs. Fortune! Are you quite all right?" Sir Charles asked in alarm.

Raven tried to smile and nod, but the effort seemed beyond her. She looked down at Jeffery's hand on her shoulder. Was that the hand of a traitor as she had come to believe and accept, or was it as innocent of those crimes as he now claimed? Or worse, she thought shuddering, was it the hand of a traitor who was trying to wipe his crimes onto another as he claimed her uncle had done?

"My wife did not know of my suspicions concerning her uncle," Jeffery said.

"Her uncle!" Sir Charles said. "Good Lord! She didn't know and I just blurted it out like that? I do beg your pardon, Jeffery. And you, too, Mrs. Fortune. I thought surely you must know ... I mean ..."

" 'Tis no fault of yours, Sir Charles. I should have discussed this with Raven ere now."

Raven looked at her husband, so solicitous of her, and thought how little she really knew of him. Yes, she thought, this was something he should have discussed with her ere now. Why had he not told her?

"Perhaps it is best that I go," Sir Charles said, rising from the table.

As if in a dream, she watched Sir Charles rise, heard Jeffery say, "I will see you to your carriage."

"No, no. You stay with Mrs. Fortune. I can find my way." Bowing, he hastened off.

"A French prize? Damage to *The Falcon*? My uncle, not you and your father, the traitor? It seems, Jeffery, that there is much you have not told me." She stared up at him, her heart feeling heavy within her. There was but one reason she could think of that he had not told her of his suspicions before he married her. "Is that why you wanted to marry me, Jeffery? To gain information about my uncle?"

"No!" He grabbed her by the shoulders so hard he hurt her, pulling her to him.

She allowed him to put his arms about her, hold her in his embrace, but it was without feeling, without response.

His arms tightened about her. "Do you think I take our marriage so lightly that I could use it to gain information? I want you so much, Raven. I want nothing more than to continue the little tryst that Sir Charles interrupted." He sighed and loosened his grip. "But I can see that that organized, logical mind of yours must have an explanation first." He set her back into her chair and pulled his close. Smiling wryly, he took her hands.

She felt the warmth of his touch but it meant nothing to her. It was as if her hands were lifeless.

"So much has happened in the last few days, the wedding, the harvest. There has been little chance for us to really talk."

She looked into his eyes, feeling bleak and empty. "Did it seem of such little importance that you could not find a spare moment to tell me? We managed to find time for . . . other things."

"Those 'other things' are indeed important, to me, Raven. Ever since I found out that you were Parkington's niece, I knew that eventually I would have to tell you about my suspicions but I dreaded that time. I was too afraid."

"Afraid?" She felt the hands that held hers tremble and she was amazed that this man who faced death so blithely could fear anything. "Of what?"

"Of losing you!" he said, and there was real pain in his eyes. He looked away for a moment. When he turned back to her, his eyes were once more the cold, glacial shards that she had seen so little of in the last few days. "Raven, my father was innocent of the charges against him. Right after the rebellion, judges sentenced so many so quickly that there was often too much haste for proper justice. My father's case was such a one. There was a mass of evidence that someone had been spying for Monmouth. There was very little to indicate who it was. There was but a sheaf of letters to and from 'The gentleman from Barbados.' Someone accused my father since it was well known he was from Barbados. Some of those letters were found in his effects."

He held her hands tightly, as if trying to erase the pain of the past. His eyes became more frighteningly cold than she had ever seen them. "But those letters were not his. There was another 'gentleman' from Barbados in England at that time—your uncle. The night before my father and I were arrested, your uncle came to call on us, which seemed strange since we had never been on very good terms. When I came into the room, Parkington was sitting at my father's desk but jumped up right away. I merely put it down to snooping, but since we had nothing to hide I made no issue of it. He stayed for only a few minutes, saying something about missing Barbados and wanting to visit with a neighbor. The next morning when they came to arrest us, those incriminating documents were found in the desk. I believe your uncle put them there."

She pulled her hands from his grasp, her own eyes

hardening to obsidian. "Why would Uncle Samuel do such a thing? Even if he were guilty, why didn't he just burn the evidence?"

"For two reasons," he said, again gathering her hands into his. "First, too much suspicion had been aroused for him to get by with just burning the letters. Someone was going to be arrested. Your uncle made sure it wasn't him by framing my father."

"And the second reason?" she asked, leaving her hands in his, uncertain whether to believe him.

"The second reason goes back almost thirty years." He smiled mirthlessly at her. "Your uncle wanted to marry my mother."

Raven started in surprise. "Your mother?"

"Aye. She inherited this land. Your uncle wanted it. Added to his, it would have made him the largest landowner in Barbados. But my mother was too taken with a certain Irish sea captain, John Fortune. Samuel Parkington never forgave her for turning down his proposal, nor my father for winning the prize he coveted."

"Why were you arrested?"

"Again, it was because of your uncle. He had made quite a few influential friends for the purpose of gaining information for Monmouth, but it was impossible to convince anyone of that. He wanted to wipe out the Fortune family then buy Fortune's Fancy for himself. So he convinced them that whatever the father was up to, the son was also. It was well known that my father and I were very close so it was not hard to believe that I would have supported whatever political stand my father made. On that evidence I was condemned."

"It seems too frail, too insubstantial, to be believed," she said, trying to pull her hands away.

"Not in England in the aftermath of the rebellion,"

he said, holding her hands more tightly. "Not with the colonies crying for labor. There was a simple solution for everyone. Every malcontent a man of influence wanted to get rid of was branded a traitor and shipped off for a life of slavery to supply labor in the colonies."

"Uncle Samuel bought you to help you," she said. "He told me so. But you were rebellious, ungrateful."

"Your uncle wanted me dead," he countered. "That's why he bought me. To make sure I did not survive too long. When I found a chance to escape, I took it."

"Crippling my uncle in the process."

"I didn't cripple your uncle. But his accident did give me the diversion I needed to make my escape. Maybe that is why he blames me."

She no longer had any respect for her uncle, but to believe there was a traitor in her own family, knowing how important loyalty was to her father, was stretching her credulity too far. She pried her fingers from his grip. " 'Tis a nice story you tell, Jeffery. But I hardly think an admitted pirate could be as innocent as you paint yourself. What do you hope to gain by trying to make me believe that my family and not yours is traitorous?"

His jaw clenched. "The truth, Raven. And the truth it is whether you choose to believe it or not."

"My father would never have countenanced disloyalty!"

" 'Tis not your father I accuse, Raven. Nor you. But you know as well as I what kind of man Samuel Parkington is."

"I have work, to do, Jeffery. You must have things to do, also," she said, pulling her hands away from any contact with his.

She felt his hands tremble in her lap, saw them

314

start to reach for hers. With a ragged sigh, he stood up. For a long moment he stood in front of her as if waiting for her understanding, but she did not look up at him, did not let her hands reach out to him. At last, he turned and strode away, his boots nearly soundless on the shredded bark path through the garden.

Chapter Seventeen

Raven watched Jeffery disappear down the path and her heart ached to call him back, but her mind set strong restraints upon her body, forcing it to be still and silent. She let him go, to leave her feeling more alone than she had felt even at her father's death.

The beacon of Barbados and a life with her uncle had been a false one that had left her on her own again. Her pregnancy had further shattered her hopes for a secure, stable world. Then she had married Jeffery. For a few days she had reveled in security and warmth. She had even been able to free a little of the love she felt for him from the cold logic of all the reasons she shouldn't. There was no need to free the passion that flared between them. It had a life of its own and could not be denied. Even now, when she thought of him holding her, desire grew within her.

She had been able to love and marry Jeffery, even though the knowledge that he was a pirate and a traitor was a constant burr scratching away at her contentment. Now would the safe haven she had found in his arms also be torn from her by deceit and lies?

She glanced away from the empty path and turned

to go back inside, then stopped, sucking in her breath in a quick gasp. Or was he telling the truth? But if he were, then she would have to accept for her own family the guilt, the shame of treason, and worse. She would have to accept that her family was to blame, not only of being traitors and spies, but of being so cowardly as to shift their guilt onto innocent shoulders. Would that be any easier to bear?

Yes, her heart cried. Yes. How she wanted to believe Jeffery innocent! It was enough that he had been a pirate. Pray God he was, at least, not a traitor!

Mechanically, she returned to her work, clearing rubble and broken furniture from the drawing room, setting aside anything that could be repaired. She did not spare herself, working to keep from dwelling on what she had learned. But every now and then she would find herself staring out the window in the direction of her uncle's plantation, wondering, wondering.

If only there were some proof of what Jeffery had told her. There were the scars on his wrists and back. But they only proved what her uncle had already admitted, that Jeffery had been a recalcitrant slave and had been beaten. It did not prove that he was innocent of the charges against him.

But would Jeffery have been so rebellious, would he have had to escape, if Uncle Samuel had truly bought him to help him as he claimed? Uncle Samuel hated the Fortune family. Was that hatred strong enough for him to have done the things Jeffery accused him of?

Sighing, she returned to her work. She pulled on the rotted drapes, and they came crashing down, shredding apart, tumbling at her feet. Was this what would happen to her marriage? Shredded by distrust and dishonor until nothing was left?

Michele Stegman

There seemed little hope of proving what Jeffery had told her. If she accepted his words as true, it would have to be on faith. But she was not sure she could do that. Could she love and respect her husband never knowing whether he was an innocent man or a traitor and a liar?

Oh, Jeffery! I want to love you and to believe you fully and completely! If only ... She let the thought die away into the land of hopeless dreams.

Jeffery did not join her for dinner and she supposed he ate with his slaves in the fields. Their food was not as sumptuous as that which Mary served, but it was decent and plentiful. She did not have to worry that he would go hungry. But she wondered why he did not come home. She had spurned him that morning. Had she turned him against her? Perhaps, then, she should have a care for her own heart, and prevent it from being hurt in turn.

Raven stood on the veranda watching the sunset, then went to bed alone.

It was late when Jeffery joined her, sliding close to her so that she could feel the warmth of his body, smelling washed and sandalwood-scented. He touched her shoulder, lightly moving his hand down her arm as if what he touched was cherished, yet fearful of waking her.

She had planned to feign sleep, to keep him at a distance her heart could manage without agony. But with that simple touch, that one gentle caress, she lost all control and all thought of control. She could no more keep herself from his arms than a waterfall could stop its torrential descent. His arms opened for her as she turned into them, fitting into that space as if it had been planned since the beginning of time to receive her.

Whether she could ever accept Jeffery as he was

or believe his story, whether their lives could ever truly be one, this part of him she had to have or she would die. She found his mouth and took his kiss with a hunger that matched his own.

His tightening embrace held her, as if he would never again let her go, and she heard a muffled sob catch in his throat. His lips brushed against her hair.

"I love you, Raven. You are breath and life to me."

They came together then with an ancient hunger eagerly, frantically devouring one another as if trying desperately to break through the walls that separated them.

Harvesting on a sugar plantation was always a busy time, but with slave cabins to repair, the mill to rebuild, the house to restore, and not enough hands for the work, Raven saw little of Jeffery. Her pregnancy gave her a need for more sleep, and he was always gone by the time she got up. Sometimes he did not return to the house until after she had retired for the night, slipping in beside her in the darkness, taking her into his arms. Sometimes he made love to her gently and tenderly. More often he fell asleep before he could even kiss her good night. But always he held her close, even in the depths of his exhaustion.

Raven was busy with her work on the house. Jeffery had found time to buy two indentured servants for her, cautioning the two Irishwomen not to let her do any heavy work or to get too tired. Meg and Katherine had taken their new master's words to heart and would hardly let her do more than sit on a chair and stitch new curtains while they worked.

But once a day she rode over to her uncle's plantation to check on the slaves. She went in the morning since his harvest was done and she no longer had to worry about disrupting the work.

This morning there had been little to do. Her uncle had been gone for nearly two weeks and there had been fewer punishments.

Raven urged Cinnamon into a canter, cutting across the fields to one of their own fields where she knew Jeffery would be working with some of his men.

The line of slaves hacking at the cane moved with an easy rhythm, their machetes flashing in the sun, their backs bent to their work. Stripped to the waist, Jeffery toiled beside his men and had she not known who he was, it would have been impossible to separate master from slave for his back was as scarred as the rest, his skin as sun-browned and sweaty. There was an easy camaraderie between them and occasional laughter. No guns threatened the slaves. No whips kept them at their work. Yet they worked with a willingness she had never seen on her uncle's plantation.

Most planters would have shuddered with disdain at the thought of working with their slaves, not only because they abhorred honest toil, but because they did not want to lose their slaves' respect and fear. But she had seen Jeffery performing every job which he asked his slaves to do, from whitewashing a cabin to feeding canes into the heavy millstones to cutting cane. And his slaves only seemed to respect him more for it.

Jeffery stopped his work when he saw her, wiping his brow with the back of the hand that held his machete. In his hand, the large work knife looked more like a saber than a tool. She grinned wryly. There would always be something of the pirate in him, she thought, no matter how long he played the honest planter.

He reached up to help her down, but she shook her

head. "I only stopped by for a minute to bring you these," she said, handing him a batch of cookies Mary had baked.

Jeffery took the bag from her, his strong fingers, work-hardened and calloused, brushing hers lingeringly. He took a couple of the cookies then handed the rest to the other men.

"You've been over there?" he asked, scowling in the direction of her uncle's plantation.

She nodded and watched his eyes harden, his jaw clench.

"I wish you'd stay away from there."

"The slaves need medical attention, Jeffery. If I don't help them, they will suffer."

"I know exactly how they suffer," he said bitterly, rubbing the scars on one wrist. "You're right to help them all you can. But I worry about you going over there alone. That man's a—"

"That man is my uncle," she interrupted.

"I know," he said tightly. "If he weren't, I'd be tempted to find an excuse to call him out and run him through as he deserves."

"Jeffery!"

He placed his hand over hers where it rested on her saddle. "You needn't worry, my love. I've no intention of killing him before I wring a confession out of him."

Looking down at him, she saw he was so adamant that it was hard not to believe in his innocence. She turned her hand to hold his. "You've been pardoned, Jeffery. Can't you let it rest?"

He stiffened. "Would you if it were your father who unjustly bore the brand of traitor?"

She let go of his hand. "No, I would not want to see anyone in my family called traitor. Must you persist in this?"

"I would see justice done, my lady."

"No matter who it hurts? To clear your father, you would sacrifice our good name."

"Would you rather see the name of Fortune continue to bear an unjust stain? I would remind you that it is the name you now also bear. The Parkington name was never yours—or your father's."

She looked away from his eyes. There was much truth in what he said. She would bear the Fortune name for the rest of her life. Did she owe it less loyalty than a name that had never been hers?

She gathered up the reins. "I must go, Jeffery. Don't forget that Sir Charles is coming to dinner tonight."

He smiled up at her, but there was more sadness than joy in his smile. "I'll come in early."

Nodding, she rode away.

Raven ran her fingers lightly over the gleaming surface of the mahogany table. It had been delivered two days ago and she had been polishing it ever since. She was glad that Sir Charles would be the first guest to sit at the table he had given them. She and the two Irishwomen had worked hard to restore the parlor and dining room, and she was proud of the results.

Jeffery came in just as she heard the crunch of gravel under carriage wheels in the drive. Still damp from washing, his hair glittered gold in the candlelight matching the gold embroidery on his white vest. His white linen coat fit smoothly, and equally white lace at his throat and wrist emphasized the tan of his face and hands.

Raven opened the door and was surprised to see Sir Charles helping a lady from the carriage. A footman was taking down a large trunk as if the woman planned to stay for some time. At first Raven thought she was a young woman, she was so girlishly slim and petite. But as she came up the walk, Raven could see that the hair Raven had taken for pure blond was sprinkled with white. It was difficult to judge her age, Raven thought, wondering who she was.

She felt Jeffery come up behind her, slipping an arm about her waist. When he saw the woman, he let out a joyful cry and ran down the walk to meet her. Unceremoniously, he scooped her up and whirled her around in a hug that Raven feared would crush so delicate a creature.

Sir Charles stood back, smiling broadly. When at last Jeffery set the woman on her feet, he said, "I ran into this woman in Bridgetown. I didn't think you'd mind if I brought her along."

Jeffery turned and Raven was surprised to see tears in his eyes. Holding tightly to the woman as if afraid to let her go, he led her up the walk to stop before Raven.

"Mother, may I present my wife, Raven Winthrop Fortune? Raven, my mother, Madeline Fortune."

Raven's eyes widened in surprise. She looked from Jeffery to the fair beauty standing beside him and could see a definite resemblance. But where Jeffery's eyes were a startling blue, his mother's were a gentle gray.

"Your wife?" Looking back to Sir Charles, Madeline said, "So this is the surprise you told me about!" She turned back to Raven. "And a lovely surprise you are, my dear! I was beginning to think Jeffery would never marry! Looking at you, I can see why he finally changed his mind." Kissing her on both cheeks, she said, "Welcome to our family."

The warmth of her greeting made Raven feel drawn immediately to Jeffery's mother. "Thank you,

Mrs. Fortune," she said, returning her welcoming kiss.

"Mrs. Fortune! La, my dear, call me Maddie. Everyone does."

Madeline looked around as she stepped inside, nodding her head in approval. "I expected to find the place in ruins, Jeffery. It's beautiful."

"Raven has done the work of restoring the house, Mother. I'm afraid I've been too busy with the harvest to help."

Raising her brow, she looked anew at Raven, her glance lingering for a moment on Raven's hands.

Blushing, Raven tried to hide her hands behind her back. They were roughened from her plastering, pricked from her sewing, and her nails were splintered and broken.

But Maddie took her hand and patted it, drawing Raven close as they walked into the parlor. "Your hands tell me a great deal about you, my dear," she confided. "I'm happy to see you're not one of those beauties who think work is beneath them. On a place like this, a man needs a woman who isn't afraid to do her share."

When everyone was settled, Jeffery and his mother on the sofa, Sir Charles and Raven in chairs facing them, Raven smiled at Maddie and asked, "How long has it been since you saw Jeffery?"

"Why, seven years. Not since ..." A sadness came into her eyes and her voice hardened. "Seven years," she finished flatly.

"My mother has been living with distant relatives in England, Raven. Given the circumstances, we have only been able to exchange letters."

"And he sent money. Quite a lot of it. Through a good friend, Alex Jamison. I do hope I'll get to see Alex before I return to England." She smiled at

Raven. "Have you met Alex?"

"I...I..." Raven stammered. Her eyes met Jeffery's and found them hard.

"They've met," he answered shortly.

Maddie looked from one to the other then tactfully changed the subject. Looking around, she said, "I like the colors you used in here, Raven. Your home is nearly as lovely as you are."

"It is your home, too, Maddie," Raven replied. "There is no need for you to return to England."

"Yes, there is." Maddie rose and went to stand by Sir Charles's chair, her hand resting familiarly on his shoulder. "I think it is time to announce our surprise," she said.

Sir Charles smiled up at Maddie, squeezing her hand. Turning to Jeffery, he said, "I told you I had known your father. But I didn't meet your mother until two years ago."

"When Parliament kicked out James and King William ascended the throne, I went to Sir Charles to ask him to plead your cause to the king. Everyone else had turned a deaf ear to me, but Sir Charles agreed to help. It was he who was at last able to obtain your pardon, Jeffery."

"For which I again thank you, Sir Charles," Jeffery said.

Sir Charles shrugged and grinned at Maddie. "I could not refuse to help so lovely a lady."

"Or such a persistent one," Maddie added.

Sir Charles laughed. "Very persistent. But I grew to love your mother, Jeffery. I have asked her to become my wife and she has at last agreed."

Jeffery stood to offer Sir Charles his hand and his congratulations then hugged his mother.

"I was going to wait in England until after I was sure Sir Charles had given you the pardon and you were settled. Then he was to send for me. But I couldn't wait. Two weeks after he left England, I did, too."

"I'm so glad you've come, Maddie," Raven said, adding her own hug of congratulations.

Mary called them in to dinner, and wedding plans were made while they ate.

Later they sat in the parlor again, and Raven listened as Jeffery and his mother told each other about the events of their lives since their last meeting and reminisced about Jeffery's boyhood.

The next few days, while Jeffery finished the harvest, Maddie and Raven had a lot of time to talk and to get acquainted. Maddie, Raven found, was full of decorating ideas and eager to help restore the house but was quick to defer to Raven when their ideas clashed.

"La!" Maddie exclaimed one morning when they were choosing curtain material for a guest bedroom. " 'Tis your house, now, Raven. If the yellow print is to your liking, then that is what we'll use. I'm sure it will look as good as the green." She paused, eyeing the room and its furnishing. "Maybe better," she conceded.

They measured and cut the material then sat together sewing. Raven squirmed in her chair, trying to ease the ache in her lower back. After a long morning with no chance to lie down, it was bothering her. The nausea had finally stopped, but now her back ached if she did not lie down for a few minutes in mid-morning.

Handing her a pillow, Maddie said, "I always found that a well-placed pillow did wonders for my back when I was pregnant."

Raven started and her hands flew to her stomach. "How could you tell? I'm not showing at all yet."

Maddie smiled. "The way you walk, I guess. The way Jeffery looks at you. Just how far along are you?"

Raven had never been one to back away from the truth, even if it meant shocking this woman she had come to care very much for. "Almost three months."

Maddie's brows shot up. It was not difficult to calculate that the pregnancy had happened before the marriage. Maddie grinned. "You'll be needing new clothes soon. And I think the next room we work on should be a nursery."

"Oh, Maddie," Raven said, putting her hand on the older woman's arm, "thank you for not condemning me!"

Maddie chuckled. "If I did that, I'd have to include that son of mine, now wouldn't I?"

Tears welled in Raven's eyes. She had never met anyone so totally accepting. She loved her son, trusting that whatever he had done had been for a good reason.

"Is it because he is your son that you can be so forgiving, in spite of all he has done?" Raven wondered aloud.

"That's part of it, of course. But I happen to know Jeffery is innocent of any traitorous doings. And if he was forced into piracy, it is more the fault of that despicable . . ." She jabbed the needle viciously into the seam. "I'm sorry, Raven. I know the man is your uncle, but I can't help despising Samuel Parkington for what he did to my family."

Raven sewed quietly for a few minutes. Could it all be true, after all? Was her uncle really the traitor? Even if he were and had done all Jeffery had said, did that excuse Jeffery's piracy?

"Tell me, Raven, just how did you and Jeffery meet? If you are already three months along, it must have been before he was pardoned."

Michele Stegman

"I happened to be on a Dutch merchant ship Jeffery...ah...intercepted."

Maddie's eyebrows almost disappeared under the soft waves of her blond hair. "Now *that* sounds like an interesting story."

Raven laughed and told her the whole tale, how Jeffery had captured her, how she had been frightened of him at first. But, she assured Maddie unnecessarily, he had treated her with respect and courtesy. She told Maddie how Jeffery had kept her in Tortuga and how she had begun to fall in love with him and how she made her escape. She left out only the part about Alex's seduction.

"I saw no future for us. I did not want to be anyone's mistress and marriage was never mentioned. So I made my escape."

"But when he came to Barbados and found out you were pregnant, he asked you?"

"As a matter of fact, he didn't know I was pregnant when he asked me. It was the first thing he did when he arrived in Barbados," Raven said, remembering Jeffery's first proposal.

"He must love you very much," Maddie said softly.

"Is that why he waited until I made my way to Barbados to ask me to marry him?" Raven asked, a nagging bit of suspicion still clinging that Jeffery married her only to get information about her uncle.

"But, my dear, Jeffery couldn't have married you sooner. Not without implicating you in his crimes."

Raven shook her head in puzzlement. "I don't understand."

"If you had married Jeffery, knowing he was a pirate and a condemned traitor who had escaped from slavery," Maddie explained, "you could have been tried for harboring a fugitive and implicated in any acts of piracy he committed after your marriage.

It is why he refused to let me join him on Tortuga. He didn't want me to take the risk of hanging, too."

"I never knew all that," Raven said softly.

Maddie gave a quick nod. "Neither did I until Jeffery explained it all in a letter. It was hard not to see my son all those years when I knew he was in such trouble. But I figured that I could help him best by continuing to keep his case before the court—after King James was deposed, of course."

"And that was how Jeffery finally got his pardon?"

Maddie nodded. "With the help of Sir Charles."

"Which reminds me," Raven said, putting down her sewing, "Jeffery should be back from Bridgetown soon with Sir Charles and Lieutenant Mason. I must see how Mary is coming with dinner."

Maddie reached out and caught Raven by the hand, giving it a gentle squeeze. "Pregnant or not, I'm glad Jeffery married you, my dear."

"Thank you, Maddie." Bending, she gave her mother-in-law a kiss on the cheek. As she left the room, she saw Maddie wipe a tear from her eye.

Raven smiled, urging another piece of chicken on Lieutenant Mason. That worthy officer of the king reached as delicately as his ham hands would allow to take the bowl from her, first wiping his fingers on the napkin tucked at his throat.

Jeffery had finished his meal, too excited to eat much, pushing his plate aside to lean eagerly on the table.

"The last of the supplies will be brought aboard *The Falcon* in the morning," he said to Sir Charles. "We can take her out at noon with the tide."

The smile on Raven's face remained politely in place for the sake of her guests, but it did not reach her own heart. Was Jeffery so anxious to go a-roving again? She noticed that Maddie was not eating much either, and a worried frown creased her brows.

Maddie asked the question that was also plaguing Raven. "How long will you be gone, Jeffery?"

He looked surprised at the question. "Why only two or three days." He looked from one woman to the other, patting his mother's hand and smiling reassuringly across the table to Raven. "It's only a shakedown cruise. To make sure all's well with the ship and to whip the crew back into shape." His brows arched as if with a sudden inspiration. "Why don't you and Raven come along?"

Raven's smile became a genuine one. "Could we really, Jeffery?"

His eyes, even more than his words, told her how much he wanted her with him. "I don't see why not. I will have to leave early tomorrow, but you ladies can come later with Sir Charles and Lieutenant Mason."

"Make that one lady," Maddie said. "I just spent over a month at sea. I'll stay on dry land for a while, thank you." Turning to Raven, she added, "I'll finish those yellow curtains while you're gone."

Making plans for the cruise, Raven's heart was light. They all retired early that night, and she lay within the circle of Jeffery's arms, glad that he had asked her to go with him tomorrow.

She was almost asleep when a low chuckle rumbling up from the broad chest she rested against woke her.

"I was just thinking," Jeffery said, and she could hear the teasing tone in his voice, "it will be nice having my captive back on board *The Falcon* and not have to sleep in a hammock."

"Why, Captain Fortune," Raven answered in mock horror, "surely you don't intend to ravish me once I am helpless aboard your vessel?"

He rose above her, securing her beneath him, his voice husky with desire. "Every chance I get!"

His mouth found hers in the darkness and tasted her quick response. "Perhaps I will not have to ravish this maiden. Perhaps she has finally become that 'shade more willing' and will fall breathless into my waiting arms."

Arching enticingly beneath him, Raven said, "I think, Captain Fortune, that you will find this maiden more than willing. In fact, if you don't spend a lot of time in your cabin, you may find yourself chased all over your ship!" Reaching up, she grabbed him by the hair and pulled him back down to her, before he could do aught but respond to the hunger of her mouth.

The next morning when Jeffery rose, Raven yawned and also swung her feet over the side of the bed.

"There's no need for you to rise so early, my love," Jeffery told her, fondly tousling her hair. "You don't have to leave for Bridgetown for some hours yet."

"I know," she answered, stifling another yawn. "But I want to ride over to my uncle's before we leave. There are a couple of slaves I want to check on."

Jeffery stiffened and the hand that a moment before had been playfully caressing her hair, now grasped it tightly, holding her close to him, and she wondered briefly if he would forbid her to go. "I worry about you going there," he said tightly, and she knew he was hoping she would not go. "I know he is your uncle, but you are also the wife of the man he detests."

"I haven't seen my uncle since our wedding. Yesterday, one of the overseers told me he has been gone from home for more than two weeks. So there's no need to worry about me."

His hand relaxed its grip, but the tension did not leave his eyes. "If you are late coming to Bridgetown, I'm coming back for you."

Touched by his concern for her safety, she rose and twined her arms about his neck, molding her body to his and lifting her mouth to be kissed.

He took her gift and returned it a hundredfold. Groaning, he pulled away from her. "If you keep that up, you won't have time to make your medical rounds!"

Laughing, she twirled away from him and began to dress. His eyes, she noted, never left her and she made it well worth his while to watch her, letting her nightgown fall slowly away from her shapely shoulders and slide seductively over her rounded hips before landing in a billowing heap at her feet. He groaned as she pulled her chemise over her head and tugged it over her breasts, grown even rounder and fuller since her pregnancy.

"You're a witch," he said, shoving his arms through the sleeves of his coat. "If I don't leave now, I will fall so heavily under your spell that *The Falcon* will rot at anchor ere I reach her."

Heaving an exaggerated sigh, Raven said in mock sadness to his retreating back, "So. You are leaving me for another woman."

He turned back and gathered her once more into his arms. "Never!" And his mouth once more covered hers, rousing, tormenting, promising.

It was she who finally found the strength of will to push him away, herding him out the door with a laugh. "I've a desire to see this other lady who draws you to the dock, and to sail the seas with you this day, not just warm a bed."

"And I have merely a desire," he answered. "Assuredly, we will sail the seas this day, but much of that voyage will be in a bed!"

"Your crew may wonder why they see so little of their captain," she warned.

"When they see the captain's wife, the crew will know why they see so little of their captain."

Kissing the tip of her nose, he at last left and she hurried to finish dressing.

After tending to her patients, Raven was mounting Cinnamon when she caught sight of the whipping post between the barracoons. Ever since she had learned that Jeffery had been a slave here, she could not see that post without seeing him bound. Shuddering, she turned Cinnamon toward Fortune's Fancy.

Had Jeffery suffered as a slave through no fault of his own? Would he have lied about his innocence? Now that he was pardoned, she could see no reason for him to. Unless he truly wanted to clear his father's name. And he could only do that if his story were true.

Raven shook her head. Maddie had told the same story as her son. Somehow, in spite of Jeffery's piracy, Raven had to believe the story both mother and son told. But her belief would avail Jeffery not at all. Only solid proof would stand up in court and clear his father. And where would he find any proof?

With a sudden gasp, she reined Cinnamon up short, making the chestnut mare prance. If there was any proof at all, she knew where it must be. And she could get it.

Chapter Eighteen

Glancing at the sun, Raven was assured that she still had some time before she had to leave for Bridgetown. Pulling Cinnamon's head around she leaned forward, sending the well-trained mare into a canter toward Uncle Samuel's house.

Skidding to a stop at the porch, she jumped down from the saddle and ran up the steps into the house, thankful to find it unlocked. At the door to her uncle's office, she hesitated with her hand on the latch, swallowing hard to regain her courage. If the proof she sought were truly in that desk, cluttered with a lifetime's collection of papers, did she really *want* to find it?

She shoved the thought aside as she pushed open the door. Looking over shelf after shelf of papers, boxes overflowing with papers stacked along the wall, and the overstuffed cubbyholes of the desk, she wondered where to begin her search.

Sitting at the desk, she rummaged through a few of the cubbyholes. The papers were recent ones, bills for the slaves' salted cod, receipts for sugar deliveries. Kneeling on the floor, she opened one of the boxes. More bills and receipts, a few letters, most dating back twenty years. The next box was more recent, filled with papers from fifteen years ago. There were so many boxes! So many papers!

She was beginning to feel overwhelmed. She did not have much time to search before she would have to leave for Bridgetown. But her uncle could return any day. Who knew when she would have another chance to rummage through his papers?

"Think!" she muttered, rubbing her forehead. She glanced at the two boxes she had opened. It seemed hopeless, but there was some semblance of organization. Papers of about the same time were put together. She just had to find the ones from seven years ago and look through them. Checking several boxes, she at last found the one she wanted. Every paper was dated from five to seven years ago.

She thumbed through the papers. There were bills for food, lumber, bills of sale for slaves, receipts, all pertaining to the running of her uncle's plantation. There was nothing incriminating.

Disappointed, she was about to shove the box back into place when it dawned on her that she had seen not one single paper in the box concerning Fortune's Fancy. She looked through them again. Every paper was for her uncle's plantation. None were for Jeffery's. Her uncle had been given the king's commission to run the neighboring plantation. Where were the bills and receipts for Fortune's Fancy?

The king's commission! Her uncle had showed it to her once. She scrambled across the floor to open the lower drawer in her uncle's desk. There was the box where he had kept the commission. With trembling hands, she opened it.

Paper after paper dealing with Fortune's Fancy sifted through her fingers, most of them for the sale of slaves or other moveable properties. She rifled through the entire box, all the way to the bottom. Nothing.

Raven bit her lip in disappointment. What had she expected, after all? She started to replace the papers when her eye caught something. The bottom of the box was uneven. She pushed on one corner and was surprised to see it lift at the other corner. The bottom was not a bottom at all, but a close-fitting piece of wood placed over more papers to form a poor false bottom. Removing it, she lifted out a sheaf of papers and with trembling fingers began to read.

"To The Gentleman from Barbados," it began. One after another bore that salutation. There were letters of thanks for information and information the "Gentleman" was asked to pass on. There were troop movements, lists of supplies, places, dates. The last was a list of code names. Next to "The Gentleman from Barbados" was listed the name of Samuel Parkington.

She let the sheaf of papers fall into her lap, and buried her face in her hands. *How the mighty are fallen*, she thought. *I was once haughty enough to set myself far above Jeffery Fortune, traitor, pirate, slave. Now it seems that the guilt for his crimes must rest on my own family. He knew the truth all along, yet he did not spurn me as I would have spurned him.*

If there had been any doubt that Jeffery was innocent of treason, it was gone now. If he had been a slave, it was through no fault of his own.

She clutched the papers. But no one had forced him to turn pirate, she thought. He might have had to escape slavery to survive, but did he have to become a pirate? To prey on the helpless? There was much that Jeffery Fortune was unjustly accused of. But there was also much for which he could be held accountable.

Raven looked at the papers in her hand. What should she do with them? If she gave them to Jeffery, he would certainly use them to prove his father's and his own innocence. What then would happen to Uncle Samuel? Would he be tried, condemned, hanged? Or would a crime of treason against a king who had later been deposed by Parliament still be considered a crime? Could she let these documents be used to salve the pride of a former pirate and a man long dead and take the chance that it would mean her uncle's death? Was a pirate's pride so important, even if that pirate was her husband? Even if she bore the same stained name?

She shoved the papers deep into her medical bag. *I'll decide later*, she thought. *After I think about it, maybe I'll know what to do*. After straightening the desk, she took her leave of the cluttered office. The hour was growing late and she would have to hurry.

When she arrived at Fortune's Fancy, she found the carriage ready and waiting, her small trunk already strapped on the back. Giving Cinnamon into the care of Jenkins, she said her good morning to Sir Charles and Lieutenant Mason, and the lieutenant helped her into the carriage.

She sat next to Sir Charles, facing Lieutenant Mason. Her medical bag rested on her lap and it was almost as if those incriminating documents burned her hands through the leather of her kit.

Here is your chance, she told herself. *An officer of the king sits before you. In one moment you could put these papers into his hand and clear the Fortune name. Of treason, never piracy*, she reminded herself. But at what cost to her and hers? Clenching her teeth, she put the bag on the floor and kicked it under the seat.

* * *

Jeffery was waiting for them aboard *The Falcon*, dressed for the sea in a white shirt open at the throat and rolled to the elbows, a red leather baldrick cutting diagonally across his chest to support a saber at his hip. The ends of his red silk sash fluttered in the breeze and he leaned his arm across his knee, one booted foot resting on the railing.

For a moment, Raven could imagine herself back on Tortuga, about to be taken aboard this pirate's vessel. Then Jeffery saw her and waved, a broad grin of happiness on his face.

It's where he belongs, she thought, and remembered that his father had been a sea captain, too.

When she walked up the gangplank onto *The Falcon*, Jeffery greeted her as warmly as he had parted from her. A twinge of guilt tweaked her conscience but she ignored it.

"Shall I bring this, Mrs. Fortune?"

She looked down to the dock. Lieutenant Mason was holding up her medical bag with its cargo of guilt. It was ironic, she thought. The king's officer already held in his hand the means to clear Jeffery. But neither of them knew it. Should she let him bring the bag and the papers along? Or would it seem suspicious if she left behind the bag she usually took with her everywhere? Suspicious? Already she was feeling like a criminal. Why should she feel this guilt? She was guilty of nothing.

"I...I..."

"Bring it along, Lieutenant," Jeffery answered for her. He looked down at her with a fond smile, his arm around her shoulder. "We can always use a good doctor aboard."

When Lieutenant Mason came on deck, he held out the bag to Raven. She started to take it but curled her fingers away as if its contents would burn her hand. She smiled sweetly at the lieutenant. "Would you put it in the captain's cabin for me?"

The lieutenant moved off and she shivered.

"Chilled?" Jeffery asked worriedly.

She shook her head. "No. Just excited. About the voyage, I guess."

"So am I," he said, bending to whisper in her ear, "though for a different cause. 'Tis your nearness."

She turned to smile at him, but his attention was already on his ship, calling orders to get underway. The gangplank was hauled in, and *The Falcon* was edged away from the dock with sweeps. Sails were set, there was a fair breeze, and they soon cleared Carlisle Bay.

Raven leaned on the ornately carved quarterdeck railing to watch Jeffery as he bounded from one end of his ship to the other, full of life and joy. Lending a hand, hauling on a sheet, or standing beside her on the quarterdeck nudging the whipstaff a little to the right or the left as the wind shifted, his was a contagious kind of vitality. She could not help but smile proudly as she watched him, sensing that he was master of his element.

When Barbados lay astern, Jeffery began putting his ship and his men through their paces, tacking, coming about, sending the men scurrying up and down the ratlines as if, in truth, their lives depended on the speed of their maneuvers.

It was on the starboard tack, when the strain on the mizzenmast was greatest, that a crack sounded so loud that, at first, Raven thought someone had fired a gun. But if she were puzzled by the sound, Jeffery was not. At his instant order, the bonnets were let go to shorten sail and he leaped to lend a hand himself. The ship slowed, and the crew gathered to assess the damage to the mizzenmast.

Michele Stegman

Jeffery ran his hands over the mast, sending men aloft and below decks to check it. Ed, the ship's carpenter, made his report.

" 'Tis not so bad as it sounded, Cap'n. The mast itself is still sound. 'Twas the mast step that cracked. I'd say she could still carry a bit of sail in an emergency, but I'd hate to risk it until that support can be repaired."

"How long to make a repair, Ed?" Jeffery asked.

Ed shrugged. "In port, two days. Out here, it can be makeshift at best."

Jeffery nodded and clapped Ed on the shoulder. "Do what you can, then. After a little gunnery practice in the morning, we'll head for Bridgetown. 'Tis late today, at any rate. Joe, dismiss the men to their supper. And issue an extra ration of rum. They did well today."

"Is it serious?" Raven asked, coming up behind him.

He smiled to set her at ease and put his arm about her shoulders. "Nothing that cannot be set to rights. Tomorrow we shall have a bit of gunnery practice and then head home," Jeffery told Raven as he led her down to dinner.

"Where will you find a Dutch merchantman to practice on?" she asked, looking up at him mischievously.

" 'Tis not the Dutch I'll be seeking, but the French," he said, giving her a squeeze.

"I will worry about you when you go off privateering, Jeffery," she said seriously, leaning on his arm.

"I am right glad to hear it, though you may be assured that I'll have a care. I've more to come home to now than ever I had before." Briefly, he took her into his arms and kissed her before he opened the cabin door.

Sir Charles and Lieutenant Mason had preceded them to the cabin, and the lieutenant was already making inroads into the decanter of wine that Rodney had set out. A few drops had spilled on his rumpled cravat and he brushed at them ineffectively.

They were well into their meal when Jeffery informed Sir Charles and Lieutenant Mason that tomorrow he would begin gunnery practice.

"Glad I am to be on this side of your cannon, Captain," the lieutenant said, his voice muffled by the roll he was chewing. "The skill of your gunners is well known in the Caribbean. I must admit to a few moments of unease when your ship hove to in Carlisle Bay and us with no warships to protect us and our fort still in a state to be of little service. It was a great relief to me to see the pardon dangling from your hand and to know you're now on our side."

"It is no less a relief to me, Lieutenant," Jeffery said with a chuckle. "Piracy is not a very pleasant occupation."

"Then why did you turn to it so readily?" Raven asked.

Jeffery looked at his wife in puzzlement. "What else could a condemned criminal do? No English port was safe for me nor would I have been welcome in a Spanish one. Only Tortuga offered a refuge. And to live there, there is but one occupation to support a man."

"Yet one that seemed to suit you well enough when I saw you at it," Raven added.

Jeffery shrugged. "One makes the best of what he has."

"You certainly made the most of your piracy. To become a captain of your own ship in such a short time seems to me to be no mean accomplishment. Was it because you fit so well into the mold of buccaneer?" She threw the words at him, a challenge he was not loath to accept.

"There are many advantages to being the captain of one's own ship. I at least had some control over the rapacity of my crew. I could make sure that as few lives as possible were taken. And with a captain's larger share, I could make fewer voyages."

Raven stirred the peas around on her plate, her resentment of his past piracy for the time allayed. It was true that he had treated her with courtesy and the Dutch crew had fared better since they met up with Jeffery. Van Doorn seemed quite happy commanding one of Jeffery's ships.

"If you will excuse me, my dear," Sir Charles said, rising from the table and bowing, "I will take my leave of you."

Grabbing a last hunk of cake, Lieutenant Mason also left, and Raven rose to look out the stern windows while Rodney cleared the table. She heard Rodney leave and the bolt lock the door. It did not take Jeffery long to cross the cabin to encircle her with his arms.

"Is something wrong, Raven?" he asked, nuzzling deep into the dark waves of her hair.

Raven bit her lip. *Aye*, she wanted to cry out. *You were a pirate, even if you had little choice. Now I hold the means to clear your name but I know not what to do.* She saw her medical bag stowed in one of the sections under the window seat. In an agony of indecision, she turned away from the sight of it, forcing a smile to the lips she lifted to be kissed until her mind forgot all else but his touch.

Grinding her hips into his, she lifted her brows in a look of innocence, saying, "Should I not be concerned, Captain Fortune? I heard the bolt lock us in. Though you vow you try to keep the rapaciousness of your crew in check, I fear that it does not apply to you. Already I can see the lust growing in your eyes."

" 'Tis not the only place it is growing," he growled, placing his hands on her buttocks to press her hard against him. "I give warning now to this pretty maid who pretends such innocence—I will sleep in no hammock this night."

She twined her arms about his neck. "I was hoping you would say that, Captain."

Lifting her into his arms, he carried her to the bed in which she had slept alone and fearful of what she now looked forward to with great anticipation.

Laying her down, he made short work of her clothes. His followed quickly and he sought the silkiness of her skin. Matching every part of her with every part of him, he urged her into a duet of love.

A warmth blossomed in her loins and, like a flower opening to the rays of the tropic sun, she welcomed him within her, arching to meet his desire with her own. The heat continued to build in wave after wave that had little to do with the temperature of the sultry night. His hand was a brand upon her, his mouth a fire, searing her throat and her pink-peaked breast. His ardent kisses were a scorching, unquenchable flame igniting the dry kindling of her need.

They clung to each other as want answered want, need answered need, and their passion erupted in a volcanic blaze flowing over them. At last sated, their desire banked to a controllable smolder, they slept, wearing no other wrapping than each other's arms.

Jeffery kissed her to wakefulness, the sun's morning rays a golden blanket over her creamy skin. She turned into the pillows to burrow back to sleep but his tongue on her spine was a lash, rousing her. Groaning, she curled into a ball, but his hand kneaded the smooth roundness of her buttocks and found the secret place between them. She turned and straightened, lifting her arms above her head in a languid stretch and he carried his attack to new territory—the mounds of her breasts and the dark delta that so invited his touch.

Dropping her arms onto his shoulders, she tugged him onto her, urging quick completion of that which had caused her waking. But he held back, taunting, teasing, tormenting, until, unable to contain her desire, she pushed him onto his back and rose over him, coming down upon him. In smug satisfaction, she rode him, teasing him in turn until neither could hold back the tide that rose within them. Surging, cresting, they were lost in a whirling vortex until he moaned beneath her, shuddering at last in release.

Propping her head on her hand, she looked down at him. "That, my pirate captain, will teach you not to meddle with an innocent maiden in your power."

"I think, fair maid, that I am as much your captive as you are mine. Mayhap we can strike a bargain."

"Now that you are helpless beneath me you are willing to bargain," she chided, pulling at the golden strands of hair curling on his chest.

With a growl, he grabbed her and rolled on top to capture her. She yelped and struggled but he held her easily. Grinning down at her, he kissed her face, saying, "Now will you bargain?"

"What bargain do you offer, buccaneer?" she asked, laughing.

"I promise never to make love to you more than ten times a day if you promise the same."

She chewed her lip a moment as if in thought then

looked up at him forlornly. "Does that mean no more than a total of twenty times a day?"

"Insatiable wench!" he said, getting up and smacking her bottom playfully. "Out of bed with you!"

They dressed with many a playful pat and pinch between them. Jeffery opened the door to Rodney bringing them a breakfast tray.

Raven sat at the table and nibbled a croissant, and Jeffery nibbled at her fingers. When Jeffery got up to leave, she again caught sight of her medical bag under the window seat and a pang of guilt shot through her. But could she give those documents to Jeffery if it meant that her uncle would hang?

"Jeffery?"

He stopped with his hand on the latch and turned back to her.

Chewing her lip, she asked, "If you succeed in proving that my uncle was the traitor and not your father, would Uncle Samuel hang?"

His brow clouded. "Probably not, more's the pity!"

Hope sprang into her heart. "Why not? Your father was hanged."

"My father was condemned under King James. That tyrant was deposed three years later when the rest of the country had at last had a bellyful of him. I doubt that anyone who stood against him in '85 would be condemned now."

"I see." Raven's eyes strayed to the bag and she started to speak when they were interrupted by the lookout's call.

"Sail ho!"

Jeffery bounded up the companionway two steps at a time, calling, "Where away?"

Raven was not far behind and found Jeffery with a foot braced on the ship's rail, a telescope in hand.

For long moments he studied the distant ship. Sir Charles stood by his side.

"Can you make her out?" Sir Charles asked.

Jeffery put down the telescope, snapping it shut. "She's still hull down and she flies no flag."

"Pirate, do you think?" Sir Charles asked with concern.

" 'Tis not likely in these waters."

"Why not, Jeffery?"

He turned to her with a reassuring grin. "Barbados is too far out of the way and there's naught here but sugar merchants. The pickings are better outside a Spanish port. The Spanish have a liking for shipping gold and silver bullion."

"I'm sure you would know about these things, Captain," she said archly. But today her tone was less barbed, and her words were accompanied by a disarming smile.

"Aye, I do," he admitted, turning back to study the ship. "But even if I'm wrong and she's pirate, I doubt she would attack a well-armed frigate. There would be little profit in it."

"Sail ho!"

"Another one?" Jeffery called aloft.

"Aye, sir."

Jeffery again lifted his glass. Raven shaded her eyes and could just make out the top of a second vessel, closely following the first.

"They've spotted us, Captain," the lookout called. "They've changed course to intercept us."

A puzzled frown creased Jeffery's brow. "Now why . . ."

Raven moved closer to Jeffery. If he was puzzled, so was she. She could think of no reason why a ship would want to intercept them this close to land. In mid-ocean, two or three weeks from the nearest port, vessels would sail close and exchange news and letters. But here, only a few hours from either Barbados, St. Vincent, St. Lucia, or several other islands, there was usually only one reason for a ship to change its course to intercept another vessel. Attack.

"Could they be French warships?" she asked, trying to steady her voice.

Jeffery did not answer, but continued to peer through his glass, leaning over the rail as if that would make it easier for him to see the lines of the two ships bearing down on them.

Lieutenant Mason shuffled up behind Sir Charles, a buttered croissant in his hand and crumbs on his cravat. "What's to do?"

"Two ships heading for us, Lieutenant," Sir Charles explained. "They changed course to intercept us, but we've no idea who they are."

"Frenchies, d'ye think?"

Sir Charles only shrugged.

Raven watched Jeffery, waiting for his report. She saw him stiffen. When he turned to look at them, his face was grim and winter shards of ice had invaded his eyes.

"DeLessops!"

Chapter Nineteen

DeLessops!

When Raven heard that dreaded name, the memory of her capture came back to her. His evil eyes leering at her, his grimy finger tracing along the scoop of her gown while she was helplessly bound to the mast. Then, in Tortuga, it was he whom Jeffery had fought to save her. He, who had sworn vengeance on Jeffery Fortune. Her knees suddenly felt weak and her hands trembled. Jeffery's arm came around her waist to steady her and give her strength.

"Methinks I've heard that name," Lieutenant Mason mused.

"Well you should as an officer of the law," Jeffery said to him. " 'Tis a name that is infamous from Panama to Port of Spain, from Nassau to Cartagena. Through the length and breadth of the Caribbean, the depravity of his deeds would shame even those of L'Ollinais."

"But why is he coming after us?" Sir Charles asked, looking with renewed interest at the approaching ships. "As you pointed out, there is little for a pirate to gain in attacking a well-armed ship when there is no chance of a profitable cargo."

" 'Tis not cargo or riches that marauding minion

of hell is seeking," Jeffery said grimly, "but vengeance!"

"Egad!" Lieutenant Mason gulped, nearly dropping the croissant he had pulled from his pocket. "You don't mean to say he's going to attack us to settle some old score with you?"

"I mean precisely that," Jeffery answered. He smiled at Raven but it was hardly a reassuring smile. It was more of a grim twisting of his lips, and his eyes had frozen into chilling chips of ice.

"Is there any chance of outrunning them?" Sir Charles asked, looking up at the full, billowing sails above him.

"Ordinarily, I would say yes," Jeffery answered. "But with that cracked mast step, our sailing speed will be severely diminished. Besides, you will note that *The Demon* is directly between us and Bridgetown."

"Then we must fight," Sir Charles stated calmly.

"Aye," Jeffery said softly, looking into Raven's eyes, a worried frown clouding his brow. "We must fight."

"But what chance have we?" Lieutenant Mason sputtered. "We're one crippled ship against two sound ones!"

"That is true," Jeffery said, again returning to his study of the approaching ships. "But we may find some advantage yet."

"Advantage! What advantage can you find in this situation?" the king's officer yelped. "We cannot sail and we cannot maneuver!"

"DeLessops has ever been negligent in the maintenance of his ship," Jeffery said, squinting through the telescope. "Do you note how labored she is sailing?"

349

The lieutenant shook his head. "I do not remark it, sir."

" 'Tis my guess *The Demon* is long overdue for a careening. A barnacle-befouled bottom is as cumbersome as a sea anchor. And too, *The Demon* may be larger than *The Falcon* and carry more sail, but this ship has sleeker lines and has just been careened."

"If she carries more sail, she probably carries more guns as well," the lieutenant remarked in dismay.

"She does," Jeffery said. "But they are not as new as mine or as heavy. And we have one other advantage," he said, finishing his survey of the approaching enemy. "*The Falcon* rides lower in the water. De-Lessops will be sending a lot of shots into our rigging, which is not much help to us anyway. While I shall be aiming at his hull—at the waterline. Gentlemen, if you will excuse me, I have work to do. DeLessops will be in range within the half-hour.

"Rodney! Barnes! Clear for action! Run out the guns!"

Jeffery's orders brought a flurry of action from his well-disciplined crew. Sabers and pistols began to appear, and someone handed Jeffery his weapons.

"Helmsman! Bring her two points to starboard!"

"Two points to starboard!" Lieutenant Mason yelped, tugging at Jeffery's sleeve. "Are you mad? That will put us right between them!"

Jeffery shook off the lieutenant's hand. "And on a direct heading for Bridgetown. They mean to catch us in a crossfire anyway. They will not be expecting me to sail into it—and through it. If we can hold our own for the exchange of a few shots, we will be past them. They will have to come about before they can fire on us again. In that time, I hope to put a few miles between us. The closer we can get to Bridgetown, the less likely they are to close in on us again. They may not know there are no British warships to come to our aid."

" 'Tis a risky plan," Lieutenant Mason worried.

"Do you have a better one?" Jeffery snapped.

"Can I help?" Sir Charles asked. "I was quite a swordsman in my day. I'll not shirk a fight."

"I thank you, sir. If it comes to that, if they board us, we will need every hand."

"My sword is in my cabin, I think," Lieutenant Mason stammered. "I'll go and look for it."

Jeffery pulled Raven close to him as the lieutenant went off in search of his elusive sword. "I want you to stay below, love. Sir Charles, will you stay with her?"

"Jeffery, I—"

"Shh, my love. DeLessops shall not have you while there is yet breath in my body."

Did he not understand? It was for him she feared the most. She leaned against him, savoring his hard strength, taking comfort from his calmness.

Kissing her long and lingeringly, Jeffery gave her into Sir Charles's keeping and the two of them went below, leaving Jeffery to do battle.

"Are we really going to run straight into their teeth, Cap'n?" Rodney asked.

Jeffery tore his eyes away from the trim figure of his wife disappearing down the companionway. A cocky smile spread over his face and a twinkle leaped into his eyes as if he anticipated the battle ahead. "Aye, Rodney. But mayhap we can knock some of those teeth out before we're caught in them. Load the forward guns with grape. But hold your fire until I give the order."

"Seems we'll get a bit more target practice than we planned, eh, Cap'n?" Rodney said as he hurried off to give Jeffery's orders to the gunners.

Standing at the bow, Jeffery saw the puffs of smoke from DeLessops's cannons and laughed as he heard the sound of shots and watched DeLessops's angry efforts fall far short of Jeffery's ship. "That's it, DeLessops," he whispered. "Spend your shot and overheat your guns before we're even in range. You always were one to let your anger control your sense."

There was a pause of several minutes while De-Lessops let his guns cool and reloaded. The next shots found them well within range, but went wide of their mark.

"Their next shot'll find us, Cap'n," Rodney warned.

"Nay, Rodney. They'll not have time for another shot from their forward guns before we're abreast of them."

"But there's nothin' wrong with the rest of their guns," Rodney worried. "I've no liking to be caught between a double broadside."

"Then let's pull a few of those teeth! Mr. Barnes!" Jeffery called to his chief gunner. "Aim the forward guns at their gun deck. Wait until I give the order to fire."

Long, quiet moments passed aboard The Falcon with the only sound a muttered, "What the 'ell's the cap'n waitin' for? They're so close now I could spit on 'em!"

"Now, Mr. Barnes!"

The Falcon's guns thundered devastation into the gun decks of the two attacking ships. Moments later The Falcon was between its attackers and loosed a broadside into each of them. A few answering shots from DeLessops's two ships thudded into The Falcon's hull and skimmed through the rigging. One further shot was exchanged by their stern chasers as they passed, causing little damage to anyone, then *The Falcon* was in the clear.

Jeffery's crew gave a lusty cheer and Jeffery joined them, though he knew that the battle was far from over. DeLessops would waste no time coming about and giving chase. He had taken some damage to both vessels, but if Jeffery were any judge, the man would only consider it a further insult to be avenged. There was little time to be lost before the next attack.

"Mr. Leach, check below for damages. Mr. Alden, see if you can rig a patch on the foremast mainsail. We're losing too much wind through that hole. Mr. Henderson, clear that dangling foreyard. Any wounded?"

A swirl of blue silk at the head of the companionway caught his eye, and he went to meet Raven. She clutched at him, pressing her trembling body close to him.

"I had to see for myself that you were all right. Is it over?"

"No," he whispered, inhaling the fragrance of her hair, a welcome relief to the acrid sting of gunpowder. "They'll come about and give chase."

She lifted her head from his chest. "Was anyone wounded?"

He shook his head.

"I'll set up a sick bay," she said, and he could feel her trembling cease as the cool head of a battle-experienced surgeon took control. "We may not be so lucky the next pass."

"Thank you, Raven."

She headed for the companionway then turned back. "Jeffery, be careful. I'd not like to number you among my patients."

He gave her a smile full of cheer he was not feeling and a pat on her bottom as she went below.

Reassured that Jeffery had not been wounded, Raven returned to the cabin for her medical bag. Lieutenant Mason, who had at last found his sword and elected to stay below to protect her, jumped when she entered. Sir Charles, in shirtsleeves and vest, was buckling on a sword he had found.

"I'm going to set up a sick bay," she told them.

Sir Charles nodded. "You will probably be safer there, my dear. Those two ships are closing fast and the stern of *The Falcon* will be their first target," Sir Charles said, nodding toward the stern windows where DeLessops's ships could be seen all too close. "I am going up on deck, Raven, but I shall station myself at the head of the companionway. If they board us, I shall come down to you."

"Do have a care, Sir Charles," she pleaded, placing a hand on his arm.

Giving her hand a squeeze, he left. Lieutenant Mason blushed, fumbling with his sword. "I . . . I think I'll go help him."

Raven bent to get her medical bag and froze, mesmerized by the sight of the two ships bearing down on them. Shaking her head, she took her bag and left the cabin. Raven found the room she had previously used as a sick bay when last aboard. The six narrow cots lining the wall were freshly made. She checked the surgical instruments, rearranging them into a more convenient order, and laid out bandages and sutures.

The room was quickly set into an order that even Raven approved of. Then there was nothing more to do until the next attack. She looked around, searching for something more to occupy her but there was nothing. She rearranged the instruments again, and then again, trying not to listen for the roar of cannon, the crashing of timbers, the thudding of shot. Squeezing her eyes shut, she leaned her head against the wall and clenched her fists to keep from trembling—or screaming. The waiting was so hard!

She lifted her head and took a deep breath. The brief engagement had been far worse, with the ship lurching, never knowing if the next moment a cannonball would come crashing through the wall. Never knowing if Jeffery were alive or dead.

What if DeLessops should prevail? she wondered. Jeffery had told her that that scourge should not come near her while there was breath in his body, but what if Jeffery were killed? She fingered a scalpel, razor-sharp and shining. It would be far better, she thought, to use it on herself than to fall into those grimy claws again.

Shaking, she put the scalpel back into its place. As wise as that decision might be, she was not certain she could carry it out.

That was when she heard the first cannon. Answering fire was not long in coming. The ship shuddered as the shot found its mark, nearly knocking her off her feet. Biting her hand to suppress a scream, she sat on one of the bunks, her medical bag cradled in her arms. She wished she had something to do besides wait and listen to the sounds of battle, the sounds of feet running overhead, cannons, shouts. It seemed to go on forever.

There was a grating, crunching sound and she heard the shouted call, "Prepare to repel boarders!" and she knew that DeLessops had pulled alongside. Even now grappling lines would be thrown, and savage, half-naked pirates would be surging onto *The Falcon*'s deck. Once again fingering the scalpel, Raven could only pray that Jeffery's greatly outnumbered crew could somehow, miraculously, defeat DeLessops.

Michele Stegman

* * *

When Raven disappeared below, Jeffery turned his attention to the ships following him. With them coming up fast astern, sick bay was the safest place for Raven. He put the glass to his eye again, studying the oncoming ships for any weakness he could use to his own advantage but could find none. With the damaged mizzenmast step, he could not even outrun those barnacle-belabored ships.

Snapping the glass shut, he ordered the stern chasers loaded with solid shot and aimed at DeLessops's waterline. A good hit there might slow him down enough for *The Falcon* to show them a clean pair of heels. It would be a difficult shot with only the narrow, pointed bow as a target. He would have to wait until they were well within range and his own ship in danger even from DeLessops's indifferent gunners.

Even after DeLessops came into range, her guns kept silent. "Learned a bit of a lesson, did ye, DeLessops? Do ye think to use your guns to better affect this time?" Turning to Mr. Barnes, Jeffery said, "Take careful aim, sir. I want a shot right at her waterline. See if you can't scrape off some of those barnacles for him!"

"Aye, aye, Cap'n!" Grinning, Barnes knelt to his gun, checking the distance and the elevation. Then, with a smoldering slow match held on a linstock, he sighted along the barrel for a full minute, before laying the match to the vents of both stern chasers.

There was an explosion of sound and Jeffery had his glass to his eye before the smoke cleared enough to see.

Barnes peered at their target, straining to see if their shot had been good. "Cap'n?" Barnes asked, but he knew the news was not good when his captain put down his glass and he saw his face.

"A hit, Mr. Barnes, but a glancing one. She's shipping water, but not enough to slow her sufficiently. We'll soon have company aboard, I'm afraid."

Barnes had never seen his captain so worried and he wondered if it was because his wife was aboard or because their situation was really as desperate as it seemed. True, the captain had pulled them out of some tight spots, but Barnes could see no way out of this one. Barnes looked to his guns. It would be some minutes yet before they were cool enough to reload. When he looked back at Captain Fortune, he was heartened to see the old look of cocky self-assurance. Maybe things were not so dark after all. Maybe the cap'n could pull 'em through again.

Though Jeffery put on a good face to encourage his crew, he was far from feeling the confidence he showed. Two sound ships against one crippled one were not odds to his liking. DeLessops was close enough now that Jeffery could see his men hanging from the rigging, anxious to board, and could hear their shouts. The foreward guns of *The Demon* and her fellow ship sang out at once and *The Falcon* shuddered from the blows. Splinters of wood flew in all directions.

Jeffery grinned. "Now that they've used their foreward guns, let's swing around and give 'em a good broadside!"

Sails were turned and before DeLessops could guess their intent, *The Falcon* swung sideways across the path of the oncoming vessels and poured a devastating broadside into them. DeLessops's flagship, *The Demon*, suffered the most damage but was now close enough to throw grappling lines.

"Prepare to repel boarders!" Jeffery called to his crew.

Grappling lines were cut and pistols were kept

busy, but boarding a ship was a trade well known to DeLessops and his crew. His second ship grappled onto the other side of *The Falcon*, and pirates began to overrun Jeffery's crew.

Jeffery hacked at the lines with his crew, running through one overanxious boarder who attacked him.

Distant guns thundered, and DeLessops's ship lurched into *The Falcon* with a crunch of breaking timbers.

Sword in hand, Jeffery leaped to the railing for a better view of the distant vessel that had fired the shot. A broad grin spread itself across his face. "Alex!" Never had the sight of *The Brigand*'s widespread sails looked so good!

DeLessops's ship was now crippled and taking water, but his second ship was in better circumstance, having been sheltered from Alex's guns by both *The Demon* and *The Falcon*. Having more sense than courage, her captain cut the lines binding her to *The Falcon* and warped away, setting her sails to run while she could still get away.

The Demon was sinking and DeLessops's crew threw curses at their fellow ship which had abandoned them to a fight they now had little chance of winning.

The Brigand's guns continued to tear at *The Demon* until, by the time Alex's ship came alongside, there was little left of DeLessops's ship. Her remaining crew now leaped to *The Falcon* as much for refuge as for the fight which had now turned against them. They desperately fought hand to hand with Jeffery's crew. Their only chance was to win a ship to replace the one they'd lost.

Alex nosed his ship into the bow of *The Falcon*, and his crew began pouring aboard to join the fight. Alex came, cutting a path to Jeffery's side, where the fighting was the heaviest.

With his friend fighting back to back with him, Jeffery soon found the battle easier going. "What took you so long?" he asked, grinning over his shoulder at Alex.

" 'Tis a long sail from Tortuga!" Alex answered, shrugging and smiling his lopsided smile as if this were but a pleasant afternoon's exercise.

DeLessops's crew, what was left of it, was pushed back and cornered at the stern, but they still fought on since surrender meant hanging. In a last, desperate bid for victory, DeLessops drew a pistol and took careful aim at Jeffery. In the split second before he fired, another shot rang out and a feminine scream shattered the air.

DeLessops saw Jeffery go down and saw the smoking pistol in Alex's hand only a moment before he realized that that pistol had sent him to his death. The last thing he saw was his own blood pooling on the deck.

Unable any longer to huddle in sick bay, Raven made her way to the forward companionway. She had to assure herself that Jeffery was still alive. The sounds of fighting were coming from the stern and it should not be too dangerous for her to peek out the forward hatch, she thought. Her hand trembling on the latch, she forced herself to a calmness she did not feel. Opening the hatch, Raven swept the deck with her eyes, searching, with heart-stopping anxiety, for that one, tall, golden form. Jeffery's back was to her as he swung his saber, plowing his way into that attacking horde. A second familiar and well-loved form fought by Jeffery's side, and, with a start, she recognized Alex, wondering where he had come from. But she could have wept with relief. If Alex were here, surely the odds would be more in their favor.

The fighting was becoming more ragged as De-Lessops's crew was pushed farther and farther toward the stern. That was when she saw DeLessops. He was pulling out a pistol, aiming it at ... She screamed and her scream became one with the shots that rang out.

Lifting her skirts, Raven flew across the deck, but to her, it was like a nightmare. Her legs were leaden, the length of the deck seemed to stretch endlessly before her, and Jeffery crumpled in an agonizing slowness, a red blotch spreading on his chest.

"Dear God, no!" she cried. And in that moment of uncertainty before she reached his side, while she ran the length of that endless deck, Raven knew beyond any doubt that she loved Jeffery. It no longer mattered what he was or had been. Even if his crimes had been entirely of his own doing and his piracy taken up with eager hands, it did not matter. What mattered to her at this moment was that Jeffery yet lived, that he would hold her in his arms yet another time, that he would someday smile into the face of the child she carried.

Kneeling at Jeffery's side, she cared not that DeLessops's disheartened crew were now throwing down their arms, that DeLessops lay dead in a pool of his own blood, that the battle was won. It only mattered that Jeffery live and that he know she loved him wholly and unconditionally.

Alex knelt on the other side of Jeffery. "Is he ..."

Raven touched Jeffery's neck to feel for his pulse. It was there, strong and steady. Her hands tore at Jeffery's shirt, frantic to expose the wound.

Jeffery moaned and his eyes fluttered open. His eyes

focused on Raven and he smiled.

"Thank God!" Alex said.

Pausing, Raven looked at Alex, his pistol still smoking in his hand. "Thank *you*," she said.

She returned to her work, carefully examining the wound. The bullet had passed completely through Jeffery's shoulder, missing the lung by a fraction of an inch. There was little for her to do but staunch the bleeding and apply a bandage.

"I knew I was lucky to have a doctor aboard," Jeffery rasped, struggling to sit up.

Lieutenant Mason and Sir Charles had come up and now helped him lean against the mast, but Raven pushed him back when she saw him start to stand.

"This is as far as you go until you are *carried* to your bed, Jeffery Fortune," she said in a tone that brooked no argument.

"Bed?" Jeffery laughed, but the laugh was weak and he winced.

"Bed! For at least a week."

Jeffery grinned up at her. "Only if the good doctor comes with me."

"You're incorrigible!" she chided. She moved closer to him and her eyes grew soft. She would wait no longer to tell him how she felt. "Oh, Jeffery, I love you so."

He gasped, joy leaped into his eyes, and he reached for her. His hand trembled and she knew not whether it was from his wound or from the emotion she saw stirring in his face at her first declaration of her love for him. He pulled her to him and they shared a kiss, brief, but full of promise.

Alex had left to see to DeLessops's crew and to salvage what he could from *The Demon* before she sank. He came across the deck toward them now, and Raven's eyes widened when she saw who he was dragging along by the scruff of his neck.

"I fished this rat out of the bilge of *The Demon*," he said, giving the man a shake.

"Parkington!"

"Uncle Samuel! What are you doing aboard DeLessops's ship?"

"Trying to bring an untimely end to the Fortune family," Alex answered. "DeLessops was recruiting men and a second ship when I was on Tortuga. It took very few questions to find out what he was up to. He and Parkington made little effort to keep their plans secret."

"You, Uncle?" Raven asked unable to believe what she was hearing. "In league with a pirate?"

"Not 'in league,' Raven," Alex said. "Your uncle was the instigator of the whole enterprise. He came to Tortuga to seek out enemies of Captain Fortune, to hire them to lie in wait outside Carlisle Bay to attack the unsuspecting *Falcon* when it emerged. It did not take him long to find DeLessops. I was on my way to warn you, Jeff, when I heard the sounds of the battle."

"Uncle Samuel," Raven said, a frown of disbelief on her face, "can this be true?"

"Of course it's true, you twit!" her uncle snarled. "I've been trying to get rid of the Fortunes for years. But someone always comes along to interfere." He nodded toward Alex. "Just like that fool judge seven years ago. He hung the father but only transported the cub. Said the letters I planted were not evidence enough to condemn him, too!"

"Then it's true!" Sir Charles stepped forward. "My apologies, my boy," he said to Jeffery. "There has always been just a shadow of a doubt that the story

you and your mother told was true. But Parkington's
as much as confessed to it!"

Jeffery leaned back, content. "Then my father's
name will at last be cleared!"

"Maybe, maybe not," Lieutenant Mason said, his
hand bravely rattling his sheathed saber. "A confession such as that, uttered in anger and in haste, may
not hold up in court. We've witnesses enough to his
act of piracy against a ship commissioned by the
king, but I think you will need further proof of his
former crimes."

"Oh!" Raven exclaimed, suddenly remembering
the papers stowed in the bottom of the medical bag
at her feet. Jerking the bag open, she pulled out the
papers. There was no longer any doubt in her mind
or her heart as to just where these papers belonged.
Her heart pounding, her hands trembling, she placed
the bundle in Jeffery's hand. "I found these in Uncle
Samuel's desk," she said. "I think you will find
enough evidence there to clear your father's name
and to convict my uncle of the crimes he tried to
blame on the Fortunes—*our* family."

Puzzled, Jeffery scanned the papers, his eyes widening, his lips setting into a satisfied line. Silently,
he handed the papers to Lieutenant Mason.

That worthy officer of the law looked them over,
nodding. "Solid proof enough!" he declared.

"You wretched—" Her uncle jumped at her, his
hands curved into claws, but Sir Charles and the
lieutenant grabbed him, hustling him away to join
DeLessops's crew in the brig.

His eyes shining, Jeffery took Raven's hand in his,
lifting it to kiss her fingers. "Thank you, Raven. I
know what giving me those papers must have cost
you. To have sacrificed your own family name for
mine."

She placed her fingers across his lips to silence him. "I gave up my family name for yours when I married you. It has just taken me this long to realize where my loyalty—and my love lie."

"Then I will count on you to help me build the Fortune family to a throng. Beginning with taking care of the little one now within you. I think you ought to rest a few days. Who knows what damage all this could do to you in your condition?"

"In her condition?" Alex asked blankly. Then his eyes widened and his lopsided grin broadened his face as he realized just what his friend meant. "I had heard of your marriage, Captain and Mrs. Fortune," he said, sweeping them a bow. "It seems further congratulations are in order. You didn't waste any time did you, Jeff?" He laughed, offering his hand to his friend.

Jeffery frowned at Alex's hand. "Perhaps you are the one to be congratulated instead."

Alex's brow wrinkled in puzzlement. "Me? I don't understand?"

"He knows, Alex," Raven said, blushing deeply but holding her head up proudly. "I told him about that night in your cabin."

Alex shook his head. "The night in my cabin?"

A look of annoyance briefly crossed Raven's features. "Yes. When you . . . and I—"

"But nothing happened!"

Now it was Raven's turn to look puzzled. "But I remember." She rubbed her forehead. Just what did she remember? "We had dinner together. I drank too much. The next morning, I was in bed, undressed."

"And from that you assume I was cad enough to—" He looked with astonishment from Raven to Jeffery, then he shrugged. "I can't say I wasn't tempted. I had even planned to seduce you and take you away from Jeff. But I wasn't very successful. I even got you drunk. But you kept calling me Jeffery and saying how much you loved me—or rather Jeff." Shaking his head and sighing, he continued, "Your feelings for me were more...brotherly. So like a good brother, I took off your gown and shoes and rolled you into bed. So help me God, that's all that happened between us."

Raven smoothed her hand over her barely protruding belly and smiled happily at Jeffery. "So the babe that grows within me..."

"Is undoubtedly mine, my love. And Alex is..."

"Our very good friend," Raven finished for him, smiling up at Alex.

Jeffery cocked a brow and looked up at Alex sheepishly, holding out his hand. "I'll accept your congratulations now, Alex, if you're still offering them."

There was no hesitation on Alex's part and he grasped his friend's hand firmly.

"Alex! You're wounded," Raven cried, eyeing a red stain on Alex's thigh.

" 'Tis nothing, Raven."

"I'll have a look at that leg," Raven said in her best no-nonsense surgeon's voice, pushing him toward a hatch cover.

" 'Tis but a scratch, Raven," he said, giving her his reckless smile.

"Now, Captain Jamison!" she snapped. "I'll not be put off."

She stood over him, glaring until he sighed and sat down, extending his leg. "A bossy wench, isn't she?" he said to Jeffery over her shoulder.

"She does tend to take the bit in her teeth at times," Jeffery agreed, speaking of her as if she weren't there.

"Maybe I was lucky not to get stuck with her after

all," Alex said, wincing as Raven cut away his blood-ied pants leg. "What ever will you do with her?"

Raven turned to glare at Jeffery, her brows raised waiting for his answer.

He grinned mischievously, leaning his head back against the mast to look at her most appraisingly. He shrugged. "If she's more trouble than she's worth, I suppose there's always Maricaibo."

SPEND YOUR LEISURE MOMENTS WITH US.

Hundreds of exciting titles to choose from—something for everyone's taste in fine books: breathtaking historical romance, chilling horror, spine-tingling suspense, taut medical thrillers, involving mysteries, action-packed men's adventure and wild Westerns.

SEND FOR A FREE CATALOGUE TODAY!

Leisure Books
Attn: Customer Service Department
276 5th Avenue, New York, NY 10001